LOVE MINUS EIGHTY

Mira dreamed she was running on a trail in the woods. The trail sloped upward, growing steeper and steeper until she was running up big steps. Then the steps entered a flimsy plywood tower and wound up, up. It was dark, and she could barely see, but it felt so good to run; it had been such a long time that she didn't care how steep it was. She climbed higher, considered turning back, but she wanted to make it to the top after having gone so far. Finally she reached the top, and there was a window where she could see a vast river, and a lovely college campus set along it. She hurried over to the window for a better view, and as she did, the tower leaned under her shifting weight, and began to fall forward. The tower built speed, hurtled toward the buildings. *This is it*, she thought, her stomach flip-flopping. *This is the moment of my death.*

Mira jolted awake before she hit the ground.

An old man—likely in his eighties—squinted down at her. "You're not my type," he grumbled, reaching over her head.

By Will McIntosh

Soft Apocalypse
Hitchers
Love Minus Eighty

LOVE
MINUS
EIGHTY

WILL McINTOSH

orbit

www.orbitbooks.net

ORBIT

First published in Great Britain in 2013 by Orbit

A CIP catalogue record for this book
is available from the British Library.

ISBN 978-0-356-50214-4

Printed and bound by CPI Group (UK), Croydon, CR0 4YY

Papers used by Orbit are from well-managed forests
and other responsible sources.

MIX
Paper from
responsible sources
FSC® C104740

Orbit
An imprint of
Little, Brown Book Group
100 Victoria Embankment
London EC4Y 0DY

An Hachette UK Company
www.hachette.co.uk

www.orbitbooks.net

For my wife, Alison Scott

Prologue: Mira

AD 2103

The words were gentle strokes, drawing her awake.

"Hello. Hello there."

She felt the light on her eyelids, and knew that if she opened her eyes, they would sting, and she would have to shade them with her palm and let the light bleed through a crack.

"Feel like talking?" A man's soft voice.

And then her mind cleared enough to wonder: who was this man at her bedside?

"Aw, I know you're awake by *now*. Come on, Sleeping Beauty. Talk to me." The last was a whisper, a lover's words, and Mira felt that she had to come awake and open her eyes. She tried to sigh, but no breath came. Her eyes flew open in alarm.

An old man was leaning over her, smiling, but Mira barely saw him, because when she opened her mouth to inhale, her jaw squealed like a seabird's cry, and no breath came, and she wanted to press her hands to the sides of her face, but her hands wouldn't come either. Nothing would move except her face.

"Hello, hello. And how are you?" The old man was smiling gently, as if Mira might break if he set his whole smile loose. He was not that old, she saw now. Maybe fifty. The furrows in his forehead and the ones framing his nose only seemed deep because his face was so close to hers, almost close enough for a kiss. "Are you having trouble?" He reached out and almost stroked her hair. "You have to press down with your back teeth to control the air flow. Didn't they show you?"

There *was* an air flow—a gentle breeze, whooshing up her throat and out her mouth and nose. It tickled the tiny hairs in her nostrils. She bit down, and the breeze became a hiss— an exhale strong enough that her chest should drop, but it didn't, or maybe it did and she just couldn't tell, because she couldn't lift her head to look.

"Where—" Mira said, and then she howled in terror, because her voice sounded horrible—deep and hoarse and hollow, the voice of something that had pulled itself from a swamp.

"It takes some getting used to. Am I your first? No one has revived you before? Not even for an orientation?" The notion seemed to please him, that he was her first, whatever that meant. Mira studied him, wondering if she should recognize him. He preened at her attention, as if expecting Mira to be glad to see him. He was not an attractive man—his nose was thick and bumpy, and not in an aristocratic way. His nostrils were like a bull's, his brow Neanderthal, but his mouth dainty. She didn't recognize him.

"I can't move. Why can't I move?" Mira finally managed. She looked around as best she could.

"It's okay. Try to relax. Only your face is working."

"What happened?" Mira finally managed.

"You were in an accident," he said, his brow now flexed with concern. "You were working on an engineering project for the military. Evidently a wall gave out." He consulted a readout on his palm. "Fairly major damage. Ruptured aorta. Right leg gone."

Right leg *gone*? *Her* right leg? She couldn't see anything except the man hanging over her and a gold-colored ceiling, high, high above. "This is a hospital?" she asked.

"No, no. A dating center."

"What?" For the first time she noticed that there were other voices in the room, speaking in low, earnest, confidential tones. She caught snippets close by:

"...neutral colors. How could anyone choose violet?"

"...last time I was at a Day-Glows concert I was seventeen..."

"I shouldn't be the one doing this." The man turned, looked over his shoulder, then up at a black screen she could just see, set into the wall behind her. "There's usually an orientation." He turned back around to face her, shrugged, looking bemused. "I guess we're on our own." He clasped his hands, leaned in toward Mira. "The truth is, you see, you died in the accident..."

Mira didn't hear the next few things he said. She felt as if she were floating. It was an absurd idea, that she might be dead yet hear someone tell her she was dead. But somehow it rang true. She didn't remember dying, but she sensed some hard, fast line—some demarcation between now and before. The idea made her want to flee, escape her body, which was a dead body. Her teeth were corpse's teeth.

"...you're at minus eighty degrees, thanks to your insurance, but full revival, especially when it involves extensive injury, is terribly costly. That's where the dating service comes in—"

3

"I have a sister," she interrupted. "Lynn." Her jaw moved so stiffly.

"Yes, a twin sister. Now, that would be interesting." The man grinned, his eyebrows raised.

"Is she still alive?"

"No," he said in a tone that suggested she was a silly girl. "You've been gone for over eighty years, Sleeping Beauty." He made a sweeping gesture, as if all of that was trivial. "But let's focus on the present. The way this works is, we get acquainted. We have dates. If we find we're compatible"—he raised his shoulders toward his ears, smiled his dainty smile—"then I might be enticed to pay for you to be revived, so that we can be together."

Dates.

"So. My name is Alexander—call me Alex—and I know from your readout that your name is Mira. Nice to meet you, Mira."

"Nice to meet you," Mira murmured. He'd said a wall collapsed on her. She tried to remember, but nothing came. Nothing about the accident, anyway. The memories that raced up at her were of Jeannette.

"So. Mira." Alex clapped his hands together. "Do you want to bullshit, or do you want to get intimate?" The raised eyebrows again, the same as when he made the twins comment.

"I don't understand," Mira said.

"Weeeell. For example, here's a question." He leaned in close, his breath puffing in her ear. "If I revived you, what sorts of things would you do to me?"

Mira doubted this man was here to revive anyone. "I don't know. That's an awfully intimate question. Why don't we get to know each other first?" She needed time to think. Even just a few minutes of quiet, to make sense of this.

4

Alex frowned theatrically. "Come on. Tease me a little."

Should she tell Alex she was gay? Surely not. He would lose interest, and maybe report it to whoever owned the facility. But why hadn't whoever owned the facility known she was gay? Maybe that was to be part of the orientation she'd missed. Whatever the reason, did she want to risk being taken out of circulation, or unplugged and buried?

Would that be the worst thing?

"I'm just—" She wanted to say "not in the mood," but that was not only a cliché but a vast understatement. She was dead. She couldn't move anything but her face, and that made her feel untethered, as if she were floating, drifting. Hands and feet grounded you. Mira had never realized. "I'm just not very good at this sort of thing."

"Well." Alex put his hands on his thighs, made a production of standing. "This costs quite a bit, and they charge by the minute. So I'll say good-bye now, and you can go back to being dead."

Go back? "Wait!" Mira said. They could bring her back, and then let her die again? She imagined her body, sealed up somewhere, maybe for years, maybe forever. The idea terrified her. Alex paused, waiting. "Okay. I would..." She tried to think of something, but there were so many things running through her mind, so many trains of thought she wanted to follow, none of them involving the pervert leaning over her.

Were there other ways to get permanently "revived"? Did she have any living relatives she might contact, or maybe a savings account that had been accruing interest for the past eighty years? Had she had any savings when she died? She'd had a house—she remembered that. Jeannette would have inherited it. Or maybe Lynn.

"Fine, if you're not going to talk, I'll just say good-bye,"

Alex snapped. "But don't think anyone else is coming. You're a level eight-plus."

Mira opened her mouth to ask what that meant, but Alex raised a finger to silence her.

"What that *means* is your injuries make you one expensive revival, and there are many, many women here, so not even your nine-point-one all-original face and thirty-six-C tits, *also* original, are going to pry that kind of treasure from any man's balance." He stepped back, put his fists on his hips. "Plus, men don't want women who were frozen sixty years before the facility opened, because they have nothing in common with those women."

"Please," Mira said.

He reached for something over her head, out of sight.

I: In the Minus Eighty

AD 2133

1

Rob

The woman across the aisle from Rob yammered on as the micro-T rose above street level, threading through the Perrydot Building, lit offices buzzing past in a colorful blur. He should have taken his Scamp. Public transport was simpler, but he always seemed to share a compartment with someone who didn't have the courtesy to subvocalize.

For no reason except that she was annoying the shit out of him, Rob decided to scan her to see how much work she'd had done on her face.

As his fingers danced over the skintight system on his left arm, the woman glanced his way and curled her lip—a microexpression that was there and gone in a flicker. Now he had another reason to dislike this complete stranger. No, his style wasn't elegant and seamless, and he was tired of being judged by the technological glitterati as lacking some vital core because he only cared about making his system function, not how he looked doing it.

A flashing grid superimposed itself over the jabbering woman's face. He grinned, satisfied. Nose work, lip work, eye work, chin work. There wasn't much to her that was original. It was petty of him to check, even more petty to take satisfaction in her artificiality, but she was truly bugging him.

"I wasn't the one who told him," the woman was saying to some guy's screen. "Ask Corrie if you don't believe me." She was naked except for her skintight system running upper thigh to midchest, which was a 5/5 Manatee—totally state-of-the-art, glittering like blue-green jewels on her skin.

The screen she was speaking to, which was huge and floating two feet from Rob's head, was muted. The unshaven face framed in it looked sleepy, or maybe just uninterested.

"Since when don't you like Corrie?" the woman asked in response to something the guy said. "So you don't like any of my friends, is that it?"

She had no class. If a conversation was going to be intense, you did it in person. She probably showed up for weddings and funerals via screen. He could mute her, but her gesticulating form would only be more distracting if her mouth was moving soundlessly. Rob decided to go to screen himself, and see what Lorelei was up to. Of course that meant working his system again, and another contemptuous microsneer.

Lorelei was in their bedroom. She was utterly surrounded by screens. Rob was stunned at how many people were watching her, and she was adding more by the second. Onlookers' eager screens jockeyed for the best vantage point, rolling and shifting like rectangular gnats, scooting low to corners of the room, all shrunk to palm-size to accommodate the crowd. Yes, Lorelei was a total attention hound, but she'd never scored (he called up the stats on his screen) one hundred eighty-two simultaneous viewers before.

Lorelei actually looked nervous, kneeling on her bed in the midst of the storm, probably terrified she might blow it by saying something stale or letting the pace of whatever she was doing drag. What *was* she doing? Rob zoomed in on the stack of greeting cards in her hand, just as she activated the one on top.

"Aw, how cute: 'Love to Robby, from Grandma on your sweet sixteen.'" She grunted, flipped the card over her shoulder, toward a scattered mess that Rob recognized as his journals, remote photo files, all the personal stuff he kept in his lockbox. As Rob's heart began to hammer, Lorelei activated the next card. "Oh, here we go. I knew it."

He could see it was the one from Penny, the one Rob had almost thrown out when he moved in with Lorelei. A rush of rage, threaded with tendrils of guilt, hit him as Lorelei read the card aloud:

"'To Rob. Okay fine, if it'll make you happy. XX(X). Penny.'"

No! Rob subvocalized to Lorelei as she activated the video, holding the card at an angle as the screens swooped and rose, bumping up against Lorelei's privacy perimeter, jockeying to see.

"This should be choice," she said, ignoring Rob. As the video started, Rob set his screen to lurk, hoping no one had noticed his brief presence. Of course they hadn't; all eyes were on Lorelei. She was scoring more and more eyes—her stunt was going viral.

Penny's video was etched in Rob's memory from a hundred viewings. Penny was sitting on her bed, one leg tucked under her, dressed in a high-necked, double-button blouse and demi-jeans. Her gaze dropped shyly as she lifted her hands and began unbuttoning the blouse.

There was no sound, so Lorelei provided slutty

11

"buh-buh-buh-bah" stripper music for her audience as Penny exposed first one, then the other small, erect-nippled breast.

That was all; Penny stopped there and blew a kiss, a kiss only Rob was meant to see.

"I *knew* he was keeping secrets from me," Lorelei hissed. She tried to sound outraged, but undertones of triumph and excitement leaked. "Let's see what else we've got." She picked up the next card.

Shaking with rage, Rob cut the feed and returned to the train, and the loud chick still arguing with her bored boyfriend. Stabbing sensors on his biceps, Rob submitted a destination change, hoping the microrailcar would plot a reroute that was inconvenient for the woman, who never seemed to need to take an inbreath.

Lorelei looked up when Rob burst into their room. She made no attempt to hide what she was doing.

Without taking his eyes off Lorelei, Rob gestured toward the screens with his chin. "Block them."

"No. It's *my* apartment. They're my guests."

Rob looked at the sea of floating faces, all of them waiting to see what would happen next. Messages were surely flying among them—reactions, predictions, snide asides.

Rob spotted his friend Mort in the crowd. When he saw Rob had noticed him, Mort looked away sheepishly, then tucked his frame out of sight behind some others.

Rob realized there was no way he was going to get Lorelei to block the eyes, because she was loving this; it was her finest hour.

"Fine. Can you and your friends go somewhere else so I can pack my things?" As he said it, the certainty of it sunk in. They were through; there was no walking this back, not after what Lorelei had done. Despite himself, despite what Lorelei was doing, he felt a lump of pain forming in his chest.

Lorelei folded her arms and pouted dramatically. "So you still have a thing for Penny. I guess that makes sense, since she ditched you, not the other way around."

"You're rummaging through my stuff without my permission." He gestured toward the wall of small faces watching them. "In front of *hundreds of people*. And you think *I* should feel guilty for keeping a card from my ex-girlfriend?"

She put her hands on her hips. "A card? She's *stripping*."

He opened his mouth to defend himself, but most of the defenses that came to mind were lies. *I forgot I had it. I never watched the video again, once I met you.* He looked down at his private things, strewn on the floor like candy wrappers, or used condoms. Yes, he shared some of the blame here, but what Lorelei had done...

"This is just sick." Rob waved the closet open and pulled out a duffel bag. Kneeling, he scooped a double-handful of his stuff off the polished granite floor, set it gently in the bag.

"I found the porn holos as well, by the way. How lovely. When did you find time to"—she cleared her throat suggestively—"use them?" Her words, cutting as they were, still came in that beautiful rhythm, Lorelei's signature vocal style, injected with subvocalized asides to her friends that sounded like soft susurrations and gulped exclamations that she somehow made sexy.

"At least they're convincing when they fake their orgasms," he said, wanting to humiliate her in front of her viewers.

Lorelei grabbed the back of his collar and yanked, nearly sending him sprawling. "I don't have to fake them when a man actually excites me."

His anger boiling over, Rob sprung up, meaning to... what? Shove her? Hit her?

13

And then, suddenly, he got it. This was Lorelei's climax, the finishing touch that would leave her viewers eager to return to witness more of her fascinating and tumultuous life. She didn't care about Penny's card; it was just a useful prop, a ratings boost.

He took a few deep breaths, willing himself to stay calm, just until he got out of there. He went back to packing. Lorelei had over eight hundred sets of eyes now; the room was teeming with screens. As he scooped another handful of his things into the duffel, he realized how pathetic he must look to all these people.

Rob stood, leaving the duffel where it was. "On second thought, I'll pick up my things later." Despite his best efforts to deny her audience the satisfaction of seeing how hurt and angry he was, his voice was shaking. "I'm out of here."

The only things he grabbed were his lute, and a stack of his publicity photos that were sitting on top of the lute case. At the bedroom door he paused to take a last look at Lorelei, so absurdly tall (yet wanting everyone to believe no genetic trickery was involved), her face a perfect balance of Asian, African, Anglo, her jet-black curls rolling down her shoulders.

As he turned away, it occurred to him that Lorelei might have been planning this from the moment they met at The Skyview. Was it possible? Would anyone build a relationship and then wreck it solely to draw eyes?

"Why don't you see if Penny will take you back."

Rob felt something ricochet off his shoulder. He didn't turn—he already knew it was Penny's card. He kept moving, through the living room and down the glass corridor to the tube.

To his relief the door to the tube opened immediately. Breathing hard, arms at his sides, he glared at the sea of frames hovering outside the tube door, wanting a good look at the rube who'd just been disemboweled by super double-nifty Lorelei. He set a total block to keep them from squeezing into the tube with him as the door slid closed.

One, two, three, he counted silently to give the tube time to get moving, out of auditory range of the gawkers, then, as the familiar three-hundred-sixty-degree view of Manhattan's Low Town spread out far below him, he screamed so loudly his ears crackled. He dropped the photos and his lute case, pounded the glass wall of the lozenge-like compartment, spun and slammed his back against it, pummeled it with his elbows, pounded it with the soles of his spear boots, which Lorelei had bought him. It felt good. He went on slamming the glass until he was exhausted, then, panting, he slid to the floor.

What had just happened? For the past eight months, everything had been skintight. No drama, their relationship exclusive but not escalating, everyone happy. Or so he'd thought.

Fortunately the tube didn't stop at any of the other apartments spread out along the lift line, like beads threaded on a string, hanging from the underside of High Town. This was the last time he would take this trip, he realized. No, the second-to-last time—he still had to collect his stuff. Maybe he could get Gord or Beamon to do that for him.

If this was his last trip, he wished he could enjoy the view, drink in the rooftops below, dappled in sunlight filtering through High Town. He couldn't, though. He was too hurt, too angry, too sad. He honestly wasn't sure what he felt, whether he was glad to be rid of her or devastated to lose her. Both. Lorelei was brilliant in her own way, dynamic, utterly unpredictable. It was fun to be with her. He'd been aware of her cutting edge, had felt it graze him from time to time, but never thought she'd cut so deep.

Rob knelt, collected his photos scattered on the floor, and

grabbed his lute as the lift opened onto Rogers Street—the shopping district. He stepped into bright sunlight, looked left and right, not sure where he was going. One of the photos slipped between his damp fingers. As he stood there panting, a twenty-three-dollar fine rolled off his account balance in the corner of his vision. In High Town the incivility cameras were always rolling. Rob flung the rest of the photos at the sky and stormed off, as several hundred dollars in fines thinned his balance further. He headed west, away from the garage where his mini was stored, toward Skyview. He needed a drink. No—he needed six.

Skyview was nearly empty. Ignoring the breathtaking view of the outer burbs provided from the tables, Rob slipped onto a bar stool, smiled at Ellie as she came over.

"What *happened* to you? You look terrible."

Rob tried to wave away the question. "Nothing. It's stupid."

Ellie folded her arms. "Clearly it's not, or you wouldn't look like someone just stomped your favorite puppy wearing four-inch spiked heels."

Rob surprised himself by choking up. He shook his head, looked down at the bar, felt Ellie's hand on his shoulder. "I'm gonna go out on a limb and guess you're not having absinthe?"

A coarse guffaw escaped him. "No, no absinthe." Absinthe was Lorelei's drink. He'd gotten into the habit of drinking it, hanging with her. Suddenly it was way too expensive for him. This entire bar was suddenly too expensive for him without his girlfriend and her rich parents.

A vodka martini appeared directly below his hangdog face. "First one's on me, sweetie. And don't repeat this please, but I think you're better off without her."

"Yeah, I know. But even though I know that, even though

she did something so"—he reached for a word to encapsulate the wretchedness of what Lorelei had done to him, but came up empty—"so *shitty*, it still hurts. You know?"

Ellie sighed, leaned on the bar. "I know."

"I didn't do anything to her. It was like she just decided to shit on me for kicks." Rob lifted the martini and took a long swig.

2

Rob

Rob was going too fast when he hit the long, rainbow-curved ramp out of High Town, and his mini was slowed by the ramp's governor. High Town, pulsing silver, teal, salmon, and lemon yellow on a backdrop of black night, slowly disappeared out of his rearview mirror as he descended.

He knew he was leaving High Town for good. Sure, he'd take day trips, maybe be lucky enough to play gigs up there one day, but he'd never live there again. Musicians couldn't afford to live in High Town. Rob didn't mind, though. As he curved back around, Low Town spread out before him, the fork of the Hudson and Harlem Rivers flickering in the mottled blobs of lamplight. In some ways he preferred the tightly packed, aging stone and steel of the old town to the shiny glass and carbon fiber of the new. It suited him. It felt more honest.

As he reached ground level, the smoothness of the ramp was replaced by the rattle and bump of old blacktop. Rob hung a left onto 192nd Street. The streets were nearly deserted at this time of night. He'd have to crash with Beverly or his folks until he could find somewhere to live. Which reminded him—he'd put a block on his link. He removed the block and found six messages waiting for him. Three were from Mort. "Dickhead. Asshole," Rob hissed. He'd better have left a damned sincere apology after scoping Lorelei's little ambush party. On second thought, Rob didn't care how sincere the apology was; there were no words sincere enough to forgive such backstabbing. He was tempted to delete the messages without watching them, but decided to see the first at least, just to satisfy his curiosity.

Mort didn't sound apologetic, he sounded frantic. "Brother, hey, are you seeing this? You need to get back there. She's ditching all your stuff. Shit. *Not okay*. Get back up there, okay?"

Ditching all his stuff? A sick dread crawled up his spine as he set his frame for one eye only so he could see to drive while peeping Lorelei's bedroom, expecting that Lorelei had already blocked him. But she hadn't. No, of course she hadn't—she wanted him to see.

Lorelei was leaning out the window. Rob tried to maneuver closer, but a thousand frames were crowded around her, forming a porous, semicircular barrier. Rob peered between the cracks, his stomach clenching. Lorelei was holding a storage clip lightly between her thumb and forefinger, dangling it out the window.

"*Adiós*, photos age seven to twelve. *Sayônara. Tot Siens. Da svidaniya.*" She opened her fingers and the clip dropped toward the roofs of Low Town.

She transferred something to her right hand, from a stack in her left, held it up to examine it. "Early recordings: original compositions."

Rob howled in fury as she extended her arm, the disk dangling loosely between her fingers. Some of this stuff he had backed up, but a lot of it...

Rob's eyes flew open as a woman came off the curb, and he realized he'd taken the turn too wide. He slammed the brake, jerked the steering pads.

The woman, her arms raised defensively, disappeared under his Scamp. He felt the thud right into his teeth. The vehicle bucked violently once, then again, throwing Rob partially into the passenger seat as the air emptied from his lungs in a long, involuntary scream. The Scamp rolled on until it collided with a light post. Then everything was still, except for the feed from Lorelei's bedroom.

Although he'd lost all interest in what Lorelei was doing, his left eye remained there.

"*Arrivederci. Paalam na po.*" Lorelei let another bit of Rob's life slip from between her fingers.

Rob disconnected the feed. Lorelei winked out.

He wanted to remain just as he was—his head and shoulders crammed toward the floor on the passenger side, one leg twisted between the seat backs, the other stretched across the driver's seat. He wanted to stay there forever, frozen, never to move forward in time.

The mournful wail of an ambulance rose in the distance. Rob straightened himself into the driver's seat. He should get out, but he didn't want to see the woman.

So he sat there, his breath coming in quick gasps, telling himself he had to move, had to check on the woman, try to stop the bleeding if there was bleeding, give her mouth-to-mouth if she wasn't breathing, pull off his jacket and bunch it under her head. Act like a human being.

Outside, screens were popping up by the hundreds as word spread and virtual rubberneckers rushed to see. Two people ran past looking alarmed, shouting. Rob opened his mouth to tell the door to open. Nothing came out but a moan.

3

Veronika

Veronika took a break from feeding her client witty words to impress a guy who was totally wrong for her, and watched Nathan work. She liked to watch Nathan. Since he was sitting right across from her, Veronika hoped it didn't appear as if she looked at him an inordinate amount of the time, though Nathan certainly didn't look at her as much as she looked at him. So maybe she shouldn't spend so much time looking at him.

Instead she surveyed the Donut Hole Caffeine Emporium, which was busy for a weekday afternoon, its cup-clutching clientele swirling around tables sprouting here and there like mushrooms, talking, working their systems, all of it silent because Veronika had muted everything. She and Nathan were at their usual table—fifth level, on the edge of the hole that ran right down the middle of the shop and gave it its name.

She looked back at Nathan. She loved how he worked his system, loved his vocal style, and the way he always seemed to have three days of stubble on some parts of his face, and only one on others. She also loved how his jaw and chin were chiseled and masculine, but his nose and dark, smoky eyes were soft and pretty in an almost feminine way.

Nathan wasn't his usual high-energy, talkative self today. He seemed almost morose, which was supposed to be Veronika's role. She took a sip of her almond bean brew. It was getting cold.

Work this into the convo, she subvocalized to her client. *"Sometimes I'm baffled by how you can be so deep and so shallow at the same time."* Her client, Sylvie, barraged her with frowny-faces. Sylvie liked this guy and was hoping they'd escalate to Romantic Interaction Face-to-Face soon, and because of that she was getting tight, in danger of blowing it.

I'm telling you, you need to neg this guy a little if you want to keep his interest. Romance 101, Sylvie!

My friend Suk thinks it's a mistake.

Does Suk have a master's degree in Interpersonal Relationships from NYU? Veronika shot back. She didn't like playing the degree card, because this job was so much about instinct, but the comment got her hackles up.

After a pause, Sylvie sent back, *Give me something else. Something nice!*

"Oh for God's sake," Veronika said aloud. "This bird needs to get out of my nest and flap her own damned wings. Too much longer and it's going to be *so* obvious she had a coach when they finally meet in person."

Nathan chuckled sympathetically, breaking the chuckle into two parts as he wove it around the subvocalized conversation he was having with one of his own clients. Nathan's vocal style was a variation on La Lune—very jazzy, very sexy.

"I hate working in real time," Veronika said, while feeding

23

Sylvie a few flirtatious lines. "When you're having a live screen conversation, you're implicitly claiming all of your material is original. At that point using a coach is cheating."

"It's all cheating," Nathan said. "Getting us to create their profiles in the first place is cheating."

"It's cheating, but it's not *dishonest* cheating. It's like nudging other people's systems so you look ten pounds lighter and an inch taller to them. Everybody does it."

Nathan didn't take the bait. Definitely not himself; normally he couldn't resist a good argument.

"You okay? You seem a little down."

Nathan sighed heavily. "I thought I was masking it. Guess not." He took a sip of coffee. "I'm not ready to talk about it. I need to work through it first. Unpack it."

"Oh. Okay. I understand." This was going to bother her now. She knew herself. She'd spend half the night running through scenarios of what it might be.

"So how are you?" Nathan asked, lacing his hands behind his head and stretching. "Been on any hot face-to-faces?"

Veronika felt herself flush. "Yeah. A different bronco every night last week."

Nathan sighed a little tune. "Get out there. See some men."

Veronika didn't bother to respond. Nathan knew she wasn't dating, and she didn't want to hear yet again how weird it was for a dating coach to be so starkly single. Yes, it was pathetic. Yes, if her clients ever found out, they'd dump her immediately. And yes, it had been almost five years since Sander smashed her heart, way past time to climb back on that old horse. She was sick of hearing it. There was enough stress and disappointment in her life as it stood. Working behind the scenes for someone else was like a fluid puzzle, but a face-to-face, sitting across from a man, live, was a different story. Her wit abandoned her.

The deep, relentless melancholy that was her default condition was as evident on her face as a fist-size pimple.

Nathan's fingers flicked the air, probably tweaking a profile for one of his clients. "Maybe you should hire a coach." It was an old joke between them.

Veronika's cup chirped, indicating her seat-time was up. She checked the time, decided she had plenty, and let the cup chirp down until it defaulted to a refill and automatically debited her account.

"How about you? Any new prospects?" She watched his face. She was fishing, hoping to get a clue to what was bothering him. "What am I saying? You've always got new prospects lined up; it's like a conga line." Nothing—not even a smile.

Nathan shrugged, shook his head. "I'm taking a break for a while, too."

Veronika studied his face. "You can't still be getting over that teacher, can you? It's been, like, two days."

Nathan covered his mouth with both hands and looked down at his coffee. Veronika canted her head, studying his face. He looked close to tears.

He cleared his throat, raised his head to look at Veronika. "She died. Winter died."

"Oh my God." She'd only met Winter a couple of times, but still, the words knocked her back. "What *happened*?"

"She was hit by a Scamp." He cleared his throat again, trying to steady his voice. "She was out jogging. Two nights ago."

A sonorous pseudovoice whispered in her ear that her brew was ready for pickup. She ignored it. "Oh, God, Nathan. I'm so sorry."

"We'd only been seeing each other for three months, but she took it pretty hard. She said it surprised her; she thought things were going well." He pinched the bridge of his nose, right where tears were threatening to break loose. "So now I'm thinking, she went out jogging to feel better. Because I made her feel bad."

Veronika scooted her chair, wrapped her arms around Nathan, feeling slightly guilty at how much she was enjoying the hug, the feel of his muscular shoulders. Finally, Nathan let go and straightened up, nodding that he was okay.

"I'll be right back," Veronika said, and went off to pick up her drink.

When she returned, Nathan was back to work. "This guy rejected the entire profile I wrote for him. Says it's not him at all. Of course it's not you, asshole, that's why you might actually get a few hits." He sighed heavily, fixed Veronika with his smoky-brown eyes. "Do you ever wonder if this job makes it harder to fall in love? I mean, it forces us to approach things so objectively: attractiveness ratings, desire to procreate, BMI, cognitive patterning, IQ, emotional stability quotient. Sometimes I think I've lost the ability to sit across from someone and just *know* what I feel. That I feel something, or I feel nothing."

Veronika didn't feel that way at all, but she didn't think Nathan was looking for input. He was working through what happened with Winter, and just needed to talk it out.

"I don't know. Maybe what I'm really afraid of is if I ever settle into something stable, I'll lose my edge as a coach. That if I'm not out there myself, I'll lose interest in the whole dance." He looked at Veronika, as if remembering she was there. "Do you ever worry about that?"

Veronika sipped her brew; it scalded the tip of her tongue, just the way she liked it. "I already hate this job. Being less miserable in my personal life isn't going to make me more miserable at work." She looked out the window, down through an oval light-filtering hole just outside that offered her a crescent-shaped glimpse of Lemieux Bridge spanning the Hudson, crowded on both sides by the black roofs of Undertown.

"Do you follow *Spill Your Secrets*?" she asked.

Nathan shook his head.

"It's an anonymous voice-only feed. People post their darkest secrets. A few weeks ago someone posted that they were planning to jump off the Golden Gate Bridge."

Nathan frowned. "Wait. You're not saying it was you."

"No, *of course not*." The comment stung like he'd smacked her. "Do I really seem suicidal to you?" Sometimes she struggled to gauge how she came across to others. Dark and brooding? Fair enough. But did she come across as a neurotic mess who might one day have her toes jutting over the cross-beam of a bridge, looking down at the brown water hundreds of feet below? "And why would I fly to San Francisco to jump off a bridge? People jump off Lemieux Bridge all the time." Veronika looked it up. Three a week, on average, since suicide was decriminalized and the steel nets were taken down.

"Sorry. What were you going to say?"

"What I was going to say was, someone organized an event, and almost a million people from all over the world converged over the bridge, and shouted 'Don't jump.' "

"Did she jump?" Nathan asked.

"The jumper hadn't specified a time, so he probably wasn't on the bridge. The thing was, they were doing something *meaningful*. I was there. I was one of those million screens and it was…" She choked up, couldn't go on for a moment. "It felt meaningful." She pulled the napkin from under her drink, feeling dumb for crying over this after what Nathan had just confided. "Nothing in my life feels meaningful."

Nathan nodded slowly, as if he really wanted to get what she was trying to say, while he subvocalized to a client.

"I know, I know," Veronika said, shaking her head. "Veronika is feeling empty, her life a vast wasteland of ennui and coffee shops. As usual." She flipped the napkin onto the table like failed confetti.

Now Nathan's cup began to chirp. He checked the time. "I'd better get going. I'm sorry to leave in the middle of this. Maybe I can pop in on you later?"

"No, go." She waved him away. "I feel like an idiot for kidnapping the conversation and making it about me, after what happened to Winter. Leaving now would be showing mercy."

"No, really, I was relieved to move off that topic. Maybe you should join in on more of those sorts of events, like the bridge one."

"I was thinking instead of working from home, or from coffee shops, I would work from a bench on Lemieux Bridge." It sounded dumb, now that she was saying it out loud. "Then if someone comes to jump, I can talk them out of it. Save a life." She shrugged. "That would be meaningful."

"It would also be cold. It's January." Nathan leaned over and kissed her cheek, then headed for the door. Veronika watched him go.

She stayed awhile longer, since she'd already paid for the seat, and thought about the bridge.

4

Rob

On the eighth day after the accident, Rob got dressed. He pulled on his socks at the edge of the bed, whispering, "*Kwa heri. Odabo. Ha det.*" He stood up shakily, got his left foot through the pant leg on the second try as he went on reciting. "*Do pobachennya. Ajo. An lot soleil.*"

The last was West Indian Creole. When he wasn't sleeping, Rob memorized ways to say *good-bye*. He'd found memorizing a good way to narrow his attention so he wouldn't think about things. Thinking was the enemy. He now knew how to say *good-bye* in many languages. Lorelei's performance at the window had given him the idea, though Lorelei hadn't memorized her *good-bye*s—she'd been reading off a feed with one eye. Just as he'd been watching her with one eye when he ran over Winter West.

Rob pulled a New Peregrines sweatshirt over his head, relishing the darkness that enveloped him, feeling disappointed when his head popped through the neck hole and his room returned, with its sagging ceiling, its pocked walls.

He stared at the doorknob. The knob had a dent in it he'd probably put there when he was a kid. In this old house his parents had owned for the past thirty-five years, this hundred-and-sixty-year-old house meant to last fifty, you still had to grasp a knob and twist it to open a door. Right now it seemed far too definitive an act.

He saw the flicker of a shadow beneath the door, but no muffled footsteps. His mom. Or, more accurately, a holographic image of his mom that roamed the house to keep his father company, ten years after his mother's death. Rob kept expecting his father to move on, to find Mom gone one day. It hadn't happened yet.

He decided to go back to bed. Maybe tomorrow.

Dad, looking gaunt and raccoon-eyed, brought dinner. If Rob could have eaten anything—a roll, a forkful of baked beans—he would have, just to bring a shade of relief to Dad's eyes. The last thing Rob wanted was for his dad to suffer along with him. Dad had enough to deal with; he didn't need a second ghost roaming his house. But Rob couldn't eat, and didn't know how else to release Dad from sharing his misery. Maybe he should try harder to get out of the house during the day, to give Dad some relief from his presence, from the constant reminder that a woman was dead because of his son.

Maybe it would have been better for everyone if Rob had been over the legal limit, and sent to prison. He winced, recalling the DA's ferocity at the inquest, her outrage that he was going to get away with it. Should he have been allowed to walk, simply because he hadn't been *quite* intoxicated? He hadn't felt drunk at the time, but surely the drinks had affected him. He was still surprised he'd passed. Three vodka martinis seemed like a hell of a lot of alcohol, even if spread over a few hours.

Seeing that Rob wasn't going to eat, his dad sat on the edge of the bed. "So how are you feeling?"

"I'll be okay. I just need a few weeks."

Dad considered this and nodded, somewhat skeptically. "I've got to say, you don't seem to be getting better."

Rob muttered something that was incoherent, even to him, then a long silence stretched, and Rob couldn't seem to find the energy to break it.

"Why don't you go out, get some fresh air?" his dad said.

Rob opened his mouth to say he wasn't up to it, but his father cut him off.

"Even if you don't feel like it, you should go." He used that calm yet piercing tone that insisted Rob hear him. "You may have to go through the motions for a while, you know?"

Here was something he could do to ease his father's suffering: Go Through the Motions. He grabbed his jacket from the closet.

He went out the back door to avoid neighbors who might want to chat, his chin tucked against a chilly breeze. He crossed their small dirt-and-weeds backyard, vaulted a low concrete wall into the gray-water recycling canal that ran behind the houses, and headed toward the abandoned mall. He could lean up against the wall for a few hours, read the graffiti.

Each step was an effort. All he wanted was to be back in bed, memorizing salutations in foreign languages.

The Backmans' dog barked as he passed behind their house. He eyed the cluster of ancient, cracked solar panels set along the edge of the canal behind the Royers' house.

The sun felt unnaturally bright, and when he glanced up, it

stung his eyes. Better if he were in Low Town with its muted daylight, the buildings hugging the sidewalks. There was too much open space in the burbs.

"Rob?"

Rob flinched at the sound of Lorelei's voice. He spun, foolishly expecting her to be standing there in the flesh. Instead her screen was there, large enough that her face was actual size. Several hundred smaller screens flitted behind her.

"You've got to be kidding. Get the fuck away from me." He turned his back. It burned his skin to have all those eyes looking at him, judging him, in all likelihood firing comments back and forth about how utterly consumed with guilt he looked.

"Rob, I just came to say I'm sorry. I'm so sorry. I've been trying to contact you. Haven't you seen my messages?"

Yeah, he'd been eagerly reading all of his friends' and exes' messages. *Sorry you killed someone. Feel better soon.* He turned to face her. "Thank you. I appreciate your concern, I really do. Now, if you don't mind, I'd like to be alone." He looked toward the mall. It was semipublic space, there would be nowhere to go where Lorelei couldn't follow. Better to go home. He ducked around Lorelei, stormed right through the solid-looking wall of frames, rudely shattering their illusion of solidity for a moment. If he'd been wearing a system, the fine for defiling their personhood would have ticked off immediately. As it was, he wasn't sure if he could be identified and fined or not. He really didn't care.

"I can't help feeling partly responsible for what happened."

Rob glanced back. Lorelei and her entourage were following three paces behind him.

"I'm sorry. I can't help what you feel."

"Will you please stop and talk to me for a minute?"

Head down, Rob kept walking. "Didn't we break up? I seem to recall we did."

"That doesn't matter. None of this petty shit matters, after what happened."

"Amen to that." Another hundred yards, and he'd hit the block he'd set up around the house eight days ago. Thank goodness for private property.

"I'm sorry about what I did. I stopped airmailing your stuff as soon as I heard. I have it at home. Some of it."

"Toss it out. I don't want it."

"Rob, please."

If she'd been there in person, she could have grabbed his shoulder and yanked him around to face her. But as things were, there was nothing she could do to stop him from climbing out of the canal and into his yard.

Actually, if she had come in person—alone—he might have talked to her. Maybe she could have convinced him that throwing his stuff out the window had been some sort of temporary insanity. Rob still couldn't believe she'd done it. Lorelei was not your typical person, but he'd never sensed cruelty in her before that night.

Relief flooded him as he closed the back door.

Rob's father was in the kitchen, watching Lorelei out the window, his old handheld on the table. "I see you didn't get far."

Rob's mom was at the table, studiously chewing some invisible meal.

"Made it to the Royers' before she chased me back." Rob eyed the three ancient barber chairs that stood in a row in the front room, in "the Business Room," as Dad called it. They were empty at the moment, but a customer might push open the door and saddle up at any time of day, seven days a week, and Dad would power up the scissors. It was so simple, so beautifully simple. Dad carried on a pleasant conversation with his customer, and cut hair. He avoided politics and mean gossip, hiding behind a wall of polite "Uh-huh's" if a customer brought up either, and went about his days in blissful simplicity. Before the accident, Rob had zero interest in carrying on the family business, but if there'd been anywhere near enough business, Rob would happily begin learning the trade today. Snip-snip, talk about last night's boloball game.

Dad was watching him stare longingly into the Business Room, probably with no clue why. He clapped Rob's shoulder. "Come on, you could use a trim."

Before Rob could protest, Dad led him to the first chair—the one closest to his supplies, and to his Wall of Fame, plastered with hundreds of before-and-after photos of his regulars over the past thirty years.

The familiar high-pitched *wheem* of the scissors, Dad's fingers brushing his head, made Rob's throat clench with emotion. Two years ago Rob had quietly begun getting his hair cut at a swanky shop in High Town, where you could see what your haircut would look like beforehand, rather than hope Dad got it even and didn't shear off too much. Dad had never said a word about it, but now Rob could see what a betrayal it had been. He'd basically told his own father he was no good at what he did. What a thoughtless bastard he was.

No more, though. No more selfishness.

Not that he could afford haircuts in swanky salons in any case, now that he and Lorelei had broken up. The mirror allowed him to see through the doorway behind him, out the kitchen window into the backyard. Lorelei was gone. Did he feel better or worse about being supported by Lorelei and her trust fund for the past eight months? About the same. He'd felt slimy about it before, he felt shitty about it now. He'd told himself he had no choice, that Lorelei wasn't about to live in Low Town, and Rob couldn't afford to live in High Town without her help. Who was he kidding? He hadn't been able to afford to live in Low Town on what he made as a musician.

His dad set an old handheld in Rob's lap, amid the clumps of hair collecting on the barber sheath Dad had whipped around him like a bullfighter wielding a red cloak. Rob liberated one hand from the sheath and picked up the handheld.

"What's this?"

"I've gone back and forth on whether to show you."

"Show me what?" Rob was uneasy about something in his dad's tone. "What is it?" He sensed it was something that would force him to think about things he didn't want to think about.

"Just look at it."

When Rob saw Winter West's name at the top, it felt as if all of the light drained out of his head. He was sure he was going to black out, but he didn't.

It was a profile from Cryomed's dating center. The bridesicle place.

"Oh. Jesus Christ." There was a clip of Winter standing in front of the Grand Canyon. She was laughing. Not smiling but flat-out laughing, her nostrils flared like a winded colt. Her hair was striking—long, curly, deep auburn—she looked to be one of those easygoing, energetic people others love to be around. A lot of people probably missed her.

"She's in the minus eighty. She didn't have freezing insurance, but she was good-looking enough that Cryomed picked her up for the bridesicle program." Dad leaned over to look at the screen with him.

Even on this old handheld, Rob could have expanded her

profile so that she was standing right next to him, as big and bright as life itself. But it hurt just to look at her static clip on the tiny screen, like a flame on his retinas. She'd been thirty, single, a teacher. An English teacher. She'd been an avid runner, loved random-selection reality feeds and vertical gardening.

"She just made the cut." Dad pointed to her global attractiveness rating, which was eight point six, before returning to the haircut. "They only take uninsured who are eight and a half or over." Her face was all original, so the rating was unadjusted. A nose job or butt implants would have put her in the ground.

After her physical stats was a list of the damage, beginning with the major organs that would need to be replaced. Rob squeezed his eyes shut, turned his head. "You're showing me this to say that at least she's got a chance, is that it? At least she's not in the ground?"

Dad stopped cutting, stared out the window, tugging at his lower lip. "I guess that's part of it." He looked at Rob; it had always amazed Rob how open and frank his gaze could be. Maybe it was because he wasn't educated enough to learn about guile. More likely it was because he never carried on other conversations while talking to Rob, never divided his attention. It was hard to meet his father's gaze now. "What I was really thinking was, you could go there and apologize."

"*What?*" The thought filled him with electric terror. "No, no, no." It would never have occurred to him, not in a million years. He couldn't imagine anything more awful than standing over her while she lay in that drawer, and admitting he was the one who put her there. And to what end? To seek absolution? He had no business asking her to release him from his guilt. He deserved to feel awful for the rest of his life; his last breath on earth should be an uneasy one.

"You're saying I should go to the dating center, revive her, tell her I was the one who killed her and I'm very sorry, then pull the plug on her again?"

His father's tone grew soft. "She probably has some things she wants to say to you, and you should give her the chance to say them, even if you don't want to hear them. Maybe you'll find some peace that way." Rob felt his dad's hand on the back of his neck. "Even if it doesn't, I think it's still the right thing to do."

Rob had no answer. "I know you're right." But even if it was the right thing to do, it still wasn't possible. There had just been something on the macrofeeds about protests outside bridesicle centers. Visiting bridesicle places was crazy expensive, to discourage people who couldn't actually afford to repair any of the women from visiting, so it had an exclusive feel, no relatives sitting around sobbing. It cost something like six times as much to visit a bridesicle as it did a relative frozen in the main facility. Not that most people could even afford to visit their relatives.

Rob called up the local bridesicle site, which was in Yonkers, and located a fee list. Yeah, crazy expensive.

"I can't afford it, though. Even if I drained all of my savings, I wouldn't have anywhere near enough."

His father patted his shoulder. "I'll loan you the rest. Whatever you need."

"Dad, no, five minutes is like nine thousand. I have less than two, and I know you don't have seven."

His dad shushed him like he was six again. "We'll get it."

5

Mira

Mira dreamed she was running on a trail in the woods. The trail sloped upward, growing steeper and steeper until she was running up big steps. Then the steps entered a flimsy plywood tower and wound up, up. It was dark, and she could barely see, but it felt so good to run; it had been such a long time that she didn't care how steep it was. She climbed higher, considered turning back, but she wanted to make it to the top after having gone so far. Finally she reached the top, and there was a window where she could see a vast river, and a lovely college campus set along it. She hurried over to the window for a better view, and as she did, the tower leaned under her shifting weight, and began to fall forward. The tower built speed, hurtled toward the buildings. *This is it*, she thought, her stomach flip-flopping. *This is the moment of my death.*

Mira jolted awake before she hit the ground.

An old man—likely in his eighties—squinted down at her. "You're not my type," he grumbled, reaching over her head.

38

6

Veronika

As the front door whooshed closed, Veronika dropped her groceries on the counter and immediately activated *Wings of Fire*. Normally she would first dress in something to fit her part, maybe break out some pretzels, but last night she'd intentionally discontinued at a good part, and had spent all day anticipating.

She pulled on her extensions as the living room transformed into Peytr's dance studio, the program adapting each piece of furniture into some functional aspect of the set so she wouldn't bump into it. Peytr materialized, filling Veronika with a warm, comfortable glow of longing. It was embarrassing, how engrossed she was in this show. Well, not in the show itself as much as in Peytr Sidorov. For Veronika, it was always about the male lead. She fell for Peytr the moment she saw the preview for *Wings of Fire*.

"Are you sure you want to do this?" Peytr asked, picking up where they'd left off last night. "If we cross this line...if we act on what's in our hearts, there's no going back." He was slick with sweat from dancing, his musky scent magnified by the exertion.

Veronika's heart was pounding with anticipation. If she told Peytr she wanted to go through with it, as she planned to, she was fairly sure Peytr's wife, Anya, was going to walk in and discover them. All day Veronika had been planning what she'd say to Anya, trying to anticipate Anya's reply. She'd grown to despise Anya in a manner that was entirely too real.

In answer to Peytr's question, Veronika reached out and stroked Peytr's virtual shoulder, feeling his slick skin under her fingertips, though well aware the sensation was really originating in her brain. She tried to still her breath as Peytr caressed the curve of her breast, which felt just as real, causing her nipples to tense.

Peytr leaned in and whispered, "I love you."

"I love you, too," she answered. It was the first time they'd said it, the culmination of a month of anticipation building from their chance meeting at a penthouse party. Now, the first kiss. Veronika held still as Peytr leaned in, his eyes closed. Veronika kept hers open, not wanting to miss a thing, anticipating the sound of the door opening, of Anya's husky howl of surprise.

"Hey, sweetie, do you—" A male voice that was not Peytr's broke the spell. Veronika leaped from Peytr like she'd been goosed.

She spun to find Nathan gawking at her via screen. *Shit, shit, Goddamn it.* She'd forgotten to set up a block.

"Oh. Sorry," Nathan stammered. "I'll come back."

"No. It's all right. I—" She hurriedly banished the interactive as the heat recently building in her loins migrated to her cheeks. "What is it?" She felt so incredibly stupid.

"I just wanted to see if you wanted to meet up with the gang at Ponyface for a drink later on."

"Yeah, sure." Her lips felt numb.

"Great, I'll, uh, let you know what time once I know."

Nathan beat a hasty retreat. As soon as he was gone, Veronika covered her face with her hands and wished for death. How was she ever going to face him again? Yes, romance interactives sold by the millions, so theoretically what Nathan had caught her doing wasn't particularly strange, but it was still pathetic. Millions of people also masturbated, yet people didn't want others popping in while they were doing it. How could she have forgotten to put up a full block?

If it hadn't been only three p.m., Veronika would have dealt with her searing humiliation by drinking heavily, but that would have to wait a couple of hours. Instead, she decided to work. Focusing all of her attention outward, toward the plights of others, seemed like the best way to pass the next few hours. Maybe with a day or two's distance this would feel less humiliating.

She conducted some advanced searches, using her own signature algorithms to find potential matches for a client having trouble locating men on her own. It was difficult to concentrate. Pulling it up from her system, she replayed the recording of the moment she'd turned to discover Nathan floating behind her, froze the image of his face, covered her own at the sight of his thinly concealed shock and embarrassment.

Was she getting weird from being single for so long? Lots of thirty-two-year-olds were single, but some were better suited to being single than others. *Nathan* was certainly suited to being single (to Veronika's eternal dismay). But she wasn't. It always felt a little off—a little wrong—to come home to an empty apartment. It was as if her life was on hold, the real part yet to get under way. And it was making her weird. Five or six hours a day of romance interactives was a little weird.

It was also childish. Virtual environments were for children. Adults inhabited the real world.

On top of all that, there was the threat of technomie. Because of the nature of her job, Veronika already spent too much of her time interacting with screens, sending subvocalized voice messages, and texting. Instead of withdrawing further from human contact, she should be immersing herself in the real world. Maybe raw-lifers exaggerated the dangers, but the research was clear: In-person contact was vital to healthy functioning. She should give the interactives up. She should delete them all, even the new Peytr Sidorov one she'd been saving. Go cold turkey.

The thought of it swelled her eyes with tears. It would be like going through a breakup; her apartment would get so much emptier. Which was probably a good reason to do it.

No. Some other time, when she was feeling stronger. When she was back in a real relationship.

Veronika reactivated *Wings of Fire*. At first she felt silly and self-conscious, but when Anya burst into the room and discovered her with Peytr, she nearly forgot about the encounter with Nathan.

7

Rob

"Where are you going? Why are you going in there?"

Rob turned to face the screen that had been following him since he got off the micro-T—a brown-skinned woman, maybe southeast Asian, young. Until now she'd kept her distance, said nothing, but whenever Rob glanced behind him, she was there. Now she was right in his face.

"Do I know you?" Rob asked.

"No, but I know you. Why are you going in there? Don't you know she's in there?"

Rob swallowed thickly, feeling himself redden. Since he first noticed her, half a block behind him on Riverdale Avenue, he was afraid she might be a friend of Winter West. Since he wasn't wearing a system, locating him could not have been an easy task. Either she'd been watching him since he left the house, or she'd paid a locator service to alert her as soon as he passed a public security camera. That couldn't have been cheap.

"Yes, I know she's in there," Rob said.

The woman's eyes grew wide. "Then how dare you go in?"

Rob turned, continued toward the big doors to Cryomed's dating center.

The woman's screen swung around to block his way. Rob was tempted to walk right through it, as he'd done with Lorelei, but he stopped.

"Winter was my closest friend," the woman said. "I want to know why you're going in there. If you don't tell me, I'll call the police."

"The police?" The door was ten feet away. He could duck around the screen and sprint inside before the woman could react. But if he did, she would probably be waiting for him on the way out. Better to deal with her now. He was anxious enough about this without having to face Winter's friends. "Look, I'm going inside to face up to what I did. No one feels worse about this than I do. I'm doing what I can to make things right."

The woman studied him, her eyes narrowed with anger and suspicion.

"Why else would I possibly be going to see her? Do you think I want to see her, that I'm going to enjoy this? I'm just trying to do the right thing."

Slowly, tentatively, she moved aside. "All right. Tell her Idris loves her." Just before the doors swirled shut, Rob heard her add, "You bastard."

Deep in the wall, machinery hummed, and the crèche slid slowly out of the wall, like a drawer opening in a morgue. She came feetfirst, and was covered in a silver wrap that was something between a blanket and aluminum foil. Rob was relieved he couldn't see her body. He probably should have read what to expect before coming, but as soon as the money had been secured and there was no turning back, he'd wanted to get it over with as quickly as possible.

Raising the money had reminded Rob of their frantic attempts to raise enough money to save his mom when she got cancer, only this time they'd needed far less money, and had succeeded in raising what they needed.

His chest felt tight, his stomach and bowels were roiling. Another bout of anxiety-induced diarrhea was probably imminent. If he hadn't been twenty-five years old and in perfect health, he was sure a heart attack would be imminent as well.

Her face was the only part of her not covered in silver wrap; Rob stifled a moan when it slid into view. She was so terribly white, her lips gray blue, her eyelashes frosted. She was so clearly dead, and he so did not want to see her dead eyes open and fix on him. As the glass between them slid away, he considered fleeing. He could hide in the bathroom, tell his father he'd done it, fabricate a story about how well it had gone, how cathartic it had been for both of them. Of course, he wouldn't do that, not after his father had taken out a high-interest loan to get him here.

Some sort of machinery started up beneath the crèche, a whooshing, whistling sound that grew higher in pitch and then stabilized, and a separate deep thrumming that Rob felt in his lurching belly.

Winter opened her eyes.

Her pupils were fat disks, devoid of awareness, staring into eternity. Rob pulled back, leaned out of her field of vision, his breath coming in gasps as Winter blinked once, twice, in slow motion.

"I can't—" Rob whispered. He stood to leave as Winter's eyes rolled to look at him, her head perfectly, unnaturally still. Her eyes were focused now—focused on him—and they were wet with terror.

"Hi, Miss West, my name is Robert." He licked his lips. His mouth was horribly dry.

She opened her mouth. Nothing came out but a hiss of air, as if her mouth was one of those spigots that inflate your tires that you still came across, out beyond the suburbs. He watched her recently frozen tongue struggle to form a word. "Do you work here?" When he was searching for her crèche he'd heard other women speaking, so he wasn't startled that her voice was a deep, rolling, androgynous croak.

"No. This is the first time I've ever been here."

She closed her eyes for a moment, as if gathering strength. "I'm scared. I want to go home."

Rob pressed his hand over his mouth; his chest hitched spasmodically. "I'm so sorry."

Winter narrowed her eyes like she was trying to see Rob better, like he was far away. "What am I supposed to do? I don't understand. You're my first..."—she struggled for a word—"visitor."

Her first "date," she meant, but she didn't want to call it that. Rob couldn't blame her.

"What day is it? How long have I been here?"

"About three weeks."

"It feels longer." Her speech was coming easier, maybe as her lips and tongue warmed, but the awful, empty gargling quality of her voice persisted. "The woman who works here told me I'm supposed to talk to you, get to know you, not talk about this place."

"No, that's okay. I'm not..." He trailed off, the words clogging in his constricted throat. He was going to say, "I'm not here for that," but then Winter would ask why he was here, and he'd have to say, "Because I'm the one who ran you over."

"What's your name again?"

"Robert. Rob."

"Hello, Rob. You're not catching me at my best." She laughed, or maybe it was a sob. "What do you do?"

"I'm a musician."

"What do you play?"

"The lute." He took a deep breath. He stammered, starting and abandoning a half-dozen sentences. How could he broach something like this? It needed to be led up to, he couldn't just blurt it out.

"Aren't I the one who should be nervous?" She smiled, clearly trying to put him at ease. He was a wreck, blinking rapidly, his breath coming in shaky gasps. He closed his eyes, feeling like an idiot.

"I promise you, the only reason I don't seem nervous is because my heart isn't beating." Winter's own words seemed to startle her. Her mouth moved soundlessly, her eyes darting around as if seeking an escape route. "I'm really dead, aren't I?"

He didn't want to answer, but what choice did he have? "Yes."

"She wouldn't tell me much about the accident, when she woke me for the orientation."

Somehow Rob's heart found another gear. "Do you remember it at all?"

"No. Not at all. She said I was hit by a small vehicle? Does it say how I died, in my profile?"

Rob checked the timer in the wall above her head. He'd used up nearly four minutes; the remaining seconds were ticking away much too quickly. He needed to get to the point, or this would be pointless, and nine grand he couldn't afford would be wasted.

He just had to say it, let it spill out. He inhaled sharply, looked directly at her face, his heart pumping madly, and said, "There was—you were jogging, and a Scamp came around the corner too fast. The driver wasn't paying attention. And he hit you."

"It says it was a he?"

The timer was racing, the seconds bleeding away. Thirty-one seconds. Twenty-eight. "No, I know it was a he because I—" He squeezed his eyes shut, shook his head. There wasn't time. If he told her, there wouldn't be time to explain, to express how sorry he was. To ask her forgiveness.

Nineteen seconds.

"I'm sorry," he finally said.

She smiled. It was clearly meant to be a sunny smile, but with limited muscle control it looked like she was showing Rob her teeth. From her profile he knew she'd had a beautiful smile. "Sorry for what? I should be the one apologizing. You're being kind enough to visit, and all I've done is talk about my accident."

Eight seconds. She couldn't see the timer. She had no idea how little time they had.

"So you must have died instantly. No pain."

"No pain. At least, I don't remember any."

Her eyes went blank; the muscles in her face relaxed all at once.

Rob stood, stared down at her, his legs trembling, threatening to give way. "Shit. Oh, shit." What was he going to tell his father?

The window slid silently over Winter. Rob watched from

the bottom of the blackest despair as the crèche retracted back into the wall. With nothing else to do, he left.

Nine thousand dollars, wasted. He'd have to lie to his father, tell him everything went swimmingly, that Winter had been incredibly understanding under the circumstances.

Who was he kidding? He couldn't pretend everything was nifty for two minutes, let alone indefinitely. He could barely walk; he felt like there were fifty-pound weights around his ankles, a hundred-pound sack across his shoulders.

"*Idiot*." Rob punched his palm. An old man with pink hair turned to look at him. Rob resisted giving the old prune the finger. Despite how he'd dreaded this visit, he'd also felt a flicker of hope that somehow it would make things, if not right, at least bearable. However Winter had reacted, there would have been some succor in facing her. Instead he was leaving with nothing. As he reached the exit, Rob slowed. He turned to face the enormous room, the walls broken into hundreds of boxes, the farthest rows the size of postage stamps. If he had money, he could simply go back and do it again, but he had nothing. He had worse than nothing—he was nine thousand dollars in debt.

Head down, Rob stepped through the exit into a cutting wind and swirling snow. Idris was waiting for him.

"Did you see her?"

"Yes, I saw her."

"What did she say to you?"

"She told me to rot in hell," he answered without thinking, "Good for her."

Rob walked off, Idris's sobbing growing fainter with each step. He felt so disgusting, like he was leaving a foul odor in his wake that Idris could smell, even through a screen. He had to do something; he couldn't live with himself, trailing that odor. Maybe he should kill himself.

He wasn't sure he was capable of killing himself, and even if he were capable, he couldn't do that to his father.

His father had been right—the only possible absolution would come from facing Winter West. Which meant the answer was obvious. No matter what it took, he had to return and face Winter. Nothing else mattered.

He'd have to suspend his musical career for the time being, find reliable hourly work that paid. Otherwise it would take years to raise nine grand. He could cut expenses. Most of his money went to rent and system fees. He could go on living with his father, so rent wasn't a problem. His biggest expense by far was his system.

There was no getting around it: he'd have to give up his system for a few months—suspend his account and pick up some ancient handheld for the unavoidable stuff like paying tolls.

All that was left was to tell his father what had happened. It was ironic—he had to face his father and ask his forgiveness, because he hadn't been able to do so with Winter. He would, though; he would face Winter, and he would tell her. The certainty of that was all that allowed him to keep walking.

8

Mira

"Hi." It came out phlegmy; the man cleared his throat. "I've never done this before." He was a black man, maybe forty, tall and beefy. His eyes were soft and kind, jittery and shy, and he had an honest smile, though the smile couldn't mask a melancholy he all but radiated.

"What's the date?" Mira asked, still groggy.

"January third, twenty-one thirty-three," the man said. Nearly thirty years had passed since Alex had waked her. She had no idea how long ago her brief encounter with the old man had been. Unless that had been part of her dream. No—there would have been no dream unless someone had waked her.

The man wiped his mouth with the back of his wrist. "I feel like I'm doing something wrong, being here." He frowned. "Is it okay, for me to be visiting you? There's no way to ask ahead of time."

"I'm happy to have the company."

The man gave her a big, sloppy smile. "I'm Lycan, by the way."

"I'm Mira. Nice to meet you."

"I can tell you're an honest person, from your eyes." Lycan had abysmal posture; Mira wondered how he could breathe sitting so slumped.

"I like to think I am," Mira said.

"You're the oldest woman in here, did you know that?" He shook his head. "I mean, not the oldest, since you're only twenty-six, but the oldest based on your birth date. That's why I chose you."

"I see." So she really was an antique. It made her feel terribly alone, and forgotten.

"You know, you wouldn't know it from what's coming out of my mouth, because I'm so nervous, but I'm actually very smart. I'm probably the smartest person you've ever met." Lycan fell silent for a moment. "I'm talking too much. I'm sorry."

"No, I like it," Mira said. It allowed her precious time to think. When she was alive, there had been times in Mira's life when she had little free time, but she had always had time to think. She could think while commuting to work, while standing in lines, during all of the other in-between times. Suddenly it was the most precious thing.

Lycan wiped his palms. "First dates are not my best moments."

"You're doing great." Mira smiled as best she could, although she knew it must look forced. She had to get out of here, had to convince one of these men to revive her. One of these men? This was only the third person to revive her in the past thirty years, and if the first guy, the pervert, was to be believed, she'd become less desirable the longer she was here.

Mira wished she could see where she was. Was she in a coffin? On a bed? She wished she could move her neck. "What's it like in here?" she asked. "Are we in a room?"

"You want to see? Here." Lycan held his palm a foot over her face; silver netting covered his hand, flashing words and images. It transformed into a mirror.

Mira recoiled. Her own dead face looked down at her, her skin gray, her lips bordering on blue. Her face was flaccid—she looked slightly unbalanced, or mentally retarded, rather than peaceful. A glittering silver mesh concealed her to the neck.

Lycan angled the mirror, giving her a view of the room. It was a vast hall. A lift was descending through the center. People hurried across beautiful bridges as crystal-blue water traced twisting paths through huge transparent tubes suspended in the open space, giving the impression of flying streams. Nearby, Mira saw a man sitting beside an open drawer, his mouth moving, head nodding, hands set a little self-consciously in his lap.

Lycan took the mirror away. His eyes had grown big and round.

"What is it?" Mira asked.

He opened his mouth to speak, then changed his mind, shook his head. "Nothing."

"Please, tell me."

There was a long pause. Finally, Lycan answered. "I'm sorry, the last thing I want to do is make you feel bad. It's just that it's finally hitting me at a gut level: I'm talking to a dead person. If I could hold your hand, your fingers would be cold and stiff."

Mira looked away, toward the ceiling. She felt ashamed. Ashamed of the dead body that housed her.

"Is it bad?" he whispered, as if he were asking something obscene.

Mira didn't want to answer, but she also didn't want to

go back to being dead. "It's hard. It's hard to have no control over anything, not when I can be awake, or whom I talk to. And to be honest, it's scary. When you end this date, I'm going to be gone—no thoughts, no dreaming, just nothingness. It terrifies me. I dread those few seconds before the date ends."

Lycan's eyes had filled with tears; he looked genuinely distraught at her plight, so Mira changed the subject, asking about Lycan's family. He had a father and a sister, had never been married.

When Lycan asked about her, she avoided any mention of Jeannette. She told him she'd been an engineer in the military, that she loved Purple Fifth's music and old 2-D Woody Allen movies. She'd been a retro girl, loving all things old and out of fashion, dressed in baseball caps and leg warmers, decorated her apartment with covers of old print magazines. She told Lycan her father died when she was young, but her mother was still alive. Then she remembered that her mother must be long dead as well.

"What if we fell in love, and you agreed to marry me?" Lycan said when she finished. "Would people sense you were too beautiful for me, and guess that I'd met you at a bridesicle place? We'd have to come up with a convincing story about how we met."

"Bridesicle?"

Lycan shrugged. "That's what people call this kind of place."

Then even if someone revived her, she would be a pariah. People would want nothing to do with her.

"I'm afraid it's time for me to say good-bye. Maybe we can talk again?" Lycan said.

Mira didn't want to die again, didn't want to be thrown

into that abyss. She had so much to think about, to remember. "I'd like that," was all she said, resisting the urge to scream, to beg this man not to kill her. If she did that, he'd never come back. As he reached over to turn her off, Mira used her last few seconds to try to reach for a comforting memory, something involving Jeannette.

She remembered last Christmas Eve, just her and Jeannette curled up on the couch, watching an old romantic comedy starring Carly Coates and a willowy blond woman whose name Mira couldn't remember.

9

Rob

The air was filled with the rumble of conversation, spiked with drunken laughter, set over music drifting out of a dozen doorways. The narrow streets were tight with people Rob's age, the air sweet with the scent of popcorn and pastries and buttered lobster sticks, sold by shiny drones from mobile stands. How many nights had Rob spent down here with Lorelei? He had such positive associations with this part of High Town, yet tonight was turning out to be one of the most demoralizing of his life. He'd never really *needed* a job before; playing the lute had earned him what he needed, because he'd always needed very little.

Rob worked his way through the crowd of High Town Friday-nighters. The night style was heavy on checks at the moment—black-and-white checks, red-and-yellow checks. The tips on spiked boots were getting longer and sharper, and bald was getting popular, eyebrows as well as heads, though many were still sporting the giant-ball-of-hair look.

Pelicula was on the corner, bursting out from between two nondescript redbrick buildings like confetti. Rob had no reason to believe he had a better chance of landing a job there than at the last seven places he'd tried, although he used to hang out at Pelicula more than most of the others. Maybe he should have started at a superstore, or one of the factories out by his dad's house, but the crappiest job in High Town paid better than a decent one in the Low, and nightclubs were what he knew, where he felt comfortable.

At the door, the greeter looked him up and down, eyed his old handheld, shook her head before he could open his mouth.

"I'm not looking to get in," Rob said. "I'm looking for a job. Can I talk to the manager?"

The greeter shook her head again. She was perilously thin and absurdly tall, though part of that was her heels, which she boosted an additional inch as she shook her head. "They don't hire unknowns."

"I used to come here pretty often, with Lorelei Van Kampen."

That sparked her interest. "If you get Lorelei to pop over, I'm sure she can get you an introduction to the manager."

Rob folded his arms, wishing he hadn't brought up Lorelei. "I can't do that. Can't you help me out?"

"Sorry, no," the greeter said, and immediately turned to the couple behind Rob. Rob turned back toward the door, doing his best to ignore the glances from people in line who'd overheard the exchange.

Outside, he spotted a woman who looked familiar. She was small, with Anglo-Asian features, peering down the street as if looking for someone. Hadn't he met her at some point? She'd been with a guy Lorelei knew. He needed an in, a connection. There was no way he was going to ask anyone closely associated with Lorelei, but maybe he could capitalize on a loose connection.

His stomach twisting, Rob approached the woman. "Hi."

The woman looked him up and down. "Do I know you?"

"I think so. Didn't we meet in Pelicula a while back? I was with Lorelei Van Kampen."

The woman rolled her eyes. "I seriously doubt that." She went back to looking down the street.

It had been a very long night, and Rob was sick of being treated like shit just because he wasn't wearing a system and was dressed for an interview instead of a night of doing bugs and dancing. "You doubt we've met before, or you doubt I was with Lorelei Van Kampen?"

The woman sighed heavily, but otherwise ignored him.

"You know, despite your staggering beauty and obvious charm, I really wasn't trying to pick you up. I was just saying hello. We did meet before, and from what I remember, you were just about licking Lorelei's boots clean to get her attention and approval."

The woman whipped around to face him. Something scurried out of the black bag hooked to her belt, and before Rob could even identify it as a portable bodyguard, it had climbed up his pants and positioned itself right over his crotch. "What did you say?" she asked.

"Nothing," Rob said. The synthetic bodyguard resembled a black, hairless rat with a silent, rotating blade in its mouth instead of teeth. Its little claws had a death grip on the fabric of his jeans.

"Correct answer." She pressed her face close to his, her eyes blazing. "Get. Lost."

As soon as the bodyguard was off, Rob scurried away, heading for the elevator to Low Town.

Maybe he should have worn his system, although it was now nothing but a dead sheath of synthetic skin. He could have told people it had malfunctioned and he had no idea why. It would have been comforting to have it on.

The elevator let him off on Forty-Second Street, and he was met by the blandness, the deadness of the city unenhanced by a system. It hurt, being without one. It physically hurt. Without the Esthetic Visual Enhancement the steel-and-glass of Pipkin Tower was a flat, featureless obelisk. The sidewalks were a gum-stained mess, the gutters caked with crud. When he got to the suburbs, the contrast between system and no system would get even starker as the landscape got grimier.

"Excuse me." The screen of a pretty, fully-shaven woman was floating alongside him. "How are you today? Nifty?"

"Seminifty at best," Rob said, smiling wanly, wondering if she could possibly be hitting on him. That would be nice in a way, though he couldn't afford to go out with someone, even if he'd felt like it.

"I'm trying to find the Winkle Systems outlet. I know it's around here somewhere." She three-sixtied her screen, then faced him again.

Rob gave her a puzzled look. "Can't you query your system? I don't have one."

"I noticed," she said. "I was wondering why."

He shrugged, trying to look carefree but feeling like a turd that needed to be washed into the sewer, like the turds that seemed to be everywhere now that his system wasn't filtering out all but the ones in his immediate path. "I don't know, I guess I've got other priorities for my money right now."

"You know, you can get a basic one for almost nothing. Why don't you come to Winkle with me? I can show you—"

An ad. It wasn't a woman, it was a Goddamned ad. "Oh,

you're kidding me. Get lost, you lousy shit-screen." He walked away. The screen followed, launching into a flat-out sales pitch now that it had been outed. Out of habit he reached for his system to block the damned thing, but his fingers found nothing but his shirt. Without a system he had no way to block it (if he'd been wearing one, it would have filtered the damned thing out to begin with), so all he could do was ignore it as it rattled on. He broke into a jog, but the ad kept pace, speeding up its pitch, talking faster than any human could.

Mindlessly, he reached for his system *again*, trying to open a screen to escape the thing. He barked a curse. How long would it be before he finally stopped instinctively reaching for his system?

In his first break of the day, a micro-T glided down, wrapped around the outside of a tube like a butterfly clinging to a branch. Rob ran to catch it, hopped in behind the old women who had flagged it. He headed for a seat, leaving the ad on the outside looking in, its beautiful face frowning. From his seat he watched it glide away in search of another defenseless sucker.

"Sir? Please pay six dollars." The micro-T's drone operator startled him; its head was rotated one hundred eighty degrees, looking back at Rob with its big, round, lidless eyes. The micro-T wasn't moving; he'd forgotten that the old handheld he'd salvaged from a discard site didn't have automatic debit capability. It wasn't much more than a toy, really. He couldn't pop a screen with it, couldn't block anyone, couldn't alter what he saw or smelled or felt. Sheepishly Rob stepped up front, pressed the handheld's screen to the micro-T's interface.

As they pulled away, rising up, the shell twisting and turning but the passenger compartments constantly rotating to remain level with the ground, Rob noticed the old woman looking at the handheld wrapped around his knuckles. He slid it into his pocket like a dirty secret. When he'd picked it out of a ten-buck clearance bin it had been caked with dust; it had probably been dumped down a High Town recycling tube ten years earlier, and had sat on the shelves ever since.

A black despair settled over Rob as they headed toward the suburbs, the sun rising behind them. Without his system he felt slow and stupid. And *empty*. It was like he didn't recognize himself. Rob was gone, and this other guy—this *loser*—was in his place. For the hundredth time, he reminded himself that this was only temporary, that what mattered was making things right with Winter.

The micro-T cleared a ridge and the Manhattan skyline rose outside Rob's window. It was dominated by the towers of High Town—the Second Life Building, CDC Headquarters, Porter Rise—porous, colorful spirals reaching toward the clouds, caught in a vast web of bridges and platforms and tubes. Rob smiled wistfully, remembering how as a child he'd referred to them by their colors—the green building, the orange building, the pink building. Lemieux Bridge burst from the east side of High Town and touched down on the New Jersey side of the Hudson like a chrome rainbow, while light copters, flitting like silent mosquitoes, peppered the sky. Private islands crowded the river and bay, like alien invaders wading to shore.

How could he have thought for a moment that he belonged up there in any permanent way?

The clunky steel towers of Low Town, embarrassingly straight and solid, huddled in the dimness below. The amputated stubs of the Empire State Building and Freedom Tower were lost in the shadows of the underside of the platform.

He tried to picture the city as it had been a century earlier, with no High Town at all. He remembered the first time he'd seen a picture of the old Manhattan in school, in the days before dwindling oil supplies and the soft apocalypse caused people to abandon their cars and squeeze into the cities and close-in suburbs by the millions. From what Rob understood, the tubes, plus solar, wind power, etcetera, meant that the know-how was there for everyone to spread back out like it used to be, but the money wasn't there to build it all. So only raw-lifers and the very poor lived far outside the cities now.

The slowing of the micro-T snapped him out of his reverie. He was in New City, the end of the line. New City had been named so long ago that the founders had no idea what a joke the name would become. Rob didn't relish the seven-mile walk to his dad's house.

First, though, he would stop at the tubes to get some groceries. Dad kept telling him he didn't need to, but it felt wrong not to contribute. He was living rent free; the least he could do was buy some food once in a while.

Rob felt the loss of the city most keenly while wading among the tubes, which looked like brightly colored, chest-high mushroom stalks surrounded by screens sporting logos and blaring advertisements. In the city there were actual stores, with actual merchandise right there. Once, there'd been stores in the suburbs as well, but as he'd learned in school, they died during the soft apocalypse. Their corpses were everywhere, some rotting, others converted to housing. Now if you lived far out of the city, your stuff was shot to you at high speed in maglev tubes. Unless you lived too far out, in which case you were fucked. Although if you lived that far out, you probably couldn't afford to pay anyway.

He headed straight for the biggest tube, the only one that

had a line. The line for Superfood, the fed's answer to hunger, purchased from vast ocean farms. It didn't taste that bad, really, despite all the jokes. Even paella would probably begin to taste bad if you ate it three meals a day. When it was his turn, he worked the screen—which had no words, just pictures to serve a semi-illiterate clientele. Then he slumped onto a bench and waited while some drone twenty miles away assembled his order.

A blue jay flapped by, searching for breakfast. Instead of enjoying its flight as he used to do, Rob watched it with envy. Along with guilt, envy was a common emotion these days. He envied everyone, everything. He was used to bad things happening, used to setbacks. How many times had he auditioned for a gig and been turned down? His natural response was to shrug it off, stay positive. He never imagined a situation where he screwed up so badly it would be impossible to make it right, it would be unthinkable to shrug it off. Running someone over required him to stay in a perpetual state of mourning. If he laughed too loud, no matter the situation, it would seem insensitive. Not that he ever felt like laughing.

When the orange light flashed, Rob pushed himself up from the bench. He swiped his index finger over the ID port and his groceries dropped down the delivery chute.

With the straps of the disposable grocery pack digging into his shoulders he walked along the churned-up blacktop of Route 304, the solar plant rising to his left, the collectors like hundreds of giant magnifying glasses raised on poles, the ground below a smooth silver field. To his right, the sun was setting behind pod-style apartment high-rises, the pods worn and cracked, stacked haphazardly along zigzagging walkways. Beyond the pods, the reclamation center sat at the base of Ramapo Mountain, the gargantuan mountain of trash.

He'd once read that ninety percent of the mountain was actually composed of discarded microchips, but that was hard to believe.

Rob stopped, set the groceries in the road, swung one arm and then the other in a big circle to ease the burning in his shoulders as he stared at the reclamation center. Vince, his friend since childhood, worked at the reclamation center, and could probably get Rob a job there. Lots of hours. Shitty pay, but not as shitty as the other options available to him. Walking distance from home. It made perfect sense, even if it was grueling, tedious work under extremely unpleasant working conditions, from what Vince had told him. It was probably time to call Vince. Rob picked up the groceries and kept walking.

Two miles later, he passed one of the enormous pilings that supported Percy Estate, and the pink sky disappeared. Many of the residents of these private estates that stood high above the clustered burbs never set foot in the towns beneath—they flew back and forth to High Town in copters. Rob rarely noticed the latticed roof over his old neighborhood anymore, just took as a given that all of his childhood memories were set in a mottled half-light, and sometimes in full shadow, because at times even the filtered sunlight vanished, hidden behind the stables, the guesthouse, or the main tower residence of Percy Estate. Occasionally the sun would move behind the Percy Estate's pool, and Rob's neighborhood was bathed in a shimmering, dreamlike bluish light. When that happened, kids in the neighborhood used to send messages to each other and they'd all run outside, thinking it was the coolest thing.

10

Mira

Lycan came back. He told her it had been a week since his first visit. Mira had no sense of how much time had passed. A week felt the same as thirty years. It didn't feel as if *no* time had passed, though. It wasn't an eyeblink, although by all rights it should be, since she was dead in the interim.

"Just out of curiosity I visited a few other women. They weren't nearly as interesting as you. Modern women can be so shallow, so unwilling to seek a common ground. I don't want a relationship that's a struggle—I want to care about my wife's needs, and have her care about mine."

"I know just what you mean," Mira said, in what she hoped was an intimate tone. As intimate as her graveyard voice could manage.

"That's why I sought you out. I thought, why not a woman from a more innocent time? The woman at the orientation said choosing a bridesicle instead of a live woman was a generous thing—you were giving life to someone who'd been cheated of hers. It's nice to think I'd be doing something good for someone, and you've been in line longer than anyone here."

Mira had been in line a long time. Although it had only been, what, about half an hour since she died? It was difficult to gauge, because she didn't remember dying. Mira tried to think back. Had her accident been near the city, or had she been on remote assignment? Had she done something careless to cause the accident? Nothing came, except memories of what must have been the weeks leading up to it.

"It's so easy to talk to you," Lycan was saying. "Out in the world, I'm so uncomfortable around women. My heart races. But I open up with you. If you weren't in that drawer, you probably wouldn't give me a second glance, though."

Mira could see he was fishing, that he wanted her to say he was wrong, that she would give him a second glance. It was difficult—it wasn't in her nature to pretend that she felt something she didn't. But she didn't have the luxury of honoring her nature.

"Of course I would. You're a wonderful man, and good-looking."

Lycan beamed. "Some people just spark something in you, make you breathe faster, you know? Others don't. It's hard to say why, but in those first seconds of seeing someone"—he snapped his fingers—"you can always tell." He held her gaze for a moment, something that was clearly uncomfortable for him, then looked at his lap, blushing.

"I know what you mean," Mira said. She tried to smile warmly, knowingly. It made her feel like shit.

There was a constant murmur of background chatter this time.

"...through life and revival, to have and to hold..."

"What is that I'm hearing? Is that a marriage ceremony?" Mira asked.

Lycan glanced over his shoulder, nodded. "They happen all the time here. It's kind of risky to revive someone otherwise."

"Of course," Mira said. She'd been here for decades, yet she knew nothing about this place.

11

Rob

Vince met him outside the front gate of the reclamation center. "Nifty?"

"Not even close," Rob said, falling into step beside Vince. His back still ached from the previous day, and he felt unnaturally drowsy, like he'd been drugged or was getting sick. Vince didn't look tired, though he'd been working at the reclamation center since he finished his last year of free education at sixteen. "Do you adjust to this after a while? I'm so tired I can barely keep my eyes open."

Vince shrugged. "I wouldn't say you adjust. You just get used to being tired."

Ramapo Mountain loomed beyond the reclamation center. It was conically shaped, if you discounted the huge bite taken from the left side. Vince had said they'd have the whole thing processed in another ten years, and move on to another site. Maybe that was why the building looked temporary, constructed of a molded quilt of plastics and metals they were reclaiming from the mountain, the ceiling barely a foot above Rob's head.

In the staging room Rob stashed his clothes in a locker, pulled on a hazard skin, and fixed the filter over his mouth and nose. Then it was out to his station on the floor, past the drones doing the heavy work, tearing open plastic shells and steel cases to expose corroded batteries, circuits, magnets, all the tasty morsels Rob and his superior human fine motor skills would remove and sort. Not that there weren't drones that could do what he did, but they were so expensive to purchase and operate that it was cheaper to pay Rob.

The chubby, ruddy-cheeked woman who'd worked the night shift nodded to Rob as he took over her spot and got to work. The hazard skin's built-in system color-coded the various crap, so all he had to do was use the suit's various extensions to extract the stuff and drop it into the correct color-coded mobile bins. The tough part was that his employers demanded speed. So far he'd been docked at least ten percent of each day's pay for insufficient pace. Vince said that was common for beginners.

The torn-open thing he was working on was big and round and unidentifiable. Rob's best guess was that it was a solar cell, but it didn't matter. Pluck out the components glowing red, drop them in one bin, the green components in another, and so on. The mindlessness of the work allowed him plenty of opportunity to think. Much of the time he rehearsed what he was going to say to Winter. He'd tried out so many possibilities that the words were beginning to lose meaning, to decompose into word salad.

The important thing was, he had saved three thousand

dollars. His father was letting him defer the seven thousand Rob owed for the first visit, and was footing the bill for the interest out of his own earnings. His father was a saint. No grown man nine years out of school could reasonably expect the sort of help his father was giving him. One day, Rob would make it up to him. He would never forget.

12

Veronika

At lunchtime Veronika pulled the cook cord on her Thai boxed meal. When it finished heating, she popped over to Bourbon Street in New Orleans and people-watched. She needed to be around people while she ate, otherwise she would wallow in self-pity that she was eating alone, and she would get depressed. Watching others have fun on Bourbon Street didn't completely insulate her from the tightness in her chest that always came with eating alone, but it helped. After three hours on the bridge, she was seeing the downside: people came and went, but they passed quickly and anonymously, hunched against the cold. Vehicles whizzed by, their drivers paying no attention to Veronika. She was basically all alone.

A climate-controlled full body suit kept her body warm, but her face was icy cold, and the wind was constant and made it difficult to work. Still, the view was lovely. The choppy black water far below; the river, glimpsed here and there winding among old brick-and-steel toward the horizon;

one massive pillar of High Town so close it seemed she could reach out and touch it; the strings of apartments hanging like jewels from the underside of High Town, swaying slightly in the stiff March breeze. Beautiful.

It had been the right decision to come here, despite the isolation. She felt alive, and vigorous. She'd come back tomorrow, and the day after, leaving only to hang out with Nathan for their afternoon coffee.

Her social life revolved so heavily around Nathan. Why did she have so few friends? It was a question she obsessed over, but there on the bridge, with the water lapping far below, she felt an uncommon clarity. It wasn't because she was abrasive, or because she was an outsider. She used to have friends, other outsiders who hung out at coffee shops until late into the night, trading witty barbs. Without realizing it she'd shed some of those friends when she met Sander, even more when Sander left her for Jilly. The truth was, she hadn't tried to make friends since Sander left her for her sister. She hung out with Nathan, played with her interactives, worked. She was alone because she'd chosen to be alone.

A pedestrian stopped at the apex of the bridge, enjoyed the view for a moment, then continued across. Veronika was ready, though. Eventually someone would come to jump, and she would be there, a light against the darkness of their despair. Maybe she wouldn't be able to convince all of them, but if three people jumped per week on average and she could stop one, she'd be saving a life a week.

13

Rob

When the worst of the disorientation cleared, Winter smiled. "I thought I'd totally blown it with you, and here you're back. You must like your women anxious and needy."

Rob tried to laugh, but only managed something that sounded more like a dry cough. He was so nervous, the muscles in his face felt tight, and his lip was twitching.

"I wish I was here for a date. I really do." His voice was a harsh whisper.

Winter studied his face, her smile fading. "What do you mean?"

Rob stared at the floor, trying to muster his courage. He couldn't blow it this time. He'd worked his fingers to the bone, double shifts for three months, for this opportunity. He had to tell her, right now.

"I'm here to talk to you about your accident. That's why I came the first time, but time got away from me. I lost my nerve, I guess."

"I don't understand. Did you see my accident?"

He forced himself to look at her. It was by far the hardest thing he'd ever done. "Miss West, I'm the one who hit you."

It didn't seem to register. A few precious seconds ticked by. Then confusion spread across Winter's face. The lines of confusion melted away, and she stared at Rob with a startled lucidity that made her look almost alive.

"You're the one who killed me?"

He'd looked away again, was staring at his hands. He forced his gaze back to her face. "Yes. I came to tell you how sorry I am." The words sounded absurd leaving his lips, like so many puffs of air sent out to heal a broken spine, a burst aorta, a mile of crushed intestine.

Winter sounded like she was choking, then Rob realized it was a laugh. "You're sorry."

"I know it's worthless, but it's all I have to offer you."

"Were you drunk?"

He looked at the timer. Three minutes left. Three more minutes of this to endure, then he could go back to bed and die there. "I'd been drinking, but I wasn't drunk. I was under the legal limit."

"So you were only slightly impaired. I guess that should make me feel better?"

"No. I didn't mean it that way. I'm not trying to make excuses. Yes, I'd been drinking, and I wasn't paying attention to where I was going, and I fucking hate myself."

She stared at him, her eyes bright and wet. He didn't think the dead could actually cry. "I don't know what to say to you. You have *no idea* what a nightmare this is. You get to leave. I have to stay. Maybe no one will ever wake me again, and I'll stay in this box, in this wall, dead…" She made a sound in her throat that made Rob want to clap his hands over his ears.

"I'm so sorry. If there was anything I could do, I would. I would gladly change places with you." He glanced at the timer. "Oh, God, I only have one minute."

Her eyes opened wide, like a wild animal caught in a trap. "Please. I don't want to go back in there. Let me stay alive for a few more minutes. Just a few."

The dread in her voice, the pleading tone, bored a hole right through him. He sobbed, put his hands over his face. "I can't. I don't have any more money."

Winter made that terrible sound again. "Please. Please don't—" Her eyes widened farther, and all at once she went silent. For a moment Rob thought the refreezing process had started, but there were nineteen seconds left.

She looked at him. "You said you'd do anything. Did you mean it?"

"Yes."

"Then promise me you'll come back. Promise you'll visit me from time to time, so I know I won't spend forever dead in this drawer."

"I will," he said immediately. Her words were like a life-line. He could do this, at least. "I promise. I swear." The relief he felt was like a vise loosened from around his soul. "I will."

The timer reached 5:00; the light drained from Winter's eyes as if they were connected to a power source. Her pupils dilated as the glass cover slid silently over the top of her crèche. Rob turned away. Behind him, he heard her crèche retracting into the wall.

He'd noticed very little on his last visit, cocooned in his own fear and depression, but now he walked a little easier. Not easy, but easier, his boots clicking on the heavy marble floor as he passed row upon row of bridesicles in the long room, their crèches nothing but rectangles set into the walls in floor-to-ceiling grids. He passed what looked like a family sitting around a crèche. The cloak was drawn up so tightly around the woman inside that she seemed nothing but a disembodied head.

There was a smell in the air, something vaguely familiar that would have been pleasant if he'd felt more relaxed. Just a hint of it on a slight artificial breeze. Toasted coconut, maybe? It reminded Rob of some of the swankier restaurants Lorelei had taken him to, where scents were piped in like an olfactory concert.

His dad had been right: look Winter in the eye, own up to what he'd done, do what he could to make it right. He'd do whatever it took to keep his promise. Keep working long hours, spend nothing.

Down an open lift, he reached the vast main room of the facility, the only room that wasn't long and narrow. There was a supplement bar and dine-in restaurant tucked into one corner, and in the center a breathtaking multilevel fountain resembling a vertical maze.

He passed a screen hovering over an open crèche—a virtual date, no doubt—and caught a snippet of conversation as he passed.

"I've done a lot of good for this community—"

He'd have to abandon his dream of making it as a musician. Performing in Low Town bars didn't pay enough to make it worthwhile. The thought of giving up his music hurt almost as much as the idea of giving up his system. Not having his system the past few months had been like not having his right hand. No, worse; he'd rather lose his right hand than his system. Maybe he could allow himself that one indulgence.

He stopped walking.

No. He wasn't going to start making compromises on this

promise. Full effort. No bullshit. He wanted his father to be able to look him in the eye and feel proud, or at least not feel ashamed. If he lived at home and gave up his system, he could visit maybe three times a year. And he would; he would keep his promise, no matter what.

Rob sent a message to his manager at the reclamation center to see if he could pick up some extra shifts.

14

Veronika

Veronika turned her face toward the sun, enjoying the heat on her cheeks, trying not to think of the wrinkles her older self would have to endure. Ultralight copters flitted less than a hundred feet above, looking so much like giant, brightly colored dragonflies. It was worth the substantial toll she and Nathan were paying to lounge on such a high, isolated platform. It was rejuvenating, to be so far from the dense crowds of the city. Almost like a spiritual retreat.

"You know what's missing from this?" Nathan gestured at the view.

"Nothing?"

"Masseuses."

"Oh." She dropped her head. "I was perfectly content two seconds ago, now you've pointed out a shortcoming in my paradise."

Nathan shrugged. "I'll just have to plug the hole in your paradise."

Nathan's fingers flew across his system as Veronika wondered. Massages? That was an awfully intimate suggestion. Downright romantic, almost.

"So I paid Winter a visit," Nathan said.

Veronika jolted. "Oh my god. You're kidding. What happened?" It had never occurred to Veronika that visiting Winter was even possible, but she was in the minus eighty, so of course it was.

Nathan rolled onto his stomach so he could face Veronika. "I felt like I owed it to her, to pay my respects. After the timing of her death and all." He reached up to work his system. Veronika was pretty sure he was working with a client. "Anyway, it was a mistake."

"How so?"

He half whispered his answer, like he was saying something obscene. "She wanted me to visit regularly, like I was a part of her family or something."

Veronika remembered lying in bed when she was twelve, trying to imagine what it would be like to be a bridesicle. She'd just learned about the program that afternoon, from her friend Marcy Tayback, and imagining herself in one of those crèches had filled her with such awful dread. "I know you can't afford to do that, but I can understand her being desperate enough to ask." She couldn't imagine visiting someone there; the idea made her skin prickle. "It would be rancid hell to be a bridesicle. Not that I have anything to worry about." Veronika didn't expect Nathan to argue, since getting selected for the program was based on physical beauty.

"At least she has a fighting chance at getting revived," Nathan said. "One day she could be walking around down there again." He gestured toward High Town, far below. On a teacher's salary, Winter hadn't lived in High Town, but if she was revived, she'd be married to someone who lived in High Town, or on an island estate.

The tube at the far end of the platform hummed, then the door rolled open and the masseuse drones rolled out.

As soon as the drones flashed a green *all clear* to indicate they'd set up a camouflage field, Nathan pulled his shirt over his head, then wriggled out of his pants. Veronika's view was masked, of course; to her it appeared Nathan was wearing a white cylinder from waist to thighs. Still, he was really in his underwear, and a moment later so was she, and they both knew it.

Veronika moaned with pleasure as the drone worked on the knots in her back with soft grips while simultaneously running curved rollers down her arms and legs.

"See?" Nathan said, almost purring. "It wasn't really paradise yet."

"It is now, though." She pointed an accusing finger at Nathan. "Don't you dare come up with something else that's missing."

Through the mesh floor, Veronika watched throngs of people gliding here and there through the Market District, creating fluid patterns, their silent movement leaving Veronika feeling peaceful, her mind temporarily silenced. The next time Veronika was down there in that crowd herself, she needed to remember what it looked like from up here.

Nathan grunted, dismayed. "This guy insists I include a clip of him with his shirt off. How do you tell someone their shirtless torso is definitely not going to draw women."

"Let me see."

Nathan uncloaked the feed he was viewing, revealing a meter-high hologram of a ferret-faced guy tossing a bolo. He was so scrawny you could play his ribs like a xylophone.

Veronika couldn't suppress a bray of laughter. "Yeah, definitely not helping himself. He needs to be in a jacket and tie."

"That's what I told him."

A text alert flashed in the corner of Veronika's vision. She froze when she saw it was from her sister. "Abort. That's all, I'm finished," she told the massage drone as she reached for her neatly folded clothes. Something had to toss her out of paradise, didn't it? God forbid she should have an hour of bliss.

"What's the matter?" Nathan asked, raising his head, but remaining on the table.

Veronika eyed the message like it was a mine. What the fuck did Jilly want? Hadn't the phrase *zero contact* been clear enough for Jilly? One of their parents must be sick, or dead. If that was it, would she attend the funeral? No. Death didn't change anything. So why even open the message? What could be in it that wouldn't cause her pain?

Nathan stopped his drone and sat up. "What is it? You look like someone died."

"Someone may have," she muttered. If she didn't open it, she'd wonder and wonder until she had no choice but to open it just to break the cycle of guesses and speculation spinning in her head.

So she opened it.

It was an invitation to her nephew's second birthday party, on the roof of her parents' condo building. The attached message from Jilly was short and to the point. *Please come.*

Growling in anger, Veronika deleted it.

"Come on," Nathan said, waving his hand in a beckoning motion. "Let's hear it."

"My sister invited me to her son's birthday party."

"I didn't know she had a son."

"Neither did I." Although that was a lie. One weak and

lonely night, Veronika had checked up on Jilly and Sander, hoping to discover they'd divorced. Not that she would take Sander back if they divorced, but it would have been comforting to discover they weren't living happily together. Evidently they were.

"What are you going to do?"

Veronika gaped at him. "What do you mean, what am I going to do?"

Nathan shrugged. "You have a choice: you can go, or not go. If you don't go, you have another choice: tell Jilly you're not going, or ignore the invitation."

"Thanks. I understand the basics of human social interaction." All she'd asked is for Jilly to leave her the fuck alone. Evidently even that was too hard.

"I think you should go," Nathan said.

Veronika's hands balled into fists, totally on their own. "Are you insane?" She waited for a response, but Nathan just looked at her. "That should be *my* child. *I* should be planning a birthday party, not Jilly."

"Do you even want kids?"

"Yes I want kids. Why would you think I wouldn't want kids? I love kids." She was shouting; she could hear she was shouting, but seemed unable to control the volume, just like she was unable to unclench her fists.

Nathan held up his hands, like a boxer trying to stop the fight. "I'm not saying your sister is right and you're wrong. She was wrong. You were right. But Vee, you've let her drive a wedge between you and your parents. You've let her steal your parents as well as your fiancé."

"My family drove that wedge, not just her. They condoned what she did." Still shouting. She took a huffing breath. This had been such a perfect afternoon.

Nathan let his head droop for a moment, then he lifted it. "I think 'condoned' is a little strong. They tolerated it."

Veronika sputtered, words escaping her.

"I never bring this up, because I know it's a painful topic for you, but just for a minute, try to step back from it."

"I don't want to step back from it. You think I'm the one who's being unreasonable, don't you?"

Nathan waved his hands, shaking his head emphatically. "Let's drop this. I didn't mean to suggest I was on their side. It's none of my business; I should have kept my mouth shut."

Fighting back tears, Veronika lunged forward and hugged Nathan fiercely, feeling his bare chest and belly against her. "I'm sorry. I didn't mean to take it out on you."

She felt Nathan nod, his chin brushing the top of her head.

"But I can't go. Even if you're right, I can't sit there while Jilly and Sander cuddle with the son that should have been mine while my parents beam."

Another nod. "That's a perfectly understandable sentiment." Over Nathan's shoulder, Veronika watched the drones, who were watching them, waiting for instructions.

"What if I went with you?" Nathan asked.

Veronika stepped back, mildly stunned as she reeled out the implications of his suggestion. What if he went with her? No one in her family knew Nathan, or knew she hadn't been out with anyone since Sander betrayed her. She didn't have to show up as the lonely loser she was—she could make a grand entrance, turn everyone's head, turn Jilly lime green.

"Would you act like I'm the most fabulous woman you've ever seen?"

Nathan opened his mouth, feigning surprise. "You *are* the most fabulous woman I've ever seen."

"No, really. The only way I could stand to be there is if it looks like Jilly did me a favor by stealing Sander. If I showed up totally flash, a gorgeous guy on my arm…" The image in Veronika's mind set her heart racing. She grasped Nathan's arm at the biceps and squeezed. "You'd really do yourself up? Be utterly gorgeous? Charm the living shit out of everyone in sight?"

Nathan spread his palms, flashed that gorgeous grin. "Lead me to the fray."

Oh, this was going to be magnificent.

15

Mira

It was their fifth or sixth date in just a few weeks, and they'd been talking about Tarrytown, Mira's hometown, which Lycan had visited, or not exactly physically visited but had seen by opening some sort of remote portal, if Mira was understanding him correctly. Her parents' house was gone, but the lighthouse was still there, and the park where Mira had broken her arm doing a backflip. Mira had grown fond of Lycan, which was a good thing, because the only thing she ever saw was Lycan's face. He was her life, such as it was.

"There's something I have to tell you," Lycan said.

"What is it?" Mira asked.

He looked off into the room, sighed heavily. "I've never enjoyed a woman's company as much as yours. I'm afraid you won't want to see me again, after I tell you what I have to tell you."

Mira tried to imagine what this man could possibly say that would lead her to choose being dead over his company. "I'm sure that won't happen, whatever it is. You can trust me."

Lycan put his hand over his eyes. His chest hitched. Mira made gentle shushing sounds, the sort of sounds her mother had never made. "It's okay," she cooed. "Whatever it is, it's okay."

Lycan finally looked at her, his eyes red. "I really like you, Mira. I might even love you. But I lied to you. I'm not a rich man. I'm well-off, enough to afford these visits, but not the kind of rich where I can afford to revive you. Not even if I sold everything I owned."

She hadn't realized how much hope she was harboring until it was dashed. A black despair overtook her and swelled until even the room seemed to darken. "Please. You have to get me out of here."

"Mira, I can't. We're talking millions and millions of dollars." He whispered the amount, as if it were too obscene to say aloud.

She wanted to cry, but no tears would come, her chest wouldn't respond. She was left with nothing to express the rising panic she felt except a gargling sound in the back of her throat. "I can't stand this. I can't be here any longer." She looked at Lycan, who looked away, ashamed. "You have to get me out of here. *Please.*" She was blowing it, driving Lycan away with her hysteria. She knew that, but the words poured out anyway.

Lycan covered his face with his hands again. "I'm sorry I lied to you. I did a terrible thing, raising your hopes." He let his hands drop. "It's just that I was so *lonely.*"

The women here must all be kind to him, must hang on his every word in the hope that he'd choose them and free them from their long sleep. Where else would a man like Lycan get that sort of attention?

"But now I see how selfish I've been. I'm disgusting." He swallowed thickly, shook his head. "Do you know, I've tried half a dozen social-anxiety stabilizers? But they all make my depression worse." He laughed humorlessly. "That's the thing, isn't it? There's always a catch, always a cost that's too steep."

The self-hatred in his tone, the flatness in his eyes, shocked her. It was as if he'd suddenly undergone a complete personality change. He'd been coming to this place to escape the man he was in the real world, she realized. He was dropping the pretense now, and he would never be able to face her again.

"I'd miss you terribly if you stopped visiting me," she said. The truth was if Lycan didn't visit, Mira would be incapable of missing anyone. No one else was visiting, or likely to stumble upon her among the army of bridesicles lined shoulder-to-shoulder in boxes in this endless mausoleum.

Lycan wiped his nose on his sleeve. "I'm sorry, Mira. I'm so sorry for what I've done."

"Lycan, please—" was all she could get out as he reached above her.

16

Rob

It was stupid, but Rob found himself hurrying to get to Winter's crèche. For months he'd been rehearsing follow-ups to their previous conversation—new, more upbeat lines of conversation. Mostly, though, he'd agonized over the months that had passed since he last visited her. Pressure had been building in his chest from the moment he made his promise, and this visit would release that pressure. Or some of it, at least.

He understood that Winter was beyond time, beyond impatience as she waited for an opportunity to live for a few minutes. What concerned him was that someone else had waked her since his last visit. If so, she would have asked this visitor how long she'd been dead, and when she heard it had been months, she'd assume Rob had lied, that he told her what she wanted to hear and slunk off to enjoy his life. He didn't want her to think that, even for five minutes.

On the other hand, he had no idea what they were going to say to each other. That part made him nervous, which was why he'd been rehearsing possible things to say while he'd plucked color-coded bits of technology from century-old husks for the past four months.

The seat was waiting for him, as usual. Squeezing his hands together, he waited while the crèche rolled out of the wall.

Winter's eyes fluttered open. The timer began to roll. It was unfair that the timer began as soon as Winter was conscious; it would be fifteen or twenty seconds before she was lucid. He would pay about five hundred dollars during that time.

"You came back," Winter said.

"Of course. I promised."

They looked at each other, the seconds ticking away.

"I wanted to say again how sorry I am. If it's any consolation, there hasn't been a moment since it happened that I haven't been miserable."

Winter bit her lip thoughtfully. The gesture made her look more animated, almost alive for a moment. "How can I put this? That you're miserable doesn't make me feel better. What does make me feel better is knowing someone will wake me from time to time. If you do that, then there's no need for you to be miserable. Fair enough?"

Rob nodded, though he wasn't sure it was that simple.

"Is there anything I can update you on that you'd enjoy? The news, your favorite interactives? Your profile said you're a Cubs fan—do you want to hear how they're doing?"

"*No*," Winter said. If she were capable of shouting, Rob thought she would have shouted it. "I can't put the 'why' into words, but, no." She thought about it. "I don't want to be reminded that the world is moving on, that time is passing."

There was something unsettling about her face, and Rob finally realized what it was. She didn't blink.

"How much time *has* passed?" she asked.

"Four months." He felt guilty admitting it had taken him that long.

"Though someone woke me a month after your last visit, so three months."

Rob raised his eyebrows. "Oh?" He knew the odds of any one bridesicle being chosen for repair and revival were long, so he hadn't dared hope.

"My ex-boyfriend." Her eyes moved stiffly up, then down. She may have been trying to roll her eyes. "He broke up with me the day of my accident. Evidently he feels guilty now that I'm dead."

"*He* feels guilty?" Rob looked toward the ceiling, shook his head.

"I asked him to visit once in a while as well. Nathan promised he would."

Rob nodded. If someone else visited, maybe it would be all right for Rob to visit less often. He wondered if the guy really would, and if Winter knew how much it cost to visit. He glanced at the timer: almost two minutes gone.

"Do you want to pass along a message to anyone? I can make sure it reaches them."

"No, thanks. My parents are dead, and I don't want to upset my friends."

"You don't have brothers or sisters?"

"I have a brother, but you wouldn't be able to find him. He's a raw-lifer, way out in the wild."

Rob nodded understanding. One of his favorite interactives was a raw-life show. You had to figure out how to make new shoes when your old ones wore out while also trying to learn how to avoid dead spots and people who weren't living way out in the ruins by choice.

There was a date going on nearby, maybe one level down.

Rob couldn't quite hear their words, but the murmuring was distracting.

"I wish I could see the sky. Trees."

"There's a window down there." Rob looked over his shoulder at the picture window down the hall. It looked out on the tops of gorgeous hybrid cypress yaupons.

"I can't see it." She couldn't turn her head at all. He wasn't allowed to touch her to turn her head, and surveillance cameras were monitoring them. He wasn't sure he could bring himself to touch her even if he'd been allowed.

"It feels like my head is a block of stone," she said. "All I can feel is my face."

Rob nodded, not sure how to respond.

"Tell me something happy," Winter said. "Something warm. I don't want to think about my life." When she saw Rob struggling, she added, "What do you love to do?"

"Play the lute."

"The *lute*? That's right, you're a musician. I didn't know anyone played the lute."

"No one else does," he laughed. "When I was ten, I heard an old man playing one in a park near my house, and I..."—he cast about for words—"it just called to me. I can't explain it."

"You're an old soul, then. You must have played one many lives ago."

He smiled, not sure if she was speaking figuratively, or if she really believed in reincarnation. "When I'm playing, everything else fades away. It's the purest joy I know." He spoke quickly. He felt like every word should be meaningful. Winter was speaking quickly too; as quickly as she could, given the stiffness in her jaw and mouth.

Eighty seconds left. Five minutes was an astonishingly brief period of time.

"Will you bring your lute next time, and play for me?" The hope in her eyes told him it was not an idle request.

"Absolutely."

"Maybe you could play while I'm waking? I'm so disoriented then. Music would give me something to focus on."

"Do you have a favorite song?"

"No, nothing I know. Something ancient, from the time when lutes were popular."

He nodded. "I can do that."

Thirty seconds now. He wondered if he should tell her. "Is it easier if you don't know when the time is up?"

"Oh, God. The time is almost up?" The panic in her voice was unnerving, somehow made worse by the distortion. "How much do I have?"

Rob glanced at the timer. "Only thirteen seconds."

She whimpered. "I want to go home." She looked at Rob. "Promise you'll come back soon?"

"I will. Don't worry. It'll seem like an instant."

That didn't seem to comfort Winter. "It won't. It's not like sleeping—"

The fear drained from her eyes, leaving emptiness.

As soon as Rob got outside, he took out his handheld. She'd said her ex-boyfriend's name was Nathan. Maybe Nathan would be willing to coordinate visits with Rob, if Rob could locate him. There was only one possible way to locate him with nothing but a first name. He scrolled to the text message he'd received from Winter's friend Idris the day after she confronted him at the entrance to the dating center.

I miss her so much. You have no idea who you took from us.

He had never replied to the message. Now he did. *Can*

you please tell me the last name of Winter's ex-boyfriend Nathan? I need to contact him, for Winter's sake.

Idris appeared via screen before he made it to the end of the block. "What do you mean, for Winter's sake?"

Rob explained what he was doing, and how Nathan might help.

17

Veronika

Two teenage girls passed Veronika, one wearing a falsie—a skin that looked like a system but didn't actually do anything. She was speaking in inflected speech, her subvocalization nothing but nonsense syllables. Her friend, who didn't even have a falsie, seemed impressed.

As the girls passed out of her view, Veronika returned to watching the Hudson creep by between the chrome slats of the bridge while helping Dora McQueen swap text with a guy who was completely wrong for her. FaceQ had Dora rated a four point four. She was a squat, stubby-legged woman with a big head and thin hair. The guy she was flirting with was a solid six point two, and Veronika knew the type—he was looking for someone who would not only happily do it doggy-style on their first face-to-face, but agree to wear a collar and a leash and let fifty of his friends watch. Most of her clients eagerly took her advice about how to meet someone, but so few listened when she offered expert advice on *whom* to meet.

Across the bridge and down a ways, a pedestrian caught her eye. Like countless others who'd stopped over the past six months, he was taking in the view, but there was something about his posture—a tightness, an unease.

He put a hand on the rail, and lingered.

He looked around and, spotting Veronika sitting on her portable chair on the other side of the bridge, quickly looked away. Even from this distance Veronika could see he was a big man, six-five or taller.

As Veronika pretended to work, he kept glancing over; soon Veronika was reminded of kids attempting to cheat on tests, back in the days of her brief, disastrous stint as a high school teacher. A glance to see if she was looking, then a quick look away when he saw she was.

Her heart began to thump. He might well be planning to jump. After all this time, finally.

She leaned forward in her chair, intending to stand, to go over and talk to this man, then sat back. It would be a long, awkward walk over there, and all the things she'd imagined saying to a potential jumper now seemed absurd.

The man glanced at her yet again. Veronika rotated her chair so she was facing away, toward the water, then discreetly opened a screen up in the rafters of the bridge.

When the man saw she was no longer facing him, he pulled a handheld from his pocket, worked it for a moment, spoke a few words into it.

Then he dropped it over the railing and watched it tumble, growing smaller until it splashed into the Hudson. He looked around, lingering on Veronika, evidently making sure she wasn't about to turn around. He grasped the railing with both hands.

Shit, he was really going to do it. Barely able to breathe,

Veronika leaped from her chair and rushed toward him. The deafening bleating of a microbus horn startled her; she'd stepped right into traffic, was nearly clipped by the bus as it sped by. Shaking both hands impatiently, she waited for a break in traffic as the man struggled to get over the railing.

"*Wait*," Veronika called, waving at the man, whose front leg was on the outer girder, his back foot still hooked by the rail. Veronika skirted across a thin opening in the traffic and sprinted down the curve of the bridge. She reached him just as he set his second foot on the girder.

"Wait. Hang on," she said, breathless.

The man turned. His entire face was trembling. "What do you want? Get away from me."

She grasped the rail with both hands. "Don't do this. It's a mistake. I know you're feeling hopeless right now, but that feeling will pass."

The man gaped at her. He was a black man, with a boyish, innocent face that seemed out of place on his tall, powerful frame. "Leave me alone. This is *personal*." He looked over his shoulder, down at the river.

Veronika was taken aback by his reaction. She'd expected sadness, despair. That she understood. But he was angry. He also seemed embarrassed.

"What's your name?" Veronika asked.

He reacted as if the question startled him. "I'm not telling you my name. Go. *Leave*."

"Let me buy you a cup of coffee. Let's talk. You can always come back later."

"What is *wrong* with you?" he growled. "Just get the hell away from me. Do you understand? I don't want you here."

Veronika took a step away, feeling foolish. "I'm sorry." She wanted to go, wanted to escape this man's angry glare, but her feet wouldn't move. He was going to *jump*. How could she walk away from another human being, knowing he was going to kill himself? She held her ground. "If I was the one standing where you are—and that's not totally inconceivable—I would hope someone would care enough to try to stop me, even if I didn't want them to."

"Well, that's beautiful. Why don't you go write a book of beautiful platitudes?" He squeezed his eyes shut for a moment. "Look, I've thought this through very carefully, and I'm at peace with it. Every moment you stay here, you're just stretching this out for me. So please, I appreciate your good intentions, but give me my privacy."

She'd known this was going to be hard, but this was hard in a way she'd never anticipated.

"I can't," she said.

A screen popped up, out over the water a dozen feet from them. It was a middle-aged woman with raccoon-eye tattoos. She didn't say anything, just hung there, watching.

The man glanced over his shoulder, noticed the screen, just as another popped up. And another. Rubberneckers. Someone passing on the bridge must have alerted her friends.

The man looked back at Veronika as a dozen more screens popped into existence. "You've made my last few minutes on this planet even more intolerable than they would otherwise have been. Thanks a lot."

Then he turned and jumped.

An icy, paralytic shock filled Veronika as the screens shifted as one to face the river so they could watch the man plummet. Veronika was left staring at the thin slices of the tops of the screens—a hundred of them now—her mouth still cranked open to beg the man to stop, to wait, to think about how beautiful the world was, if you could just get out of your own head.

The screens began to disappear. The show was over.

Her paralysis finally lifted, Veronika ran, her breath coming in tight gulps that threatened to turn into sobs as she avoided looking between the slats, afraid she might catch a glimpse of the man floating on the river, the man she'd been speaking to just a few seconds earlier. She didn't ever want to set foot on this bridge again. While she ran, she sent a message to Nathan. She needed to see him, needed his confidence. Only he could convince her she hadn't just done an awful, unforgivable thing.

18

Rob

People glided by on the sidewalk. Rob could feel a slight breeze as each passed. He felt like a big, dopey lunk, plodding along in his Low Town shoes. The two hundred dollars he'd gotten for his gliders didn't help the Winter cause much, but Rob could imagine what people would think if he glided by in High Town shoes while claiming that he was taking a vow of poverty to make reparations for what he'd done. He wasn't afraid to admit it: part of his reason for doing this was to redeem himself in the eyes of his friends and family. It wasn't the only reason, or even the primary reason, but it was part of the reason.

As he walked, he kept reaching back to massage his neck. It ached, sent bolts of pain into his shoulders if he turned his head too quickly. Spending ten-hour shifts bent over discarded electronics was wreaking havoc on his back and neck. His fingertips were finally developing calluses, so at least he was past the point of walking around with raw, bleeding fingers.

Club Aishiteru wasn't hard to find. The entrance was

raucous, pulsing, brightly colored—like a silk-gloved fist that grabbed you and tried to pull you inside.

They wouldn't let Rob in without a system, so he had to rent one. He watched ninety precious dollars roll off his bank balance, on top of sixty for the cover charge. He sure hoped this guy Nathan showed up. He hadn't sounded eager to meet.

It was a cheap system, and since it wasn't custom-fit nor did it have a body-adaptive function, it hung from his arms like an old man's sagging skin.

Then Rob had to create at least a minimal profile before the greeter would let him in. Did he want kids, or have any that he knew of? Was he interested in women of any ethnic mix? If not, he had to specify the maximum tolerable percentage of whatever ethnicities he found undesirable in a mate. Then he had to report his own ethnic makeup (fifty-four percent Asian, twenty-eight Anglo, eighteen Latino, not that it was anyone's damned business).

As he passed through the checkpoint into the bar, his height and weight (evidently he'd lost nearly twenty pounds since the accident) were measured and added to his profile automatically. Rob was surprised they didn't insist he drop his pants so they could measure the length of his dick.

A singles meetup was not the sort of place Rob would have preferred to meet, but Nathan had made it clear that if Rob wanted to talk to him, this was where he'd be. It was difficult to tell how big the place was, because the walls had been replaced with visual links to sister bars in other cities, which gave the impression that it stretched out almost to infinity in every direction. The idea was if you saw someone interesting in one of the other bars, you could pop over remotely and say hello.

People visiting remotely weren't in screens—they were here in full head-to-toe, three-dimensional virtual splendor. This was a private business, so the public regulations that required people to use screens so they wouldn't be confused with live bodies didn't apply. And it *was* confusing. Most of the nearby patrons were zombies—virtual images their owners weren't monitoring. They were completely still, expressions frozen on unblinking faces. Evidently people set up in multiple locations so they could be seen, and waited for someone to approach them.

Scanning the bar, Rob spotted Nathan talking with a virtual woman. Rob hung back and watched, waiting for the conversation to finish. Nathan had a Mediterranean look, with pretty, long-lashed eyes and a three-hundred-dollar haircut, complete with stylish white highlights. Rob fumbled with his unfamiliar system, called up the profile of the woman Nathan was talking to, curious about what kind of woman Nathan went for. Ms. Petra Knox. Twenty-eight, compared to Nathan's (Rob called up his profile) thirty-eight. She was a transportation analyst (whatever that was), didn't want kids, an atheist from a Methodist family. Ratingsmart certified her attractiveness at eight point nine, FaceN at eight point seven.

The ratings firms used highly scientific programs to arrive at their ratings, but Rob was sure the programs missed important aspects of beauty they couldn't teach a computer to recognize. There was no way Petra Knox was more beautiful than Winter West. Petra looked like a thousand other beautiful women; she had an elegant face, perfect cheekbones, a long neck. She was perfect to the point that she looked artificial. Even dead and frozen, Winter's face was so much more expressive. When Winter smiled, the lines that formed around her mouth, and the way she seemed to show far too many teeth, made her look warm and real and unique. Also, Winter was more cute than classically beautiful, and from what

Rob could tell, the programs never awarded a "cute" woman a score approaching nine, no matter how achingly cute she was. Higher scores were only for women with aristocratic faces, faces that indicated superior breeding, but did nothing to make the heart skip a beat.

Petra Knox's screen finally swiveled away from Nathan, and Nathan immediately turned and headed toward Rob. Either he'd spotted Rob watching him, or had set up a facial-recognition program to alert him when Rob showed up.

Nathan extended a hand as he approached. "How did you get my name again? You said you were a friend of Winter's?" He looked to be carrying on at least two remote conversations, maybe three, while speaking to Rob. His style was impressive; Rob didn't even recognize the vocal rhythm he was using, and his fingers worked the air so deftly Rob could almost see the virtual keyboard he was working, in lieu of working directly on his system.

"I got it from Idris Badini, one of Winter's friends. And I *am* a friend of hers, not was."

Nathan looked Rob up and down, not missing a beat. "You've got a rented system and out-of-style boots, but you've got the juice to be friends with a dead girl at eighteen hundred a minute? Okay, suddenly you got interesting. Give me some context."

If he told Nathan the truth straight-out, would Nathan punch him? Rob wasn't sure. Nathan wasn't a thick-browed hyper-masculine orc, but he had a restless, high-energy style that might translate into violence under the right circumstances. Rob opened his mouth to tell some credible lie, but couldn't think of a damned thing. What would explain his situation, besides the truth? He took a subtle half step back from Nathan.

"I'm the one who hit her."

Rob watched Nathan take this in, his face slack with surprise, his other conversations dropped. It was strange to have someone's full attention (someone other than his dad, anyway).

"Hold on," Nathan finally said. "Let me get this straight: *you* killed Winter? You ran her over?"

Rob looked Nathan right in the eye, fighting the urge to look at his shoes. "That's right."

"And then you thawed her out for a visit?" He was shaking his head, incredulous. "Did you tell her who you were?"

"Yes, of course. Why else would I go there?"

"I don't know. I can't believe you went there, period." His fingers were flying again, his Adam's apple bobbing as he resumed his secondary conversations, probably encouraging his friends to listen in. Fortunately, they couldn't simply pop open screens and gawk because of the cover charge.

"You went there, too," Rob pointed out.

"She told you that?" Nathan seemed surprised.

"She mentioned it, yeah."

He studied Rob for a moment. "I want to hear the whole story. You've got beach balls, Cousin." He put his arm across Rob's shoulders, turned him toward the bar. "Come on, I'll buy you a drink."

Rob began at the beginning, with Lorelei. He wanted Nathan to have the full context for the accident. If he was going to convince Nathan to commit to visiting Winter, and hopefully coordinate with Rob to spread out their visits, he needed Nathan to like him. When he mentioned he'd been living with Lorelei, Nathan's already animated features lit up further. "Lorelei Van Kampen?"

"You know her?"

"Indirectly. Three degrees." It took Rob a second to get it, that Nathan knew someone who knew someone who knew

Lorelei. Three degrees of separation. "She's got a trillionaire grandfather, but she's mostly cut off, right?"

"Right. So, she's throwing everything I own out the window with three hundred screens looking on. My photo files. Recordings of songs I composed—"

"Yeah, I can see what you mean about all the eyes—she's got quite a following. She's one rare bird, though. Gorgeous."

Rob's stomach lurched. "Are you watching her right now? Live?"

Nathan nodded, his attention clearly compromised.

"Please don't do that. I don't want any connection to her, not even once-removed."

Nathan flashed a wide smile, nodded. "No problem, I get it. I take it there's no chance of me getting an introduction, then?"

Rob laughed. "No, we're not on speaking terms." This guy was something.

Rob went on with the story, careful to avoid foisting responsibility for Winter's death onto Lorelei, or onto Winter herself. From the start it had been tempting to claim Winter came out of nowhere. Given Winter's breakup with Nathan that day, Rob could have weaved a convincing story of a heartbroken and careless woman not watching where she was going. Maybe he could have even convinced himself. But Rob had been the one who came out of nowhere, drunk, driving too fast. He skipped the part about being drunk.

When he told Nathan about the promise he'd made to Winter, and how he planned to keep it, Nathan stopped him. "Wait a minute. You're giving up everything, including your dream of becoming a famous musician, just so you can visit Winter?"

"That's right."

"For how long?"

Rob shrugged. "Until she's out of there."

Nathan tilted his head, as if maybe he hadn't heard Rob correctly. "Cousin, she's not ever getting out of there. She's a cutie, no doubt, but there are many, many cuties on ice in that place."

"Then I'll visit her for the rest of my life."

Rob looked at Nathan, daring him to question his commitment.

Nathan groaned, rolled his eyes. "Shit. We're about to have company. One of my coworkers just touched base and she's completely unglued, babbling about someone jumping from a bridge. Hey, I'm sorry about this."

Rob waved off the apology, quickly got to the point. "The reason I'm here is because Winter said you were planning to visit occasionally as well—"

Nathan's smile vanished. Suddenly he looked grim, pained. "I see where this is going. Not a chance, Cousin."

Someone in the bar pinged Rob; Rob sent a quick decline, wondering who would be interested in talking to a guy with a rented system, a guy who was so scrawny he looked like bait for stray cats. "But you promised her you'd visit."

"Of course I promised her. What was I supposed to say? 'Hell, no, Winter. I can't afford it? I can't imagine anything more depressing than visiting my dead ex-girlfriend every couple of months?'" He craned his neck to look around Rob, maybe at a woman who had pinged him. "I'm sorry I went there in the first place."

A dark-haired woman appeared in the entrance, her eyes red, her lower lip trembling. She looked utterly out of place, her baggy, multipocket pants and red sweatshirt not intended to show off her figure. It had to be Nathan's friend.

Rob talked faster. "I understand what you're saying, but these visits mean the world to her; she clings to them like a lifeline. I thought if you—"

"They're not a lifeline, because she's not alive." Nathan put a hand on Rob's shoulder, lowered his voice as the woman approached. "I don't mean to be cruel, but Cousin, you snipped her lifeline."

The woman rushed into Nathan's arms, sobbing. "Give me a sec, Veronika," he said, prying her off far enough to offer Rob his hand. "I admire what you're doing. No—'admire' isn't strong enough. I'm in awe." The woman clinging to Nathan turned to look at Rob, her eyes wet, but curious. She was on the chunky side, her brown hair a great unkempt tornado, her eyes squinty. Despite all of that, she was cute, in a shy, intellectual sort of way. Rob wasn't sure if he should introduce himself, or if that would seem insensitive, given her agitated state.

"I just sent you nine hundred toward your next visit," Nathan said. "I'll help when I can. That's the best I can do." He gave Rob's hand a final squeeze and let it go.

"Thanks. That helps more than I can say."

"Yeah, well, it's guilt money. I figure I'm ten percent responsible for what happened."

Nathan turned his attention toward Veronika, and Rob headed for the exit. He was disappointed, but with an extra nine hundred in his account it hadn't been a total loss.

"And Cousin?" Nathan called. Rob turned back. "Let me buy you a drink sometime. I'd like to see if some of whatever it is you have rubs off."

"I'd like that," Rob said.

Nathan nodded. "I'll be in touch."

As he left, Rob heard the woman breaking into sobs. Nathan had said it was about someone jumping off a bridge. Rob wondered if he'd meant it figuratively, or literally. It would be rude to linger, so he'd probably never find out.

19

Veronika

All night, Veronika saw the man leap off the bridge. She'd doze from time to time, and wake feeling sure the whole incident had been something she'd seen on TV, or in an interactive, and then with a jolt she'd realized that no, it had actually happened. Then when that jolt had just about played itself out, she remembered she was going to see Sander and Jilly in the morning, and a fresh jolt of adrenaline would hit her. When she dragged herself out of bed at six, she was exhausted.

There was no way she could see her sister. She needed to be at her best for that encounter, otherwise she'd be a twitching, nervous mess. As she showered and dressed, she went back and forth, came close to telling Nathan to stay home half a dozen times, finally decided she would let him show up, then suggest they get doughnuts instead.

All of her anxiety evaporated when the door opened and Nathan let himself in. He was perfect. His haircut probably cost more than Jilly's car, the points on his boots were a foot long and rapier-sharp, and his eyes were auburn to match his silk cravat. He'd opted for a full system, wrists to shoulders to breastbone, like he was prepared for battle.

A glow of triumph washed over Veronika, erasing much of the awfulness of the previous day, returning her thoughts to an older, long-festering trauma. The prodigal daughter returns. Jilly would feel like so much river scum when Veronika made her entrance.

"Remember, you have to act like my boyfriend. Like you're madly in love with me."

Nathan shrugged. "No problem. You can't be a good dating coach if you're not a good actor."

That stung a little, but Veronika didn't let it show. "Give me a minute." She hurried off to put on her outfit—a six-piece ensemble constructed of bright primary colors to fit the mood of a child's birthday party.

When she paused in the doorway, Nathan clutched his heart. "My God, you're ravishing!" There was a playfulness to his tone, but still, he looked at her toe to head, the way you look at a woman rather than a buddy.

"Ready?" He offered Veronika his arm. The door adjusted to allow them to leave side by side. Nathan's biceps felt like marble under her fingers.

"How are you feeling, about the jumper?" Nathan asked as his vehicle hit the ramp to Low Town. He grasped the control stick.

"A little better, I guess. I mean, at least I tried to stop him. Fifty people in screens just watched."

"Absolutely. That's what I was trying to tell you last night. It's a shame the man died, but you should feel proud."

"I was also thinking that it's possible I did save someone.

I spent over sixty hours up there, and there was only one suicide attempt during that time. Last year there were seven in that same period, so either it's a fluke, or my presence discouraged approximately six people from jumping to their deaths."

"Or they came back when you weren't there and jumped anyway." Nathan laughed.

Veronika raised a finger. "In which case we should see a surge in the prevalence of suicides during the hours I'm not there, as compared to previous years. And you know what?" She reached over and flicked his earlobe. "We don't."

"Ow." Nathan clapped his palm over his earlobe. "That was uncalled for." He reached out, tried to twist her nipple, but she was ready for it and parried, both of them giggling. "You know, it would have been easier for me to be madly in love with you for this party if my ear wasn't throbbing."

"I'm sorry." Veronika made a show of examining his ear for bruises or bleeding.

Veronika looked out at the crowded streets of Low Town, the mélange of pedestrians, bicycles, Scamps, minis, cars, buses, tubes winding through mottled patches of sunlight mixed with dim stretches. It was hard for her to believe she'd spent most of her life here.

"Have you thought about what you're going to say to your sister when you see her?"

The question set Veronika's heart pounding. She'd thought of a thousand things she might say to Jilly, none of them quite right. "I think I'm going to go with, 'Hello.'"

"That's good." Nathan nodded. "Pithy, to the point."

"I think so."

He slowed. "There's a spot."

"Now, don't open your door. People could be watching,"

Nathan said as the vehicle slid into the tight space horizontally. He got out and went around to her door.

The party was on the roof; Veronika thought she heard the screeches of kids having fun through the traffic noise, but wasn't sure.

She was breathless from nerves by the time they stepped into the elevator. It was almost inconceivable that she was about to see Jilly, her parents. Sander. They seemed like part of some other lifetime.

"Relax, it's going to go fine. I promise." Nathan's voice helped calm her, reminded her that she wasn't going into this alone.

"Thank you for doing this."

"*De nada.*"

The elevator opened onto the roof. Heads turned, most of them people she didn't know, many hovering near young kids or holding babies. Nathan's hand slid around her waist, his fingertips pressed to her hip bone. He guided her forward, out of the elevator, toward a table stacked with presents. Veronika added hers to the stack. She'd obsessed over how to sign the ID tag, finally settling on her first name, sans *Love*, or *From*, or *Aunt*.

For a moment she didn't recognize the woman heading toward her, hands clasped in front of her, wearing a sundress that looked like it had spent the winter crushed at the bottom of a drawer. It was Jilly, smiling nervously, circling Veronika as if waiting for permission to come closer. "I'm so glad you came."

Veronika didn't want to say she was glad she'd come, because she wasn't sure about that yet. "It's good to see you" also seemed like a stretch. Her damned heart was racing, making it hard to think. "Hi, Jilly," she managed through dry lips.

"God, you look beautiful. I can't believe it's you." Jilly

finally stepped forward, misty-eyed. She looked so much older than Veronika remembered. She turned, called, *"Mom?"*

Her mother looked the same—squat, bow-legged, her eyebrows pursed in a perpetual V of concern. While Mom approached, Veronika spotted Sander, watching from a distance, clutching a toddler as if he was prepared to use the kid as a shield if it became necessary. He also looked older. Or maybe not older so much as exhausted.

Nathan released Veronika long enough to introduce himself to Jilly and kiss her cheek, then he came right back, pressed his hip against Veronika's, his hand on her back.

Like Jilly, Mom stopped at a safe distance. "Hello, Mom," Veronika said, nodding tightly.

Mom nodded back, just as tightly. "How are you?"

Nathan surged forward, hand outstretched. He grasped her mom's hand in both of his, said something Veronika couldn't hear, causing Mom's face to uncloud. Then he turned to Veronika. "Sweetie? Should we go see the birthday boy?"

"Sure."

Nathan took her hand, then leaned in toward her and kissed her. It was a warm, wet kiss so unexpected she started to recoil before catching herself and recovering her composure.

She was floating as they walked, hand in hand, toward Sander and little what's-his-name. Other guests watched as they crossed the roof.

"Now, this isn't so bad, is it?" Nathan said under his breath.

"This is fucking awesome."

Veronika gave Sander a one-armed hug, then knelt to say hello to the birthday boy, who had jets of yellow snot protruding from both nostrils, as Nathan shook Sander's hand, introducing himself as Veronika's boyfriend. She patted the boy's enormous, apple-shaped head as he stared at her, openmouthed. "Hi there." She looked up at Sander. "Can he talk yet?"

"A few words. Ike? Can you say hello to Aunt Veronika?"

Ike put his finger in his nose.

As Veronika stood, Nathan put a gentlemanly hand on her elbow, then lightly kissed her neck. "You want something to drink?" He gestured toward a folding table set out with soft drinks and disposable cups.

"Some water would be great, honey." It felt a little goofy saying "honey"—not something she'd actually say to a boyfriend, but in this context it felt right. Hey, she was a dating coach; she could act, too.

"He seems wonderful." Veronika turned to find Jilly at her side.

"Yeah, he is."

"You look great, Veronika. You look so happy."

The view from her seat on Lemieux Bridge flickered in her mind, unbidden. She gave Jilly her brightest smile. "I am happy."

"Can you watch him for a minute?" Sander broke in. "He keeps heading for the edge, and I need to bring the cake up."

"Sure," Jilly said, lifting Ike, who wrapped his legs around Jilly's waist and buried his runny nose in her dress.

Nathan was back with her water. "If you need me, I'm over there talking to your dad."

Her dad. She hadn't even said hello, and Nathan was already having a conversation with him. "Okay." Let him wait.

"I'm so glad you came," Jilly said as Nathan walked off.

"Me, too." It was true. She felt like Cinderella at the ball— beautiful, worldly, complete with handsome prince.

"As you can tell, Mom's still her same warm, radiant self."

Veronika laughed. "Yes. I thought she was going to crush my ribs with that hug."

To Veronika's relief, Jilly didn't bring up the whole issue of her and Sander. Veronika didn't want to wade into that mess. Another time, maybe. Seeing them together, imagining herself coordinating this dreary birthday party with Sander, was a balm for the sting of their betrayal. Let Jilly have this life—Veronika didn't want it. She wanted...well, not her life, either. She wanted the life she was pretending to lead for the benefit of her family, with a kid of her own tossed in.

She scanned the roof for Nathan, spotted him talking to her mother. Excusing herself, Veronika headed over. She wanted to soak in Nathan's affection while she could, wanted to feel his breath on her hair, to entwine her fingers with his.

"...no question, she's still hurting, but I think if the family reaches out—" Nathan spotted her, lifted his arm to draw her in. "Come join us, your mom was just telling me about what you were like when you were a little girl."

There's an art to seamlessly changing the subject when the subject shows up unexpectedly, and Nathan clearly hadn't mastered it, but Veronika was touched that he was trying to broker peace between her and her family. It meant he cared.

As the elevator closed, Nathan withdrew his hand from around her waist. The void there was like a blast of frigid air.

"So, how'd I do?" Nathan asked.

"You did great. It was one of the best hours of my entire life. Thank you so much."

Nathan reached out, and for a moment Veronika thought he was going to put his arm back around her, or draw her in and kiss her, like he'd done at the party. Instead, he patted her shoulder. "I'm so glad."

20

Rob

A woman in a nearby crèche was having an emotional meltdown. Rob was surprised more women here didn't have them, given their circumstance. A man with a red, multilevel beard was shushing, trying to calm her. Rob waited beside Winter's sealed crèche, his lute in his lap. He didn't want to begin their visit until it was quiet. He was eager to play for Winter.

"I can't, I can't," the woman was wailing. It occurred to Rob that music might soothe the woman, or at least distract her, so he lifted his lute and played a tune as light as soap bubbles. The woman stopped wailing. She asked her visitor a question Rob couldn't hear over the lute, maybe where the music was coming from. Her visitor murmured an answer.

Rob played on until the woman seemed in a better state of mind, then paused long enough to revive Winter before returning to his song.

Winter's green eyes fluttered open. They darted around, unfocused, lost, finally fixing on the lute. Rob watched lucidity creep back into them, and thought he could pinpoint the exact moment when memory returned.

She smiled. Her face was still stiff from cold, so the smile looked more like a grimace, but it was wonderful to see. Rob played on, allowing one precious minute to bleed away before setting the lute aside.

"I've never heard a more beautiful sound," Winter said. "Thank you."

"You're welcome. How are you?" The question came out automatically, and he kicked himself. Dead—she was dead, that's how she was.

"I'm good," she answered.

Now that he wasn't playing, Rob could hear the conversation between the recently agitated woman and the guy with the red beard, and understood why the woman had been saying, "I can't."

"I'll slap your ass while you suck me. Would you like that?" the guy was saying.

"Oh yeah. Spank my ass," the woman answered, her voice thick with embarrassment.

He could tell from Winter's expression that she heard it too, and felt himself turning red. There was a way to block sounds. It took him three or four precious seconds to figure it out and activate it.

"I brought something else I thought you'd like." Rob picked up the mirror he'd borrowed from his dad's barber room, held it over Winter's face, and slowly tilted it toward the big window at the end of the hall. "Tell me when."

"Oh. *When*." Winter laughed with delight. Her laugh was a beastly croak rather than the musical laugh she probably had when she was alive, but a chill of delight ran up Rob's spine nonetheless. She admired the green-leaf-and-blue-sky view for nearly thirty seconds before she was satisfied.

"So, what do you want to talk about?" Rob asked.

Winter considered. She had such beautiful, remarkably expressive eyes. The attractiveness-rating services had cheated her out of a half point, at least. It gave him hope that she would eventually be chosen by one of the men who came here.

"Do you believe in an afterlife?" Winter asked.

The question caught him off guard. "I don't know. I haven't given it much thought." He didn't want to say no, because it was probably an important issue for her, but he thought cryogenics had answered the question pretty conclusively. Forty years ago, when Georgio Moldovar became the first dead person to be successfully revived, most religions withdrew to the position that the afterlife, or reincarnation, begins after the body decomposes. Some Christian denominations pointed out that the Bible actually says everyone goes into the ground until Jesus comes back and takes everyone to heaven. Rob figured he'd find out when he was dead.

"I haven't given it much thought either. I wonder if I should have passed on this second chance at life. Maybe I'm putting myself through this misery when I could be somewhere wonderful."

"Maybe." He wasn't sure what to say to that. It felt wrong to encourage her to change her mind and go into the ground, just because he had a vested interest—that would release him from his promise. And he still held out hope that Winter would be rescued and given a second life, which would be the ideal resolution for both of them. "Do you have any particular religious faith?" Her profile had a blank under religious affiliation.

"I'm kind of a sampler," Winter laughed. "I used to rotate—I'd go to Jewish services one week, Zen Buddhist the next, Quaker, Catholic Mass, even Raw Life. Each fed my soul in a different way—I didn't feel obliged to choose one."

Rob opened his mouth to reply, then noticed the time. "Oh, shit."

"What?" The dread in her tone told Rob she knew what. "How much longer?"

"Thirty seconds."

She laughed with a panicked urgency. "I just tried to nod. I can't feel my body, but I keep reaching for it, you know?"

Rob nodded, feeling guilty that he was able to.

"How about this? I'll just *tell* you when I'm nodding, or shaking my head, or punching you."

"Oh, no," Rob laughed, "are you planning on punching me often?"

"We'll see."

Rob couldn't help glancing at the timer, though he knew it would only make Winter more aware of what was about to happen. Seven seconds.

"I keep expecting this to get easier, that it will start to feel as if I'm going to sleep. But it doesn't. Maybe it's not possible to get used to dying."

Rob reached out to comfort her, then remembered it was forbidden and drew back. If not for the surveillance, Rob would have reached under the silver cover and taken her hand, cold and stiff as it would have been.

21

Veronika

As she stood on the bottom step outside her apartment building, waiting for an opening in the flow of human traffic gliding by at morning rush hour, Veronika felt simultaneously exhausted and energized. It was the three-month anniversary of the Red Letter Day, as she thought of it, and still, that flurry of events occupied most of her waking thoughts. The man on the bridge, her semi-reconciliation with Jilly, her intimate playacting with Nathan, Rob's struggle for redemption. She had spent her days cycling from pain to longing to joy to curiosity, riding a merry-go-round of emotion.

She stepped onto the sidewalk, quickly got up to speed with the other pedestrians, a cool morning breeze blowing her hair, which was unsatisfactorily frizzy this morning. She was only half watching the sidewalk, her attention focused for the moment on Nathan. Those hours spent pretending to be his girlfriend had been some of the best of her life. The problem was, now she was back to her normal life. It felt so dreary by comparison. Until now, she'd only been able to fantasize about what it would be like if she and Nathan were together. Now she knew exactly how his strong arm felt wrapped around her waist, saw how people looked at her when they thought Nathan was her boyfriend.

Rationally, she knew this crush on Nathan was absurd. But love wasn't rational, and there didn't appear to be any way for her to *stop* feeling what she felt, or even to tone it down so that it wasn't so all-consuming. Dwelling on his many flaws—his narcissism being front and center on that list—did nothing to cool her ardor.

Up ahead, a man was standing motionless in the middle of the sidewalk, clogging traffic, forcing people to push past on either side of him. He was a black man, tall and huge. He was glaring at Veronika with lunatic rage.

Although she knew it couldn't be the man who'd jumped off the bridge, she was certain it was him.

Veronika jolted to a stop, her momentum almost causing her to tumble forward. Heart pounding, she ran a facial match with the recording from the bridge her system had made, sure she must be mistaken.

The match was confirmed. It was him.

The man stepped toward her. He seemed livid, though uneasy with his rage, unsure whether to clench his fists and grit his teeth or leave his hands and mouth open.

"So here I am, alive. Are you happy?"

"Hey, come on," a passerby growled after bumping into the man.

People passed on either side, brushing against Veronika's coat. "I don't understand. You didn't survive the fall, did you? You couldn't have."

The man made a guttural sound of disgust, squeezed his

eyes closed, as if the sight of Veronika was just too much for him. He stormed off.

Veronika was relieved to be out from under his angry stare, but couldn't just let him walk off. She ID'd his fast-retreating form, was surprised to discover he didn't have a privacy block on his system. His name was Lycan Hill; he worked at a place called Wooster.

Had he survived the jump? Maybe he was wealthy enough to afford complete revivification insurance. If so, why did he kill himself without canceling the insurance first? This was going to torment her.

Veronika took off after him.

"Lycan?" she called when she was right behind him, almost running to keep up with his long, brisk strides.

Lycan turned, again grunted with disgust when he saw it was her.

"Look, I just wanted to help. I didn't mean to make things worse."

"All right." He kept walking.

"Can we talk?"

"What about?"

"I don't know. I just want to make sure you're okay."

"I'm okay."

Huffing from exertion, Veronika stopped. "*Will you just please stop walking?*"

Lycan stopped, turned to face Veronika, waiting for her to say something.

"I have to know how you were saved."

Lycan sighed heavily. "When I canceled my freezing insurance, I neglected to indicate in my will that no one *else* could revive me." He shook his head grimly. "Evidently I'm valuable enough to my company that they footed the bill to drag me back."

Veronika looked around at the flow of pedestrians. "Can we sit somewhere?" She gestured toward a little fenced park jutting over a drop.

Lycan rolled his eyes. "I have to go now."

"Just for a minute. Please?"

Lycan heaved a sigh, looking defeated. "By all means," he said with mock enthusiasm. "Maybe we should order tea and cakes."

Veronika led him to a couple of seats in the park, then wasn't sure what to say. After what happened on Lemieux Bridge, something should be said. Something. She wasn't sure what, though.

"What do you do, that you're so valuable to your employer?" she asked. If Veronika jumped off a bridge, she'd be lucky if L-Dat sprang for flowers.

"What's the difference?" Lycan said.

Veronika shrugged sharply. "I'm just asking. You know, I didn't push you off that bridge. Stop acting like I did."

Lycan relaxed a bit, though his pinched expression suggested he wasn't conceding her point. "I'm a neuropsychologist. I'm working on a project with some commercial potential." He grunted softly. "Evidently more commercial potential than I knew. They paid almost thirty million to revive me." There was a note of pride in his otherwise acid delivery as he stared down through the latticework of the sidewalk at the black rectangles of Low Town roofs, at the frenzy of traffic, the barely discernible moving specks that were people. The braided material that formed the floor of the park was designed to maximize the amount of light that filtered down to Low Town, but it also served to make sitting in the park an ungrounding experience, as if you might fall at any moment.

"I was an expensive fix because when I hit the water, my

ribs punctured most of my vital organs." Lycan's tone, and the look he gave Veronika, suggested this was somehow her fault. "They missed my heart, however, so it was a much more painful death than I'd anticipated. Almost as painful as the moments leading up to it."

"I'm sorry. I meant well."

He watched Low Town for a moment, then looked back at Veronika. "I know I shouldn't be taking this out on you, but you were so certain that it was your business. You were so concerned that I stay alive. Well, I'm alive. Now what do I do?" There was no anguish on Lycan's face as there had been on Lemieux Bridge. He seemed not so much despondent as genuinely lost, as if he expected an answer to his question. Which was not good, because Veronika didn't have one. That life was better than death seemed obvious to her, but that didn't mean she thought life was particularly awesome.

He waited for her answer, his wiry eyebrows raised. When it didn't come, he stood. "I have to get back to work." He turned to leave, then paused. "You're right, though. It wasn't your fault at all." He made the sign of the cross in the air with his hand. "I absolve you of the residual guilt you're obviously feeling. Good-bye."

"Hold on." He obviously wanted to be left alone, but somehow Veronika couldn't let him go.

"What?"

"Why did you do it?"

Lycan rolled his eyes toward the sky. "I don't owe you an explanation."

"I know that, but…" What was the "but" here? A vague plan formed in Veronika's mind. "You asked me, 'What now?' I can't tell you why life is worth living, but maybe I can show you, if you'll let me."

Lycan's cheek protruded where he poked at it with his tongue. "What are you planning to show me, exactly?"

Veronika looked around. "Where were you headed right now?"

"To lunch."

"Let me take you to lunch, somewhere you'd never go on your own. Let me show you the world with fresh eyes." She'd heard that line somewhere, maybe in *Wings of Fire*. Lycan didn't seem the type to have a plagiarism detector on his system.

Lycan burst out laughing. "You're going to take me to lunch?"

"That's right. Come on."

When Lycan made no move to follow, Veronika grasped his sleeve and tugged. "Come on."

Reluctantly, Lycan took a step. "At least they're unlikely to fire me if I take a long lunch," he muttered.

The only thing was, Veronika wasn't sure where to take him. She knew most of the restaurants in High Town, and quite a few in Low, but what sort of restaurant choice could possibly constitute a life-affirming change in one's usual humdrum routine? As they walked, she frantically scanned recent articles on restaurants in Manhattan.

"So, what do you study?"

"I study the links between the brain and consciousness."

Veronika gave him a look. "I know what a neuropsychologist is, I mean specifically."

"I'm not at liberty to talk about the specifics. You probably wouldn't understand what I was talking about, in any case."

"Ooh, so you're like a secret-agent neuropsychologist." Veronika couldn't resist the sarcastic retort, even though she was supposed to be showing Lycan why life was wonderful.

She found what she'd been looking for: it was an article

on the cuisine of Undertown, titled "The Edgy Side of Local Cuisine." That would be an adventure—eating in some seedy corner walk-up that served authentic Undertown fare. Veronika headed for an elevator. Maybe this would help Lycan and maybe it wouldn't, but it was certainly lifting her muddled mood. There was something liberating about being with someone even more lost than she, being the one who had it together, relatively speaking.

In the silence of the elevator, Veronika noticed that Lycan was making an odd sound—an atonal humming. She glanced at him and found that he was studying her, his expression suggesting he was trying to determine whether he was in the hands of someone who was deranged. Typically when you looked at someone and caught them staring at you, they looked away, but Lycan went on looking until Veronika felt so uncomfortable she looked away. He went on humming. Maybe humming wasn't the right word for it. He went on making noises in the back of his throat.

When they reached the subway entrance that would take them into Undertown, Veronika paused, reconsidering. The eatery she'd picked out, Biryani Burger, was about a five-minute walk through a dodgy underground neighborhood, and big as he was, Veronika didn't think Lycan would scare off potential muggers and rapists with his round-shouldered gait and baby face.

"You're not thinking of going down there, are you?" Lycan asked, motioning toward the subway entrance up ahead.

Veronika spotted five largish men wearing High Town boots heading for the subway. She grabbed Lycan's elbow and tugged him toward the men. "Come on."

Over Lycan's hissed protests, Veronika got in step behind

the men, close enough that the casual murderer might assume they were all part of the same party. She squeezed into an elevator with them as they descended from the train level down to the market level, where Biryani Burger was located.

As the elevator opened, they were hit with the clattering, the claustrophobia, the jostling and dimness of an Undertown market. Veronika's system was set to filter unpleasant sensory input, but the system seemed overwhelmed, unsure how to filter when everything was an eyesore. It was dimming the cacophony, but various sections of the market flickered from artificially serene scenes of well-dressed shoppers to the real scenes of desperately poor, filthy people engaging in commerce that bordered on brawling.

"Oh, no, no, no," Lycan said, eyeing the scene. "Let's get out of here."

The big guys who'd unknowingly been serving as their bodyguards had gone left out of the elevator, and they were going straight, so Veronika and Lycan were on their own.

Veronika pulled Lycan into the crowd. "Just act like you come here all the time." He looked at her as if he'd definitely decided she *was* deranged, but didn't resist.

"What's the farthest you've ever been down?" Veronika asked as they passed through the labyrinth of the market, around stone pillars, past booths cut into the solid stone that comprised the entire foundation of Manhattan.

"*This* is the farthest I've ever been down." A topless woman motioned to Lycan from inside a booth that held nothing but a bed. Lycan held up a hand to the side of his face, blocking her from view. "Can we get out of here? This is crazy."

"Yes, you might get killed," Veronika said, deadpan. "You've never even taken an armed tour farther down?"

"I'm not a tour kind of person," Lycan said.

Veronika and Sander had once taken a tour *way* down, to an underground river twenty stories below street level, where there was nothing but a rat warren of grimy corridors and sewer lines. She was stunned to see people living down there, their homes crevices and long-forgotten pumping stations.

Ahead, Veronika spotted a flashing sign for Biryani Burger. As the article had said, it was nothing more than a bricked-in corner. Veronika poked her head inside the one small square window in the bricks. Two feet to her left, a sweaty Asian man in a dirty apron stood over a filthy fryer. He looked Veronika's way and raised his eyebrows.

Veronika consulted the article, which had explained the correct way to order. "Two big ones with plenty of everything."

"Thirty-six," the man said. Although the article advised her to grow irate when told the price, because regulars and Undertown residents paid around twenty for two big ones, Veronika just tapped her system and transferred the thirty-six.

The man nodded curtly and turned back to his grill.

Veronika lingered in the opening for a second longer, taking in the tiny enclosure, devoid of any decorations save for several paper pictures stuck to the wall, two of them maybe of the cook/owner's children, four others she recognized as characters from an old TV show called *High Town Gardeners*.

When the food was ready, the cook simply thrust his hand through the window clutching a half loaf of French bread packed with a paste that resembled sewage, and Veronika took it from him. A moment later, his hand reappeared holding the other.

Lycan accepted his like he was being handed a dead rat. "What are the odds we're *not* going to contract botulism from these?"

"Fifty-fifty." She took a big bite. It wasn't bad.

Eyeing her accusingly, Lycan took a much more tentative bite, almost a dainty bite. "My father's a gastroenterologist. If he saw me eating this, he'd have a stroke."

"Nice guy, your father?" Veronika asked.

"He had to sign off on my revival. Whether that's evidence of how much he loves me or how much he hates me, I couldn't tell you."

"That was only two days ago." Veronika shook her head in wonder. "It's hard to believe we're standing here now."

"That's for sure."

A big dollop of her sandwich's innards dropped out, just missing her boot. It didn't matter, there was no way she was going to finish half of the thing, although it was growing on her with each bite. It wasn't all that greasy, and had a nutty, creamy flavor.

"Just for argument's sake, if you were to die down here, would your company revive you again?"

"I don't have full revival as part of my health plan, so there's no guarantee, but I think so, yes. They've taken precautions to prevent me from making another attempt on my life." He pointed in the air. "Someone's monitoring me from a cloaked screen most of the time. I'm surprised they didn't send someone to stop me when you dragged me down here."

She was curious to know what he did that was so important, but didn't relish another "I'm not at liberty" rebuttal.

Lycan looked down at his torso, prodded his sternum.

"Are there scars?"

"No. It's remarkable how advanced their techniques are."

Veronika eyed his stomach. "It's so hard to fathom that for a few hours you simply did not exist."

"I don't like to think about it." He looked around, holding

his half-eaten lunch by his side, and Veronika realized he was looking for a trash recycler.

"Finished?" A girl of about ten was suddenly standing in front of Lycan, hands out. Lycan set the food in her hands, then the girl turned to Veronika, who turned hers over as well.

"Ready?" Lycan asked.

They climbed into the elevator back to train level in silence. Neither of them said anything for a good ten minutes, but Veronika felt strangely at peace, comfortable in the awkward silence. The thing was, she was sure Lycan suffered through as many awkward silences as she, which shifted at least some of the responsibility to him.

Veronika realized that Lycan had yet to ask anything about her. He had no idea what she did for a living, where she lived, whether she had children or siblings. As they rose, he hummed atonally to himself. It was grating.

"So what's with the humming?"

Lycan stopped humming. "What do you mean?"

"You hum all the time. It doesn't seem to be a song, exactly."

Lycan put the tip of his finger in his mouth, nibbled the nail. "I don't know. I guess it keeps the demons at bay."

" 'The demons,' " she repeated as they stepped out of the elevator and headed for the stairs to the surface. It wasn't a question; she knew what demons he was talking about. The thoughts that threatened to devour you; the icy blasts of self-doubt and despair. She knew them well, and could imagine that if they got loud enough, she might try humming to drown them out too. "Are you on meds?"

Lycan laughed. It was the first time she'd heard him laugh—it had a panicked quality. "Meds. Yeah, I'm on meds." He pulled up his sleeve, showed her a silver bug attached to his impressive biceps, delivering his meds. "Zoreo. Palquin." He raised one eyebrow. "How about you?"

The question threw Veronika. Her emotional state, like everything else about her, hadn't come up in conversation. Was it that obvious? "Perion-e."

Lycan nodded knowingly. "Good old Perion-e. My verbal-complexity app pegs your IQ at one thirty-eight, so I'm guessing you're familiar with homeostatic affect theory?"

"It's one forty-one," Veronika corrected. Maybe it was petty, but she didn't want those three points deducted. "Yeah, I'm familiar with it."

Lycan shook his big head. "Meds aren't the answer."

Veronika couldn't argue. The medical research industry was still trying, still claiming that some med going through clinical trials was going to change everything, but no matter how they messed with receptor sites, neurotransmitter levels, hormone levels, the mind always found its way back to baseline.

"For a while I thought Perion-e was the answer, then I started developing facial tics," Lycan said.

"I worry about that." That was the other problem. If a med worked at all, it came with a side effect—a cost that often was as bad as the problem it was meant to solve. Or worse. They'd conquered physical illness, conquered death for those who could afford it, but the mind was another animal altogether. Screwed-up minds always found a way to stay screwed up. Maybe that was because Chan-juan Yang had devoted her vast fortune to cheating physical illness and death. Maybe some other trillionaire needed to devote the same sort of resources to overcoming anxiety and despair.

"So how did you end up on that bridge?" Veronika asked. "Why that day instead of the one before or the one after?"

"I could ask you the same question," Lycan said.

"Yes, you could."

Lycan glanced at her. "All right. What were you doing on that bridge?"

What could she say? That she'd decided to save people more screwed up than she as a way to save herself? That sounded awfully narcissistic. Maybe it was narcissistic. Was she a narcissist? No, how could you be a narcissist with self-esteem as low as hers?

"How about we call it a draw?" Veronika finally answered. "I won't ask you if you don't ask me."

They'd come to the elevator to High Town. Lycan stuck out his hand, and Veronika shook it as they stepped into the elevator.

"Of course that implies we'll have another opportunity to ask each other. What do you think? You want to meet up again some time?"

Lycan considered. "Kind of an 'I'm alive, what now' club?"

"Exactly."

Lycan tilted his head. "I actually enjoyed myself." There was surprise in his tone, as if he'd never expected to utter those words again.

Veronika was surprised, and pleased. She'd been able to sink her teeth into these last few hours and get real nourishment. The elevator opened and they stepped out, back home in High Town. Unable to hide her satisfied grin, Veronika said, "I'll meet you on the bridge—you know, The Bridge We Don't Ask About. Saturday at noon."

Lycan smiled. "All right."

They said good-bye with a wave.

As she headed home, watching copters buzz in a blue sky scattered with high, steel-gray clouds, she felt light, energized. It wasn't butterflies—she didn't feel attracted to Lycan in a romantic sense, but despite his prickly, depressive, obtuse nature, Veronika felt comfortable around him. She was sure she had just made a friend, and given the tragedy of their first meeting, that felt like magic. She would help Lycan learn to love life, or at least not despise it, and in doing so, teach herself as well.

22

Mira

An old woman peered down at her, squinting, frowning suspiciously, as if trying to penetrate some veneer.

"Hello," Mira said.

"Hello." There was even suspicion in her tone, as if Mira had come to her door uninvited and might be selling something.

"I'm looking for a companion." She held up her hand as if Mira had tried to interrupt her. "Not a lover or anything like that. I'm too old for lovers, and for that I would need a man, in any case. I'm looking for a different sort of companion."

"Okay," Mira said when it was clear she wasn't going to elaborate. "A friendship, you mean?"

The woman shook her head impatiently. "No. Deeper. Like family."

That was perfect. A relationship she wouldn't have to fake. Hope flickered uncertainly in her. Could she convince this woman that she was best suited out of all the women here? "I think I understand. Like a daughter, or a granddaughter?"

"No. I don't want to put a label on it."

Mira was fairly sure "like family" was a label, but kept her opinion to herself. "Oh. All right."

"Do you think you could love me"—she glanced up at the readout on the wall—"Mira? Could you love me so much you'd weep beside my deathbed?"

Mira's first inclination was to blurt, *Yes, absolutely*, but that must be what everyone here said to her. It must sound profoundly insincere for a complete stranger to assure you that she would love you like family.

"I know I'm capable of loving deeply. My heart is open. I'd only know if I could love you for sure by spending time with you, cooking dinner with you, hearing about your life, sharing mine with you."

The woman studied her, breathing heavily through her nose, her head bobbing with the palsy of old age. "Well, you're out. Do you think I'd pay all that money with no guarantee?"

Mira could only get out one word as the woman reached up to send her back to oblivion, and the word was, "Shit."

23

Rob

Central Park was alive with joggers, loungers, buskers, chess players, hustlers. As Rob crossed Strawberry Field toward the steps to High Town, he barely noticed anyone. He was deep in thought, thinking about how much his life had changed since the accident. It was as if he himself had died, and had been revived into an entirely different, far more unforgiving existence. When people asked what he did for a living, he couldn't honestly answer that he was a musician, so he answered that he was a manual worker. He didn't feel the swell of pride he used to feel telling people he was a musician. What friends he had were new as well. When he'd moved in with Lorelei in High Town, her friends had become his friends. He'd kept in touch with his burb friends, but if friendships took place primarily via screen, they tended to atrophy, because you don't talk about core things, intimate things, via screen. When he broke up with Lorelei and moved back home, he lost most of his new High Town friends, and because he'd given up his music, he lost touch with the friends he'd made playing Low Town clubs. What little time he had to socialize now he spent with Nathan and Veronika. They were High Towners, but they'd gone out of their way to cultivate a friendship with Rob. He was also friendly with some of the people at work, people on the opposite end of the economic spectrum from Nathan and Veronika, but besides Vince, he wasn't sure he'd call them friends.

And then, of course, there was Winter.

He reached the bottom of the endless, twisting staircase leading up to High Town, grasped the railing, craned his neck to look up at High Town, and took a deep breath. His legs were going to be jelly. Still, part of him was looking forward to the climb. Saving the eighty-dollar elevator charge was his primary motivation for hoofing it, but as he took his first springing steps, he felt a strange freedom, like a raw-lifer living among the techies.

He got raw-lifers—he understood why someone might forsake all but the most basic tech, even though he wouldn't willingly do so himself. You did gain something, always seeing things as they really were, being forced to stand face-to-face with someone every time you had something to say to them, even something trivial. People questioned whether there really was such a thing as technomie, if it did flatten out your emotions, dull your senses, to be wired all the time. He didn't doubt it. What always tripped him up about raw-lifers was how they could choose to live without modern medicine. Rob had lived without it for most of his life, but not by choice. As far as Rob could see, medicine was the one area where there were no minuses to balance out the pluses. There was no downside whatsoever to having access to all that modern medicine had to offer.

In school, Rob had been taught that Chan-juan Yang was

the greatest person of the past century, a trillionaire who self-lessly funneled her entire fortune into the medical research that ultimately conquered death. As an adult, he'd read a biography of Yang that was less laudatory. It depicted her as a selfish shut-in whose only concern was extending her own life. The book had been far kinder to Yo Wen Chan, the researcher who actually discovered how to revive the dead.

When he reached the halfway mark, winded but still feel-ing good, he cut through Brandywine Park, though it was a roundabout route to Park Avenue High and Zuckerberg, where he was meeting Veronika and Nathan, and an addi-tional toll charge to boot. He'd be damned if he was going to climb to High Town and not see Brandywine Park, though.

Three dollars rolled off his account as he passed through the gate. It was a pittance; it took him five minutes of pluck-ing parts at the reclamation center to earn that much, but in the new order of his life every expenditure was a defeat.

If anything was worth it, though, it was Brandywine Park. Rob chose a song from Six Anonymous to accompany his climb, wished he had a system to give him the full effect. With a sys-tem, the semitransparent pedestrium vanished, and you walked on air, six hundred feet above the roofs and streets of Low Town, passing islands of wilderness—copses of trees and veg-etation set among winding staircases that looked to be made of silk thread—far too delicate to support a person.

Rob tried to ignore the readout on his handheld as he stepped onto a staircase and was charged another dollar and a half. As he climbed, the vista expanded farther. He found the patch-work of buildings, roads, parking lots, and parks that stretched to the horizons pleasing to the eye, the contrast between the busy ground and the silent, open sky in beautiful balance.

When he finally reached street level in High Town, he

realized the climb hadn't been as bad as he'd anticipated. He was barely winded, actually. Having neither a vehicle nor money for public transport meant he was walking everywhere, and the muscles in his thighs felt harder and stronger because of it. There were upsides to living raw. Maybe one day he'd even stop missing his system.

Heading east, Rob suddenly felt like he was crawling as people soared by in their High Town shoes. He slowed further as he passed Backstreets on Fifth Avenue, recalling how he'd once told Lorelei that Backstreets was going to be the first club he played in High Town. He'd been so certain of how his life was going to unfold.

He spotted Nathan and Veronika up ahead. Nathan saw him, waved a greeting.

"Good to see you, Cousin." Nathan squeezed Rob's hand, looking at him like you would an old, dear friend you haven't seen in a long time.

As usual, Veronika seemed nervous, ill at ease. Something about her gave Rob the impression she was always ill at ease.

They took an elevator toward the skywalks. Rob didn't complain as fifteen dollars rolled off of his account balance—Nathan and Veronika seemed to keep track of what he spent when he was with them, and later dropped it into his account. Today that was a good thing, given that eating dinner in High Town with Nathan and his friends would cost two hundred easy, even if Rob drank nothing but water. While they rode, Nathan and Veronika resumed the debate they'd evidently been having when they met up with Rob.

"L-Dat's algorithm pegged us at point eight-nine compatibility," Nathan said. He looked to Rob. "Not that I put a lot of stock in those scores, because they assume everyone's telling the truth in their profiles, but still, point eight-nine! It seemed so promising until the first face-to-face."

Rob nodded sagely. He had no idea what point eight-nine compatibility was, but didn't want to seem ignorant.

"You just can't tell through screens. The intangibles don't come through," Nathan said.

"Which intangibles are those?" Rob asked, mostly to be part of the conversation. "You mean like chemistry?"

"Yeah, chemistry, whatever that is." Nathan waved his hands before returning them to his system, and whatever supplemental conversation he was having. "The thing is, compatibility algorithms are *fairly* effective for most people, despite their flaws. For me, they're useless. Worse than useless—they're counterproductive. I'm much more likely to click with a woman I meet in the wild. Take Winter, for example. I met Winter at work, when I went to her class to give a presentation on L-Dat."

Rob felt a jolt of adrenaline at the mention of Winter's name. He wanted to learn more about her, so he would have more substantial things to say the next time he visited, and Nathan was the person who could help him there, yet he was painfully aware of how Veronika glanced his way at the mention of Winter's name, curious of how he would react, and how the half-dozen screens watching the action from a distance (friends of Nathan's, he'd guessed) crept closer, not wanting to miss anything. He decided not to say anything; he'd wait for a less public moment to ask Nathan what Winter was like, and if Nathan seemed amenable, maybe ask to view some recordings of time they'd spent together. Rob had no doubt Nathan, who seemed like a true techie, recorded all of his waking moments. Of course in recent years who didn't, besides people who didn't own systems?

"You know, if the algorithms are misfiring that badly, I wonder if there's a disconnect between the characteristics you're attracted to in a woman and the characteristics that would lead you to a healthy relationship," Veronika said.

"Oh, is that it?" Nathan raised his eyebrows.

"Either that," Veronika went on, "or you've become so overwhelmed with all the possibilities, you're incapable of settling for any one real, and therefore imperfect, woman. It's a common problem; I see it in my clients all the time."

"So do I," Nathan said.

They stepped off the elevator, onto a skywalk, neither of them missing a beat.

"That doesn't mean you're immune to it. Just because we do this for a living doesn't mean we're aware of our own weaknesses."

Rob sensed a subtext here. He wondered if Veronika and Nathan had gone out at some point. They didn't seem like a good match—Nathan was suave and charming, Veronika kind of goofy—but he'd seen odder couples.

"And by 'we,' you mean me," Nathan said. He was sporting an easy smile, enjoying himself. Actually, they both looked like they were enjoying it. "You're certainly aware of *your* weaknesses."

"Yes, I am. I'm neurotic as hell," Veronika said without missing a beat. "That's why most of my relationships last a couple of months—it's how long it takes me to start driving a guy crazy." She rolled her wrist, flicked an accusing finger in Nathan's direction. "*Your* relationships, on the other hand, tend to last a couple of weeks. You hop from woman to woman like they're gelato flavors." She looked at Rob as if she'd just remembered he was there. "Now *you*."

Nathan laughed delightedly. "You've met Rob a grand total of, what, four times, but you've already got him pegged?"

Veronika stepped in front of Nathan, forcing him to stop. She pushed her face right up close to Nathan's—close enough for a kiss. "You doubt me, do you?"

Nathan grinned, looked toward Rob. "Not at all. Let's hear about Rob's love life."

They went on walking as Veronika offered her assessment of Rob. "Most of your relationships have lasted more than a year, and when you're not seeing someone, you don't see too many women a second time. If you're not feeling it, you move on."

Rob smiled, shrugged. "You got me."

Veronika rolled her eyes toward the sky. "It's so obvious that you're disgustingly well adjusted. You'll be trolling the listings one day, discover a woman who's a point nine-two match, fall in love, and be completely faithful to her for the rest of your life. And you'll do it all without a coach. Makes me sick."

Rob held up his finger. "Ah, you missed there. I don't use dating services."

Dual cries of surprise lit the air.

"Don't tell me, you're a closet raw-lifer," Veronika said.

"Not at all. I never took my system off, when I had one. I'm just old-fashioned when it comes to love." It was the one realm where he had completely turned his back on the modern approach. Somehow it was important to him that he meet a woman in the course of his day-to-day life. "In the wild," as Nathan put it. Technology felt like cheating.

Veronika smiled. She had a peculiar smile—her lips all but jumped from her teeth, forming a big *Sardonicus* grin. "I'm going to fix you up."

"No, I don't—"

Veronika waved away his protest. "I'm going to find the perfect woman for you, on the house. The honor of my trade is at stake."

Rob wasn't the least bit interested in meeting a woman at this particular juncture, but it seemed rude to refuse when Veronika was being so insistent. Hopefully she'd forget about it.

Up ahead, a bunch of screens that hadn't been there a moment earlier caught Rob's eye. He pointed. "What's going on?" More and more were popping up between the Second Life Building and the Hilton.

The screens were swirling, trying to organize into a pattern, but having trouble. Rob searched the net for information as the three of them jogged out to get a better angle, but he couldn't find anything. Maybe they didn't have a permit to gather in such large numbers, so they hadn't posted any public info that might tip off the police.

"Look at that—they're spelling something," Veronika said.

They were. The first word was *Save.* That much was clear. The rest was an indecipherable mess of swirling screens.

They watched as some of the letters formed. The third word was long, and started with a *B.*

" 'Save the bumpercrops,' 'Save the bicycles,' " Nathan said.

" 'Save the bicycles.' Yeah. That's probably it," Veronika said.

An *r* and a *d* fell into place, and with a jolt, Rob got it. " 'Save the bridesicles.' "

They watched as the remaining letters formed.

" 'Save the bridesicles'?" Nathan said. "I didn't realize they needed saving."

The skywalks were filling with people coming out of towers to watch.

"I've always wondered why there are no groomsicles," Nathan said.

Veronika clicked her tongue. "And you call yourself a dating coach? There were, early on, but the program folded from lack of business."

"I didn't know that," Nathan said. "I wonder why it folded?"

"My guess is it's the same reason there aren't many hetero male prostitutes: women just aren't into the sort of power and dominance that keeps the bridesicle program going."

"They're not?" Nathan asked, eyebrows raised.

A chant was rising up from the screens, intentionally low at first, slowly building.

"What about gay men? And gay women, for that matter?" Nathan asked.

Veronika shrugged. "Probably just too small a market. The straight program is relatively small as it is—a niche industry with a limited but extremely wealthy clientele. I also doubt gay women have any more interest in that sort of setup than straight women do."

"What are they chanting?" Rob asked.

Veronika stopped talking. They listened, and soon it became clear: "Women aren't salvage. Women aren't salvage."

"Not sure what that's supposed to mean," Rob said.

Rob spoke the phrase into his pathetic little handheld, feeling self-conscious as he manually sorted the results. The group was called Bridesicle Watch. He brought up their site, and was met by a familiar face. It was Lorelei's stepmother, Sunali. He laughed out loud. "Oh, you're shitting me."

"What?" Nathan asked.

Rob externalized the image so Nathan and Veronika could see it as well. A crawling line of text beneath Sunali identified her as a founding member of Bridesicle Watch, and a bridesicle herself. Nathan and Veronika were looking from the clip to Rob, trying to understand his reaction.

"Look at the name," Rob said, highlighting it for them.

"Van Kampen. Is that Lorelei's mother?" Veronika asked.

"Her stepmother," Rob said. After considering whether he wanted to go into a long explanation, he reluctantly added, "And her great-grandmother."

"Come again?" Nathan said.

Rob took a deep breath. "Sunali was a bridesicle for something like seventy years. In the meantime, her son, Kilo, became a trillionaire techie, but wouldn't revive Sunali, because he hated her guts. Kilo's *daughter* went through an ugly divorce, and to spite her and Kilo, her ex-husband revived Sunali. And married her."

It wasn't surprising that Lorelei was a little fucked up, when you laid out her family's story in a nutshell like that. Not that it excused what she'd done.

More screens were joining the protest. Rob couldn't believe Sunali was one of the people behind this. Not that it was out of character—she was as brash and blunt and tough as nails—but this was a big event; they'd convinced thousands of people to join an illegal protest that would probably cost each of them an instant two-hundred-dollar fine.

"So what are they protesting?" Nathan asked. "At least bridesicles have a fighting chance to be revived, which is more than you can say for most people in the minus eighty."

Rob pulled up Bridesicle Watch's goals and read: "'We want the dead to be afforded the same rights as the living. We want marriage contracts that are nothing short of indentured servitude banned. We want Cryomed's outrageous upcharges on revivification abolished so that reviving people is more affordable. Most importantly, once a human being is put in the minus eighty, we demand regulations that make it the equivalent of murder to remove her.' "

Rob felt a chill as he read the last part. "They can remove people?"

"I read about that in a magazine somewhere," Veronika said. "If a bridesicle doesn't draw enough paying suitors, they pull her from the program."

"But if they move them back to the main cryo facility, aren't they paying just as much to maintain them?"

Veronika hesitated. "No, I mean the women who don't have freezing insurance." *Like Winter.* Veronika didn't say it, but Rob could tell she was thinking it.

"I assumed you already knew that," Veronika said as Rob searched deeper into the Bridesicle Watch site.

"*I* didn't know that," Nathan said.

Rob read aloud: " 'Cryomed charges a great deal for bridesicle visits because they want to create an atmosphere of exclusivity that will encourage men who can actually *afford* to revive bridesicles to visit. Loved ones crying over lost daughters and mothers is bad for business—' "

"They should stop referring to them as 'bridesicles.' It's derogatory," Veronika said.

"It would have taken a lot more screens to write 'cryogenic dating center resident' over the city," Nathan said. "Plus, no one would have known who they were talking about."

Rob was only half listening. He scrolled farther, until he found what he was looking for. "What's less well advertised by Cryomed is their barbaric policy on what they refer to inside the organization as 'salvage.' 'Salvage' refers to women who don't have cryogenic insurance. While only attractive women under forty are recruited into the bridesicle program from the main storage facility, Cryomed incurs very little extra cost, because these women must be stored in the minus eighty in any case. Women without cryogenic insurance are selected for the program only if they're especially young and beautiful. If a salvage case doesn't prove profitable because not enough men are visiting, she's 'Released from the Program'—Cryomed's euphemism for thawed and buried."

Rob felt like he'd been punched in the stomach.

"We treat our stray dogs better than that," Veronika said.

On the website, Sunali's picture grew ghostly pale, her lips tinged blue, her hair and eyelashes frosted over. Her eyes welled with tears.

How long was it before they pulled the plug on an unprofitable salvage case? Decades? Years? *Months?* Rob was paying to visit her, so she was bringing in some income, but was it enough? Was anyone else visiting her?

Rob felt a hand on his shoulder, turned to find Nathan at his side. "Holy, holy, shit. I'm sorry, Cousin."

"I have to find out how long she has," Rob said.

Veronika worked her system, after a moment shook her head. "I can't find any numbers."

Rob could barely feel his feet. Despite the dizzying view and wide-open sky, he felt as if walls were closing in around him. She was going into the ground. If no one wanted her, she was going into the ground.

It was not solely guilt that caused that image to shake him to the bones. He knew her now.

"I have to go," he said. "I'm sorry. I have to find out." Before they could answer, he turned and jogged toward the elevator.

Sunali might know, or be able to find out. As he ran along the crosswalk, he tried to contact Sunali on his handheld. She had a complete block in place—no visitors, no messages, no info on her current location.

He tried the public address for Bridesicle Watch, and was told Sunali was out of the office for a few days, on personal business. He left a message for her.

"*Shit.*" He wanted to punch something, or scream at someone. How could they simply bury someone? It wasn't murder, because Winter was already dead, but surely it was *something*.

Lorelei would be able to get in touch with Sunali, but God, he didn't want to contact Lorelei, especially about this. Maybe there was some other way to get the information. In the meantime, he'd keep trying Sunali.

24

Veronika

"Hey Rob, this is Veronika." Veronika paused the recording, looked at the ceiling. She wasn't sure of her own motivation here. Was she doing this because (a) Rob was a thoughtful, genuine, remarkably principled guy she'd like to cultivate a friendship with, and (okay, unlikely) possibly more? Or because (b) if Nathan saw her hanging out with Rob, he might think there was something percolating between them and get jealous, even if he had caught Veronika kissing a virtual hunk from an interactive?

Option (b) reflected the thinking of a disturbed individual who should seek psychiatric attention. Of course Veronika was already receiving psychiatric attention on a weekly basis, so she was covered there. She closed her eyes, tried to listen for that tiny voice of truth anchored within the swirling mass of chattering and anxiety that passed for her mind.

The truth was, it was both, but it was sixty percent (a) and forty percent (b). Veronika decided she could live with that.

She checked the time and jumped off her sofa. She was supposed to meet Lycan at the Broadway High micro-T stop in three minutes. The message, checking on Winter's status and simultaneously inviting Rob to coffee with her alone, would have to wait.

Veronika threw on her boots and bolted for the elevator. She really should invite Lycan on some outing with Nathan and Rob, rather than having it always be just the two of them. Lycan clearly saw their get-togethers as platonic, but what if he did develop a crush on her? She certainly wasn't sending him signals that she *wasn't* interested.

Taking the walk-up steps two at a time, she hit the sidewalk and glided off, threading past slower walkers.

Was she interested? No, not seriously. She needed a man she could spar with, a man with a sharp sense of humor. Maybe that was why she was reluctant to bring Lycan along on a jaunt with Nathan. Lycan wouldn't fit in—he was too earnest, too serious.

Weaving slightly like a tall tree in a breeze, his hands dangling awkwardly at his sides, Lycan was waiting at what appeared to be the exact center of the station. He spotted her and smiled, raised his hand to wave, then inexplicably aborted the wave and let his hand drop.

"I thought you'd changed your mind."

"Just got caught up in other things. Sorry."

"So where are we going?" Lycan sounded excited.

Veronika paused for effect. "Into the wild." On their last two outings they'd seen a concert, and visited the vertical gardens on Roosevelt Island—both beautiful things. It was time to revisit the other end of the spectrum.

Lycan frowned. "You mean, literally?"

"As far out as we can get."

"*Why?*" Lycan sputtered. He seemed flabbergasted that anyone would voluntarily leave the city.

"Just for the adventure." She grabbed Lycan's elbow, tugged him toward a waiting micro-T.

Three nubile twenty-something women got the last three spots, but another was already in sight, so Veronika couldn't hate them too much, though she hated them slightly for being nubile and having a combined twenty screens tagging along behind them. Veronika looked into the empty air surrounding her and Lycan. No screens; not one between them. Not even her mother was interested in seeing where she was going.

They got off in Westchester and rented a vehicle, a big road-eating Geely that Veronika struggled to keep between the lines when it wasn't on autopilot. Lycan sat with his hands awkwardly in his lap, saying nothing, but looking at Veronika once in a while.

She hoped Rob was all right. It was inconvenient that she couldn't get in touch with him when he was at work.

"Remember my friend Rob?" she asked Lycan, mostly to break the silence.

"Sure. His story's hard to forget."

"Well, now it turns out Winter, the woman he hit, could be thawed and buried if she doesn't have enough dates." Veronika sighed in exasperation. "Dates. It makes her sound like a prostitute, but that's what Cryomed insists on calling them."

"My God," Lycan said. "That's terrible. They can do that?"

"I'm so worried for him, and for Winter." And for herself, if she was honest. If Winter was buried, a small, warm something inside her would be snuffed out. It was childish to hang anything on the small role she played in Rob's promise to Winter, but that small part she played kept her going in a way.

"I'll tell you something."

Her serious tone caused Lycan to turn and look at her. "You want to know the real reason I was up on the bridge that day? It was because I wanted to do something that mattered. I was starting to feel like I was invisible, you know?"

Lycan nodded. He was listening to her, really listening. Feeling a silly swell of gratitude, she continued.

"My clients never see me. I had one friend at the time, and most of the time when we were together IP, most of his attention was on his system. I wanted to do something *real*. I wanted to grab a *real* arm, pull someone down from a *real* bridge."

"What you're describing sounds a lot like technomie. Do you think you spend too much of your time inside screens, playing interactive?"

"Of course I do. If I didn't, I'd spend too much time alone, staring at the walls of my apartment."

Lycan laughed harshly. She got the sense he knew just what she was talking about.

"But anyway," she said, "instead of harassing people on Lemieux Bridge..."—another bark of laughter from Lycan—"I help Rob now. I give him money so he can visit more often. And it feels good to help him...maybe like some people feel when they give money to their church, I don't know." She balled her hand into a fist, thumped her forehead. "I know that's so not the point of why you help someone, and it is *so* self-centered for me to think of Winter's awful plight in this light, but if she dies..." She couldn't finish the thought. She shouldn't even have started it, she realized.

"If she dies, that connection to something real dies with her."

"Exactly."

The terrain was getting bleaker, and blanker. It was sort of like traveling into the past; it seemed as if every mile they traveled away from the city, the shops, houses, even the roads, were a few years older. Veronika expected Lycan to say more, but he fell silent. She realized she'd been hoping Lycan would offer to help Rob and Winter as well, but he didn't. If his company had paid thirty million to revive him, he must make a substantial salary. It bothered her a little, that he didn't offer to help. Maybe if he got to know Rob better, he would. She really needed to include Lycan once in a while.

"So what got you up on that bridge?" Veronika hadn't planned to ask, it just came out.

"I wonder where those tubes go," Lycan said. A cluster of several dozen tubes of varying sizes and colors ran alongside the highway. Veronika couldn't care less where they went.

"Really. What got you up there?"

Lycan looked around, almost as if he was seeking an escape route. Veronika let the silence stretch, waiting. Lycan was humming again.

"Come on. *I* told *you*."

He was pressed right up against the passenger door, his face almost touching the window.

She was taken by surprise when he finally spoke. "A lot of the time I'm fine. I work, I read. Then I'll hit a rough patch. The thought of going through another day, and then another." He shook his head, watched a twenty-story cattle farm pass by. "Sometimes the thought of getting through even an hour is intolerable. Not as much lately. Lately, I've felt better."

"But why? What's at the root of the rough patches?"

He looked at her, frowning. "The root of it? There's no root of it. It's not a rotten tooth."

"If you could change one thing, what would it be?"

Lycan barked a laugh. "The way my brain functions."

"No." Veronika tapped his shoulder with her fist. "No fair. One thing in your life."

Lycan sighed heavily. He was looking out the window. Maybe it was easier for him to open up if he didn't have to make eye contact. That was nifty with Veronika; she found eye contact exhausting.

"I'm forty-three years old," Lycan said.

Veronika waited for him to continue, but that seemed to be it. "So?"

He fell into another long silence. Outside, Veronika's system showed her nothing but perfectly manicured grass and generic buildings that could be warehouses, stores, homes. She knew they were none of those things—they were whitewashed to camouflage something that couldn't simply be spruced up. Piles of trash, maybe, or a shantytown constructed of old electronics housings.

"I'm forty three," Lycan repeated. He pinched his temples. "Do you want to have a family someday?"

"I do. Someday. Is that the core? That you want a wife, a family, and you feel like you'll never have them?"

Lycan shrugged noncommittally.

"So the core is that you want to meet someone."

Lycan was clearly uncomfortable with the direction the conversation had taken. Of course that discomfort with talking about personal things was part of the reason he couldn't meet anyone.

They'd have to work on that.

"I'm going to help you," Veronika said.

Lycan looked at her, frowning.

She held her arm out. "Lycan, this is what I *do*. I coach people who aren't good at meeting people." She hiked herself up higher in her seat, grinning. "I knew there was a reason we met on that bridge. You *are* going to meet someone, because this is what I do and I'm damned good at it."

"If you're so good at it, how come you're still single?"

Veronika felt her blood pressure surge. She so hated when people asked that. But Lycan had asked without malice. Just an honest question—and a fair one, given the context. "I go out a lot, I just haven't found the right person. I have high standards."

Lycan nodded, considering this.

"What, are you suggesting I shouldn't have high standards?"

"What?" Lycan looked profoundly confused. "No, of course not. I would expect you to."

She set up the scaffolding for a new profile. "Can you give me access to your nonprivileged data? I'll also need your complete DNA code."

Lycan looked pained. "Do we have to start now? I'm not even sure I want to do this."

Veronika stopped working. "Why not?"

Lycan shrugged his big shoulders. "I don't like dating sites."

"It'll be great. Trust me."

Lycan didn't reply, but his head dropped in defeat.

While his head was conveniently within reach, Veronika opened a brain scan program, set Lycan's head in the bull's-eye and set it running. "Keep still."

Lycan looked up, but kept his head still. "What is this for?"

"It's an MRI."

"I know it's an MRI. I'm a neuropsychologist. What's it for?"

She opened her mouth to say, "To get a sense of how you think about the world," then reminded herself Lycan had a Ph.D. in neuropsychology. "To examine your habitual cognitive patterns by measuring the relative strength of your various neural networks."

He seemed surprised. "You actually match people based on something that sophisticated?"

"Sweetie, you have no idea. Do you record? I could use some random clips from your POV for characteristic analysis."

"No, I don't record," he said, sounding disdainful of the very idea. He started to lift his head, but Veronika reached out and moved it back in place.

"That's okay, I can work from some of mine." She could work up a full profile for him when she had more time; right now she was eager to see what sort of rough compatibility matches she could find, just to capture his interest.

Twenty minutes later she was ready to run a raw search. She expanded the three best matches so Lycan could see them.

"What do you think?"

Lycan looked up at them without raising his head, then dropped his gaze. "I don't know."

"What don't you know?" They were attractive women with intriguing careers. One had oversize eyes indicating an epigenetic misfire, but she was still a cutie. All had high IQs.

"I don't know if I want to do this."

Veronika decided not to push it. She would let him get used to the idea, bring it up again later.

There was a particularly large whitewashed area to their

right; Veronika took manual control of the car, turned down the next exit ramp.

"Where are we going, exactly?" Lycan asked, peering at the landscape.

"I don't know. It's an experiment."

"I take it we're not in the control group."

Veronika rolled her eyes. "Very funny, Captain Science."

They were rolling along in a vast, empty parking lot. Veronika stopped the car. "Let's go."

Lycan looked outside, then back at Veronika. "You're kidding, right?"

"No, I'm totally serious. Come on." She opened her door, stepped out. After a moment, Lycan followed.

Veronika switched off her system's sensory filter. The bright, bland building morphed into a semicollapsed Macy's. They were in the parking lot of what had once been a shopping center.

"Switch off your sensory filter," Veronika said.

"Do I have to?" Lycan said as he switched it off. "Oh." He folded his arms, took in the Macy's, nodding. "Now I see why you drove us almost an hour away from the city. You wanted to go shopping."

"Very funny." The building didn't look safe, so Veronika headed around the side, skirting the ruins. Her system informed her it was the Mohawk Commons Shopping Center, constructed in 1998, finally abandoned in 2066. Some of the signs on the stores were intact: Foxy Friends, The Soft Parade, Marathon Games.

It grew difficult to find a path through the trash and debris.

"You haven't told me why we're doing this yet," Lycan said from behind.

"Relative deprivation. By coming to the outer suburbs, we

become more grateful for the lives we have. Basic psychology." Actually, she'd just come up with that. The original idea had been sketchier.

"People," Lycan said.

Veronika looked around, spotted four people coming out of a store called Fashion Xpress.

"Why don't we get out of here?" Lycan said.

"We can't *run*," Veronika said, with more certainty than she felt. "They're just people." People heading right toward them; not running exactly, but moving with purpose.

It was a mix of men and women, all adults, thin the way people who eat little but Superfood are, and in need of a bath. Veronika had seen plenty of movies, TV shows, and interactives set in the outer burbs and beyond, but she'd never been out here before, alone, in the presence of locals. Her heart was pounding, although none of them was carrying so much as a stick.

"What are you doing here?" a woman with bleached-blond hair said as she approached.

"Just..." Veronika couldn't think of a sane response. She felt incredibly overdressed, absurdly clean and shiny standing there amid slabs of concrete, rotting fabric, discarded fast-food containers.

"My family used to live near here," Lycan said. He pointed. "Over that way, about a mile. I wanted to see it again."

"Which street?" an old guy with thick white sideburns asked.

The slightest delay, a surprisingly deft flourish of Lycan's fingers told Veronika he was calling up a map. "Barnhart Place."

The old man squinted one eye, pointed in the direction Lycan had been pointing. "It's off of Grady Street, about half a mile down on the right."

Lycan studied the road in the distance as if it was vaguely familiar. "That helps. Thank you."

"You have any cash you can spare?" the blond woman asked.

Veronika tapped her system. "Oh, sure. Give me your account link." Then she froze, realizing what a stupid thing that was to say.

"No, *cash*," the woman said. "Do you have any cash?"

Out here, there was still a distinction. She looked at Lycan, who shook his head.

"I'm sorry, we don't," Lycan said.

Veronika tried to think of anything of value she had, beyond her clothes. There was nothing, and nothing back in the rental.

"Oh, come on," a younger man said, stepping around to their left, between them and their rental. "You're telling me you have twelve-hundred-dollar boots, but you don't have twenty dollars on you?"

Lycan stepped between Veronika and the man. "We don't. We almost never carry cash."

"That's bullshit—"

The old guy cut him off. "Trent, that's enough. Let it go."

"*You* let it go," Trent said.

Veronika hit Emergency on her system.

A police officer in a screen materialized almost instantaneously. "What's the problem?" he asked, doing a three-sixty.

"You called the *police*?" the blond woman said. "We didn't do anything to you but offer directions."

"He was acting in a threatening manner, because we don't have any cash to give them." Veronika pointed at Trent.

"Oh, *bullshit*," Trent said.

"What are you doing out here?" the police officer asked Veronika.

Veronika sputtered, then remembered Lycan's cover story. She pointed at him. "He used to live near here. We were looking for his house."

The police officer took this in without a word. "All right. All of you"—he gestured toward the locals—"leave the vicinity immediately." He rotated to face Veronika and Lycan. "You two—"

"This *vicinity* is where we live," the old guy interrupted.

"Where are you, in Yonkers?" Trent added. "What are you gonna do, *fine* us?"

"What I'm going to do," the officer said, clearly losing patience, "is tag you with a zombie, send a drone to bring you in, and throw your ass in jail." He turned back toward Veronika and Lycan. "You two get in your vehicle, and go home."

"Yes sir. Thank you," Lycan said. They stepped past Trent and hurried toward the car as the officer stayed with the locals.

"You have some nerve," the blond woman called after them. "We were nothing but kind to you."

Veronika felt like complete shit. "I panicked. I shouldn't have called the police."

"It was a tough call," Lycan said. "I have to admit, I was nervous."

"I feel terrible, though. That woman was right. Beside Trent's little hissy fit, they were being nothing but kind."

"Why don't we get going?" Lycan suggested.

Veronika nodded, started the car, and pulled out. "What if I sent my drone out here tomorrow with some cash for them? Do you think that would be okay?"

"I think that's a great idea," Lycan said.

25

Rob

Rob felt as if the shoulder of Route 304 were listing side to side as he staggered along. He was so tired. All he wanted was to sleep.

No. He was hungrier than he was tired. In fact he wasn't sure he could make it all the way home without something to eat. Which meant stopping at the tubes.

He was so tired of this life. Not that it was a life, really. Tired of this existence. At the end of each shift, the voice in the back of his head got louder; early on he'd been able to ignore it, but now it was deafening.

Quit. Run away. Start over where no one knows you, where no one knows what you did.

He could move to Philly, or Pittsburgh, start a new life. What Winter was asking of him was too much. Did she even know how much it cost to visit her? Too much; it was just too much.

Leave in the morning. Philly.

He thought about Winter, who would wonder what happened to him when she was waked for a date. She'd know he let her down. Without his visits, she'd probably be kicked out of the program even more quickly.

In the distance he could see the turnoff for the tubes. He was so hungry. Superfood wasn't going to do it—he needed fat, something dripping with grease, like burgers or biscuits. Of course that would take money. Rob checked his account on the handheld. He stopped in his tracks.

There was an extra nine thousand dollars in his account.

He brought up the transaction, checked the routing, found nothing but a simple notation:

"Anonymous."

Chuckling to himself in an exhausted, slightly delirious way that might make a passerby think he was unhinged, Rob resumed walking. Who the hell would give him that kind of money, and do it anonymously? That the amount was exactly what it cost to visit Winter made his benefactor's intentions clear. Nathan and Veronika had been open about helping, but he doubted they had that kind of money to give away in any case, so it probably wasn't them. For most of his longtime friends, nine thousand was two or three months' pay. Sunali? Rob mulled that one. Possibly. Bridesicles were her passion, so it wasn't inconceivable, especially given Lorelei's role in this whole mess. In case it was Sunali, Rob would have to start thinking nicer thoughts about her.

In any case, the discovery, and the possibility of visiting Winter, sent a fresh jolt of adrenaline through Rob's veins. He would indeed grab a bite at the tubes, then catch the train to Yonkers. As he headed for the train, he tried Sunali again.

She was still completely blocked; he couldn't even leave a message. Since Cryomed had been unwilling to answer questions about the policy on "salvage," he was running out of options. The thought of having to contact Lorelei and ask for a favor made him cringe.

Winter didn't comment about Rob forgetting his lute, which made him feel better about forgetting it.

"How long has it been?" she asked.

"Believe it or not, less than three weeks. Some kind soul deposited the fee into my account anonymously. Isn't that incredible?"

Winter tried to smile, her stiff lips trembling. "Unbelievable. Do you have any idea who it was?"

He was tempted to mention Sunali, but didn't want to eat up precious time explaining who she was and how Rob knew her. "Not really. I don't know many people with that kind of money."

"Well, if you find out, tell them thanks for me."

"I will."

"For a second I thought it might be Nathan, my ex, but then I remembered he doesn't even know you."

"Yeah, probably not him." Rob felt unsure whether he should tell Winter he and Nathan were now friends. She might think it was weird that Rob had sought out her ex, even if it was only to try to convince him to visit her.

"I guess Nathan isn't coming back," Winter said.

"He hasn't visited again," Rob said, half statement, half question. The topic gave him an opening. He tried to sound casual. "So, have you had other visitors?" He swallowed, hoping his nervousness, his eagerness to hear the answer, didn't show.

"A few. Two dates." She grunted. "Dates. What a strange word for it." She studied Rob's face for a moment. "They're not like your visits, though. I have to let the client lead the conversation. I have to act all warm and peppy and fake. This is the only time I have to think, to talk about what *I* want to talk about."

Rob suspected Winter was worried he might visit less often if he thought others were visiting. Maybe she even sensed that he was having moments of weakness, when he thought of abandoning her altogether. He promised himself he would never give in to that weakness. "Well, I'm glad my visits help, because I have no plans to stop."

She seemed to relax. "I appreciate that."

A few seconds ticked by; Rob was distracted trying to decide whether two visitors, plus his visits, was enough.

"You know, I don't know anything about you," Winter said. "Where do you live?"

"With my dad." He didn't add that it was a new arrangement.

"You must get along with him okay?"

"I do. He's a barber, out in the suburbs."

"How far out?"

"Not too far. New City." Of course the name of the town itself wasn't the issue; asking how far out someone lived was a way to gauge how poor they were.

It felt like a frivolous waste of time, to be talking about himself, but it made sense that Winter wanted to learn more about him. He was a complete stranger. "Mom died ten years ago. Dad has a simulation of her running all day long. All day." Rob shook his head. "It's like her ghost, wandering the halls, sitting at the table with us, eating invisible food."

"That's beautiful, in an unsettling way. He must have loved her so much. How did she die, if you don't mind me asking?"

"Cervical cancer."

"Head nod. I'm sorry."

There was no need for Rob to elaborate. She'd died of a curable disease. Winter would know they did the usual desperate things people do to try to raise money when a loved one gets a curable terminal illness. Both Rob and his dad had worked second jobs, they'd appealed to friends and relatives, posted a donation site on the web, sold everything of value. By the time his mom died, they'd raised close to fifty thousand dollars. They were seven hundred thousand short.

"Your profile said both your parents are gone?" Rob asked.

"In the ground. Dad in a construction accident. Mom died in her sleep."

Rob nodded. Autopsies cost money.

"Although it's more complicated than that makes it sound. My mom was married seven times, if you count the four times she married my father."

Rob winced. "Sounds like a rough childhood."

"Shrug," Winter said. "Not as bad as some. How much time?" Winter asked.

"Two minutes."

"Can you do something for me?"

"Anything."

"One of the men who visited said I would be a costly bride, but he wouldn't elaborate. Can you tell me what injuries I have?"

Rob felt like he'd been socked in the stomach. He still remembered the first few items on the list, the ones he reached before he had to stop. "Are you sure you want to know?"

"I do."

He tried to think of some way to say no, to run out the clock, but he could think of no polite way to do that.

Reluctantly, he read off the profile set in the screen on

the wall. "Severed spine between the third and fourth lumbar. Crushed kidney. Crushed liver." Winter's eyes got huge, her mouth an O of surprise. Rob took a breath, tried to run through the rest of the long list as quickly as possible. "Forty percent of large intestine gone. Shattered pelvis, broken left femur, broken left knee, shattered—"

"*Stop*," she shouted. "Oh my God." Her eyes darted left and right. "I have to get out of here—"

"It's all right," Rob said. But it wasn't all right, it was the exact opposite of all right.

"I can't—" Her eyes went blank, her face slack. Air hissed between lifeless blue lips.

"We apologize for cutting your time short," a disembodied woman's voice said. "You had twenty-one seconds left. We've reimbursed the prorated amount. You're welcome to visit Miss West again at your convenience."

"Thank you," Rob said, not knowing what else to say. He rose on wobbly legs, feeling suddenly tired beyond words. He had no idea how he would make it home, let alone to work in seven hours.

26

Rob

Rob's handheld woke him at five a.m. for work. Even as he struggled toward consciousness, he was accosted by images of Winter, terrified, pleading to get out.

He had to find a way to get her out of there. Dragging himself out of bed, Rob pulled on the same flannel pants and shirt he'd worn the day before. At the recycling center, no one noticed any one particular foul odor.

In the Business Room, his dad was giving a haircut to an ancient guy in weathered frankenboots. The man had no arms. In all likelihood he was, like Rob's own long-dead grandparents, one of the ten-percenters. That must have been some time to be alive, when ten percent of the children born were deformed, and grew up to be a very angry generation indeed when the cause of their suffering was discovered to be a food additive—a chemical that coagulated ice cream so it could more easily be eaten off a stick without melting.

Through the mirror, the old guy saw Rob standing in the doorway. He nodded, and Rob nodded back.

After a night of little sleep, he was beyond tired; he was in that wired, headachy zone that was becoming so familiar, between the long hours of work and the relentless anguish.

He stepped into the kitchen and tried to contact Sunali again.

Blocked. What could she be doing? From what Rob could remember, she'd been pretty active with her system, especially for someone who'd stepped into a strange, unfamiliar future after being dead for ninety years.

When Lorelei had first explained that Sunali was both her stepmother and her great-grandmother, Rob thought she was bullshitting in order to draw more eyes. But no, she wasn't.

Lorelei. If he wanted to get in touch with Sunali, it seemed to be Lorelei or nothing, didn't it? Cursing silently, Rob opened a screen into a place he was sure he would never visit again.

He found himself swimming among fifty other screens, all of them watching Lorelei brush her hair. For most people, it was polite to ping for permission to open a screen, but not Lorelei; she was open to the public most any time of the day or night.

She must have been carrying on a dozen conversations at once, her speech was jumpy and mostly incoherent. Rob pinged her to get her attention.

Her eyes opened wide with surprise. "Rob?" She slid from her stool, turned and searched for him. "It's so good to see you. How *are* you?"

"Hi." It made him twitchy to speak to her. He'd almost stopped thinking of her as a real person; in his mind she was fixed in time, still dropping his life from her window. "Look, I'm here because I need your help. I have to speak to your mother, and she's completely blocked."

"Yeah, I know. She's with my grandfather." She gave *grandfather* the same inflection most people give to words like *dysentery* and *pedophile*. "He's dying again."

It took Rob a moment to digest this. "You can't mean Kilo. Do you have another grandfather?"

Lorelei laughed. "No, just the one."

"But—" Rob stammered, flabbergasted. *But Kilo left your mother to rot on ice for ninety years, when the cost of reviving her would have been minuscule to him.* The only reason she was alive was because Lorelei's father made a grand parting fuck-you to the Van Kampen family by using money from his divorce settlement to revive her. Sunali was probably the only bridesicle ever revived out of spite.

"Yeah, I know. Stepmom says even the biggest asshole in the world shouldn't die alone." She threw back her head and shook her hair, an all-too-familiar gesture. "Although I don't know, you might have a different opinion on who's the world's biggest asshole."

Rob didn't take the bait. He did want to understand why Lorelei had done what she'd done—he was desperate to understand—but right now he needed to talk to Sunali. At the same time, he had to be polite, because he needed this favor. "How many times has he died now? Five or six?"

"This will be number eight. He died six weeks ago." She put her hands on her narrow hips and started pacing. "The old fucker is going to squeeze every possible second out of his life. In the end they'll be reviving him so he can live five more minutes, then one, then ten more seconds." She shook her head and laughed, though clearly she found none of this amusing. "He's close to a hundred and twenty. Can you believe that? His telomeres are totally played out, but he won't let go."

Not that it mattered to Lorelei. Kilo was leaving everything to Lorelei's biological mom, who had a new family and wanted nothing to do with what she saw as the spectacularly incestuous arrangement between her grandmother and ex-husband.

"So why do you want to see Sunali, if you don't mind me asking?" She was being uncharacteristically polite. It was so difficult to reconcile this Lorelei with the psychopath dangling his things out a window (although to be fair, it was also difficult to reconcile the psychopath Lorelei with the one he'd known while they'd been together). Despite her new manners, he *did* mind her asking, but what choice did he have except to explain his very private story to her and a hundred others?

So he did.

When he finished, Lorelei stood without a word. Her lips were pursed in her best "Don't fuck with me" expression as she dug into her closet and retrieved an umbrella. "Meet me outside the Damark Revival Clinic. I'll take you in to see her. How soon can you get there?"

He got there as fast as the micro-T would take him, hopping off into a light rain before it had completely stopped. He hurried along the porous sidewalk, where puddles never formed, escorted by a few dozen screens—friends (or fans, or whatever you'd call them) of Lorelei. As the revival clinic came into view, he slowed so he wouldn't be out of breath when he reached Lorelei. He could see her standing under a tear-shaped umbrella, half a foot taller than everyone who passed her. Hundreds of screens buzzed around her.

She met him with open arms and hugged him with all her might, evidently choosing not to notice how unenthusiastically he returned the hug.

"Come on." She turned toward the entrance, held out her hand so naturally that he took it before realizing what he'd done. She led him through a sumptuous waiting room, past imposing security, both human and mechanical. Lorelei seemed different now that they were inside, less ebullient, older, and it took Rob a moment to identify what it was: her entourage was missing, blocked from entering the private facility.

Lorelei led him down a hall that reminded him of the lavish bridesicle hall sans the crèches, through an archway, into the room where Kilo Van Kampen was dying.

He hung suspended in a warm saline pool like a shriveled salamander. The cradle holding him was attached to the walls on a dozen strands that stretched like snot. A nurse and what looked like a couple of personal assistants hung back, while Sunali sat beside him in a chair that reminded Rob of a giant spider.

Kilo's eyes rolled to follow him and Lorelei as they entered. His mouth hung open, his perfect white teeth glowing obscenely in the wrinkled mess of his face. Sunali turned, then leaped from her seat when she saw Lorelei. Rob had almost forgotten how curvy Sunali was, seemingly all hips and breasts, how sharp her cheekbones were.

"What are you doing here?" she whispered sharply.

"Well, I'm not here to visit Grandpa, that's for sure," Lorelei said at full volume.

"Mom."

They turned in unison toward the cradle at the sound of Kilo's weak, phlegmy whisper. It was bizarre, to hear this old man call Sunali "Mom." Rob wondered how it made Sunali feel.

She went to the cradle, reached into the thick, tepid water, and took Kilo's hand. He and Lorelei watched in silence as she brushed stray strands of blond hair out of his face.

The irony. Rob wondered if Kilo got the irony in this situation.

Kilo swallowed, winced. "Throat hurts."

Before his lunging nurse could get there, Sunali retrieved his dangling water tube and slid it between his lips. He sucked impotently, groaned as it slipped out of his mouth.

"Try to rest. You'll feel better."

"When?" Kilo asked.

"In a few hours you'll feel better, is what I'm saying." It was clear she was straining not to sound impatient.

"Just what I need. Platitudes." He grunted, the sound rich with anger, betrayal. "It's not fair."

Sunali sighed heavily. "You're such an asshole."

"You're an asshole," Kilo tried to say, but ran out of breath and only mouthed the last syllable.

Sunali turned back toward Rob and Lorelei. "What do you want?" From her sharp tone, Rob realized it had probably been a mistake to come, but it was too late now.

"I'm so sorry to disturb you, Ms. Van Kampen. I asked Lorelei to bring me here." He swallowed thickly, launched into his story.

As soon as she realized this was about a sister bridesicle, she softened a bit. She didn't become warm, exactly, but she stopped looking angry and put-upon. It reminded Rob of war movies, where soldiers will do anything for a fellow soldier. Sunali worked her system as she told him someone would contact him. Then she turned back to her son before Rob could do more than call out "Thank you" to her retreating back.

As they walked the long corridor to the exit, Lorelei slowed to a stop.

"What is it?" Rob asked.

She considered him for a long beat. "So now what? You put a block on me again?"

That had pretty much been his plan. He sighed, leaned against the wall with his arms folded, staring at his feet. He wasn't sure what to say. Surely she wasn't suggesting they get back together; what she wanted was a postrelationship platonic friendship. Normally that was very much Rob's style of breakup, but he just couldn't see himself laughing over a drink with Lorelei.

"Do you want to know why I did it?" Lorelei asked.

"I know why you did it. You wanted more attention."

She looked off down the hall, shaking her head, her silky black hair swaying. "Eyes are never the goal."

"Oh, I know the attention-hound party line. Living in front of witnesses compels you to live your life fully, to never let precious moments pass in wishy-washy beige dullness, etcetera, etcetera. So, you're saying you decided the best way to live vividly in that moment was to jettison my personal possessions out a window?"

"No. I decided to break up with you before you broke up with me, and that seemed the most memorable way to do it."

Rob looked up at her.

Lorelei shrugged. "What? It's true."

Rob put his hands on top of his head, incredulous. "Why would you think I was going to break up with you?"

Without taking her eyes off Rob, Lorelei worked her system. She called up a recording from one evening in summer, when Rob was playing his lute at the Beer Yard, a Low Town bar. The hallway vanished and they were watching Rob, evidently on break from playing, talking to Dougie, the owner.

"I mean, sure, if I fall in love with a woman who wants to stay in New York, I'll stay, but—"

"That was the night before we broke up." Lorelei shut off the recording. "You never used 'we' when you talked about the future—it was always 'I.' I never said I wanted to stay in New York, so who is this hypothetical woman you might fall in love with?"

He opened his mouth to argue, to explain what he'd been thinking when he made that comment, but realized he had no explanation. It was true.

How many times, lying in bed, had Rob interrogated himself about his motives for going out with Lorelei? She'd lifted him into High Town, paid his way, but at the end of each self-interrogation Rob cleared himself of the charge of using Lorelei. She was gorgeous, had rocket fuel for blood, was witty and modern-cool. He would have gone out with her if she was broke. But only for a while. The thing was, he'd always assumed Lorelei was on the same page. Part of the reason he'd gone out with her was because he'd been so surprised and flattered that she was interested in him. He never expected it would last, because he was certain she would eventually ditch him and move on.

When he didn't answer, Lorelei nodded, satisfied. "Sooner or later you were going to leave me sitting at the side of the road, and I didn't want to play that part, so I rewrote the script."

She was waiting for him to say something.

"I won't block you. I won't stop talking to you. And I sincerely appreciate the help you gave me today."

Lorelei broke into a beaming smile. "I'm a good friend. You might think I would make a shitty wife, and maybe I would, but I'm a good friend."

Somehow Rob felt like he was betraying Winter a little by reconciling with Lorelei, that he was simultaneously betraying Lorelei by pretending he didn't still despise her for what she did. What would his dad say, the first time Lorelei popped in to say hello? What would Veronika and Nathan think? Well, Veronika, anyway. Nathan would be thrilled. How many times had he asked Rob to introduce him?

"You know, I have a friend who wants to meet you," Rob said.

"You want to fix me up with your friend?" Lorelei laughed. "He must not be much of a friend."

She offered her hand, and Rob took it. They headed back outside, where a hundred of Lorelei's friends were waiting to find out what had happened.

27

Veronika

Nathan had made the entire outer wall of his condo one-way transparent so that he could watch people glide along Pierre Street, waiting for his first glimpse of Lorelei.

"I'm kind of nervous," Nathan said, rolling his shoulders like an athlete getting loose. He sounded pleased about it, as if nervous was a good thing. Maybe when you were as cool and confident as Nathan, it was.

Veronika wasn't nervous, she was miserable. Utterly, utterly miserable. She'd been dreading this dinner all week.

Rob walked into view, his pace glacial because of his cheap shoes. Then he paused, turned, and waited, wearing a stiff, very un-Rob-like smile.

Then *she* glided into view, partially obscured by screens buzzing around her like she was the queen fucking bee. She was wearing a green drape that trailed to a half-dozen tails at her thighs, partially obscuring a gold-colored system that was just barely high enough to cover her nipples.

"Oh, God, now I'm really nervous." Nathan dragged a hand down his face, let it drop loosely to his side.

Rob and Lorelei were still talking; they'd made no move toward the walk-up to the lobby. Veronika could only hope they were discussing reconciliation.

"Don't you want to hear what they're saying? Maybe Rob is telling her all about you."

Nathan frowned. "I'm not going to eavesdrop on their conversation."

Veronika gestured toward the screens. "Two hundred people are eavesdropping on their conversation."

"True." He told his apartment to activate sound on Pierre Street. The hum and whoosh of passing vehicles lit the air, along with Rob and Lorelei's low voices.

"I met him through Winter," Rob was saying.

"Who?"

"Winter." Rob waited, offering no more.

Lorelei suddenly made the connection, gasped. "Oh, *Winter*. How does he know Winter?"

Rob folded his arms, stared at the pavement for a moment. Finally, he lifted his head. "He went out with her."

Lorelei looked positively delighted. Her eyes sparkled with an inner light that had to be system-driven. "He went out with Winter? Well, isn't this bizarre."

Now Veronika felt fully justified in hating her. *I'm being fixed up with the guy who used to go out with the woman my ex-boyfriend ran over because I was distracting him with my total bitchery? How bizarre, how modern!* She was an attention whore, right down to her rotten core.

Veronika watched Nathan gape at her gorgeous legs as she struggled to match Rob's nonaugmented pace. Veronika snapped her fingers in front of his face; he pushed her hand away.

As they disappeared momentarily, Veronika wished she could freeze time. She didn't want to live through the moments that would come after Lorelei's grand entrance. She dreaded shaking the woman's hand, hearing her voice, seeing Nathan fall all over himself to impress her.

Nathan told the front door to let them in, and seconds later Lorelei was inside, arms wide to hug Nathan, laughing brightly as Nathan whispered something in her ear. Rather than squeezing through the door after her, her entourage popped into existence inside the room, her higher-status followers assuming their proper places at the front of the crowd.

Maybe Veronika should pretend to get sick. Maybe she would get sick, watching this fiasco.

As Rob gave Veronika a hug, he gave her a quick look that said he was enjoying this about as much as she. At least she wasn't alone in her misery.

"And you must be..." Lorelei paused ever-so-slightly, checking her screen because she'd forgotten Veronika's name, or, more likely, because she wanted to make it look like she'd forgotten Veronika's name—a little dramatic pause to establish that Veronika was short, and of little consequence in this performance. "...Veronika."

Nathan led them into the living area, and the furniture cruised into place, a Polupu sofa rising to meet Lorelei's perfect ass, a Bo Pu chair sinking to house Veronika's frumpy one.

Lorelei and Nathan showed off their slick vocal stylings and fingerwork, but kept their side conversations to a restrained level in deference to their "just met" status. Veronika had trouble following the conversation because of the volume of her inner dialogue, and because she felt like a little mistake who shouldn't take up much of anyone's time by speaking.

As Nathan and Lorelei launched into the predictable "let's

seek out interests we have in common" phase of the first face-to-face ("*Oh, I love Two Boots Checker Face, too!*"), Veronika had to escape.

She went to the bathroom, washed her hands for a long time, asked the house if it would unlock Nathan's medicine cabinet so she could snoop (no), paced the bathroom, again considered feigning illness, and finally dragged herself back to the living room.

Nathan and Lorelei looked to be on their second glass of absinthe. Rob just looked miserable.

"This is so cozy," Lorelei said, scrunching her shoulders.

"Yes, very cozy. Just the hundred and fifty of us."

Nathan gave her a look. Veronika knew it was a rude thing to say, like an actor in a play pointing out the audience, but she hadn't been able to help herself.

The cheery smile never left Lorelei's face. "Just imagine how crowded it would be in here if you had friends who were interested in *your* life."

The comment would have hurt, except the way Lorelei delivered the line, the crispness of the phrasing, was so familiar. Someone was *coaching* her. Veronika smiled, let the silence stretch out for a few ticks. "You need to get a better writer. Whoever's feeding you your lines is beyond stale, on the way to moldy."

Lorelei's eyes narrowed. "Whoever's feeding *you* needs to go easy on the butter. And just for the record, all of my lines are my own material. You. Fat. Whore."

The venom in the words rocked Veronika back, but she didn't let it show. Straining to keep her voice light, she said, "Now, that last line definitely *was* yours, because it was simple and childish—"

Rob's fingers tightened around her upper arm. "Let's get

some air." Veronika let Rob lead her onto the veranda. At the moment it overlooked a vast sea of molten lava, which was apropos, given how Veronika felt.

"I don't like her," Veronika said through gritted teeth as they stood at the railing, looking out on the bubbling, steaming window dressing that masked a mundane view of a side street.

"I don't either," Rob said. "Although I don't hate her as much as I used to."

Something rose out of the lava, then flopped back under the surface before she could identify it. "Were you trying to stop me from making a scene, or just looking for an excuse to get out of there?"

"Both."

Inside, it was quiet. Hopefully the exchange had at least served to make things tense and awkward between Nathan and Lorelei.

"You don't like her, but you like *him*, don't you?"

Veronika gaped at Rob, thrown off guard. Denial seemed the best approach. "*No*. Nathan? Why would you think that?" She laughed, going for an "Oh, how silly" tone, but felt herself reddening.

Through his polite smile, Veronika could see he wasn't buying her act.

"Is it that obvious?"

Rob shrugged. "It is to me. And I'm not all that astute."

"Do you think it's obvious to Nathan?"

Rob considered. "I would think so. I kind of figured whatever was going on between you two was out in the open. You guys are always so flirty. You've never talked about it?"

Of course Nathan knew; how could he not? Of course, he probably assumed any woman he met was attracted to him.

The smarmy bastard. "It's dumb, really. Even if he was interested, our compatibility rating is pitiful."

It was still quiet in the living room; Veronika imagined them making out like adolescents, and felt a little sick.

"When you said Lorelei needed to get a better writer, what was that about?" Rob asked.

"Someone is feeding her lines."

Rob looked shocked. "How could you know that?"

Veronika sighed theatrically. "I know because I feed people lines for a living." In the living room, Lorelei suddenly squealed. Then it sounded like they were having a pillow fight. "Some of what comes out of Lorelei's mouth is trite, then she snaps off some insightful observation, or a good comeback. A funny line. I've been doing this for ten years. I have an ear for lines."

Rob seemed genuinely stunned by the idea. "So you're saying she's got someone monitoring her all the time, giving her interesting things to say?"

Veronika shrugged. "Not necessarily all the time, only when she's doing something that's drawing a lot of eyes."

"She could have been doing this the whole time she and I were together."

Veronika waved the door into the living room open a crack. Lorelei and Nathan were watching a recording from Lorelei's life, something involving her stepmother and grandfather. She scanned the screens watching Lorelei and Nathan watch the recording, focusing especially on the ones out front.

"What are you doing?" Rob whispered.

"Seeing if I can spot her coach. He probably has his screen blinded, but you never know." The faces in the most prominent screens all held the blank, wide-eyed expressions of people being entertained. None looked like they were working.

Her gaze was pulled back to Nathan and Lorelei. Their knees were touching.

It was utter masochism, the way she lived in fear of Nathan getting serious with someone. Veronika was a placeholder, a surrogate for the girlfriend who would eventually replace her as Nathan's default social partner. But how many times had it looked like she was about to lose him, only to have his relationship du jour crumble? She'd seen less of him while he was seeing Winter (though not a lot less, because his thing with Winter hadn't gotten very serious), then just like that, it was over. Maybe Nathan was too afraid of commitment to ever stay with one woman for long.

Over on the couch, Nathan looked like an eager-to-please puppy. It was sickening. Veronika pulled up the personal data available on Lorelei—which was extensive, because Lorelei lived about as publicly as anyone Veronika had ever met—and ran a quick and dirty compatibility protocol against Nathan's profile.

She suppressed a laugh of glee, though a bright little bark escaped. Point four-six. It wasn't the worst score she'd ever seen, but it was nowhere near high enough for a lasting relationship. Not a chance. It made her feel a little better.

A package was pending when Veronika got back to her building. Veronika requested delivery at the building's tube, and a moment later she opened the holding cube and lifted it out.

When she opened the box in her apartment, a tiny plush flamingo tottered out, and said, "I'm afraid we got off on the wrong foot. I'm sorry. We'll do better next time."

No name, as if none were needed. Veronika kicked the flamingo across her living room, and stomped on it before it could right itself.

28

Rob

Lorne was eating a pink onion pear, skin and all, while Rob scratched at an ancient gum stain on the arm of the barber chair. He'd always wondered why his dad had three barber chairs when he always cut hair in the same one—the one closer to the Wall of Fame. He was about to ask his dad about this when the front door squealed open and a man poked his head inside.

"You have time for a haircut?" He was lanky and loose-limbed, his hair a crazy, unkempt ball.

Lorne waved him toward a chair. "Always time for a hair-cut. I only need one hand to eat."

The guy, who looked to be in his forties, took a seat. His system was impressive; it looked to be made of standing water that defied gravity. He was a stranger, and judging from the system, not from the area.

As Rob's dad wrapped a cloak around him, the man said, "I'm Peter."

They introduced themselves, then Peter and his dad had a brief discussion about how the haircut should go. Rob eased himself out of the chair. He would leave the guy to his haircut.

"So I understand you're interested in the bridesicle program?" Peter said it so conversationally, it took a minute to register. His dad had stopped cutting.

"'Interested' isn't the word," Rob said when he'd recovered some of his composure. He eased back into the chair. "Can you help me?"

"That's why I'm here." He pointed at his head. "And to get a haircut, of course."

"Of course," Rob said, his lips slightly numb.

"From what I understand, you want to know about someone's status? Someone who's uninsured?"

Lorne resumed cutting Peter's hair, as if the conversation was none of his business.

"That's right," Rob said, climbing out of the chair. "You can check her status?"

"I can't check it directly, but the algorithm is fairly straightforward, so I can give you a ballpark. Assuming you know how many men have visited her, and how many times?"

"I've visited four times. I think there've been two others. Wait, three." He'd almost forgotten Nathan.

Peter worked his system. "Give me her date of entry and attractiveness rating."

Rob provided them.

Peter had a "This is not good" expression on his face that made Rob feel a little sick. "Last thing. Do you know if any of her other visitors are like you—people who definitely can't afford to revive her?"

"At least one was. I don't know about the other two."

Peter nodded, subvocalizing as he entered information. He stopped all at once, spent a moment staring at a readout only he could see. "I hate to say this, but it may be as little as a few weeks."

Ever so slowly, Rob put his hands over his face. The edges of his vision were going gray; he thought he might pass out. *Do you want a second chance at life? It'll be terrifying, and humiliating, but now that we've waked you and made you aware that you're dead, how could you possibly say no?* Rob dropped his hands. Weeks, he'd said. "How many weeks?"

Peter studied the output. "Two or three? Like I said, it's an estimate."

He'd be lucky to raise enough to see her once more before then. Then she'd be dead, for good and all, her death squarely on his shoulders with no way to make amends.

Peter was nodding sympathetically. "The thing is, if they leave your friend there when no one's visiting her, some other young woman misses her chance to live again. There's only so much space, after all."

Rob lifted his head to look at Peter. "You work for Cryomed?"

Peter nodded.

"I thought you were on our side."

Peter canted his head, smiled not unkindly. "I am on your side. I'm here, aren't I?" Dad finished running the vacuum over Peter's head to remove stray clippings, and Peter stood.

"So why are you here?" Rob asked.

Peter sighed, considered Rob. "Because I'm not a fan of how Cryomed runs the program. I'd like to see some of their policies changed. For personal reasons."

From the look on Peter's face, Rob imagined those personal reasons involved someone close to him.

"How can I save her?" Rob asked.

Peter put a big hand behind Rob's head, drew their faces close. "Unless some rich guy takes a shine to her, you can't. If you get her more visitors, you can nudge the termination date, but not much." He squeezed Rob's head, let it go.

Termination date. Rob had never heard such an awful phrase.

Peter tried to pay for the haircut, but Lorne waved the offer away. "Are you kidding me?" He grabbed Peter, gave him a half hug, and clapped him on the back.

Rob met Peter at the door, shook his hand. "Thank you for your help. At least we know what we're dealing with."

Peter dropped his chin. "I wish I had better news for you, Rob. I really do."

The door clicked closed, and Rob and his dad stood, unmoving, for a long moment.

"What are we going to do now?" Dad asked.

"I don't know. Something." He had no idea what that something was. They had no money, no time, and they needed someone to step up and pay a fortune to revive her.

He sent a message to Veronika. *Bad, bad news. Can we meet?* It helped to talk to Veronika. Strange, but lately he felt more Veronika's friend than Nathan's.

29

Veronika

She resisted trying to find out what Lorelei thought of Nathan for an entire day, but as she stood on the sidewalk outside her apartment waiting for Nathan to pick her up, the anxiety of not knowing finally overtook the potential pain of finding out. Veronika searched for clips of Lorelei from the past twenty-two hours that included a mention of Nathan.

She had her choice of seventy-eight clips, mostly identical, gathered by Lorelei's fans. Bracing herself, Veronika chose one of the shorter versions and activated it.

Lorelei was on the floor of her living room, doing yoga, wearing very little. An older woman who Veronika guessed was Lorelei's yoga instructor was going through the same contortions beside her. They were talking about Nathan, or rather, Lorelei was, and the instructor was listening. Lorelei made reference to the obvious complications involved if she went out with Nathan (she said this with her head between

her legs), but said he seemed fun and was kind of cute. Ultimately she decided that she couldn't decide.

"I think I'll leave this one in your hands," she said, addressing the screens watching her yoga lesson. "You haven't steered
me wrong yet. What do you think, should I see him again?"

It was all so obviously staged that Veronika wanted to
vomit, yet Lorelei's fans lapped it up. Her eye count shot from
three hundred to five hundred in a matter of seconds, and the
votes registered in real time, in the air over Lorelei's head.

The vote was sixty-three percent to thirty-seven percent in
favor of Lorelei seeing Nathan again. The clip was oddly reassuring. If Lorelei was letting her fans decide, she was clearly
going out with Nathan simply to boost her ratings. But that
also meant she was likely going to break Nathan's heart, and
that pissed Veronika off.

Nathan pulled up in his brand-new Chameleon, the wheels
tucked, the maglev drive engaged. He was beaming.

"She likes me."

"You've talked to her?" There were a dozen screens hovering in the backseat. Christ, they were probably Lorelei's fans.
Nathan was drawing spin-off attention.

"Not yet. But did you see the vote?" He pulled into traffic,
the Chameleon utterly soundless.

"What vote?" No way was she going to admit seeing it.

"She let her friends vote. Sixty-three percent said she
should go out with me."

"So her friends like you, is what you're saying."

He waved away the clarification. "If she didn't like me, she
wouldn't have let them vote."

Veronika wanted off this topic immediately. "You heard
about Winter?"

"Yeah. Rob told me."

"I've been trying to think of something we can do to help."

The car shifted to automatic as Nathan took his hands off the wheel and leaned back. "I know." Nathan was carrying on a second conversation through his system, and that bugged Veronika.

"I'm as worried about Rob as I am Winter," she said. "Do you see how stooped he is? It's like he's physically carrying Winter on his back. If she's pulled from the program, he's going to feel like he killed her all over again."

"I know."

Veronika couldn't help thinking Nathan's responses were clipped because his mind was on Lorelei, not Winter. Well, that was his choice. She wondered if Rob should warn Winter that she was almost out of time. Rob thought it best that Winter not know, but Veronika wasn't so sure. While she was thinking about it, she shot another five hundred dollars into Rob's account.

A moment later, a text message came from Rob:

Thank you! My anonymous benefactor also made another generous contribution!

Awesome! she shot back. Generous. Rob must mean he'd received another nine thousand, so he'd be able to visit right away. That was good, given the uncertainty about how long she would be there.

She shivered, imagining what it must be like to be in Winter's place, aware that you're dead, helpless to do anything about it. Why were so many people paying through the nose for the privilege of occupying one of those coffins? Why was *she* paying through the nose for freezing insurance?

"I think I'm going to cancel my freezing insurance," she said.

Nathan smiled at her like she was joking. "No, you're not."

"Yes, I am. How long is your contract for?"

"A thousand years, I think. I just increased it. How about you?"

"Twelve hundred."

"See, you're all set."

"But what's the point? Who would possibly revive us?"

"No one," Nathan laughed. "If you can't afford twenty or thirty million to revive yourself, why would some relative pay it a hundred years from now?"

Veronika swatted Nathan's shoulder. "Exactly my point. That's why I'm canceling my insurance. I might as well use the money now, while I'm alive."

Nathan sighed. "You really don't understand the true purpose of freezing insurance?"

"The true purpose?"

Nathan looked around, like he was checking to make sure no one could overhear, studiously ignored the seven or eight screens hovering in the backseat. "It's about coping with our fear of death."

"Oh, really?"

Nathan nodded as he pulled into the parking stacks across the street from Venus de Milo's. She suddenly wondered why they always went here, of all the restaurants in High Town.

"Think about it," Nathan said as they got out. "If you're frozen when you die, there's only a minuscule chance you'll ever be revived, but there is *some* chance." He held his thumb and forefinger close together. "That tiny millimeter of chance takes the edge off our fear of death. As the lights are going out, you don't know for sure it's the end, so it's not as terrifying."

Veronika nodded tentatively.

"Picture yourself as a corpse in a coffin, buried in the ground, decomposing."

She didn't want to picture herself as a corpse in a coffin. If she did, there was less chance she'd cancel her freezing insurance. "So you're saying people break their backs, some working two jobs, so they can afford a hundred and fifty thousand a year in insurance, all to cope with the existential terror of nonexistence."

Nathan considered. "I wouldn't use all of those jewel-encrusted NYU-grad-school words, but yes, that's exactly what I'm saying."

"That's what having kids is for. Plus they're a heck of a lot cheaper, and give you pleasure while you're alive."

Nathan made a sour face.

30

Rob

Rob played "The Boy in the Gap" until Winter's eyes clicked into focus, then he set the lute aside. He would not cry, would not do anything that might tip Winter off that in a few weeks they would bury her. The first time he'd come to this place, he'd carried a secret, and hadn't been able to bring himself to tell it, though she had to know. Now he carried a different secret. This one he needed to keep from her.

"How long has it been?" Winter asked in that terrible graveyard voice that so contradicted her lovely, gentle face.

"Only two weeks. Our anonymous benefactor came through again. And how about this: I contacted Nathan, and he helped out a ton. He went around and got his friends to help as well."

"Head shake. Who would have thought Nathan had this hidden fund-raising talent. He just needed to find the right charity." There was bitterness in her tone.

"He's still never paid you another visit?"

"Head shake again," Winter said without a hint of mirth.

"I'm sorry to hear it. Have you had any other visitors?" He tried to sound nonchalant.

"Head shake yet again, combined with a heavy sigh. Other than you, I've only had three visitors the entire time I've been here. None of them visited more than once. Shrug. Tough crowd."

A man in a white full-body system sauntered by. They waited for him to pass out of earshot.

"So tell Nathan to keep those donations rolling in. You're all I've got." Her voice got very low, a gargling whisper. "If you stopped coming, I would cease to exist."

Rob swallowed, trying to push back the emotion welling up. If she only knew. Looking at her lying there, as lucid and alert as anyone walking the streets outside, it seemed impossible that they could simply drag her out and let her body—. He pushed those thoughts away. "I would never stop visiting you." Rob stroked the oiled wood of his lute, an excuse to look away, to seek refuge from the intensity of her gaze. "I look forward to seeing you. I mean—" Again, he choked up, took a few deep breaths to get himself under control. "There's no one in the world I'd rather spend time with. If I stopped coming, I'd miss you." The words surprised him, but they were true, he realized. He prayed she didn't pick up the subtext behind his words. He was grateful for the opportunity to say these things, to tell her that he cared for her, before it was too late.

"I'd miss you, too," Winter said. "More than I want to admit."

A few precious seconds ticked off the clock as they sat with their words hanging in the air between them.

"Tell me about that day," Winter said.

Rob wanted to ask, "What day?" to pretend that day wasn't always right there, playing in a loop over all of his other thoughts and memories. "What do you want to know?"

"Just, I don't know, where you were coming from, where you were going." She must have sensed his reluctance, because she added, "It's not about blame, Rob. It happened. When you've got time, look up the Zen parable of the rowboat. That's how I think about it now. In my best moments, anyway. But it's still my death. I want to understand it."

Rob told her about his breakup with Lorelei, how she had been airmailing his past out her window. He tried not to sound like he was trying to shift the blame, but the temptation was strong. He wanted Winter's last thoughts of him, if he couldn't manage one last trip after this, to be good ones.

Winter was making a choking sound that Rob now recognized as laughter. "What?" he asked, smiling. "What's funny?"

"Both of us had just gone through breakups, and we were all set to pull out the sad songs and marinate our broken hearts in alcohol. As it turned out, neither of us had the opportunity to do much pining."

Rob grimaced. "The guaranteed cure for heartbreak: find pain that's much, much worse." He glanced at the timer, knowing he wasn't going to like what he saw. Six seconds. five, four, three...

He reached out and brushed her cheek. "Good-bye."

Outside, Rob looked up the Zen parable about the rowboat on his handheld.

A monk is rowing on a lake. Another boater, listening to loud music and not watching where he's going, is heading straight for the monk's boat. The monk shouts and curses, finally has to lean over the side and deflect the other boat to avoid a collision.

Later, the monk notices an empty boat trailing a broken mooring line, pushed along by a stiff wind. The empty boat is heading straight for the monk's boat. Serene and smiling, the monk leans over and gently deflects the empty boat.

Rob wondered if the monk would have been so serene if the empty boat had been a loose cargo ship that cut his rowboat in half and drowned him. It impressed him that Winter could, during her best moments.

"Rob. Wait up."

Rob turned, and immediately recognized Peter, head down, hurrying to catch up.

"Let's walk a little," Peter said, pressing Rob's shoulder.

"How did you know I'd be here?" Rob asked as they walked along Ashburton Avenue.

"I didn't. I set up a facial-recognition protocol, and it alerted me."

That would be expensive. Rob wondered what was so important. Peter just went on walking, saying nothing.

"So are you coming from work?" Rob asked.

"Yes. But I don't work at the dating center, I work in the main facility." Peter looked up at the towering, shining wall of the dating facility as Rob waited for him to say whatever he'd come to say. "My late wife is in there."

That explained a lot. Rob tried to imagine knowing your wife was in there, going on "dates" with rich men. "I'm sorry to hear that," Rob said. "It must be incredibly painful."

Peter nodded. "My twelve-year-old daughter, Emma, was nine when her mom died. But her mom is gone and not gone; it's possible she'll be back, maybe sharing joint custody of Emma, and Emma's aware of that." At the corner they turned left, toward the river. "I visited her once, but I couldn't stand to see her go through that awful fear, paralyzed, desperate." He shook his head, as if trying to banish the memory. "I tried to convince her to leave the program, go back to the main facility, but she wouldn't. It's hard to give up that chance for a second life, when the alternative is oblivion. It's cruel, reviving someone and forcing them to make that choice."

Rob didn't know what to say. "Sorry to hear it. That's why you're helping Bridesicle Watch."

"I want to see the program shut down. I want Marlene, and all the rest of them, to rest in peace. Maybe it's wrong, since it's not what Marlene wants." He took out a pack of gum, offered a piece to Rob, who refused, then popped a piece into his mouth. "All this to say, it may seem like I'm bringing you bad news, but maybe it's really not."

Rob stopped short, looked at Peter, waiting, his heart pounding slow and hard. He thought he knew, and he wasn't sure he wanted to hear it.

"I had someone check your friend's account. She's being removed Tuesday."

"*Tuesday?*" He didn't mean it to sound like an accusation, but it did. "*Tuesday?*"

"I thought you might want to say good-bye."

Rob turned away from Peter, trying to digest this. He'd known Winter didn't have much time, but not knowing the exact date had allowed him to assume she still had two or three weeks, enough time for a miracle.

"You said she had three weeks, and that was less than two weeks ago."

Peter put a hand on Rob's shoulder. "I'm pretty sure I said two or three."

Four days. He had four days. Rob turned to face Peter. "There has to be something I can do."

Peter closed his eyes. "Raise twenty or thirty thou, get a few high-net-worth individuals to visit her, you *might* push the date back a month." He squeezed Rob's shoulder, almost hard enough that it hurt. "You did everything you could. Let her go." Not waiting for an answer, he walked off.

31

Veronika

Lycan was smiling, actually smiling when Veronika waved her door open.

"So where are we headed?" Veronika asked, reaching for her jacket.

"That's top secret." Lycan canted his head. "Almost literally."

Veronika's system signaled an incoming voice-only call, which meant a call from Rob, since she didn't know anyone else who owned a prehistoric handheld. She answered as they headed toward the door, but as soon as she heard Rob's voice, she stopped. Something was very wrong. She opened a screen on the street corner in Yonkers, where Rob was leaning against a building, then pinged Nathan, and Nathan opened one as well.

"My source at Cryomed contacted me," Rob said. "She has four days. They're going to bury her in four days." He seemed barely able to stand; his breath was coming in thin

197

whoops, his whole face shaking. Veronika couldn't imagine how hard this must be on him. She wished there was something she could do. In a screen, she couldn't even hug him.

"This is too serious to handle by screen in public," Nathan said. "Rob, I'll swing by and pick you up. We'll meet over at Vee's place."

Twenty minutes later they were at Veronika's door, Nathan's hand on Rob's slumped shoulder. Nathan nodded grimly to Veronika, greeted Lycan with a handshake as Rob sat down hard on a capsule seat, as if his legs were finally giving out.

Nathan sat beside him. "Our boy here says we can delay the inevitable by a week or so if Winter has some visitors," Nathan said. "I'm sending out appeals to friends and family, along with kicking in everything I can afford."

Veronika noticed that Lycan had moved near the kitchen, was hovering at the periphery of the room, as if he didn't want to intrude. "Lycan, you're welcome to join us."

Lycan nodded, took a seat beside Veronika.

"I can come up with three thousand," Veronika said. She looked at Lycan. "Can you help at all?"

"Sure," he said. "I'll give three."

"Peter said she'd have more time if the men had higher income profiles, instead of just me," Rob said, clearly trying to control the tremor in his voice.

"Well," Veronika said, looking at Lycan, "we have a man here with a decent income profile. How about it, Lycan?"

Lycan looked mortified. "I'm happy to contribute, but I'm not going into that place. I'm sorry."

Surprised, Veronika said, "But you'd be helping Rob and Winter."

"I know. I just can't go in there. It's complicated." Lycan wouldn't look at her, wouldn't look at any of them.

"What's complicated about it?" Veronika asked. "You go in, you chat with Winter for five minutes, you leave."

Lycan stared at his hands. "I just don't want to."

Though Lycan had just agreed to contribute money, Veronika couldn't help feeling angry. It was a life they were talking about. Maybe this was why Lycan had no friends, because he didn't know what it meant to *be* a friend.

"Rob, if I could make a suggestion?" Nathan said. He clasped his hands, leaned forward. "I care about Winter, but buying her an extra week in the freezer doesn't do anyone much good. Use all the money we can raise to visit her yourself. Let her spend her final minutes with someone she knows and likes." He bit his lower lip, shook his head. "Then let her go. I hate to say it, but I think we're beat."

Veronika nodded agreement. He was right—Winter's final minutes were better spent with Rob, ironic as that was.

Finally, Rob nodded, though it was clear he didn't like the fatalistic note in Nathan's thinking. It was true, though. What could possibly change in four days, or ten, that would save Winter? Rob winning the lottery? A brilliant protest cooked up by Lorelei's mother suddenly shifting public opinion? Sad as it was—and it was tragically sad—Winter was going into the ground.

Nathan stood. "Shit, I'm sorry, I have to get going." He clapped Rob on the back. "You did everything you could, Cousin. You should feel proud—not many people in your shoes would have done what you've done."

Rob's breath was coming in shaky gasps. He may have nodded slightly to acknowledge Nathan's words, Veronika couldn't tell for sure.

"Well, have a good time." Veronika managed a stiff smile. She was sure he was leaving to get ready to go out with

Lorelei. Nathan didn't hear her; he was deep in conversation on his system as he strode out of the apartment, clearly nervous.

"I should get going as well," Rob said.

"There's no hurry. Stay as long as you like," Veronika said.

Rob stood. "Thanks, but I have to go to work. The more I earn, the more time I have with Winter." He headed for the door, then paused, shaking his head in wonder, smiling grimly. "Well, at least I won't have to rush my last visit. My anonymous benefactor just deposited fifteen thousand dollars into my account."

Veronika whooped, almost pointed out that Winter might get a few days' reprieve for that kind of money, but decided not to.

A pulse on Veronika's wrist reminded her that she had an appointment in five minutes. A new client who was willing to pay her fifty-percent-up-front fee to coach a face-to-face on short notice.

Lycan was still standing in the middle of the room, his fists under his armpits.

"Well, I've got a meeting I need to focus on," Veronika said.

Lycan looked up. "So, I guess we're not going on my top-secret outing?"

She'd forgotten all about it. "I'm sorry, I can't. I really need to give this client my full attention." The truth was, she didn't really feel like going. She couldn't shake her resentment at Lycan for being so unwilling to help. Veronika wondered if he would have offered anything at all if she hadn't flat-out asked.

Lycan was still there, making no move to leave. Her hint that he should go hadn't been particularly subtle; the guy really was socially clueless. Now her choices were to either tell him directly that he had to go, or let him stay. He looked like an orphan, standing there. A big, dopey orphan.

"You can stay for a while if you've got nowhere else to go," she said.

"Oh. Okay. I guess I'll stick around. Have a good meeting."

"If you want to play anything, feel free." She uncloaked her interactive library and ducked into the bedroom. The wall shifted to expand the room as the bed submerged into the floor. She plopped into her trusty old flex-chair and pinged the client to let her know Veronika was waiting for access. This client was a persnickety one; she wouldn't let Veronika have access to any of her personal data, said she just wanted real-time help with lines. It was a hell of a lot harder on Veronika when she had to jump in cold, with no context, no data on her client or her client's companion. People just didn't grasp that coaching was a science, and scientists worked with data.

The client pinged her back, authorizing Veronika to join them via cloaked screen. Veronika opened a screen.

Nathan was sitting across from her.

"It's complicated. There's a lot of Eastern philosophy involved," her client was saying.

Lorelei. Her client was fucking Lorelei. That double bitch. Conniving attention whore.

There was a rap on her bedroom door. "Are you all right?" Lycan called in.

Veronika hadn't even realized she'd shouted. "Fine. Go away." Her heart was racing a thousand beats a minute. Her first inclination was to terminate, to leave Lorelei hanging. Though Lorelei wouldn't be hanging—she had another coach who was probably feeding her lines at this very moment. So why had Lorelei sought out Veronika? Probably because Veronika knew Nathan better than Nathan did.

No, that wasn't it, she realized. Or wasn't all of it, anyway. Having Veronika as a dating coach was good theater. Although if Lorelei let her audience know Veronika was coaching her, Nathan would find out as well. Eight hundred viewers couldn't keep a secret for three seconds.

Maybe she should uncloak her screen and show Nathan what Lorelei was up to. Surely he would be outraged.

Right. Nathan would ditch Lorelei the goddess in a fit of righteous indignation if he knew she was using his best friend as a coach. Outing Lorelei wasn't a serious option anyway. Violating client confidentiality would be a serious breach of Veronika's professional ethics. She could lose her job.

"So convince me," Nathan was saying. He leaned back in his seat, waved a hand toward his chest. They were at Bluefin, a seafood restaurant with a glass ceiling under the Hudson River.

"All right." Lorelei canted her head, as if she were thinking, though Veronika was sure she was just waiting for a line from her coach. "Every word counts in my life. None of them are lazy filler. I've committed myself to living a life others will find interesting enough to watch. I can't lie around in disposable pajamas playing interactives."

A rush of adrenaline shot through Veronika. Had Nathan told Veronika about catching her playing *Wings of Fire*? He wouldn't. Not in front of hundreds of screens.

Nathan nodded, squinting like he was considering what she'd said. What her coach had said, actually. "I don't disagree with that." He leaned toward Lorelei, smiling. "So how do we make this moment worth watching?"

Jump in any time, Coach, Lorelei subvocalized to her.

Veronika had forgotten Lorelei knew she was there. Now

was the time to tell Lorelei she was terminating the contract and refunding Lorelei's advance, but...

There was a but there. What was it?

Lorelei had challenged her. If she terminated, she would be tucking tail and fleeing. She didn't like to flee.

We could put on disposable pajamas and play an interactive, Veronika suggested.

"We could put on disposable pajamas and play an interactive," Lorelei said to Nathan, her delivery flawless.

Nathan laughed like it was the funniest thing he'd ever heard. "Not exactly what I had in mind, but I bet we could make it interesting."

Well, what did you *have in mind?* Veronika sent.

"Well, what did *you* have in mind?" Lorelei parroted. It was standard flirtation; nothing fancy, but Nathan would eat it up.

It occurred to Veronika that she could use her familiarity with Nathan to subtly turn him off. But what could possibly turn Nathan off to this woman? Her face was a little too long, her lips a bit too full, her eyes a centimeter too big for her face, but the quirks added up to a face that was not only beautiful but fascinating. Veronika hated her, absolutely hated every molecule that comprised her.

Maybe her best bet was to go in the opposite direction—knock Nathan's socks off. Then when she pulled out after a few face-to-faces, Lorelei and her coach would seem stale. And if Nathan ever found out Veronika was the voice behind his first scintillating encounters with Lorelei, he'd look at Veronika with new eyes. Like Roxane with Cyrano.

She stayed for the entire meal, positioning her screen just over Lorelei's head facing Nathan so she wouldn't have to see Lorelei, and could feel like she was the one sitting across from Nathan.

After a while she fell into a rhythm, and almost forgot Lorelei was there. Almost. It reminded her of those blissful few hours when Nathan had pretended to be her boyfriend for the benefit of her family, rekindling that heady mix of joy and longing.

When dinner ended, Veronika followed them out, trailed behind as they glided along Chan Avenue. They ended up walking along the Harlem River, the glowing colors of High Town reflecting off the water, creating a stained-glass tapestry.

"So did you ever walk here with Winter?" Lorelei asked. It was the first thing Lorelei had said in a couple of hours that didn't come from Veronika, and Veronika sent a frown. Bringing up exes, especially dead ones, was not the way to end a face-to-face.

"Here?" Nathan said. He thought about it. "I think I do remember coming here with her. Why?"

"No reason. It's just that she's what connects us, if you think about it. You were seeing Winter and I was seeing Rob the day before the accident. There's an interesting harmonic that we should be walking here."

Correction: these weren't Veronika's words, they were her coach's. *Interesting harmonics*. It was definitely a man, a man who read books about Carl Jung, but wasn't smart enough to read books *by* Jung.

"It's touching, what Rob is doing. Don't you think?" Lorelei said.

"Rob's not a better angel, he's the best angel." Nathan put his arm around Lorelei, drew her close in one deft, casual motion. "You know what amazes me most about him?"

"What?"

"He doesn't even know it. He doesn't know he's a saint."

Sometimes Veronika forgot that Nathan was a dating coach himself. He was good. Not as good as she, but very, very good. What a lovely thing to say. Lorelei's screen count was soaring, and Veronika suspected that the path to Lorelei's heart was through that screen count. If Nathan was good television, he'd get a second face-to-face, and soon he'd get into her indigo undies. Veronika would bet money they were indigo. Nathan had a head start to being good television, because the situation was so compelling. Lorelei had laid out the context for her dimmer viewers with that harmonics comment.

Maybe it was unfair to assume Nathan said what he said about Rob to improve his chances with Lorelei. Veronika was sure he genuinely believed it. She wondered if it unsettled him, if he compared himself to Rob and felt diminished by that comparison. It unsettled Veronika, but she was used to comparing herself to others and feeling diminished.

A soft rap on Veronika's door startled her out of her zone. Veronika waved the door open. Lycan looked crestfallen; she'd gotten so sucked in she'd forgotten he was out there.

"I'm going to go home," he said.

"I'm sorry things didn't work out," Veronika said. "Can we go another time?"

Lycan managed a smile. "Yeah. Sure." He turned to leave.

"Lycan?"

He paused.

"I still don't get why you wouldn't visit Winter."

Lycan's brow clenched. "I'm not talking to a dead person. I'm just not." He left before she could reply, not that there was much to say after a pronouncement like that.

Lorelei and Nathan were saying good night on the corner

of Chan and Thirty-Ninth, which, Veronika quickly confirmed, was the midpoint between their apartments. Standard etiquette, though Veronika didn't peg Lorelei as a traditionalist. Veronika blocked her screen so she wouldn't see the kiss. Watching it would hurt way too much.

Then Nathan was off, and it was just Veronika, Lorelei, twenty-two hundred fifty-four viewers, and Lorelei's invisible coach.

Well, that went swimmingly, don't you think? Veronika sent.

Lorelei was carrying on so many conversations at once that there was a delay before her reply.

Perfect. Can I count on you for our next face-to-face?

Veronika had planned to express her outrage at being blindsided when the face-to-face was over. She'd planned to say she'd only gone along because she was a consummate professional, that she was now terminating their professional relationship. If she agreed to work a second one, then she was complicit. If she didn't, she would be on the outside, looking in.

If my schedule is open.

How would Nathan react, if he found out? Knowing Nathan, he'd be amused. Maybe flattered. It wasn't as if she was spying on him; if she wanted to watch, she could join Lorelei's throng. It was all public.

32

Rob

As they rose in the tube from the parking lot deep below the Cryomed facility, past floor after floor of underground crèches holding Cryomed's non-bridesicle clientele, Veronika looked up at Rob and smiled her odd, square smile, obviously striving to be reassuring. Rob nodded. He was glad she'd offered to come. She was proving to be a good friend. Winter was their reason for becoming friends, but he hoped they'd remain friends after Winter was gone.

The thought caused his stomach to clench. Two days. How could a person's existence or nonexistence be so clearly and coldly determined? Today, Winter existed; the day after tomorrow, she wouldn't.

"You okay?" Veronika asked.

"Mm-hm. I'm okay."

What do you say to someone, when *you* know this is the last time you'll ever speak to *her*, but she doesn't? There were things Rob wanted to say. He wanted to tell her that over the months, his reason for coming had shifted. He wasn't visiting out of guilt or obligation, he was visiting because being with her was worth every dollar, worth all the work and sacrifice. Could he say that? Would she suspect something was wrong?

"What are you going to talk about? Have you thought about it?" Veronika asked.

"I was just pondering that. I have a whole fourteen minutes, but I can't use it to say good-bye, because I don't want her to know what's happening." Was that the right thing? Until that moment, he'd been certain hiding the truth from her was the right thing to do. Now he felt uncertain. "I don't, right?"

The tube came to a stop on the main floor. They stepped out.

"You don't. If she had six months to live, maybe you could make a case for her right to know. But telling someone they have fourteen minutes to live? I think that would be cruel." Veronika tsked. "And it's not technically fourteen minutes *to live*, is it? She's not technically alive."

"Fourteen minutes *awake*. That's how Cryomed phrases it, anyway. I keep expecting them to change their mind, to suddenly realize they can't simply drag Winter out of that crèche. But they're not going to change their mind, are they?"

"No, I don't think they are." Veronika squeezed Rob's forearm. "I'll be here."

Rob nodded, turned toward the row of women behind the long receiving desk. They were always women. Maybe Cryomed figured that made the setup seem less barbaric. He paid his fee, turned, waved to Veronika, who was sitting at a reclining kiosk, working her system, and was ushered through.

As Winter's crèche slid out of the wall, he played "Free

Spirit," an old soft postal tune by Running On, and went ahead and sang the lyrics that went with it.

The crèche's cover whisked off silently; a moment later, Winter opened her eyes. They were blank as a doll's button eyes, or a shark's. Slowly, awareness bled into them; they focused on Rob, then, as always, there was that moment of recognition.

He set his lute down, expecting Winter to say something kind about his singing voice, because that would be a Winter thing to do, but she just looked at him.

"We have *fourteen minutes* this time. Rob and Veronika really came through," he said.

"What's wrong?" Winter asked.

Startled, Rob tried to laugh it off. "You mean, besides my inability to carry a tune?"

Winter studied his face. "You look like you did the first time I saw you. Your eyes are red and puffy. You look like you haven't slept in days."

He shrugged. "I'm sick. A cold. I probably should spring for rhino eradicator—"

"We're way past bullshitting each other, Rob. Aren't we? I hope we are." Her unblinking, unwavering gaze was like a spotlight.

Rob put a hand over his mouth. He should have known. All Winter ever saw was his face, so she looked closely, saw what others missed. "It's not something you want to know. Please, trust me on this."

"Someone died. Someone I know." Her lips moved soundlessly. "Is it Nathan? Idris? Tell me who died."

"No one died."

She studied his face, his hands, as if the truth was hidden somewhere in view. "Then what?"

This wasn't how it was supposed to go. He'd planned out the entire fourteen minutes, and this definitely was not part of the plan. "Let's talk about good things—"

"Tell me."

Rob closed his eyes. He couldn't simply refuse, and he couldn't think of a feasible lie. And if she was this close to the truth, maybe she had the right to know.

He took a deep breath. "They're taking you out of the program."

Winter frowned. "What do you mean, out of the program? Where else would I go?"

He couldn't bring himself to answer. Tears leaked down his cheeks; he clenched his chest, stifling the sob pushing to come out.

Winter's eyes went wide. "Wait. What does that mean? What does it mean when they take you out of the program?" She knew. He could see it in her eyes.

Another visitor—a tall, spidery man with tiny ears— looked up at Rob from beside a nearby crèche. The man was probably curious why Winter sounded so alarmed. Rob stared back at him until he went back to looking down at his date.

"I've tried everything," he said in a harsh whisper.

Winter's lip was quivering, her eyes wild with fear. "When?"

"Days."

"How many?"

"Two."

Her white tongue poked out of her mouth and tried to lick her lips, but Rob could hear the dry futility of it. "This is it, then. How much time do I have left?"

Rob checked the timer. "Nine minutes."

"Nine minutes."

Five seconds of that nine minutes vanished as Winter digested the news.

"I want to use them well, but I don't know how. What should I do?" She looked at him pleadingly. "What would you do?"

Another three seconds melted away. "I'd spend my last nine minutes thinking about you. Thinking about things you said, remembering you as the wisest, funniest, most grounded person I've ever known. And trying to forgive myself."

"Head shake. *No guilt.* We're good, you and me. I admit it, I hated your guts the first few times you visited. I resented the hell out of you. But we're good now. You kept your promise. Now make another: no guilt. Promise you'll get on with your life now."

Rob hesitated. "I promise I'll try." It occurred to Rob that he'd somehow turned it around so they were spending her precious moments talking about him. That was not acceptable. "I promise. I promise."

"But all that other stuff, about remembering me as wise and funny and grounded?"

Rob nodded.

"It's mostly wrong, but remember me that way anyway." She tried to smile, and Rob tried to laugh, but it was forced.

Six minutes. The timer seemed to be racing toward zero. Rob felt like slamming his fist through it.

"Tell Idris I love her, that I thought about her. I hope her little girl is a wonder."

"She's going to name her Winter." It just came out. When had he learned to lie so easily?

"That's nice." She whispered unintelligibly, her gaze far away. "Tell Nathan I apologize for demolishing the Baneth

One. I hope he gets there one day, if that's what he really wants."

"You apologize for demolishing the Baneth One," Rob repeated, having no idea what she meant, since the Baneth One Building was doing fine. "I'll tell him."

"It's perfectly natural, what's happening to me. It's how things are supposed to be. The wheel turns. The wheel turns."

"Sooner or later, we're all going to be right where you are now," Rob said. "In the scheme of things, I'm just an eye-blink behind you."

Winter went back to whispering, and Rob couldn't help stealing a glance at the timer. Five minutes, twenty-three seconds.

Twenty-two.

Twenty-one.

"This is for the best," Winter said. She sounded breathless, but that didn't make sense, because her heart wasn't pounding. "I won't have to be afraid anymore. This is how it's supposed to be—an end, a clear line. No more halfway, no more being scared." She looked at Rob, as if remembering he was there. "You've been a good friend. Thank you for being a good friend." Her forehead creased, her mouth stretched, as if she was starting to cry, but no tears came.

"I'll never forget you," Rob said, hating how trite that sounded. "I—I love you."

She smiled, whispered, "You love me. That's—" She searched for words. "That's the last thing I expected you to say. An Easter egg in my basket."

For some reason Rob wanted to hear her say that she loved him, too. But she had—he glanced at the wall—two minutes, twelve seconds left in her life, and he wasn't going to waste any of it asking.

"I'm so scared," Winter said. "I wish you could hold my hand. I wish I could feel my hands."

Rob reached out and lifted a corner of the silver mesh covering Winter from the neck down, exposing a white breast, a patchwork of rough black sutures that crisscrossed her skin, trailing from just below her breast, out of sight.

"Mr. Mashita, please let go of the sheath and step away from Miss West," the voice of Cryomed said from somewhere above them.

"Please fuck off," Rob said.

Winter's hips were canted at an impossible angle, one hip bone almost centered where her belly button should be. He turned his head, kept his gaze on Winter's face, slid his hand along her arm until he found her hand, slid his fingers between hers and lifted it. It was freezing cold, small and perfect.

Winter was looking at her hand. "That's better. You're a good guy. I wish—"

The final second slipped off the timer, and she was gone. Rob set her hand on top of the mesh and stood, just as a Cryomed representative—a man, for this job—was jogging toward him.

"I apologize. I forgot," Rob said as the man approached. He was tall, obviously muscular under his white suit, but not quite thuggish.

"Of course, Mr. Mashita. In the future, please remember, you absolutely may not touch the guests."

"Don't worry, I have no reason to ever come here again." With that Rob turned to find Veronika.

He stared at his feet, his expression flat, controlled, as he crossed the wide expanse of the main foyer.

Veronika rose tentatively when he approached her in the waiting room. "You okay?"

"Skintight," he answered. "Let's get the fuck out of this place." He was numb; he knew that what he'd lost hadn't fully registered yet, and when it did, the pain of that loss would cut him into cubes.

They rode the tube in silence, waited for Veronika's Scamp to rotate into view, then rode the vehicle elevator up into the sunlight.

Veronika pulled onto Ashburton Avenue. "Do you feel like you got some closure?"

"I really don't want to talk about it right now." Rob tried to mask the impatience he felt, but the words came out clipped, almost angry. "I appreciate you coming with me, but I can't think about this right now. Can we talk about something mundane?"

"Of course."

"Anything. The weather. The best pizza place in the city. Boloball."

They passed a man with catatonia standing on the corner of Ashburton and Nepperhan, his hand in the air as if he was waving good-bye to someone, his eyes staring off beyond the horizon.

"If you want something mundane, I could tell you about this client I was just helping."

"Perfect. Just keep talking."

"So she's been in a twenty-two-year PCR—"

"PCR?" Just what he needed—to feel both dejected and stupid.

"Sorry. 'Platonic-companion relationship,' with another straight woman."

"Got it."

"So they break up, because my client has realized she

wants to find true romantic love. She has no clue how modern dating works, so she hires me. She pays me four thousand dollars to set up her profile... and a week later wants me to help her get her PCR back."

Rob laughed in what he hoped was an appreciative manner, though he was so distracted by flashbacks from his fourteen minutes with Winter that he was having trouble following Veronika's story. "People pay you four thousand dollars to create their profiles?" That much he'd heard, because he couldn't believe Veronika made four thousand dollars for a couple of hours' work.

"Oh yeah. Minimum. The profile's the key, the absolute key to modern dating. If you can get quality people to look at your profile, it becomes a numbers game. The more views, the more hits. The more hits, the more the odds climb that you'll meet a compatible mate. Go on fifty face-to-faces, if you can stand it, and odds are ninety-two percent that one of them will result in a relationship of at least five years. Assuming you don't get sidetracked going out a second and third time with people who clearly are not compatible—"

Veronika went on, talking rapid-fire about PCRs, compatibility scores, intangibles, but Rob's mind was stuck on what she'd said about dating. *If you can get enough people interested in you, it becomes a numbers game.* Winter was going to be buried. He would never see her again, ever, because not enough rich guys had been interested in her. It had been a numbers game, much like the game Veronika was talking about, only the stakes were higher.

The profile is the key, Veronika had said. The absolute key. The thought spun around and around...

"Are you saying if Winter had a better profile, it would improve her chances of getting men to visit?"

Veronika draped her free arm over her head, scratched at her scalp. "I wasn't really thinking of Winter, because bride-sicle profiles are pretty blah and uniform, but, sure."

"Couldn't you improve her profile? I'd pay the four thousand." Rob's heart was pounding. There were still two days...

Veronika was shaking her head. "The money isn't the issue. God, you know I'd do it for nothing in a heartbeat. Cryomed doesn't farm out any profile work. It's all in-house. You can't just go in and edit one of their profiles."

"What if I got Winter's permission?"

Veronika looked pained. "Rob, sweetie, it's just not possible. Cryomed's a very insular operation. They don't let outsiders edit their profiles. Period."

"Their profiles suck."

"That's because they have hacks knocking them out four an hour. They suck, but they suck uniformly."

As Veronika pitched the last shovelful of dirt on the hope that had begun smoldering in Rob's heart, his mood crashed. He stared out the window. They were climbing the ramp from Low Town to High, the old rusted George Washington Bridge out his window.

Cryomed was an insular operation. That was an under-statement; you had to have secret meetings just to know when someone close to you was being—

Peter. He'd forgotten about Peter.

"*Holy shit.*" He tapped Veronika's thigh. "Can you get Lorelei in here? *Holy shit.*" Lorelei could get access to her stepmother much faster than Rob could directly.

"What? What is it?" Veronika swung the car over to the service lane.

"You'd put together a profile for Winter if I could get it posted? Like, immediately?"

Veronika turned her palms up. "If you can figure out how to post it, I'll write the best fucking profile you've ever seen."

"Men will start visiting her? Immediately?"

Veronika gave him a "Do not doubt me" look.

Rob gestured at the backseat. "Get Lorelei in here."

Veronika looked pained and a little disgusted, like Rob had asked her to bring him a steaming turd.

"Can you keep a secret?" Rob asked. "She's not my favorite person, either. But I need her help."

"Yeah, yeah." Veronika subvocalized to her system, contacting Lorelei. "Someone's life is on the line, blah, blah."

"Tell her to come alone. Complete block." The last thing he needed was one of Lorelei's fans tipping off Cryomed.

"She's not going to like that," Veronika said under her breath. While she engaged in an energetic, subvocalized exchange, she added, "She's not happy about the block."

"I don't care. Tell her to get her ass in here right now. *Now.*"

Lorelei popped into the backseat via screen. "*Kamusta!*" Despite lacking a system, Rob knew that meant "Hello" in Tagalog. His memorizing during the dark days had paid off. Her screen rotated to face him. "Okay, Bobby, this better be hairy awesome. I lose credibility with my people when I shut them out."

"I need to get in touch with your stepmother. Right now. I have an idea that might save Winter."

Lorelei pressed her hand to her forehead. "This is *platinum.* I'd break twenty thousand eyes if my people were watching this. Can't we lift the block and start again?"

"*No.*"

"Why not?"

"*Because what I'm planning is illegal.*" He pointed at

Lorelei's two-dimensional button nose. "You have to keep this quiet."

Lorelei huffed, but seemed to be working her system while she swiveled to face Veronika. "So how are you, Veronika? Good to see you."

Veronika looked pinched as she engaged in small talk with Lorelei, but she kept at it while Lorelei carried on at least one secondary conversation, presumably with Sunali. It felt like forever before Lorelei finally swiveled back to face Rob.

"There's a frozen-fruit place called L'Orange Dreams on the Upper West Side of Low Town. Seven p.m."

Rob nodded. "I'll be there. Tell your stepmom 'thank you.' She may be saving a life."

Sunali popped into the backseat next to Lorelei. "Tell me yourself. What's going on?"

Rob filled her in, painfully aware that time was passing.

"I love it," Sunali said when Rob finished. "Keep me posted. Wait, you don't have a system." She swiveled to face Veronika. "*You* keep me posted." She made it sound more like a directive than a request, and disappeared before Veronika could respond.

When Sunali was gone, Lorelei said, "I've got to get back to my people. I feel lonely without them." A quick "*Yadalanh*" (Apache), and Lorelei vanished as well.

"She feels invisible without them, is what she means," Veronika muttered as she pulled back into traffic.

"Hold on," Rob said. "I'll drive. You need both hands to start working on the profile."

Veronika pulled over and they swapped places. It was the first time Rob had driven since his red-letter day. He felt slightly out of control, as if the car might spin out and slam into something, or someone, at any moment.

When they reached Veronika's apartment, Rob asked, "What can I do while I'm waiting to meet with Peter?" The hours were going to crawl if he spent them doing nothing.

"I need a few really torrid clips of Winter, each no more than thirty seconds long. We need to depict her as youthful, full of energy, happy, sexy."

Rob frowned. "Where am I going to get clips of Winter?"

Veronika blinked slowly, as if she was dumbfounded that Rob had to ask. "Let's see." She pressed a finger to her lips. "Do we know anyone who records everything and once spent a lot of time with Winter?"

Rob put his hand on top of his head and laughed. "Nathan."

Veronika worked her system. Nathan popped up.

"*Guten Tag.* What's the context?" Evidently Lorelei's foreign-greeting thing was catching on, at least with Nathan.

"We need you to send Rob every second of recording you have with Winter in it."

Nathan waited, maybe for them to burst out laughing so he knew it was a joke. When they didn't, he said, "What for?"

"I'm creating a profile for Winter. Here—" She rummaged through a cluttered drawer in the wall, retrieved a portable boost bracelet. "Download it into this."

"Hang on," Nathan said. "Cryomed won't let you change Winter's profile—"

"We're way past that." She waggled the boost bracelet. "Every second. In here."

"Give me some time to edit first. I'm not sure what's in there."

Veronika closed her eyes, turned her face toward the ceiling as if requesting patience from the divine. "Fine. You've got three seconds! Winter's crèche is on its way to the thawing room in fifty-six hours, Nathan."

The image chilled Rob to the core, to have it broken down into hours. It was true, wasn't it?

"You don't think they reuse the crèches, do you?" Veronika asked Rob. "That would be gross."

Rob ignored the grisly question, looked at Nathan's screen, waiting for his answer.

"It's done. For your eyes only, Cousin, okay?"

"Absolutely. Thank you." Rob wondered what else Nathan thought he would do with recordings of himself and Winter.

Nathan's screen swiveled to face Veronika. "Let me see what the profile looks like so far. I knew her—I can give it a personal touch."

"I'm giving it a personal touch," Veronika said, sounding miffed.

"Let him help, if it'll get done quicker," Rob said.

"It might be quicker, but it'll suck more," Veronika snapped, but she waved her readout so that it was visible.

As Rob slipped out of Veronika's place to find somewhere private to go through Nathan's recordings, the two of them were hard at work, bickering like an old married couple as they composed. Rob chuckled, shaking his head as the door slid closed.

33

Mira

In a twilight state between dead and alive, Mira heard a woman's voice, and was sure it was Jeannette's. She struggled against the confusion tugging at her, reached for the waking world where Jeannette waited. She couldn't remember what had happened. Was it an accident? Was she in the hospital?

Then she remembered, and felt a terribly familiar cold dread.

The woman sitting beside her wasn't Jeannette. She was older, maybe forty, with dark hair, cocoa skin, and a harsh beauty.

"Hello Mira. My name is Sunali Van Kampen." Her voice was raspy, fitting her face, but her tone was gentle. "I used to be in a crèche right over there." She turned, pointed behind her, although Mira couldn't actually see what she was pointing at. "I was there until just a few years ago."

"So some really do get out."

Sunali nodded. "But only a few."

Mira almost asked if Sunali was here to get *her* out, but she knew better. She was never getting out.

"I've come to ask for your help, Mira. I'm part of an organization trying to make things better for the women in here. We think you should have more rights, more say in this process."

"How can I help?" Mira asked, talking over Sunali's last few words in her eagerness.

Sunali licked her lips, as if she was nervous, though she struck Mira as the sort of woman who was rarely nervous. "Mira, you were frozen in the early days, before it was even possible to revive people. Before this place even existed."

"I know. I remember."

Sunali folded her hands like she was going to pray, and leaned closer. "We've been doing research. We're pretty sure you've been frozen longer than anyone else here."

She thought of Lycan, telling her that's why he'd chosen her, because she was the oldest. "One of the men who visited told me that. Another said I was an antique—that I was becoming a curiosity stored in the basement, not a viable partner for anyone."

"That's not true—there's always hope. I was here for ninety years, and here I am." She pressed her fingers to her chest, over the spot where her heart was beating.

"How can I help?"

"We're developing a series of profiles of women who are here, to raise awareness of your situation. We'd like you to be one of those women, if you're willing."

"Yes, of course."

Sunali leaned back, seemed to relax. "Oh, that's wonderful. I'd like to hear some of your story—who you are, how you got here, how it feels to be here."

Mira smiled. It was a chance to be alive for more than a minute or two. Time to think. "Whatever you want to know." She'd give lengthy answers, to stretch the time.

"Let's start with your time here. Can you tell me how many times you've been visited?"

"Let me see." She went back over the brief flashes that made up her time here, counted nine—six of them visits from Lycan—then went on pretending to count while she thought about Jeannette, about the time they went low-G skiing and two teenage guys tried to pick them up. The world outside the rectangle that comprised her world—even memories of it—seemed impossibly far away. Had she really once done those things, been in those places?

"Nine," she said when she thought delaying further would seem suspicious.

"And how many of those nine would you guess were the standard five-minute visit?"

Mira couldn't imagine why that mattered. She waited maybe half a minute before answering. "Probably three. One was only a few seconds, five were longer."

"How much longer, would you say?"

"Ten or fifteen minutes."

Sunali tapped on her palm for a moment. "In other words, over the past hundred and ten years, you've been alive a total of about ninety minutes."

"Yes," she said, barely above a whisper. Now she saw why it mattered. Phrased like that, it was chilling. She didn't want to think about it.

"What about before you came here. Was there anyone in your life, besides your sister and mother? A lover? A close friend?"

"A close friend. Her name was Jeannette." She hoped

Sunali wanted to talk about Jeannette, that she wanted Mira to reminisce about her life at great length. That would be comforting.

"What was Jeannette's last name?" Sunali asked.

"Zierk."

Mira had the most astonishing thought. She couldn't believe it hadn't occurred to her until now. Jeannette had worked for the military, just like Mira. Preservation had been part of Jeannette's benefits package, just like Mira's. "Sunali, would you do something for me?" It felt as if everything rode on the question she was about to ask.

"Of course. What is it?"

"Would you search for her, to find out what happened to her?"

"I was just about to suggest that. When was she born?"

"Two thousand four."

Mira was not as anxious as she thought she should be as Sunali checked, probably because her heart could not race, and her palms could not sweat. It was surprising, how much emotion was housed in the body instead of the mind.

A smile spread across Sunali's face. "She died in twenty forty-five, twenty-two years after you. She's in the main cryo facility."

"She's *here*?"

"Well, not here in the dating facility, but nearby. You didn't know?" Sunali consulted the readout, pulling her palm close to her nose, then pointed. "She's about a thousand meters that way."

Mira wished she could lift her head and look where Sunali was pointing. "Can you do something for me? Can you wake her, and give her a message from me?"

Sunali looked surprised. "Mira, I don't know…"

"Please?" Mira said. "It would mean so much to me."

Sunali tilted her head to one side, then the other. "Okay. Sure. I guess. I'll have to end our session—it will take a while." She stood, paused. "What message should I give her?"

Mira wanted to ask Sunali to tell Jeannette she loved her, but decided against it. Better that no one knew, not even someone who understood what it was like to be in this place. "Just tell her I'm here, that I'm close. Thank you so much."

Mira woke to Sunali's smiling face. "Jeannette was excited to get the message. I mean, out-of-her-head excited. I thought she'd leap out of her crèche and hug me."

"What did she say?" Mira tried to sound calm. Jeannette was near. Suddenly everything had changed. She had to figure out how to get out of here.

"She said to tell you she loved you."

Mira sobbed. She had really talked to Jeannette. What a strange and wonderful and utterly incomprehensible thing.

Then Sunali asked more questions. During the pauses, when Sunali was thinking or even taking a breath, Mira thought about Jeannette, who had just told Mira she loved her, even though they were both dead.

34

Rob

By the time Rob got home from meeting with Peter, it was after eleven. He went directly to his room to continue watching Nathan's recordings.

As Winter leaped to life in his room, Rob recalled how horrified he'd been the first time he'd seen her face on his dad's little handheld. Now, despite the sting he felt seeing her so vibrantly alive, there was also pleasure. He was the cause of all the horror that had befallen her, but he was more than that now. Exactly what he was to her, and what she was to him, he wasn't sure. But it was something substantial, unlike any connection he'd ever had with another person.

He watched Nathan and Winter's first face-to-face. Evidently Nathan pulled out all the stops the first time out—he'd finagled virtual passes to watch someone brought back to life. Rob had seen a hundred recordings of revivals (who hadn't?), but few got to witness such a personal moment in real time. Rob had no idea how Nathan had managed it. After that, they went to dinner at an underground restaurant called Beneath, where the food was harvested from vertical gardens that ran right through the restaurant and even deeper underground.

It surprised Rob that Winter always seemed to be laughing. Veronika had said to find clips where she was happy; that would be no problem. Laughter came effortlessly to her—*not* laughing seemed more of an effort. He should have expected the living Winter to be profoundly different from the dead, terrified Winter he knew, but it was still a shock. He barely recognized her, as if the serious, somber Winter he'd been visiting in the minus eighty was a completely different woman. It was a little disturbing, actually, but watching her made Rob ache to see her again, in the bridesicle place, if that was the only option. To see her alive, breathing, laughing...that would be indescribable.

This had to work.

Because Nathan recorded all the time, most of the clips were nothing more than the two of them riding somewhere in Nathan's Xero, or sitting at a bar. With time short, Rob sampled random slivers, backing up to watch potentially interesting ones in their entirety, seeking the few gems that would bowl over potential suitors.

It was a jarring experience, because as it turned out, Winter had been a human being, fraught with the usual flaws and quirks that you rarely saw visiting someone in the minus eighty. She had a quick temper to match her easy laugh. Once Nathan and Winter took Nathan's nephews to a zero-G park. Nathan took off with the older nephew, who was maybe fourteen, to experience the wilder attractions, ditching the sulking seven- or eight-year-old. Winter was right to chide Nathan for hurting the little guy's feelings, only she didn't chide him, she got in his face and screamed at him.

And then there was her spending habits. She didn't care much about clothes or vehicles or other material things, but she would drop three hundred dollars on a meal, another two on a play, then pull Nathan into a club with an eighty-dollar cover for a quick drink. Rob had no idea how she could afford her half on a teacher's meager salary. At one point she joked about being hauled off to a debt camp, and Rob wondered just how much debt she was carrying when she died.

None of this dampened the urgency Rob felt to save Winter, but it did make him wonder if he'd professed his love for her based on an idealistic image of who she was.

At around three a.m., Lorne came in carrying a Superfood omelet. "How's it going?" He handed Rob the plate and sat down.

"All right," Rob said without looking away from the recording. "Tell me what you think of this."

Rob paused from wolfing down the omelet to show a clip where Winter called Nathan into her kitchen, opened the cabinet above the sink to reveal a space neatly divided between brightly colored cereal boxes on one side and liquor bottles on the other.

"This must say something profound about my psyche," Winter said, deadpan, as they peered into the cabinet.

"What's a psyche?" Lorne asked.

"Kind of her mental makeup."

Lorne laughed out loud. "I like it. Funny."

"I think so, too." It wasn't one of his finalists, though, because not everyone would know what a psyche was. He'd had to look it up himself.

Rob went back to sampling. Lorne hung around for a while, watching silently, then slipped out.

Winter had a distinct walk. She was slightly knock-kneed,

reminding Rob of a colt; her hands gave a little twist at the end of each step. It was an unself-conscious walk, feminine without straining to be so. She tended to walk quickly, evidently eager to get wherever she was going. Often Nathan was left scurrying to keep up with her.

He wondered why Nathan had broken up with her. Nathan clearly liked to spend money, so it wasn't that. He also seemed strong enough that he could handle her temper.

Rob came upon the recording Winter had been referring to the day before. Winter and Nathan were on one of those tour hovercrafts that cruise around Manhattan in the evening. They were on the deck, a chilly fall wind blowing, watching the city. Nathan put his arm around Winter and pointed out Baneth One, the wealthiest condo tower in the city.

"I wonder what the people in the top floors are doing right now?" he said. "One day I'm going to live there." He glanced at Winter, who was trying to keep from laughing. "What? I am."

Winter worked her system for a moment. A giant bottle of Chocolate Rocket with arms and legs sloshed out of the Harlem River, roaring like a dinosaur, the virtual image set so that only the two of them could see it. It headed right for Baneth One and smashed it to pieces.

"That's vicious," Nathan said, shaking his head.

Winter was laughing hysterically, so hard she was fighting for breath. "I can tell you what the people in there are doing right now. They're cutting their toenails, and arguing about stupid things."

Rob was giving her a pained look. She leaned in and kissed him lightly, playfully. "They're just people. They may have a shitload of money, but they're still just people."

And suddenly Rob thought he understood why Nathan had broken up with her. The things he aspired to meant nothing to Winter, and Winter's best qualities were things Nathan didn't care about. Nathan was a modern man, while there was a timeless quality to Winter. She was a school-teacher. Was there a more timeless profession? She wasn't impressed by the flash of Nathan's technology, the glamour of his life in High Town. She wasn't a climber, seeking to expand her social network. She was grounded.

He came to a clip of Winter undressing. Not so much undressing as stripping, actually. There had been plenty of clips of the two of them making love, and Rob had mostly skipped over them, partly for propriety's sake, but mostly because they made him jealous. But this one he watched, his heart racing, marinating in guilt yet unable to stop.

This one, he thought as he watched. Veronika hadn't directed him to look for recordings with nudity. He wasn't sure why; any man who watched this recording would want to meet her.

Rob yawned, checked the time. It was three a.m. He was supposed to leave for work in an hour, but he would call in sick.

As he got toward the end of Nathan's recordings, it occurred to him that all of Winter's time in the classroom should be accessible to the public. Clips of Winter teaching probably weren't of much use for her profile, but he used his handheld to locate and download a year's worth anyway, just because he was curious.

Again, she surprised him. Teachers got paid next to noth-ing, yet Winter acted as if each class was the last she'd ever teach, her last chance to light some spark in the kids. She buzzed around the classroom, cutting up, familiar with all the interactives popular with her students. She got right up close and personal with the kids who were there physically instead of via screen. When her students got out of hand, Winter's temper was evident here as well. Her students clearly loved her, but also respected her. She was no pushover.

Veronika's screen popped into Rob's room, startling him.

"How are we doing? I've got her profile just about finished."

Rob showed her the virtual destruction of Baneth One, another where Winter played basketball with a bunch of twelve-year-old kids in a park.

"Rob, she comes across as too independent in these. Too willful," Veronika said.

"What's wrong with that? She *is* willful. A lot of men find that sexy."

"*You* find that sexy. You're not the typical bridesicle client."

Rob opened his mouth to argue, but Veronika cut him off.

"Let's say you just inherited a billion dollars, and you could easily afford to date women at the bridesicle place. Would you?"

"Of course not." The thought of sitting beside crèches with animated frozen corpses inside, desperate to please him, made his skin crawl.

"Of course not. You're not our target audience."

Rob rubbed his eyes. He was profoundly tired after the adrenaline surge of his last fourteen minutes with Winter, followed by a night spent watching recordings. He stifled a yawn. "I don't get why the bridesicle program works at all. Why would rich men come to these places? They're rich, for God's sake—can't they attract trophy wives who are still alive?"

Veronika pointed at Rob, nodding slowly. "*Now* you're asking the right question. What motivates the average bridesicle patron? Two things." She flicked up one finger where it was visible to Rob. "First, there's the knight-in-shining-armor syndrome. What man doesn't want his partner to see him as a hero charging in on a white steed to rescue her from a terrible fate?"

Actually, Rob would settle for not being the villain who put her in a position to need rescuing in the first place. But he saw Veronika's point.

Veronika held up a second finger. "Then there's the power factor. If you literally bring a woman back from the dead, she's going to be very, very grateful. She's going to do what you say. On top of that, she can never divorce you, although you're free to divorce her. You hold all the power. Some men like that arrangement."

"Ah, I see. That's why 'willful' isn't good." Rob knew men like that, who were drawn to women who, for whatever reason, put up with whatever shit they pulled.

Veronika nodded emphatically. "That's why 'willful' isn't good. There's another reason: even with legally binding contracts and stiff penalties for breaking them, these men are worried their new wives will bolt. It happens."

Rob wondered where they bolted *to*. You'd definitely have to lose your system to keep from being located. Even then, a face-recognition alert would pin down your location unless you got hold of some high-quality fake-face.

"Okay, how about this?" He called up the clip that had left him dizzy and a little ashamed. Suddenly Winter was in the room with them, smiling coyly, her fingers playing with the top button of a lavender silk blouse. The button popped open almost by accident, and Winter's hand slid down to the next.

"Damn," Veronika said. "Definitely sexy."

Winter slid her shirt off, revealing a transparent bra supporting breasts that few plastic surgeons could replicate.

"You're suggesting we include something like this in her profile?"

"Not something like this. *This*." He stabbed a finger at Winter, who was unclasping her belt.

Veronika shook her head. "It's over the line. Cryomed has strict guidelines for their profile engineers; they want to keep the place classy, to match an upper-class clientele. They're marketing expensive wives, not prostitutes."

Rob recalled the man with the red beard cajoling the woman near Winter to talk dirty, and thought maybe the line was a bit blurry. The men who visited these women were mostly old, looking for much younger, beautiful wives. Sex was clearly a big part of the draw. "What do we care about their rules? We're swapping profiles without Cryomed's knowledge. It doesn't have to pass their censors."

Veronika pointed at Winter, specifically at her breasts, which swung slightly as she bent over. "This is going to tip off clients that her profile's been tampered with. What if one of them alerts Cryomed?"

Winter's skirt slid to the floor.

Veronika snapped her fingers in front of Rob's face. "Over here, Rob."

He dragged his eyes off Winter.

"I asked, what if one of the clients alerts Cryomed?"

"I say it's worth the risk. Men have to start visiting her immediately, in numbers. Everyone who sees this is going to want to meet her."

Veronika laughed. "Yeah, no kidding. You'll be first in line. Do you think Winter would mind us showing this?"

"If you were in her position, would you mind?"

Veronika made a raspberry sound. "If I was in her position, the *last* thing that would save me is a clip of me getting naked."

Rob clapped his hand over his eyes, laughed in spite of himself. "Not true. You've got a lot of sexy going on."

Veronika blushed, fumbled to respond, then just gave up and vanished.

35

Veronika

The last thing Veronika added to the profile was the nudie clip. She shook her head as she inserted it, then spread the whole thing out, lining the various virtual pages up on her living room walls until they surrounded her, and examined them with a critical eye for aesthetic appeal.

They were beautiful. *It* was beautiful—a masterpiece. Quite a bit of it was pure fabrication, but as she'd told Rob, the point was to get butts in the seat next to Winter's crèche. Enough butts in that seat, and the odds were someone would take a shine to her even if she wasn't a rabid Pittsburgh Steelers fan like it said in her profile.

Veronika fired off the profile to the address Rob had provided, stood, stretched, checked the time, and cursed. This was going to be a long day. She put a complete block on incoming messages, muted the front-door buzzer, retracted her bed and bathroom, blacked out her windows, and dimmed the lights, all the time cursing Lorelei. Leave it to Lorelei to set up a spontaneous face-to-face and expect Veronika to drop everything.

She took a few deep breaths. "Here we go. Skintight." She opened a cloaked screen beside Lorelei, who was gliding down Amyrta Boulevard in boots set to a five-inch lift, making her nearly seven feet tall. The boots were black, the rest of her outfit shades of violet. On Veronika the outfit would have looked hilarious, on Lorelei, well, Lorelei didn't need help picking out clothes.

Hey, Cousin, Lorelei subvocalized. *Ready for anything?* Lorelei was swimming in screens. Veronika ran a count: seven hundred seventy-two viewers, and all she was doing at the moment was walking.

What's the event? Veronika replied.

Drinking and dancing.

Of course. Veronika hated dancing. She decided she needed a drink herself.

Lorelei was dancing by herself, though two men danced nearby, clearly trying to work their way in. Veronika spotted Nathan winding through the crowd, just arriving. His gaze was fixed on Lorelei. When she raised a hand in greeting, he watched her dance a moment longer, then clutched his heart. Lorelei swung her neck, got her hair to flick in Nathan's direction like a black whip.

This woman didn't need Veronika's help to lure a man. Of course, Veronika wasn't there to help Lorelei get Nathan, she was there to help Lorelei land more viewers. She had nine hundred thirty-one viewers at the moment. Another sixty-nine, and sponsorships would kick in. She'd get automatic cash from Balmoral simply for wearing their boots, by Primera for wearing their system. Veronika was sure Lorelei wasn't aiming for a thousand viewers, though—she was aiming for a million.

Lorelei danced toward Nathan; he strode confidently onto the dance floor, meeting her halfway. He didn't begin dancing right away, only took Lorelei in for a moment, allowing her to be the center of attention before finally joining her.

Nathan was a great dancer—athletic, lithe yet masculine—but Veronika had already known that. As he wound around Lorelei, Veronika felt a crippling jolt of jealousy. He looked so beautiful out there. Deep down, Veronika realized, she'd always believed that in the end, it would be her and Nathan together. How could she ever have believed that?

Nathan and Lorelei finally left the dance floor and found a table.

So you must be pretty good at this, if you make a living at it, Veronika fed to Lorelei. Lorelei repeated the line with just the right tinge of playfulness.

"Me?" He waved it off. "Even my mom doesn't find my face-to-faces worth watching."

It's a relief to know your mom isn't watching. I'm not quite ready to meet your parents. Veronika laughed as she sent it. She could be so fucking clever when the words weren't coming out of her own mouth.

Nathan burst out laughing when Lorelei delivered the line—a little too hard, in Veronika's opinion. But Nathan wasn't the only person in the bar who reacted to the line. Veronika noticed a slyly dressed man at the bar who smiled and nodded, though he seemed way too far away to have overheard. Maybe he was reacting to something a friend had said remotely, but Veronika didn't think so. His waxed head, goggles, the total lack of creases on his rolled-up sleeves all screamed *Director*.

As she fed lines to Lorelei, Veronika watched the guy's

face, watched him subvocalize, watched him watching Lorelei and Nathan. It was him, it was Lorelei's coach—there was no doubt in Veronika's mind. She got a shot of his face, ran a search.

Name: Parsons Palmer
Profession: Freelance Director

"Got you," Veronika said aloud to her dark apartment. She had no idea what good it did her to know who he was, but she felt great satisfaction in having spotted him.

Things were going swimmingly, thanks in no small part to her. Veronika checked the running conversational stats. So far sixty-eight percent of the conversation had been about Lorelei, so Veronika sent, *Ask him to tell you more about himself.*

"So, tell me more about you," Lorelei said as she swirled a color stick in her absinthe. "I know what you do for a living, and that you live in Wilmington Park."

Nathan shrugged. "Let's see. I own a virtual apartment in Second Life."

"The classic. Very nice."

"Thank you. I have a dog named Riley, and every Christmas I work as a Santa in Macy's."

"You do not."

"You're right, I don't."

Lorelei laughed as if she'd never heard anything so funny. She was coming up with some of her own lines, and they were serviceable, if not brilliant. Better than Veronika would have guessed.

Ask him if he likes to cook. When you knew everything about the target, this was too easy.

"Do you like to cook?" Lorelei asked.

Nathan leaned forward. "I *love* to cook. What about you?"

Lorelei shook her head. "No."

Let's elaborate, Veronika sent. *Tell him this: "Opening the refrigerator is a humbling and confusing experience for me. My meals are mostly failures. I eat quickly, primarily to dispose of the evidence."*

Lorelei delivered the soliloquy. Veronika half expected Nathan to grow suspicious, to recognize the self-deprecating wit as classic Veronika, but Nathan beamed.

"I wish we hadn't just eaten," Nathan said. "Otherwise I'd invite you to my place and cook something for you."

Veronika saw Parsons subvocalize something before taking a sip of his drink.

"Can't you cook desserts?" Lorelei asked coyly. Veronika cringed, not because the line Parsons had fed her was a bad one, because she didn't like where it was leading.

Nathan put his arm around Lorelei. "I make an awesome Lemon Volcano."

"Ooh. Sounds delicious."

Parsons looked pleased with himself as Lorelei and Nathan headed for the exit. Veronika signaled to Lorelei that she was going to terminate now.

No! Stay! You're doing great.

I think you and Parsons can take it from here.

Parsons sat up as if he'd been goosed. Giggling merrily, Veronika cut the connection.

36

Rob

There came a point when Rob's hands seemed to be moving on their own, plucking components flashing red, components flashing blue, components flashing yellow, green, orange, and black. They came out of vacuum cleaners, home management systems, antique handhelds, and dropped into the correct bins while Rob watched.

She might already be dead. She might be okay. Rob had no way of knowing, no way of finding out until Peter contacted him.

When he told her he loved her, she'd said, "That's the last thing I expected you to say. An Easter egg in my basket." An Easter egg was a good thing. Did that mean she loved him? No, "I love you, too" meant she loved him. "An Easter egg in my basket" meant it pleased her to hear him say it. When you're about to die, Rob imagined there was nothing you'd rather someone say than, "I love you," regardless of how you feel about him or her. If she was dead and buried, it didn't matter if she loved him. Even if she wasn't, it didn't matter. Yet he still wondered, and wondered exactly what it was he felt for her, the Winter in the crèche, merged with the Winter in Nathan's recordings. He couldn't stop thinking about her, longed to see her, worried about her. That much he knew.

"Rob, brother." Rob lifted his head. Vince was standing over him. "You going for some kind of record?"

"Just got nothing better to do right now," Rob muttered.

"Nothing better to do? How about *sleep*? I've been home, had a meal, got six hours' sleep after pulling a ten-hour shift, and I come back and you're still here."

"I can't help it if you're soft," Rob said, then burst into braying laughter.

Vince shook his head. "Brother, I'm sorry, but I'm calling it. If you don't punch out and get some sleep, I'm going to Lilly and I'm calling it."

Rob drummed his fingers on the worktable. There was no way he could sleep. Idle time was the enemy. He needed to keep moving, to stay exhausted.

"Rob, come on." Vince took him by the arm, led him toward the changing room. "What's up with you? You doing some serious bugs, or what?"

"No. Just worried about someone."

Vince led him to his cubicle, knelt and unclamped his boots. "Anyone I know?"

"Nah. A woman I know."

"I hear you. Want to tell me about it?"

"Another time. I should get home."

He clapped Rob on the shoulder. "You okay to get there?"

"Sure."

Vince nodded, headed out to start his shift.

Winter could be dead right now, Rob thought. Or she

241

could be all right. Leaving his work clothes on, Rob pulled on his shoes and headed home.

He dreamed he was at the bridesicle place, talking to Winter. Three men interrupted them, one moving Rob out of the way while the other two pulled Winter from her crèche. Her hips were twisted so badly one of her buttocks was visible from the front, her pale skin a sickening road map of black stitching. Winter screamed to Rob to help her, her frozen body still paralyzed, but the man holding Rob had a vice grip on his shoulders. They carried Winter just across the narrow hall, where there was a furnace set in the wall, the entire inside of it glowing like a hot ember. The two men tried to push her in, and suddenly Winter could move. She clutched the walls, fighting, pleading, begging Rob to help.

His handheld woke him. Heart racing, groggy, exhausted, he answered it.

"It's Peter." Peter sounded...good. As if he had good news.

Rob tamped his hopes, afraid it was his own wishful thinking. "Is she all right? Is she still alive?"

"She's still in the minus eighty, if that's what you mean. If the dead needed sleep, she'd be sleep deprived from all of the appointments she's had."

Rob's whooping woke his dad, which was all right, because Rob would have wakened him anyway.

37

Rob

There was a definite spring in Rob's step as he crossed the atrium. He looked up as he passed under the waterfall, cascading through transparent tubes.

A landslide of dates. Rob loved the sound of the words Peter had used to describe Winter's past seventy-two hours. *If the dead needed sleep, she'd be sleep deprived.*

Rob now had little doubt Sunali was his anonymous benefactor. It had to be someone who was getting timely updates on Winter's situation, because nine thousand dollars had ticked into his account while he was talking to Peter. Unless it was Peter himself? No—Rob hadn't even known Peter when he received the first donation.

His seat rose from the floor as he turned the corner onto Winter's hall. He drew his lute from its case as her crèche slid from the wall.

As Winter's eyes snapped into focus, Rob set the lute aside. She looked different, her face more animated, more alive. It wasn't her, he realized—it was him. He'd watched so many recordings of her that he knew what she *should* look like, and that was coloring his perception of her—like a system overlay without the system.

"Hey, you," Winter said.

He was nervous, almost like the first time he'd waked her. He laid his sweaty palms on his thighs. "Hi." He almost asked, "How are you?" but caught himself.

"Imagine my surprise, when I opened my eyes."

Rob grinned. "You must be having luck with new visitors?" He wanted to tell her why she was still here, but didn't know how closely Cryomed monitored visits. He didn't want to risk tipping them off to the changes in her profile.

"As in, have I gotten lucky? You know the rules about fraternizing here. No necrophilia with the customers."

"You know what I mean," Rob laughed.

"Let's see. I've had"—she closed her eyes, muttered to herself—"I'm going to say something like *twenty* visitors."

Rob leaped to his feet and punched the air, whooping like a drunk fan at a boloball game. His shout echoed through the hall.

A disembodied voice said, "Mr. Mashita, please keep your voice down."

"Sorry," Rob said, breathless with excitement and relief.

"Quite all right. I apologize for interrupting your appointment with Miss West."

Winter crossed her eyes for a second, mocking the voice's ultrapolite tone. "Evidently there are some…ahem…additions to my profile? Would you know anything about that?"

Rob lifted a finger, let it hover close to his lips while giving Winter a pointed look.

Winter changed the topic seamlessly. "I don't want to get

my hopes too high, though. Visitors don't necessarily mean I'm getting revived any time soon."

It did mean she wasn't going into the ground any time soon, though. Rob wondered how much time they'd bought. It had to be months, at least.

"One of my visitors has been back *three times*, though," Winter went on. "So that's promising."

"*Really.*" Rob had the strangest feeling—a crawling, jangling sensation that felt like jealousy. Winter had a boyfriend, and he was jealous. He laughed out loud at the absurdity of that.

"What?"

"Nothing. Tell me about the guy. Nice guy?"

She made a face. "Old guy. Eighty, at least." She scrunched her eyes closed for a second. "Dirty old guy. Wanted me to talk dirty to him."

"*Dirty* old guy. Great." Evidently there were a lot of them skulking around this place. "So what did you do?"

"Are you kidding? I was filthy. Absolutely filthy. I was afraid I was going to give him a stroke."

Rob tried to contain his laughter before he got another warning to keep his voice down, as Winter added, "Naughty, naughty stuff."

"What's his name?"

"Redmond. Red."

"Good old Red."

"Good old Red," she whispered, almost to herself. "He's a smarmy know-it-all, but he has the means to revive me, if he decides to."

"How do you know?"

"He showed me his account balance. You've never seen a number with so many digits."

Rob glanced at the timer. He'd grown adept at judging how much time was passing, would have known he had about a minute left even if he hadn't looked.

"Anyway, thanks." She kept her voice matter-of-fact, but Rob knew it was meant to be heartfelt.

"It's the least I could do."

"The least you could do was run me over and go on with your life."

He was so grateful he hadn't, so thankful to his father for discovering that Winter was in this place. If she got out, they could be friends. They could take walks, have coffee. There would be no timer racing eagerly toward zero.

He checked the timer. "Twenty seconds."

Winter looked disappointed, but maybe not terrified. Maybe she was getting used to dying. Rob didn't want to ask.

"You'll keep visiting, won't you?" Winter asked.

Rob laughed. "I'd come every day if I could."

"Good." She closed her eyes, as if Rob had tucked her in and she was going to sleep. "Then I'm not afraid."

On the way out, Rob mulled over his reaction to Winter's "dates." Had that really been jealousy? Falling in love with Winter would be pointless and masochistic, and more than a little weird. He reminded himself of his reaction to Nathan's recordings, of seeing Winter out in the world, warts and all. Sure, seeing those flaws surprised him. But on balance, seeing her alive, laughing, walking fast, destroying buildings, made her even more endearing. More real. If that Winter in the recordings cut her finger, she bled.

When he thought he would never see her again, the words that had burst from the deepest part of him had been "I love you." Had that been nothing but an outpouring of grief and sadness?

Whatever it was, it was out there, dangling between him and Winter. When he said it, he thought he'd never see Winter again, so he hadn't considered the ramifications. It had just come out.

Even though he'd just seen her, he couldn't wait to see her again. What if his anonymous benefactor didn't send more money soon? It would be months before he could raise enough to see her from his pay alone. He couldn't stand the thought of waiting that long.

The lobby smelled like wildflowers carried on a spring breeze. The scent made his chest tight, made him long for Winter. Though to be fair, the smell was engineered to make people feel that way.

He left the lobby, stepped through the exit into sunlight and the more mundane smell of Yonkers. Where he was walking was dominated by the smell of sausage, wafting from the IHOP across the busy street. The tightness was still there, and he was still thinking about Winter.

Rob stopped walking. He turned, propped a foot on a bench and looked up at the Cryogenic Dating Center, a shining bronze monolith with colorful piping resembling strips of stained glass. He closed his eyes, took a deep, slow breath. Time to get real. Winter was dead, and if through some miracle she ever stopped being dead, she'd be married. What he was feeling was absurd, and pointless.

He opened his eyes and continued toward the micro-T station. He'd try to let it go now. Who wouldn't develop a crush on Winter after spending time with her? Besides Nathan, of course. It wasn't helpful to fan those flames, though. Just let it go.

He wondered what Winter would say if he told her he was struggling with romantic feelings for her. She'd asked if he would keep visiting, and when he said he would, she'd said, "Then I'm not afraid." Was she trying to tell him something?

Rob chuckled to himself. Yes, that she was scared, and it helped to know that someone with a familiar face would be back.

When he got home, he went to his room and played a recording of Winter from Nathan's files. He watched Winter drink toasted-almond coffee. The sight of her, life-size, only a few feet away, made his stomach feel like he was in free fall.

He ran clips of her all night as he slept.

38

Veronika

Veronika stepped aside as bots passed in the hallway, transporting crates that had been delivered via tube to Lycan's new digs. She was in high spirits. She had helped save a life, even if the life she'd helped save was someone who was not currently alive.

Lycan was pacing around his new apartment, directing bots where to put things. When he saw Veronika, he grinned, rushed over to greet her.

"So, what do you think?" He raised an arm toward the heights of the condo. It was an impressive space—opulent, and very modern. It was vertically oriented to the extreme, the ground floor maybe twenty feet square, but the highest point of the ceiling a dizzying hundred or more feet above. Rooms were perched at varying heights above, some walled off, others open platforms.

"It's really something," Veronika said. "I didn't realize you were in this sort of income bracket." She tried to banish thoughts of the lousy three grand Lycan had contributed to help Rob. His self-separating recycling system probably cost more than three thousand.

Lycan tried not to beam, but failed. "It's just recently that I could afford something like this. The project I've been working on at Wooster is gaining traction, and I'm part owner in Wooster."

"What is the project again?" He'd told her, but Veronika had only half listened (actually, she had probably one-eighth listened). Now she was curious again.

"I'm spoiling the surprise, but okay, that's where I'm taking you—to see my project."

Veronika tried to look enthused. They were going to Lycan's office to see his work. Yay. "Great."

They took a micro-T that ran right through the Wooster Physionica Building. Moving through the polished lobby, then down a dizzying open-air walk to his lab, Lycan's step took on the strut of a guy in his element.

"This way." He led her into a room with a glass wall that looked onto a series of enclosed spaces, where seated people were wearing systems connected to what looked like a network of vines that twisted and stretched haphazardly, clumping into knobby growths where three or more vines connected. Except that the growths weren't vegetal, but rather slick, silvery-gray.

"What are those viney things? Are they organic?" Veronika asked.

"No," Lycan said. "It's an artificial neural network."

That's exactly what it looked like, she realized—big, interconnected neurons. Veronika considered the implications for a moment. "Are you trying to construct an artificial intelligence?"

"No, nothing that ambitious," he chuckled. "That's why I like you—you're smart enough to make that sort of leap. We're developing a means of directly communicating emotional experiences between people through their systems."

Veronika looked at Lycan, back at the network. "As in, taking what someone is feeling and letting someone else feel it?"

"The exact chemical signature." He pointed at a young woman with wild hair whose eyes were closed. "She's recalling some event that made her feel sad, or scared, or happy, and the actual feelings are interpreted as electronic impulses, transferred to another test participant and converted back into neural impulses."

Veronika peered at the woman behind the glass, trying to fathom the idea of feeling exactly what she was feeling. Or vice versa.

"This is the future," Lycan said. "Connecting people to each other *directly*. At this point we can't improve any further on the speed of information transfer, but there's lots of room to improve the *quality* of the information we transfer."

Veronika studied the shiny silver neurons disappearing into the wall. "Do you have to be connected to the neural network for it to work?"

"No, we can do it wirelessly. It's just simpler this way."

The actual chemical signature of the emotions. Which meant that a piece of the person would be transferred to someone else. "Perfect empathy."

Lycan nodded eagerly. "Exactly. You see the implications without me needing to spoon-feed you. I thought you would."

Lycan seemed the most unlikely person to be working on a project like this. He was not adept at reading other people, and his own emotions seemed rather repressed. Of course, Veronika was a dating coach. Maybe some people were drawn to understand their own greatest weakness.

"Who's 'we'?" she asked. "Are you working with a team?"

"No, 'we' is me, and my assistant. Emily. She's a graduate student. Plus some undergraduate volunteers."

Veronika put her hands on her hips, took another look at the network, seeing it in an entirely different light. "This is entirely your work?"

Lycan looked at the people working behind the glass, his expression that of a proud father looking through the glass at his newborn son. "More or less."

She shook her head slowly. "Now I understand why they footed the bill to have you revived. You're fucking brilliant. I mean, one in ten million. Aren't you?" When Lycan didn't answer, she looked up at him, asked, "What is your IQ?"

Lycan look both embarrassed and pleased by her attention. "It's high."

Veronika thought back to her first meeting with Lycan, watching him climb over the railing of Lemieux Bridge, her spastic attempt to talk him out of it. She'd been watching one of the great modern minds. He could win a Nobel Prize.

"You know, when you said we were going to see your work, I have to admit, I wasn't thrilled. I figured it would be dull. I was wrong." She suddenly saw Lycan in an entirely new light as well. His awkwardness wasn't run-of-the-mill awkwardness, it was the eccentricity of genius.

"Tell me more," she said. "I want to understand how this works."

39

Rob

Rob woke from a dream, crying. For a moment he couldn't remember the dream, only that he'd been holding something, and had felt elated. Then whatever he'd been holding had vanished. He wanted to remember what he'd been holding, wanted to relive that elation.

Then he remembered. He'd been holding Winter. In the dream she'd been alive. They were lying on a couch, their fingers intertwined, and he could smell her hair, feel her chest rising and falling. In the dream Winter had inhaled deeply, relishing it. She said it felt wonderful to breathe, that she would never take another breath for granted as long as she lived.

Rob pressed his face into his pillow, overwhelmed by the emotions coursing through him. He had to see Winter again. Now. Today. He reached for his handheld, checked his account balance.

His guardian angel hadn't visited. He set the handheld down. If he had to raise the money on his own, it would be months before he could see her again. Unless Red came through.

40

Veronika

"I'm not hearing this," Peytr said, his sailboat, tethered to the dock, bobbing behind him, the sun setting orange on the water.

Veronika struggled to come up with a reply. She studied Peytr, his virtual face perfect, his eyes in deep shadow. Sighing, she stood, pulled her sensory gloves off.

"End session."

Peytr disappeared, along with the sailboat, the sea, the sunset. She just couldn't get into it; it felt so fake. So pointless. Maybe she was finally outgrowing interactives. It made her a little wistful to think she might be leaving them behind, the way it had made her wistful when she realized she was too old for Teddy Boynkin when she turned twelve, and packed him up in a box and pushed him through the storage chute.

Lorelei pinged her; Veronika dropped the block she'd placed, and Lorelei materialized on screen.

"Tell me you're free, like right now?" Lorelei said.

Veronika wanted to tell her there was a protocol for making appointments, that Lorelei was free to pull up her schedule and set up a session, but sparring with Lorelei was too exhausting. "If you're willing to pay my special no-advance-notice-whatsoever rate, I'm free, like right now."

Lorelei shook her head briskly. "Whatever. I really need you. I'm taking Nathan to visit my dying-again grandfather. I hate my dying-again grandfather, but it's compelling stuff. 'Do not go gently into that good night,' and all that."

"Mm-hm. Got it," Veronika said. "So it's not a face-to-face per se?" She wanted to ask Lorelei why she wasn't using her regular coach, but thought she knew: it was dawning on Lorelei that Veronika was better than her regular coach. Or, maybe her coach had suggested it, recognizing that Veronika was good at keeping eyes on Lorelei. Come to think of it, maybe Lorelei invited Nathan along just so she could legitimately ask Veronika to coach her. Things were getting wonderfully complex; Veronika loved it, loved the challenge.

"Not per se, no. Talk to you in half an hour?" Lorelei's screen was gone before Veronika could reply.

While ordering a pastrami sandwich so she wouldn't starve during the session, she had an attack of guilt. She closed her eyes, took a deep, sighing breath. "What am I doing?" Lorelei was using her, and she was using Lorelei. Eventually Nathan was going to find out Veronika was coaching Lorelei, and Veronika hoped Nathan might look at her in a different light when he found out. Plus, it was just so addicting to be pulling the strings.

Lorelei pinged her, and Veronika opened a cloaked screen onto Kilo Van Kampen's deathbed. Not that it was a bed; it was more a tank of goo.

Sunali was sitting beside the tank. Lorelei and Nathan hung back at a respectful distance. Nathan seemed incredibly uncomfortable, his expression a wide-eyed "What the hell am I doing here?" that seemed apropos, given that he was witnessing the intimate death of someone he'd never met. If she wasn't hiding, Veronika could have explained to Nathan what he was doing there. Lorelei's audience was blocked from opening screens in the revival center, and taping was prohibited as well, so once outside, Lorelei had to have someone to talk to about whatever drama transpired inside.

He's died three times in the past month, Lorelei subvocalized to her, snapping her out of her reverie. *Evidently he's going for some kind of record.*

Sunali glanced back at Lorelei and Nathan. She stood, told Kilo she'd be right back, and joined them by the door.

"I'm sorry, I don't mean to be rude," she said in a low voice, directing her words at Nathan, "but this is a private matter. I don't think it's appropriate for you to be here, whoever you are."

Nathan nodded rapidly, whispered, "I'm sorry, you're right." He took a step back, toward the door, his hand still entwined with Lorelei's.

"Hold on," Lorelei said, drawing Nathan back. "I asked him to come. We made plans to spend the day together, and then Grandpa started dying again."

Sunali and Lorelei stared each other down as Nathan squirmed.

Finally, Sunali sighed heavily. "Just stay back here, and don't talk," she said to Nathan, then wheeled and returned to Kilo.

Veronika had no idea what help she could possibly be in this situation. Family dynamics were definitely not her thing.

Although she was back to exchanging awkward, carefully worded texts with Jilly a few times a week, her own family was anything but tight. But the dollars were adding up as the timer ran, and she was curious to see what happened, so she kept quiet and watched.

Lorelei squeezed Nathan's hand, then let it go and went to join her stepmother.

"Hello, Grandpa," she said in a sugary child voice.

"Go to hell," Grandpa managed. He was straining to breathe, fluid rattling in his lungs. He looked at Sunali. "What are *you* smiling at?"

Sunali shook her head sadly. "Oh, I don't know. Just enjoying a warm family moment."

Kilo's eyes rolled up until the pupils were almost out of sight. "You were a terrible mother," he muttered. "Terrible."

"I was a terrible mother. I agree." Sunali folded her arms. "Terrible."

Oh, what the hell. Veronika couldn't resist. *Jump in*, she sent to Lorelei. *Point out that Sunali is here for him now, that has to count for something.*

I'm not saying that! Lorelei shot back.

Fine, just play out the same old patterns. Remind me why I'm here again?

"You know, she's here now. That should count for something." Lorelei gave it a harsh, accusatory edge.

Kilo blinked, trying to clear his vision. He stared up at Lorelei as if trying to place her. "She's a vulture waiting for me to die, so she can spend my money."

"Oh, is that it? Don't you remember? You showed me your will," Sunali said.

For a moment Kilo looked terribly confused, as if he didn't understand what she meant. Then he nodded.

Ask her why she is here, then, Veronika sent. That would give Sunali a chance to express some kindness.

"Then why *are* you here?" Lorelei asked, making it sound like an accusation.

Sunali studied her. "Honestly, I have no idea."

Veronika threw her hands in the air. These people were hopeless. It reminded her so much of her own family. *Tell your grandfather you love him*, she sent. What the hell. Let Lorelei try to put an acid tone on that one.

What? No. Fucking. Way.

Veronika let out a frustrated growl. *You want drama? You want to be a star with a million followers? Step out of your comfort zone of petty grievances and snarky comebacks and say something truly surprising. I guarantee you, Nathan will make sure your viewers know what happened as soon as you get outside.*

Lorelei's face shifted through half a dozen emotions. She craned her head forward, as if about to expel something foul.

"Come on, sweetie," Veronika said aloud to her empty living room. "Say it. You can do it." She sent Lorelei a good, hard nudge: *Or are you happy staying a small-time player?*

Lorelei cleared her throat. "I know we haven't always gotten along, but I want you to know, I love you, Grandpa."

Veronika raised her fist as Kilo and Sunali gaped at Lorelei. Veronika knew exactly what Lorelei was thinking at that moment: she was wishing her viewers were watching this. This was platinum.

"Why would you say something like that?" Kilo finally managed.

"Because I do. Sunali loves you, too; she just can't say it. That's why she's at your side every time you go through this. She's trying to show you she loves you."

Nice! Very nice! Veronika sent.

Sunali was gaping, openmouthed, at Lorelei.

"Well, it's true, isn't it?"

Lorelei reached out tentatively, as if gathering the courage to touch something that might bite, and stroked Kilo's head once, then again, clearly not comfortable, but soldiering on.

Kilo was trembling, appeared to be holding his breath. With a squeal, he finally inhaled. Lorelei was looking at Sunali. She opened her eyes wide for an instant, urging Sunali to say something.

"I don't like to see you suffer like this," Sunali said tightly. "I know what it feels like to die. Doing it over and over..." She shook her head. "It's got to be hell—"

"It *is* hell," Kilo moaned.

"Then why don't you let it go? You've squeezed everything you can out of this life. Rest now."

Kilo was trembling, his lips drawn back from his expensive white teeth in a snarl. "You're just saying that because you want my money—"

"*I know I'm not getting your money.*" Sunali leaned forward, her triceps tensing as if she was about to shove Kilo's head under the surface of the goo. Then she relaxed.

"That's right," Kilo said. The filmy, drugged quality left his eyes for a moment, and he added, "I left it to my favorite charity."

"Tell me this much," Sunali said, leaning right over Kilo, her face six inches from his. "When *do* you plan to stop the revival order? When you get one lousy day before you die again? When the doctors can only squeeze out an hour each time? When will it be time?"

"It'll never be time," Kilo whispered.

Sunali leaned back into her seat, nodded. "Fair enough."

They glared at each other. Kilo struggled; his eyes kept crossing, his breathing growing wetter, more labored. He looked like a giant wrinkled salamander. Veronika was so caught up in the moment she was barely breathing herself.

They stood, and sat, silently, until Kilo stopped breathing. No one shed any tears.

When the techs came in to prepare him for revival, Sunali stood, looked from Lorelei to Nathan and said, somewhat sarcastically, "Well, thanks for coming."

41

Veronika

As she paced from the bedroom to the living room and back, the walls kept shifting to expand the room she was occupying. She should stop it, but the back-and-forth of the wall gave the illusion that her apartment was breathing, and somehow that was both cool and soothing.

The guilt was eating a hole in her. Every time she saw Nathan, she came close to blurting a confession, but if she did she'd lose her license for violating client privacy. On top of that, she was having so much fun, and that was probably why she felt so guilty. It felt like fun at Nathan's expense.

The thing was, she'd done some genuine good while coaching Lorelei at her grandfather's deathbed. She'd brought three people closer together, had helped heal some very deep wounds. She could be proud of that. Maybe she should pursue it further; if she genuinely focused her efforts on helping Lorelei, she could feel good about what she was doing, instead of feeling sleazy. Lorelei didn't need a dating coach, but her other relationships were a mess—especially her relationship with Sunali.

She pinged Lorelei.

Almost immediately, Lorelei appeared via screen.

"We need to talk," Veronika said.

"So talk," Lorelei said.

"IP." This issue was too personal to discuss with a bloody screen.

Lorelei sighed, as if it was a huge inconvenience for her to haul her scrawny ass over to Veronika's place.

"We need to strategize. I've got some ideas to increase your viewership," Veronika goaded.

"Fine, fine." Lorelei's screen vanished.

Assuming Lorelei wasn't going to primp much before leaving her apartment, Veronika figured she'd be there in eleven minutes. She unwrapped her sandwich and popped in on Rob. He was working his awful, soul-grinding job.

"Any word on Winter?"

Rob shook his head as he carried on working. "I'm visiting her in a couple of hours, so I'll get an update then. Every time I withdraw nine thousand from my account, it grows back like magic."

"You're going in a couple of hours? That's the middle of the night. When do you sleep?"

Rob lifted his head, gave her a flat, expressionless stare. "I haven't slept in two years." He returned to his work, plucking parts out of what might have been an antique housecleaning drone.

"Let's hope it's almost over. Big hug, sweetie." After considering for a sec, she added, "Love you."

"Love you, too," Rob said.

Even though it was a friendship "love-you," it warmed her to hear Rob say it. If she could find five, maybe six friends she cared enough about to exchange *I love you*'s, it might nourish her enough that she could live without a true love's *I love you*'s. Maybe.

The apartment alerted her to a visitor. Veronika waved the door open and Lorelei sauntered in. When her virtual entourage didn't follow, Lorelei gestured toward the door. "Can you lift your block?"

Veronika shook her head as the door folded closed on Lorelei's hordes. "Just the two of us."

Lorelei turned her face to the ceiling and sighed heavily. "What is it with you people and secrecy? If you lived your lives in the open, you'd all sleep easier at night."

"I'm sure you sleep the sleep of angels," Veronika said, then offered Lorelei a drink. Lorelei asked for a Thunder Road, and they settled in the living room while Veronika's drone fetched the drinks.

"So here I am, all by my onesies." Lorelei turned up her palms, raised her shoulders toward her ears.

"I have a suggestion for you. I think you focus too much of your time and energy on your romantic life and friendships and not enough on family ties. If your life was more well rounded, people would watch for longer, and you'd broaden your appeal outside a narrow demographic."

Lorelei sipped her Thunder Road, her lips forming a plump O. "My family life? What, like I should spend more time with Sunali, talking about the plight of the frozen?"

This wasn't going to be easy. "All I'm saying is, people respond to familial relationships. They go right to the brain stem in a way friendships and boyfriends don't. You'll build your viewer base if you round out your life."

Lorelei curled her legs under her, pressed her fist against her chin. "Sunali *hates* me. And I hate her."

"That's perfect. Maximum drama. Now you slowly untangle that messed-up relationship. Conflict resolution is at the core of all good drama; find a way to reconcile, slowly but surely, and viewers will be addicted."

Lorelei rubbed her finger across her lips, saying nothing. The wheels were clearly turning, as much as the wheels turned in Lorelei's head.

"What does your puppet master think of the idea?"

Lorelei huffed. "You know, I'm getting pretty sick of your condescending attitude. Pathetic as I think it is, I don't make snarky comments about your lifestyle. Who made you the arbiter of what constitutes an authentic life?"

Veronika had to engage all of her willpower to keep from rolling her eyes. "Arbiter? Well, Parsons, let's see—"

Lorelei stood, peeled her system off, right in front of Veronika. Naked from the waist up, she held her system at arm's length between two fingers, then opened her fingers and let the system slip to the floor. Smoothing her tiny skirt, she sat down again. "What's more real: what *you* think you are, or what external, objective reality tells you you are?"

It was difficult to take Lorelei seriously, with her small, pointy breasts right there in the open, but at least Veronika knew who she was talking to. Unless she'd memorized the question, Lorelei's verbal acuity was greater than Veronika had assumed. Maybe she usually talked dumb by choice, rather than because she was dumb.

"If you think you have a great sense of humor, but no one ever laughs, then you're not funny, you're delusional," Lorelei went on. "I choose to see everything clearly, including myself, and the way to do that is to see myself reflected in others' eyes."

Veronika waited to make sure she had finished. "I'm not criticizing your decision to lead a public life." She was criticizing her reliance on Parsons, which made it impossible for others to see who she really was, but telling Lorelei that wouldn't be constructive. "So, what does Parsons think of my suggestion?"

Lorelei retrieved her system, slid it back on. She cleared her throat. "He agrees it might be an interesting direction to go in."

All this time, she'd been speaking to Parsons as much as to Lorelei. Maybe more. It was strange to have that confirmed.

"It won't work, though," Lorelei said. "There's too much bad blood between me and Sunali. Even if I could stand being nice to her, she's not going to respond."

Veronika looked at the ceiling, seeking patience. Was she really going to have to take Lorelei and Parsons by the hand and walk them through this? Probably. "Can you think of some way? Is there something you could do that might cause Sunali to have a change of heart?"

Lorelei gave her a blank look.

"Maybe if you took an interest in some *issue* that mattered to her?"

Lorelei frowned. "You're saying I should take an interest in her bridesicle shit?" She thought about it, or, more likely, talked it over with Parsons. "She'd like that, wouldn't she?"

"What if you volunteered to work with her on the cause?" Veronika suggested.

Lorelei subvocalized something to Parsons. Veronika sighed, willing herself to be patient.

"That might be interesting. Getting into people's faces, shaking my fist. That could work. My viewers might like that."

It was a cause Veronika was beginning to believe in, so recruiting someone to it was also a good thing. Although Veronika doubted Lorelei would prove a particularly valuable addition to the cause.

42

Rob

Rob stood for a moment, pressed his palms against his kidneys, and leaned back to stretch his aching muscles. The light was beginning to fade, which meant his ten-hour shift was almost over.

Straddling his little workbench, the seat rose to support him, and he went back to gutting some sort of electronic game. Once in a while Rob came across a piece of salvage that he would have liked to examine more carefully, like this game with illustrations of old-time winged jets on the sides. Most of the things that would have provided a real glimpse into the people from the past, such as photos, food packaging, artwork, were culled earlier in the process by the drones. One day he'd love to be assigned to work on the hill, as they called it. Any different assignment would be a welcome change; he was tired of looking at the insides of old computers.

"Hey, Rob." Rob turned and spotted Bryony repairing a sorting bin that had lost a wheel. She was squatting, looking at him through the curved spokes of one of the intact wheels. "You interested in doing some bugs after? Me and Kiki are going down to the tunnels."

"Can't, have to meet someone. But thanks, another time."

Bryony nodded as if it didn't matter to her one way or another. He appreciated the invitation, and he wanted to fit in and make more friends here, but it was hard shifting from the clubs of High Town to sitting in a dirty tunnel sunk into a mountain of hundred-year-old crap, getting high on cheap bugs.

Tonight he couldn't have gone in any case, because he was going to visit Winter. In just a few hours he would find out if Red had proposed. If he had, Rob would soon get to meet Winter face-to-face, maybe sit and have coffee. He might even get to hug her, to feel her newly warm body against his for a few fleeting seconds. The thought of that sent a thrill through him.

He tried to banish the longing that it be more than a hug. Even if getting revived wouldn't include Winter being bound by an ironclad marriage contract, there was another reason he should forget about any possibility of their being anything more than friends. He had run her over. Run. Her. Over. As the months and years stretched out, it was becoming easier to overlook that aspect of the story.

Rob spotted Stellan, his replacement, winding between drones. "Your ass is free," Stellan said, pulling on his hood and fixing the breather in place.

Rob resisted the urge to sprint back to the dressing room. As soon as he was out of his protective suit and heading toward the gate, he entered a reservation to visit Winter.

He stopped walking, carefully reread the message on his handheld.

No longer available.

What did that mean, "no longer available"? Had Red revived her, or had she been pulled from the program and buried? He didn't know whether to shout for joy or sink to his knees. As second-shift workers brushed past, Rob put in a call to the dating center's customer service, was connected with an AI operator.

"Yes, I was arranging to visit a woman named Winter West, and it says she's no longer available." He was breathing so hard he could barely speak.

"That's correct," the unnaturally mellifluous voice on the line said.

"Can you tell me what that means?"

"It means she's no longer at Cryomed's cryogenic dating facility."

"Yes, I understand that." A hammer-faced woman looked at him as she passed. He was shouting, he realized. He took a breath, lowered his voice. "I understand that. But was she revived, or released from the program?"

"I'm sorry, that information is confidential."

Rob growled in frustration, nearly flung his handheld over the fence. He hurried toward the exit. There had to be a way to find out what had happened. Peter was a possibility. Maybe he should try to get in touch with Sunali, see if she could put him in touch with Peter. But the thought of waiting hours, even days, for Peter to get back to him was intolerable. He wouldn't be able to eat or sleep until he knew. She could be out there right now. She could be gone forever.

He ran through the gate, headed across the parking lot toward his house.

But if she was out there, wouldn't she have contacted him? He slowed, a wave of numbness sweeping over him. She was dead. That's why the Cryomed AI wouldn't tell him. If she'd been revived, it would have told him.

She'd had visits, though. Tons of them. Even repeat visits from a rich guy. Peter said that rolled back the clock, that it was all decided automatically. Why would they bury her just as interest in her spiked? That made no sense.

Unless they'd discovered the hacked profile.

Rob paused in the parking lot, put his hands on his knees, tried to catch his breath and clear his vision. Maybe he should contact Nathan or Veronika. He tapped his handheld. They might have an idea about how to find out—

Rob froze.

If Winter was alive, she would have a com account. Maybe she didn't want to speak to Rob, but she'd want to call others. Friends, her aunt and nephews.

Com search. Winter West. New York area, he subvocalized.

Winter's image materialized. He dropped onto his ass in the gravel lot, gaping at her smiling face, the flesh tones of life restored to it.

II: In Person

43

Rob

Staring down at his system, Rob willed Winter to ping. She was out there somewhere.

Rising from the edge of his bed, Rob retrieved his lute from the closet, went out back, brushed dried leaves and silt from an old porto-seat, and sat down. He let his fingers glide over the polished wood of the lute, then began playing "Polymnia," an ancient piece he rarely played unless he was providing dinner music at a swanky restaurant.

She wasn't going to call. If she were, she would have done so by now.

Two weeks was more than enough time.

He paused midsong. Maybe he should leave one more message? No. What could he say that he hadn't said the first three times? Leaving a fourth message would only make him seem more pathetic. He carried on with the song.

His chest ached at the thought of Winter alive, laughing, living, with him no part of her life. Where was she, right now? On Red's estate? In an ultralight copter? Rob looked up at the sliver of sky visible below the roof of Percy Estate, saw a copter flitting its way to somewhere. Winter could be in it.

It was time to move on. No more calls. How sick was it for him to persist, if she didn't want to speak to him? She owed him less than nothing.

Let her go. That's what Veronika had said. His dad, too.

"Polymnia" gave way to "Laura Soave," an aching melody, without Rob's awareness. Everything was skintight. He would go back to hanging out with his friends.

He played a modern tune by Arctic Ice, plucking the strings with a vigor that bordered on abuse, his thoughts flitting across the conversations they'd had, seeking something, some explanation. On that last visit, when she told him she might be getting out, there had been such a sense of intimacy between them. Maybe not love, but a deep, close connection.

"You ready, Eddie?" Lorne called through the door.

"Yeah." He'd forgotten they were going to the tubes for dinner. Rob stopped playing and headed up the back stoop.

The benches at the tubes were packed with diners. It was Saturday night, Rob realized. Once upon a time Rob had known exactly what day of the week it was, but when you worked every day, the distinctions became less crucial.

He had no idea why he was still working at the reclamation center. The money was decent, but so what? Maybe it was because he didn't want to play for other people, and no other options for work had presented themselves.

His dad talked an Asian family into scooting down so they could squeeze onto the end of their table, then he dug right into his burger, making appreciative grunts as he chewed. Rob's stomach was tight, wasn't welcoming of food, but he ate anyway. His dad deserved to enjoy himself. Rob forced a smile.

"Where do you think she is right now?" Lorne asked.

"I try not to think about it," Rob answered.

"All you do is think about it." When Rob didn't reply, he asked, "What's the rich guy's name again?"

"I'm pretty sure the guy's name is Redmond."

Lorne lifted his cup of water, held it there until Rob finally relented and followed suit. "Here's to Redmond. God bless his filthy rich ass." They drank. Lorne lifted his cup again. "And to my son, who, against god-awful odds, figured out how to save the damsel in distress."

Rob smiled wanly. "By posting naked pictures of her."

Lorne burst into loud, easy laughter. The young girl squeezed in beside Lorne looked up at him, then laughed as well. The laughter spread down the bench.

Someone pinged Rob; he was still so unused to wearing a system again that the sound startled him. He looked to see who it was.

There was nothing but plain, unadorned text in the upper right corner of his vision. Nothing but a name.

Winter West.

Rob leaped from the bench. "Be right back." He trotted out toward the big tubes, which were inactive at this time of day.

"Hi," he said.

"Hi." She sounded, what? Reluctant? Apologetic? Certainly not excited. The connection was voice-only; he wished he could see her.

"How are you?"

"I'm okay. I just got back from my honeymoon a few days ago."

That explained her delay in getting in touch. Part of it, anyway. "You're alive. I can't believe it."

"I'm alive."

He waited for more.

"Are you free? Can we meet?" he finally blurted, trying not to sound as eager as he felt.

"Right now?" Her tone was like a lead weight in his gut. She sounded uneasy, as if she was trying to think of an excuse to decline. "I guess. I mean, I wouldn't be able to stay long. Red's coming home from a trip around eight."

"That's okay."

"All right, then." Again, she sounded almost pained.

"Great." Once they were face-to-face, the awkwardness would melt away. They would fall into that comfortable intimacy they'd enjoyed in the cryocenter.

"Where?" she asked.

"Somewhere in Low Town? Stain's Coffee?" Rob didn't know where Winter was living, but thought it safe to assume it was in High Town.

"I don't want to meet too close to where I used to live; it would be strange, bumping into people I used to know."

He started to ask why that would be strange, then got it. She'd already contacted her closest friends. Others would be shocked to see Winter alive. Winter would have to explain how she managed to get revived, then there'd be an awkward exchange where the former acquaintance would convey to Winter that it was okay to be a bridesicle, that she had nothing to be ashamed of.

"I understand." He didn't care where they met; he just wanted to see her.

"Somewhere outside? It's hard for me to be inside, since

the crèche. When Red is away, sometimes I sleep on the roof," she laughed.

"No, I understand. How about Central Park? There's a bridge with beautiful ironwork on the West Side—"

"I know which one you mean. Give me an hour?"

"See you then." He didn't want to give her an hour; he wanted to see her that very moment. She would be walking, moving her arms, breathing.

He trotted back to the bench, saw that Lorne was about three-quarters of the way through his dinner. Rob sat, made a show of eating some banana fries, though his heart was racing and he had zero appetite.

"Who was it?" Lorne asked, studying Rob.

"It was Winter. I'm meeting her in an hour." Saying it, he felt a stupid swell of pride.

"Well, I'll be damned." Lorne shook his head in wonder. "Be sure you record this. This is really something." He looked down the bench, as if contemplating sharing the story with someone, then he clapped Rob on the back. "Go on, get going. I'll see you at home."

Rob sprung from the bench and jogged off.

44

Rob

Rob spotted the bridge ahead, a graceful curve of weathered steel spanning nothing but a walking trail, the railing decorated with ornate steel clover shapes. He stopped at the center, pressed his palm to the cool steel railing. He and Penny had broken up on this bridge. Under it, actually, on the walk that ran beneath. From where he was standing, Rob could see the little orange fire hydrant he'd propped his foot on while they talked.

He was twenty minutes early; he scanned for Winter in case she was early as well. He wanted to spot her when she was still far off, so he could watch her move without her being aware he was watching.

Rob wiped his sweaty palm on his thigh and set it back on the railing. What should he say as she approached? When he and Penny used to play romantic-comedy interactives with the scoring enabled, Rob always won, was always better at snapping off those pithy romantic lines that racked up points. Now his mind was blank.

He watched an ultralight copter flit over the lake in the distance. Maybe he should say nothing, just wait until she was standing beside him at the rail, the two of them enjoying the view in silence.

The copter rose over the trees along the trail. Rob expected it to continue rising and fly away, but it paused, then touched down on the trail a hundred yards away.

Winter stepped out. She waved to the pilot as the copter lifted off, then turned toward the bridge.

She spotted Rob, lifted a hand. He waved back. She let her fingers drop, but kept her hand raised. She was simply beautiful. Coils of deep burgundy flowed across her bare shoulders; her lips were drawn in a half smile. She dropped her head and walked toward him, in no hurry.

Rob's mouth was dry, his heart racing, as she joined him on the bridge. She was small—smaller than she'd seemed in the crèche and in the videos. There was a light dusting of freckles on her arms.

"It's good to see you, Rob." She made no move to hug him, only joined him at the railing, looking toward the spot where the copter had deposited her.

"It's good to see you, too." Not a line that would have racked up points in a rom-com interactive. "You did it. I can't believe it."

She chuckled, glanced at him, beautiful eyelashes rising over lively green eyes. "*I* did it? I could barely move my face, and I sounded like a swamp harpy. You and your musketeers did it. I'm sorry, I shouldn't have waited this long to thank you."

It was another fine moment for an embrace that didn't come. They watched a goose launch itself off the lake, honking enthusiastically.

"So what's your life like?" Rob asked.

She rubbed her forehead, smiling, considering the question. "I wake up, tell a drone what I want for breakfast, take a bath in a tub the size of a swimming pool." She shrugged. "It's an easy life. Red warned me that he's going to be gone a lot. Three of his kids live on the island—"

"The *island*? You live on one of those three-legged estates on the water?" All this time he'd been picturing her in a penthouse in High Town, when she'd actually been on an estate, a hundred feet above the water.

Winter nodded. "Out in the upper bay, close to the ocean. Along with Red's extended family—kids, grandkids, nephews, nieces."

"Nice people?"

"No." She said it flippantly, as if it didn't matter.

Rob frowned. "What do you mean?"

She sighed. "Mostly they ignore me, as if I'm a pet Labradoodle Red brought home." She shrugged. "There are worse things."

"Do they think you're horning in on their inheritance?"

Winter guffawed. "Are you kidding? I don't inherit anything; it's all spelled out in the contract. You're not in a strong negotiating position when you're in a coffin. They just see me as a low person, someone to look nice at Redmond's side at public events, and for him to fuck."

Rob winced, trying to mask his reaction. "You're on Red's insurance now, though, aren't you?"

Winter nodded absently. Rob assumed she was having a second conversation on her system, then realized she wasn't working her system, she was simply fidgeting with an emerald embedded in it. Her mind was elsewhere.

"What's it like, knowing you're guaranteed to live to a hundred and fifteen or twenty?"

The question drew Winter from her reverie. She looked at Rob, really looked at him with those green eyes, her face so very alive. "I'm not sure yet." She dug at the emerald like she was trying to pry it loose. "I haven't had time for it to sink in. It's been hard enough adjusting to being alive again. I've been in touch with other women who've been through this; they're the only people who can understand what's happened to me. That's been helpful."

Rob nodded. "Have you been in touch with Idris?"

"Oh, sure. We went shopping after I got out. I didn't have a thing to wear. Some inconsiderate person gave away all my clothes when I died." She dropped her head, thinking; her hair gliding down to frame her face. Rob wanted to reach out and touch that hair, soft across his fingers. Instead, he laced his fingers and clenched his hands together on the railing. "It's been a little awkward, trying to reconnect with Idris. She wants to pick up right where we left off, like it never happened. Like nothing's changed."

"I guess it'll take both of you time to adjust."

"I guess." She was biting her lip, gone again. If Rob hadn't watched hours and hours of Winter's previous life, he might have thought this was who she was. Maybe it wasn't surprising she wasn't the same, after all she'd been through, married now to an old man she barely knew. Rob hated that old man, utterly despised him even though they'd never met. He only hoped Winter despised Red as much as he did. If she liked him, if somehow she learned to love him... he was afraid to ask, but he had to know.

He tried to sound casual. "So, what's he like?"

"Redmond? I haven't seen him since the honeymoon. He works, spends time with his kids. He's been married five times. He spends most of his free time building his video game collection." She laughed, but dryly—not the infectious laugh he'd heard so often from her past life. "Did I mention Red has one of the largest early video game collections in the world?"

"You did not. How exciting." He tried to match her droll, mock-cheery tone.

"He does. One day you'll have to visit the island and let Red show it to you. For hours and hours."

Rob laughed, but Winter only shook her head. It seemed like he'd never get to hear her wonderful laughter.

"Big sigh," she said.

That got Rob laughing again. "You do realize your lungs work now? You could, you know, actually make a sighing sound."

Winter broke into a reluctant smile, but went on looking at her hands. "While I was dead, I kind of got used to describing my affects rather than actually carrying them out. Much easier. In fact, I'm thinking about narrating all of my movements and just sitting still most of the time. 'I stand, I walk to the window. Put my hands on my hips.'"

"Just don't try to eat that way."

"Good point."

Winter craned her neck, looking toward the underside of High Town, thick with shadows, buttresses crisscrossing the framework. "I never thought I'd be so happy to see that roof. I always found it oppressive, but now it's comforting."

Rob eyed the strings of apartments dangling below the

ceiling. He could pinpoint Lorelei's if he wanted, the place where all of this had started, leading to this moment.

He looked at Winter, the pinkness rising in her cheeks in the cool evening, the barely perceptible flutter of a pulse in the hollow of her neck. "This is incredible, being able to spend time with you without that timer hanging over us," he said.

"Head nod," Winter whispered, and for the first time, Rob felt as if he was standing next to the woman he'd grown so close to. Her eyes grew soft and teary, and he could see she was with him, fully.

Then she turned, looked off toward the lake. "Let's go on a trip. My treat. Or Red's treat, if you want to get technical."

For a moment, against all reason, he thought she meant a trip in a car, or a train, and his heart leaped at the thought of packing a bag and spending two or three days, alone with Winter. Of course, that wasn't what she meant. She was working her system. "Where do you want to go? Anywhere in the world. Pick somewhere expensive." She'd gone back to looking through him as much as at him, the feeling of connection vanished.

"Won't he be upset if you take a friend on an expensive trip?" For some reason Rob couldn't bring himself to say Red's name. It hurt every time Winter said it. Rob wished she'd call him something else. Preferably "the impotent old bastard."

Winter laughed dryly. "He won't notice. Here, look at this." She moved her readout into the air so he could see it. It included her account balance: almost a half million dollars. "That's what's left of my allowance for the month."

Rob couldn't take his eyes off the readout. "That's hard to believe."

"I know. When I died, I was twelve thousand dollars in

debt, and it seemed like so much money." She closed the read-out. "Come on, let's go everywhere."

They spent five minutes in Paris, soaring over Notre Dame, popping into the Louvre long enough to see the *Mona Lisa*; two minutes hovering beside Mount Everest, watching two climbers scale an ice wall; one minute inside the dead city of Bangkok with its eighty-foot-high walls, where no living thing had walked in forty years, thanks to the nanopocalypse. Their last stop was an open-air virtual bazaar on the moon, where screens examined virtual merchandise set on virtual tables that was being hawked by other screens. Not one particle of moon dust was disturbed, because none of it was really there.

"Wow," was all Rob could say when they returned to the relative ordinariness of Central Park.

"I know."

"How much did that cost?"

Winter checked, raised her eyebrows. "Something like eleven thousand. Not bad, really."

Almost all of it would be toll fees, set to limit the number of screens surrounding attractions like Big Ben and the Sphinx at any one time. From what Rob understood, opening a screen on the other side of the Earth cost the provider no more than opening one a foot away from you, yet for some reason the farther away you opened a screen, the more you were charged.

Eleven thousand, for a few minutes' entertainment. Rob thought of how hard he had had to work to raise nine thousand to visit Winter for five minutes.

He caught Winter looking at him. When she saw him notice, she closed her eyes, smiled a neutral, unreadable smile. He sensed that the next words out of her mouth would be that she had to get going, that it had been nice seeing him, and maybe they could do it again at some other undetermined time.

"Please don't take this the wrong way," he said before she had time to say it, "but you don't seem like the same person I used to look so forward to visiting."

Winter worked her system, as if checking on something she'd just thought of.

"Did I do something wrong?" Rob asked.

"You mean, besides running me over?"

The comment stung, even though her tone was light and ironic. "Besides that, yes."

Her fingers stopped tapping. She let them drop to her sides. "Besides that, you worked yourself to the brink of exhaustion every day for almost two years to keep a promise to a stranger, then for an encore you did the impossible—you figured out how to get her out of there." She lowered her voice to a near whisper. "No, Rob, you didn't do anything wrong."

He had no idea how she'd found out about his work schedule. Maybe just an educated guess. "Then why are you acting like you hardly know me?"

Winter covered her mouth, looked at the ground. She didn't answer.

"When you were in there, sometimes I imagined what it would be like, the moment we met out in the world. I thought—" His voice hitched; he cleared his throat. "I thought it would be incredible, the best moment in my entire life. That we'd run toward each other laughing. We'd jump up and down, screaming, 'We did it, we did it.'"

Three screens drifted by on the trail below, likely joggers running on treadmills at home.

"Close your eyes," Winter said.

"What?"

"Close your eyes."

Rob looked at her, questioning, then closed his eyes.

"Now imagine us jumping up and down."

"Okay."

"Where am I, in relation to you?"

Rob opened his eyes. Winter held her palm in front of his eyes. "Keep them closed."

He closed them. "Where are you? I don't know, you're standing right in front of me, I guess."

"Where are my hands?"

He almost opened his eyes again. Her hands were in his, but he didn't want to say that. "You're clutching my wrists."

"Okay," she said, though she sounded dubious. "Now roll the scene forward. We're saying, 'We did it, we did it.' What comes next? We stop jumping, and...?"

What came next was Winter melting into his arms, the embrace he'd imagined a thousand times. And if she let him, he would go on holding her until all was silence and there was nothing in the world but the two of them, and he could feel her heart beating against his chest.

"What comes next is we fall into each other's arms," Winter said.

Rob opened his eyes. She was watching his face, searching for his reaction. He opened his mouth to disagree, but nothing came.

Her eyes were suddenly bright with tears, her mouth tight. "The thing of it is, I'm married, Rob. I signed an irrevocable life contract. Irrevocable, as in, nothing is ever going to change it. That was the price I paid. I paid it willingly, and I would do it again." She turned to go. "I can't fall into anyone's arms but Red's."

"I understand that." He spoke quickly as she moved away. "I just want us to be friends, like we were when I was visiting you. I *miss* those visits."

She paused, wiped under one eye with the back of her wrist. "I do, too. More than you can imagine. But it's a bad idea." She scrunched her eyes, seemed to be imploring Rob to understand, then she turned and hurried away. As she stepped off the bridge, Rob heard her add, "I'm sorry."

45

Veronika

Sunali looked up when Lorelei and Veronika entered, made a sound to indicate mock surprise. It appeared as if the meeting of the Former Bridesicle Liberation Army, or whatever they called themselves, was already under way. Lorelei and Veronika were fifteen minutes early, so Sunali must have given Lorelei the wrong time.

"This is my good friend Veronika," Lorelei said as they took seats at the table, several hundred of Lorelei's cohort taking up residence in the air behind her. It was a dining room table, in Sunali's dining room—this was clearly not a big operation, nor a particularly well-funded one.

Sunali introduced them to the four other women sitting at the table. All were beautiful, of course, because they were ex-bridesicles. They ranged in age from young to quite old.

Veronika listened to them for a while, trying to get up to speed. Their idea was to do another break-in event in the air over High Town, this time using a recorded plea for help from a bridesicle still trapped in the minus eighty. They would have to make the recording secretly, since Cryomed didn't allow customers to use recording devices inside their facility. Veronika thought it was a decent idea, but Lorelei clearly didn't. She rolled her eyes and sighed heavily as the bridesicle league worked out details.

What? Veronika sent Lorelei.

Their idea is lame.

Well, tell them!

"Your idea is lame," Lorelei nearly shouted. Five heads swiveled to look at her. "A big dead face in the air, doing a PSA." She waved her hands in the air. "Ooooh, how modern. That's not going to get anyone interested. It won't get passed on, won't get picked up by the micros, let alone the macros."

Sunali raised one eyebrow. "Well. Thanks for your input. Can you guess what painfully obvious question I'm going to ask now?"

Veronika could. *Do you have a better idea?* she sent to Lorelei.

"No, I don't have a better idea," Lorelei said, propping a knobby bare knee on the table. "But what you're planning is a waste of time."

Sunali made a show of rearranging the specs suspended in the air beside her seat. "We're paying a consultant who has data that says you're wrong. We're not as out of touch as you might think, sweetie." She swept long bangs out of her eyes, turned back to her committee.

"Wait, *I know.*" Lorelei leaned forward, pressing her palms on the table. "Don't do one big one, do ten thousand little ones! And not in the sky, at ground level. Have the bridesicle go right up to people in the streets, pleading for help."

"Then they'd be nothing but ads," the oldest woman,

probably in her midsixties, said. "No one would even see them; their systems would filter out the ads."

Lorelei shook her head. "Who said anything about screens. Full figures."

Veronika winced. The league of ex-bridesicles chuckled merrily at Lorelei's naïveté.

"Do you have *any* idea what that would cost?" Sunali asked. "First, we'd have to pay a rogue programmer to engineer ten thousand illegal full-body projections, then we'd have to pay ten thousand fines of eight hundred dollars each, in advance! Plus lawsuits, because the projections are bound to cause injuries, wandering into the streets. People could die."

"You're talking about tens of millions," one of the other ex-bridesicles chimed in.

Lorelei clicked her tongue in annoyance. "You could program them to stay off the streets."

"It's still way beyond our operating budget," Sunali said.

Lorelei leaned back, folded her arms. "Fine. Then put a big frozen face in the air."

Still, it was a chilling image: ten thousand frozen, blue-skinned women wandering the streets, pleading for help. Lorelei was creative, at least. Or maybe it had been Parsons's idea.

46

Veronika

Low Town. Streets crowded with people, some of them up from Undertown, smelling dank and edgy. Vehicles untethered, at the mercy of drivers. Old, straight, square buildings. All of it set in the mottled shade of High Town. Veronika loved coming to Low Town; the grittiness of it felt exciting, a little dangerous.

She kept hoping Nathan would pop in and ask her what she was up to, just so she could say she was hanging out with Lycan again. So he knew she wasn't sitting at home playing *Wings of Fire.*

A flashing green arrow appeared in her visual field, directing her down Houston Street. They were meeting on Spring Street in the heart of Greenwich Village, at Lombardi's, the oldest pizzeria in the city.

It wasn't romantic. She didn't want it to be romantic, but she wouldn't mind if Nathan thought it was. Which was pathetic—she knew Nathan couldn't care less if her relationship with Lycan was romantic or not. Still, she'd like him to know.

As she turned onto Spring Street, she finally gave in to temptation and pinged Nathan.

What's up? he sent.

Nothing. Having pizza in the Village. Just thought I'd check in.

Excellent. Who you with?

Just Lycan. She tried to sound casual.

Is that becoming something?

I don't know. It's in that blurry area.

I know it well. Have fun.

Veronika closed the link. Mission accomplished. Yeah, he'd sounded devastated. She spotted Lycan through the window of Lombardi's, sitting at a table, sort of wringing his hands. He stood when she stepped inside. He looked… distressed.

"Are you okay? You look a little…" she trailed off, reluctant to label how he looked.

"Panic attack," he said, and gave a "What are you going to do?" shrug.

"I just love anxiety. Any idea what set it off? Work?"

Lycan shrugged. "They just happen."

Veronika certainly knew how that was. "What do you usually do to cope?"

"Usually? I row."

"You row."

Lycan nodded. "I have a rowing machine. I pick a place, maybe the Nile, or the Amazon, and I row until I'm exhausted."

Veronika broke into a grin. How many times had she passed the lagoon around Central Park and vowed to rent one of those antique fiberglass rowboats and paddle around?

A quick check told Veronika there were a few available. She reserved one.

"Come on, let's get our pizza to go," she said, standing.

"Is it helping?" Veronika asked.

"A little, yes. I always feel better when I have something to do with my hands." Lycan pulled on the oars. He seemed less awkward, less a goofy brain, now that he was pulling on oars. Veronika reclined in her seat, a slice of pizza in one hand, enjoying the sweet smell of cut grass in the air. It was delightful—the breeze created by the boat's movement, the dribble of water off the oars as they lifted out of the water, the plunge as they dug back in. She watched the oars trace an oval, Lycan's biceps and triceps alternately bunching and relaxing. The baggy clothes Lycan wore gave the impression that he was more plump than powerful, and his atrocious posture reinforced that misperception, but he was actually a muscular guy.

"I have a theory about anxiety and exercise," Lycan said between heavy breaths.

"Yeah?" Veronika tossed a piece of crust into the water; almost immediately, the water swirled and a fish plucked it away.

"I'm guessing you know that physiologically, all emotion is nothing but elevated autonomic nervous system activity—elevated heart rate, skin conductance, blood pressure?"

"Sure."

Lycan smiled, nodded. "So, emotion is just the label you place on that arousal. If someone is pissing you off, that beating heart is 'anger'; if you're giving a speech, it's 'terror'; if you're in a horse-drawn carriage with a beautiful woman, it's 'love.'"

Another rower came into view to their left. Veronika glanced at him; he looked like he was rowing for his life.

"I think rowing alleviates my anxiety because it provides a plausible explanation for my pounding heart and sweating palms. It tricks that primitive part of my brain where the fear is originating. It's not 'anxiety' I'm feeling; my heart is pounding because I'm 'exercising.'"

"Misattribution of the arousal. There's a tried-and-true method dating coaches use based on that principle: Get a couple on a roller coaster and get their hearts racing. Often they'll attribute their thumping hearts to physical attraction instead of fear." Veronika sat up, considering. "You've come up with a clever application of the theory."

"I find the key is that I have to hit a level of intensity in my exercise that matches the arousal my anxiety is creating, to fool the caveman in the back of my head."

Veronika chuckled at the analogy. To their left, the other man was rowing with all his might. He glanced back, pulled even harder.

"What's that about?" Veronika asked. She queried her system. Virtual boats appeared, along with a dozen lanes delineated by red strips perched a foot above the water. "Oh, he's racing." Evidently the other boats were in other bodies of water.

"Interesting," Lycan said, consulting his own system. "The program corrects for variations in wind conditions and water flow, so the racers are on even footing." They watched as the live rower finished third, then, huffing, slowly made his way toward shore, passing Lycan and Veronika.

"Excuse me," Veronika said as he passed, "can anyone participate?"

"You have to belong to the International Rowing Club,"

the guy said. He raised his eyebrows. "You want to race one-on-one? IP is always better, and I could use the extra work."

Veronika looked at Lycan, who was already shaking his head. "I'm not a racer."

"Oh, come on, it'll be fun. So he creams you, so what?" It was weird and wonderful, playing the role of the carpe-diem free spirit. Normally Veronika would be whining for them to go back to the coffee shop, that she was damp from the spray of the oar. "This is a perfect opportunity to get out of your comfort zone."

"I left my comfort zone when I stepped out of my apartment this morning," Lycan said.

Veronika reached over and sent a spray of water at Lycan.

"*Hey,*" he laughed. He swung one of the oars, shooting a veritable wave into the boat and over Veronika's lap. She leaped out of her seat, screeching from the cold, then leaned over the boat and splashed him a couple more times.

"How about it?" the rower called.

"Come on," Veronika goaded. "Let's race."

Lycan shrugged. "Okay, why not? Seize the day."

The rower, whose name was Russell, created two lanes and a countdown clock with his system. Lycan struggled to get their boat into the lane and relatively motionless as tiny waves nudged them. Russell used his oars to compensate for the waves, keeping his boat firmly in place. The clock hit zero.

With smooth, easy strokes, Russell pulled ahead almost immediately. But once Lycan got going, Russell didn't pull any farther away; he and Veronika hung on, about twenty feet back.

"Faster!" Veronika called. Laughing through gritted teeth, Lycan rowed faster. With each stroke, the front of the boat lifted slightly out of the water, then crashed back down onto the lake. They were moving, really moving, a stiff breeze whistling in Veronika's ears, her hair blown back in the cool blast. Veronika closed her eyes, laughed out loud. "Faster!"

She opened her eyes and looked at Lycan, who was looking right at her, grinning and grimacing simultaneously, pulling on the oars with all his might, seemingly oblivious to Russell, who was only a dozen or so feet ahead.

Veronika clapped her thighs. "*You're gaining on him.*"

Glancing at Russell over his shoulder, Lycan found another gear. His hands were a blur, his rowing smooth. Veronika saw Russell react, picking up his own tempo a notch, his forehead rippled with creases.

She'd always been a little skeptical of the evidence supporting technomie, had always suspected it was mostly trumped-up bologna created by people nostalgic for a simpler time, the same people who had once argued that picture books were wonderful for your child, but if the picture *moved*, it would rot her brain. How different was it, really, to talk to a screen instead of a live person? Wasn't a virtual landscape still a kind of landscape? But this—racing in a boat—might force her to rethink her position.

"How's that panic attack?" Veronika asked.

"*Gone*," Lycan shouted over the crashing of the oars.

They were a boat's length behind Russell. Ahead, Veronika could see the finish line—a blue line bisecting the spot where the lanes ended. "Another hundred meters. Give it all you've got—leave it all on the field."

They closed a few inches with each stroke as the finish line grew closer, closer…

Russell broke the virtual tape about four feet ahead of them, but Veronika whooped anyway. Lycan squeezed his eyes closed and laughed as their boat cruised along on momentum.

"Another twenty yards and you would have had me," Russell called, paddling alongside them. "Wow, you just don't tire."

Russell asked Lycan if he'd ever rowed competitively, invited him to join the rowing club, shot him a link.

"See?" Veronika said as Russell rowed off. "See?"

"Yes," Lycan said, smiling at Veronika, blinking away the sweat trickling down his brow. "I see."

Reading people was part of Veronika's job, and what she thought she read was that Lycan was developing a crush on her. That would do wonders for her shrunken, pathetic ego— for a genius to have a crush on her, but it also made her uneasy. It was possible she was feeling a slight reciprocal crush, but for some reason, whenever she tried to imagine herself holding Lycan's hand, or lying in bed with him, it felt wrong. Odd. Maybe because it felt like she was cheating on Nathan, and how neurotic was *that*? Chances were decent that Lycan would never move beyond harboring a secret crush, if that's what it was, so hopefully it would never be an issue.

47

Rob

The drone lowered another load of electronic crap into Rob's bin.

"Thank you, kind drone," Rob said. The drone wandered off, not equipped with a mouth. Or ears.

About twice a day, Rob decided to quit. When four a.m. had come the day after his meeting with Winter in Central Park, he'd found himself up and preparing for work. He'd just allowed his body to go through the motions out of habit, let his feet carry him to the reclamation center, let his hands pluck the color-coded electronic treats. He had no desire to touch his lute, less desire to reconnect with long-neglected friends, sipping beer, discussing the issues of the day.

The exception to his utter lack of interest in others' company was, for reasons he didn't fully understand, Veronika. He felt comforted by her. Maybe it was because she didn't mind that he was morose, often uncommunicative. She seemed at her best when faced with that kind of sadness, maybe because she lived it, pining for Nathan. If only Rob were in love with Veronika. But he wasn't.

He tossed the husk he'd just picked clean into the plastic chute and pulled his next victim toward him—one of those drone vacuums you see in old comedies, running over people's toes and bumping into shins.

Eventually he would get over Winter. Until then, best to stay busy, to be so tired at night he fell asleep before his mind could get working.

When his shift ended, he put one foot in front of the other until he was standing at his front door. He quietly let himself in.

His father was in the bedroom, speaking in low tones to Rob's "mom," telling her about his day, maybe updating her on the news. Dinner was on the stove, some sort of stew, stingy bits of meat on round socket bones. It was definitely not vat grown; something had screamed and bled so meat could make this relatively rare appearance at their table. Rob wasn't hungry, but he pulled a bowl from the dispenser and ladled in some stew. His dad had gone to the trouble of making it, some sort of animal had given its life, the least he could do was eat some.

"I didn't hear you come in." Dad got himself a bowl, filled it with stew, and sat across from Rob at the aluminum folding table. "How you doing?"

"Good, Dad. Good."

Dad ate noisily while Rob cast about for some innocuous topic of conversation to break the silence. His mind rebelled, unable to generate any topic except Winter.

"You're doing good, huh?" Dad said, eyeing him over his raised spoon.

Outside, a neighbor's dog barked hoarsely.

"No, Dad. Not good. Miserable. Wretched."

"Let me ask you something," Dad said through a mouthful of stew. He waved his fork at Rob. "If you'd met Winter at a bar—if she happened to be sitting in the seat next to you and you got talking—you really think you'd feel the same?"

Rob smiled sadly, the meat suddenly dry in his mouth. Lorne was suggesting it was their situation, not Winter herself, that caused the flame to be so hot. "I know I would."

"I just don't see that you have much in common." Lorne reached up and wiped the corners of his mouth with his fingers. "Penny and you had more in common, and you didn't even seem bothered when that ended."

"Yeah. If only we could control what we feel, and who we feel it for." Rob looked out the windows, at the tall yellow grass and the big mound of dirt in the backyard. He sighed, looked at Lorne. "Let me turn the question around. Would it have mattered how you met Mom? Wouldn't you have *known*, no matter what?"

Lorne set his spoon down. He loved to talk about the days when he was courting Rob's mom. "When I saw her for the first time, walking into town with her family, guiding an old broken-down four-legged drone that was carrying everything they could heap on it, it was like recognizing someone I already knew. It was like, 'Oh, there you are. Where've you been?'"

Rob laughed. "That's a nice way to put it. That's exactly how I feel. It's as if the universe made a mistake and forgot that we're *supposed* to be together." A lump grew in his throat. He tried to eat some stew to give it time to relax, but it was as if his chest and throat were clamped shut. It was so painful to think about Winter, yet she was all he could think about. No matter how he tried to wrestle his mind toward another topic, it fought its way back.

Lorne was staring out the window, his mouth set in a familiar tight line of grief. Rob had brought up his mom, now Lorne was off on his own loop of painful, useless thoughts.

"I know Mom felt the same about you. I think of you two and it gives me faith that two people can be in love their entire lives."

Lorne surprised Rob by responding with a dry, bitter laugh. "It's never that simple, except in stories."

"What do you mean?"

Lorne studied Rob for a moment, then folded his arms and leaned back in his chair. "Let me tell you a story about true love."

Lorne took a moment, evidently considering how best to begin. Rob couldn't imagine. "Let me tell you a story about true love?" The words sounded so strange coming from his father's lips. It just wasn't something he'd say. "Never turn away a customer," sure, or "We'll get along just fine." Not "Let me tell you a story about true love."

"Remember when you lent me that voice-analysis thing, where you could tell when someone was lying?" Lorne asked.

"Sure. Then almost immediately it became obsolete." A week after the lie-detector system app was released, someone came out with a tone-scrambling application, so whenever someone tried to use the vocal-stress application as a lie detector, the target's system scrambled their vocal tones. "What about it?"

Lorne stood, picked up his and Rob's bowls, and turned to the sink. "You let me borrow it to see whether Shorty Pepper was watering the fuel he was selling me, and it turned out he was." Spoons clinked as Lorne washed them in the bucket of water sitting in the sink, his back to Rob. "The problem was, I kept the damned thing running when I came back into the house." He shrugged. "Forgot I had it on."

Rob had no idea where this was going, but his father's distress in telling it was so obvious, Rob could barely breathe.

"Me and your mom talked for a minute about what I found out about Shorty and the fuel. Then I said, 'I love you' like I did fifty times a day, and she said she loved me too, like she always did, only—" He stopped messing in the sink, turned to face Rob, braced his hands on the countertop. "Only she was lying."

Rob shook his head emphatically. "No, Dad, you can't assume the readout was accurate. There are a hundred other possible explanations." Frantic, he tried to generate some, stammered for a moment before his brain kicked into gear. "Maybe something else was bothering her, and the stress came through in her voice when she answered."

Lorne shook his head. "The thing is, it was bothering me so much, I asked her about it, and she admitted it." Rob wanted to tell his father he didn't want to hear this, that most of the other pilings that kept his life steady had already torn loose, and he needed the few that remained. But it was clear Lorne needed to tell this, maybe more than Rob needed to believe his parents' love was true and perfect.

"She said she cared about me, but never felt that thump-thump that I feel for her." Lorne turned around, grabbed a towel off the rack. "We had a rough time for a while after that. Finally, she said she could only feel what she felt, and that it was enough for her. Always had been. And she hoped it was enough for me." Lorne cleared his throat, then cleared it again, violently, as if there was something barbed down in there. "In the end I decided it was. But it was a hard lesson."

Rob wasn't sure what to say. He looked down the hall, at the closed door to his parents' room. His parents' love for each other had always been something so tangible he could almost point to it, almost roll it around in his hand, feel how smooth and perfect it was.

"Why are you telling me this now?"

His dad considered. "We tried to keep things simple for you, but nothing's simple now. I thought you might as well know the truth. It's never as clear as it seems, no matter who you are. No matter who she is."

Lorne rose, disappeared down the hall for a moment, returned carrying Rob's lute. He handed Rob the lute. "You worked hard for your music. Harder than I've ever seen anyone work for anything. Now play, damn it. You can't have Winter, no matter how hard you work." He went into his bedroom, leaving Rob clutching his lute.

48

Veronika

I slimmed you down by twelve pounds, Veronika sent to her client, whose name was Harmonia. *Any more than that and men will know the clips are altered once you go IP.*

I have a state-of-the-art system, and I'm good with it. I'll make sure they see the skinnier me IP, Harmonia sent back.

For thirty years? And will you insist he wear his system during sex? You've got to think ahead.

Someone pinged her, and her hierarchy of hopefulness kicked in as she checked who it was. She'd only recently become aware that there was a clear hierarchy as to whom she hoped was pinging her. It was Rob, who was tied for second in her hierarchy.

She pinged back, and Rob opened a screen in her apartment. It was so much more convenient to be friends with Rob now that he had a system again.

"Where are you?" Veronika asked, while keeping up the consultation with her client.

"I'm just coming out of a Zen Buddhist service."

"Can I ask why?"

"That's what I wanted to talk to you about. Can we meet IP?"

"Pick a place," Veronika said.

She could barely see the priest from their seats, which were way up in the nosebleed section, two hundred feet above, and a hundred away, from the dais. They had the whole section to themselves, well out of earshot of other worshippers, even with the cathedral's outstanding acoustics.

"Can I trust you to keep this to yourself?" Rob asked.

"If that's a condition for hearing what this is all about, I have no choice but to say yes. I must know what's going on." Everyone knelt on the little cushions set on the floor. Rob and Veronika followed suit. "What is it about?" she added.

Rob shrugged, his head bowed. "It's about love."

For an instant, Veronika thought Rob might be about to profess his love for her, then realized how dumb that thought was. "Transfer a dollar to me."

Rob looked confused. "Why?"

"Because I'm a professional. Contract me to give you relationship advice and I'm obligated to keep it confidential."

Rob seemed amused by this, but he made the transfer. "So now it's official?" He took a deep breath, as if he was going to say something else, then stalled.

"Go ahead, spit it out. I've heard it all."

Rob smiled wanly. "You haven't heard this one."

Now she was curious. She waited patiently while Rob worked out what he wanted to say. "I'm here because I'm hoping I'll bump into Winter. She goes to a different religious service each week."

Veronika groaned. "How could I have missed it?" She was slipping—how had she not picked up on it sooner? All the pain Rob was going through when it looked like Winter was going to be buried. How ironic. How perfectly, achingly romantic. How utterly hopeless. "Does she know?"

They rose and returned to their seats along with the rest of the congregation.

"I think so. I told her I loved her, that day I thought I was seeing her for the last time."

"That might have tipped her off."

"She told me she can't ever see me again." He looked crestfallen.

Veronika reached out and rubbed his back for a second. "Shit, Rob, that's the saddest thing I've ever heard. Do you want my advice, or just a sympathetic ear?"

He looked at her, eyes like a wounded puppy. "I might as well hear your advice. I paid for it."

"Yes, you did." She folded her hands as if in prayer. "So here it is. Two thoughts. First, I think it's possible some of what you're feeling is situational. She was totally reliant on you, totally helpless. You were her knight in shining armor. It would be surprising if some transference and countertransference *hadn't* occurred."

Rob stared at the vaulted ceiling, arms folded. "I promise you, what I feel isn't because she needed me. And stop using words I have to look up to understand."

"Sorry. I'm not suggesting your feelings aren't real. I'm saying the situation magnified them."

"What's number two?"

"Hopefully this one will be worth the whole buck, right?" Veronika waited for a laugh, didn't get one. "This is a mess. There's nothing ahead for you but pain. Move on. Find someone else, even if you're not—" Veronika stopped, because Rob was squeezing his palms over his ears. "What?"

"Don't even suggest it. There's no way I could be with someone else."

"Rob, you don't have a choice. Things can't possibly work out, even if she feels the same as you. Do you even know if she does?"

"No. And I understand what you're saying—I know we can never be together. All I want is to be friends with her."

Organ music swelled, filling the church. Everyone rose for the second hymn.

"Being friends with her would just make you more miserable."

"Does being friends with Nathan make *you* miserable? Maybe you'd be happier if you cut off all contact with him?" Rob asked, his eyebrows raised.

"It's not the same."

"Why not?"

She struggled to answer, knowing it was different, but not able to pinpoint why. When the answer came, it startled her, because she hadn't fully realized it until that moment. "Because I don't really want to fall in love. Nathan is safe because he's unattainable."

"So is Winter," Rob countered. "If the best I can hope for is to be friends with her and love her in secret, I'll take it."

Rob had her. He'd run circles around her logic. Either he was right, and he was better off pursuing a hopeless half measure with Winter than being without her, or Veronika's friendship with Nathan was making her miserable. She could take her pick. It was a strange and terrifying thought, that her life would be better without Nathan in it. She was not sure she wanted to travel any farther down that road.

"But what can you do?" she asked. "Winter told you not to contact her. You don't want to become a creepy stalker, hanging out in places where, if you did bump into her, you'd struggle to explain what the hell you were doing there." She gestured emphatically at the cathedral surrounding them.

"No, I don't. I know. But I also don't want to never see her again. So where does that leave me?"

Rob was waiting for an answer, but Veronika didn't have one. It wasn't like she could contact Winter and try to intervene; she'd only met Winter a couple of times while she and Nathan were together. On top of that, Veronika was fairly sure Winter's decision to make a clean break from Rob was a wise one. Winter might well be the only emotionally healthy person in this whole situation. Veronika wished she could spend more time with her, maybe get her take on Veronika's situation with Nathan.

Then she remembered Winter had gone out with Nathan, and went running late at night to try to forget him when they broke up. Clearly, she'd had a thing for Nathan. Maybe she wasn't all that emotionally stable after all.

Veronika did feel a strong connection to her, though, after creating the profile that helped free her. Come to think of it, a lot of people had pitched in to help Winter, including Rob. A lot of people had contributed money to her cause in those frantic months. Everyone would probably enjoy a chance to bask in the success of their effort, to break bread with the prisoner they helped free. How could Winter say no to that?

The question was, wasn't it in Rob's best interest to allow Winter to keep her distance? What good would it do to get them together in a room?

Rob was watching her carefully, reacting to her facial

expressions with tilts of his head. Shit. She was overthinking things. It would make her friend happy.

Veronika smiled at Rob. "Here's what we're going to do: we're going to throw Winter a welcome-back-to-life party."

Rob tilted his head farther, as if he'd misheard her. "We're going to what?"

"We're going to throw her a party. Or actually, I'm going to throw it. You think she'd come?"

Rob thought about it. "I guess. I mean, how could she say no? She knows the part you played in saving her life."

The music rose to crescendo; people began to file out. Evidently the service was over. Rob and Veronika stood. "Do you want me to do this? I will if you want me to."

Without hesitation, Rob said, "Yes. I want you to do it."

"All right, then. I'll start sending out the invitations." A thrill went through her, imagining all of them there together.

As soon as they were outside, she pinged Nathan.

Nathan materialized via screen, followed an instant later by Lorelei.

"*Salud*," Nathan said. "What's the context?"

"I'm throwing a welcome-back party for Winter, and you're both invited."

Nathan's screen bobbed into the air. "Holy shit, what a great idea!" Veronika had no doubt that before the words were out of his mouth, he was already working his system, spreading the word to his friends before they heard it from someone else. Lorelei was probably following suit, though most of her friends would have heard themselves. Did Veronika detect a flicker of envy on Lorelei's perfectly symmetrical face? How badly did she wish this was her idea, so she could be the queen of the ball? *Too late, sweetie.*

49

Rob

Since the theme of the party was freedom, Veronika had decorated the space with blue sky and fluffy white clouds. All of the inner walls in her apartment were retracted, and to anyone with a system (which was everyone present) the perimeter of the apartment dropped off into empty sky.

Rob watched Winter from across the crowded room as she laughed with a crowd of well-wishers, who pressed around her, basking in the glow of the moment's celebrity.

A familiar-looking woman approached Rob, her hand out. "I guess I was wrong about you." Now Rob recognized her: Winter's friend, Idris. "I'm sorry I was so terribly mean to you."

"No, you had every right. I appreciate you providing me with Nathan's name. If I hadn't made that connection, Winter might still be in the minus eighty."

Smiling warmly, Idris thanked him and moved on. Across the room Winter spun, turned in the opposite direction from Rob as Veronika got her attention and introduced her to Lycan, who simultaneously shook her hand and sort of bowed, smiling his big shy smile. If there was ever a gentle giant, it was Lycan. Now that Rob had more time in his life, he wanted to get to know Lycan better. Veronika said he was probably the smartest person in the entire city, which was difficult to fathom.

It took all of his willpower to resist following Winter like a lost puppy as she mingled. He'd considered the possibility that his father and Veronika were right, that his feelings were the result of her total reliance on him while she was in the bridesicle place, and of his desperate guilt-driven desire to please her. When Rob tried peeling all of that away, all he found beneath it was a glowing certainty that he would be in love with her no matter how they'd met. And why was it so unlikely that you could meet your soul mate by hitting her with your vehicle? Why was it more likely you'd meet her at your cousin's wedding?

The door opened, and Lorelei made her entrance, surrounded by her hovering entourage, her arm draped in Nathan's. Rob could see Winter's smile tighten when she saw Nathan. He and Lorelei went right over to Winter, and she graciously shook their hands in turn. Lorelei put her hand on Winter's shoulder, whispered something in her ear. Winter nodded.

"Let me stand here so it's not so obvious you're staring." Veronika, holding a pink drink in a pouch, took up a position just to the right of his line of sight on Winter.

"It's too obvious?"

"You're standing all alone. Your face screams, 'I'm pining for that woman over there.' Yes, too obvious." She sipped her drink. "You don't have to talk to me." She waved the back of her fingers at him. "Just go on staring. Move your mouth once in a while so it looks like we're talking, in case she looks over."

Rob laughed, despite the weight lodged in his chest.

"Are you going to talk to her, after I went to all this trouble?" Veronika asked.

"I want to. I just don't know what to say."

"Want me to feed you lines?" Veronika asked, deadpan.

Nathan and Lorelei turned away. Winter looked right at Rob. Rob smiled, nodded a greeting, his heart pounding.

"Did you just nod at her? Is she looking this way? I don't want to turn around; it would be too obvious."

"Yeah, we just said hello."

Winter put her head down and made her way toward him. "She's coming over." His heart thumped slow and hard against his chest as she crossed the room.

"Hi, Rob." Winter turned to Veronika, squeezed her forearm. "Thank you again for doing this; it's an incredibly kind gesture. I'm truly touched."

Veronika patted Winter's elbow. "It's nothing." She pointed across the room. "I need to go talk to Eric. Excuse me."

And suddenly they were alone.

"So, how are you?" Winter asked.

"Pretty good. Working. Playing my lute. Working on my defensive-driving skills."

Winter burst out laughing, went on laughing perhaps a bit too long, and then fell silent.

"Listen," Rob said, "I think I gave you the wrong impression the last time we were together. The *only* expectation I had was that we might stay friends. There's nothing more to it." It was a lie that came easily, because Rob would never ask for more. What he felt inside was irrelevant.

Winter looked out at the faux-blue sky, the clouds drifting by. She sighed heavily, looked at Rob. "Do you want to take a walk?"

"Absolutely."

They headed for the door, which was the only break in the cloud-festooned illusion.

Outside, Winter turned left. Rob was barely aware of the vehicles whirring by, the people. So much of his attention was focused on Winter, right there beside him, a vague half smile on her lips.

She glanced down at her pistachio-and-white High Town shoes, gliding on the pavement. "I'm not sure I'll ever get used to these shoes."

"I know." He didn't want to talk about shoes; he doubted they were going to get much time alone before Winter felt she had to return to the party.

At the corner of Chan, they turned left.

"Remember early on, when you asked if I had any visitors besides you, and I said I did, but I never got to be myself with them?" Winter asked.

Rob nodded. He remembered pretty much every word either of them spoke during those visits. Not that there had been many.

"I wasn't being myself with you at first, either," Winter said. "I hated you at first, but I couldn't say it because I was afraid if I did, you wouldn't come back. And I resented having to rely on you—on *you*, the person who killed me." She looked toward the sky, clearly trying to keep powerful emotions in check. "I tried to stay angry, but little by little, it became so painfully obvious you were a good person who had made one incredibly stupid mistake." She was walking quickly, so quickly Rob had to make an effort to keep up.

"No, not a good person, you're a fucking saint. When you came to visit, the *pain* you felt was all over your face." Winter wiped her nose with the back of her hand. Rob pulled a tissue from his pocket and offered it to her. Winter laughed as she accepted it. "See? How could anyone hate you?"

"You have every right to hate me." Rob wasn't sure where Winter was going with this, but he suspected she was letting him down gently, again.

To Rob's surprise, Winter led him onto the elevator to Low Town. They rode in silence, admiring the lights below. There were millions of lights in the city; they grew fewer and fewer stretching toward the horizons.

"Where are we going?" Rob asked.

Winter gave him a hooded glance. "You'll see."

They stepped out into Jefferson Park, along the Harlem River. Winter pointed toward a black six-sided tower set beside the river, a few hundred yards away. "That way." She picked up her pace again, their shoes clicking on the pavement now, no longer gliding.

"I didn't realize you had a destination in mind."

"I didn't either, until we started walking."

The tower turned out to be a forty-story mausoleum. They entered a wide, arched doorway to the hollow center. Winter led him onto the elevator.

"Twenty-two," she said. The elevator shot up, intensifying the butterflies in Rob's stomach.

On the twenty-second-floor landing, Winter led him through a short tunnel, out to the railed catwalk overlooking the river. Instead of admiring the view, she turned toward the wall, which was divided into rows and rows of brass plates, marking the cremated remains set inside the honeycomb of spaces that comprised this vertical graveyard. It reminded Rob of the bridesicle place in miniature.

"There." Winter pointed at a plate about eight feet up the wall, which was illuminated by the lights of Low Town, reflecting off the river. It read WINTER WEST, 2103–2133. "My friends chipped in and bought it before Cryomed swooped in."

Rob stared at her name. How close she'd been to being ashes in a wall. "That must be chilling, seeing your name there."

Winter laughed. "I spent two years dead in a box, with only my face working." She raised her eyebrows. "You want a chill? That'll give you a chill."

Rob nodded, but Winter had already turned back to look at the plaque, so she probably didn't see.

"You know, the first time you came to visit, you were twenty-five, and I was thirty." Winter smiled, as if reminiscing about a fond memory. "Now you're, what, twenty-seven?"

"Almost twenty-eight."

"And I'm still thirty." She turned toward the river, took a deep breath of the cool air. Her sleeves were flapping in a mild breeze. "I know I can trust you when you say you only want to be friends. You're a fucking saint, after all. You would never go back on your word, you would never manipulate me." Still gazing out at the water, set in the shadow of High Town, she closed her eyes. "The problem is, I'm not a saint." She opened her eyes, looked at Rob. "I can't be just friends with you, and"—she shrugged—"I can't be more. Do you understand what I'm saying?"

A lump filled Rob's throat. He nodded, lifted her hand from the railing, held it in both of his.

She studied their hands for a moment, then gently shifted hers. He loosened his fingers to let her withdraw it, but she surprised him by lacing her fingers between his and closed her hand.

It was cool. It fit perfectly in his.

"There were so many times when you came to visit that I wanted you to hold my hand," she said. "Then you finally did."

"I reached out to take your hand one other time, then remembered they'd kick me out if I did it."

She tilted her head. "When was that?"

"The third or fourth visit. The last few seconds were ticking down, and you were so scared. You said you didn't think you'd ever get used to dying."

"I remember that. I didn't see you reaching. One's field of vision is so limited—it was always the same circle, mostly of the ceiling and someone's face." She squeezed Rob's hand. The pressure sent a thrill through him. "Except for the day you brought the mirror. You have no idea what that meant to me. Not just getting to see the sky, but the kindness of that act." She blinked back more tears. "It made me feel I had someone on my side. I wasn't all alone in that box. It's horrible, being in that place. You can't imagine."

Rob was so aware of her hand in his. He wanted to wrap his arms around her, to pull her close and kiss her and tell her he'd always be there for her. She was right there, so close, so alive, her bright eyes on him.

Her face moved closer, and for a moment he thought it was a trick of the light. Then her lips touched his—lightly, not much more than a soft brush—and for an instant, everything was perfect, the world was perfect.

Winter pulled away, looked at her hands. "I shouldn't have done that."

"I'm glad you did. Even if it never happens again."

Winter pressed her fist to her mouth, her face twisting. Again, Rob resisted a screaming urge to hold her in his arms. He was afraid he might scare her away.

"I get lost in these fantasies, of how things might have turned out if we'd met under different circumstances," Winter said.

"Tell me."

She looked down, toward the sidewalk that ran along the river, lined with benches.

"I was heading for that park when you hit me. I was planning to sit on one of the benches down there and stare at the river. If you'd parked your Scamp, instead of running me over with it, and come here too, you might have ended up on the next bench over."

"I used to come here all the time. I can see myself coming here on that particular day."

Winter looked at him. "Where *were* you going? I never asked."

Rob shrugged. "No idea. Just getting away from Lorelei. Maybe I was coming here. Go on."

Winter pressed a finger along the bridge of her nose. "I'd be sitting there"—she pointed to one of the benches—"and you'd sit down. There." She pointed to the next bench over. "You notice my puffy red eyes and say something like, 'Let me guess, you broke up with someone too?' "

"And you look at me, and see my eyes are red, too, and you laugh, and say, 'Of course. Isn't this where the support group for people who just got dumped meets?' "

Winter pulled a tissue from her pocket, blew her nose. "You say, 'If it would help to tell someone about it, I'd be happy to listen. I could use the distraction, actually.' I invite you to join me on my bench, and we trade stories. You tell me I was too good for Nathan. I ask what you were doing with a narcissistic giantess in the first place. Before we know it, it's getting dark. You ask if I'm hungry, and I am, which surprises me."

"I suggest Luigi's. Comfort food."

Winter threw a hand in the air; her tissue fluttered in the breeze. "See, and I *love* Italian. I've eaten at Luigi's at least fifty times."

Rob laughed. "I wonder if we ever ate there at the same time. Maybe you were at the next table."

"Why didn't you come up and talk to me?" Winter whispered.

They watched a squirrel, out late, digging at the ground beside the jogging trail. A screen cruised by.

Rob's head was spinning, with love, with joy, with grief. She loved him, too. That made it so much better. So much worse. "What happens then?" Rob asked.

"I'm in a T-shirt and sweaty from my run—"

"Good point," Rob said. "Luigi's isn't *that* casual."

"So we arrange to meet at Luigi's in an hour, and we eat a shitload of ziti and drink a bottle of wine. Then you walk me home. We're both suddenly, miraculously over our break-ups, wondering why we'd been so miserable in the first place, because we realize Nathan and Lorelei were just dim shadows, compared to the people we're with now, standing at the walk-up to my apartment building. But neither of us says that out loud, because we've just met."

"I ask if you want to go for a run tomorrow—"

"And I tell you I'll meet you by our support-group bench at four."

"And I can barely sleep, because I'm already falling in love with you." As soon as the words were out, Rob knew he'd made a mistake.

Winter went on staring at the bench. A boat somewhere out of sight on the river sounded a deep, belching, mournful whistle that was the perfect punctuation to this painful silence.

"I'm sorry. I didn't mean to make you uncomfortable," Rob said.

Suddenly Winter looked tired, defeated. "I think we've let ourselves get into dangerous territory." She lifted her head and looked at him, her eyes achingly beautiful. "I should have told Veronika I couldn't make it, but I wanted to see you again. It was a stupid, impulsive thing to do."

"Veronika and I came up with the whole party idea so I could see you again without looking like a stalker."

Winter threw back her head and laughed. "Seriously. And here I was thinking you're incapable of guile."

Rob shrugged. "I was desperate. I couldn't eat, couldn't sleep."

Winter studied Rob's face, maybe looking for signs he was kidding. "I should not have come. We have to say good-bye, before we get ourselves into serious, serious trouble."

"Can't we just—"

He was going to say, "...be friends," but Winter was shaking her head.

Her voice was low, trembling. "Rob, don't." She leaned toward him, kissed his cheek tenderly, and stood. "Good-bye."

Numb, he watched her disappear through the tunnel. A

moment later she was on the sidewalk below, heading back the way they'd come. As she disappeared behind a copse of trees, he saw her lift the tissue to wipe away tears.

There was nowhere to go, nothing to do but stand there. It seemed impossible that Winter had been standing right beside him just now. Already, it seemed impossible she had ever been that close, had ever brushed her lips against his. Rob kept very still, as if by doing so he could put off the anguish that would soon wash over his numb shock.

An old man passed below, walking a black German shepherd. The man was wearing a leg boost that squealed every time it straightened.

Rob looked off at the spot where Winter had been when he last glimpsed her, willing that she be there again, heading toward him. But she wasn't. He would never see her again, he knew that with a cold certainty.

What was he going to do now?

He pinged Veronika, sending a single word of text. *Help.*

Veronika appeared in-screen in a matter of seconds. "Oh, sweetie." She pulled in to get a closer look at him. "You look absolutely crushed. I wish I could give you a hug. Tell me what happened."

Rob told her, and as the numbness wore off, it was replaced by pain so acute it felt like he'd been slashed by a blade.

50

Veronika

"I don't get it. It's nothing but an empty room," Lycan said, looking all around for the exhibit.

Veronika suspended the art-exhibit feed on her system, looked around the exhibit hall. It was the exact same room. She reactivated the feed, looked around again.

"Is the feed broken?" Lycan asked.

"I'm guessing no. I think the artist is making a point about the relationship between art and reality." Veronika tried to call up the artist's statement, but the artist's statement read, in its entirety, "Artist's Statement."

Lorelei pinged Veronika.

Can't talk, busy, Veronika subvocalized.

"How profound," Lycan said. He was getting better at sarcasm. Veronika mused that he must be spending too much time with her.

This can't wait, Lorelei sent.

Later. I'll contact you asap, Veronika sent.

Lorelei materialized via screen, an entourage of at least two thousand screens squeezed behind her. "Bonjour, Lycan. Vee, we need to talk."

"I told you, I'll contact you as soon as I'm done here. Some privacy, please?" She was the rudest woman Veronika had ever met, a complete and utter narcissist.

"Go ahead," Lycan said, waving. "I'll be fine."

"No, she'll be fine."

"Kilo is dead," Lorelei said. "As in, Do Not Revive. Not coming back. And do you know who's getting all of his money?"

Veronika froze. "It's not Sunali, is it?"

"Bull's-eye. *Not* Sunali."

"Kilo told her she wasn't getting anything."

"Yes, he did," Lorelei said. "And he kept his word. Do you want to know who he left every last dollar to?"

"I'm guessing it wasn't you," Veronika said, "or you'd sound more excited and less bitter."

"Bridesicle Watch." Lorelei injected each syllable full to bursting with disdain. "Sunali's fucking *charity*. Save the fucking bridesicles."

"*What?*" Veronika and Lycan shouted in unison.

"Sunali can't touch a dime," Lorelei said. "It's all in trust to the charity."

"Why would he do that?" Lycan asked.

"He didn't say," Lorelei said.

"Because he felt shitty for leaving Sunali in the minus eighty all that time," Veronika said. "This is his repressed way of saying he's sorry, that he was wrong."

Lorelei guffawed dryly. "Right. More likely he did it to torment us, leaving all that money just out of our reach."

Veronika was reminded of something Kilo had said, the time she'd been at his deathbed. She burst out laughing.

"What's so funny?" Lorelei asked.

" 'I'm giving it all to my favorite charity.' "

"What?" Lorelei asked.

"That's what Kilo said to Sunali. Don't you remember?"

"No," Lorelei said.

"This is good," Veronika said. "You're part of that charity. *Holy shit*, you could pull off any protest you dream up." Veronika didn't want to come right out and mention Lorelei's idea—the march of the ten thousand bridesicles—in front of a thousand witnesses. If Sunali actually tried it (and now she had the money to do so), Veronika didn't want to be hit with complicity fines.

Lorelei waved impatiently. "I guess." She turned, looked up. "None of this is why I really pinged you, though. I came to tell you I'll no longer be needing your services."

Veronika tried not to show how stunned she was, but she knew it was written all over her face. Lorelei had just outed her, in front of a crowd, and she'd done it via screen.

"What services?" Lycan asked.

"Ask Veronika," Lorelei said, and vanished.

"What services?" Lycan repeated.

Several hundred of Lorelei's viewers stayed behind to watch.

"Wait. Give me a second." Veronika tried to sort out what had just happened. Parsons must have decided it was time to shake things up. She thought she'd made herself too valuable for Parsons to throw her under the bus, but evidently she'd miscalculated. Maybe Parsons saw her as a threat; he might be afraid Lorelei would begin to rely more on her than on him. So it was time to out Veronika in dramatic fashion.

Then, for an encore, they would tell Nathan.

"Shit." She opened a screen on Nathan. He was blocked—in

the bathroom of Stain's Coffee Shop. She turned to Lycan, blurted, "I have to go, I'm really sorry, I'll explain later," and took off toward the exit.

She headed toward the micro-T station, running as fast as she could, because having this conversation via screen would be very wrong. Come to think of it, Lorelei might be rude enough to fire Veronika via screen instead of IP, but she wouldn't tell Nathan that Veronika had been coaching her via screen. She had to wait until she could see Nathan in person. Which meant Veronika needed to get to the coffee shop first. As she ran, Lorelei's spin-off viewers were drifting effortlessly beside her. Her life was suddenly a spin-off of Lorelei's—what a revolting prospect.

By the time she reached the micro-T station, she could barely breathe. Wouldn't it be ironic if a second woman Nathan knew died while running?

She was almost to Stain's when Nathan finally unblocked. She set a baffle to keep Lorelei's followers from tracking her, then popped open a screen as Nathan exited the loo.

"Hey, I'm on my way to see you. Meet me halfway?"

Nathan seemed amused by her breathless condition. "No prob. Toward the micro-T station?"

"Right."

"What's going on? Why are you out of breath?"

"I'll tell you when I see you."

Screens began popping up around Nathan—Lorelei's viewers, guessing correctly that Veronika would go straight to Nathan. Still no sign of Lorelei, though.

Huffing hard, Veronika spotted Nathan up ahead, half a block from the coffee shop. "Is your vehicle around?" It was the closest location where they could escape Lorelei's spin-off viewers.

Nathan nodded, gestured down Thirty-Fifth Street.

Still no sign of Lorelei. Maybe Lorelei was intentionally letting Veronika speak to Nathan first, to build tension in her grand performance.

"So what was important enough to get you to sprint? You know, you're pretty quick."

"I'm quick. Yes, thank you. That's exactly what I am." Nathan's Chameleon opened and Veronika slid into the passenger seat. "Put up a block?" Nathan shrugged; the screens that had followed them right into the vehicle vanished.

"So here's the thing," Veronika began, as soon as they were alone. She was still out of breath, and the topic of conversation was doing nothing to calm her elevated heart rate. She took a deep breath, let it out. "Lorelei has been employing me as a coach on your face-to-faces with her."

Nathan laughed. "That'd be the day. As if she needs a coach."

"Nathan"—Veronika moved her face close to his—"I'm not joking. A lot of the things Lorelei said were lines I fed her."

Nathan tilted his head slightly, as if trying to hear her better.

"I'm surprised you didn't recognize my rapier wit."

"You're serious?" He laughed, but stiffly.

"Deadly serious. She asked me to do it, and I had reservations, but in the end, I didn't see the harm, and she was willing to pay well."

"She was willing to pay well," Nathan parroted. He bit his thumbnail, thinking. "It didn't occur to you that it might make me look pretty foolish, a dating coach out with someone who was making heavy use of a dating coach?" Nathan gestured at the screens hovering outside the one-way glass. "With a couple thousand people watching?"

"You know Lorelei did it just to ramp up the drama. That's the price you pay for going out with a screen whore."

"You could have said no. Evidently you don't mind the drama all that much, either." His tone was controlled, but he was angry. Veronika couldn't remember ever seeing Nathan angry.

"She already has a full-time coach, so it wouldn't have changed anything if I said no."

Nathan blinked in surprise, waited for her to elaborate.

She'd been anticipating this moment, she realized; she knew it would come eventually, and in her fantasy it had played out just like in *Cyrano de Bergerac*. Nathan would recognize that it was the person who'd spoken the words that he loved, not the vapid package parroting them.

Veronika propped one foot on the dashboard. "Maybe I'm just tired of playing the role of the buddy. I thought it would be nice to play a different role, even from behind the scenes."

Nathan sighed, rubbed the dark stubble on his cheek. "If you're suggesting I've been playing with your emotions, I don't think that's fair. I've always been up-front with you. I've never messed with your head."

"Yes, you have."

The sun was low in the sky, casting a blinding circle of reflection on each vehicle parked along the street. The shadows of pedestrians stretched almost to the end of the block as they glided along.

In the distance, a long, lithe figure stepped out from a side street and headed in their direction, thronged by thousands of screens. "Oh, Christ." Heads turned to watch this incredibly tall, incredibly popular woman. Who was she? She must be famous. Of course she was. If you had that many screens following you, you were de facto famous. And Lorelei knew it; she moved with the easy, confident grace of someone who was no longer striving to be famous, but simply was.

"Here she comes."

"Here she comes," Nathan agreed.

"Are you going to storm out of the car and confront her for making you look foolish, a dating coach going out with someone using not one but two dating coaches?" Veronika knew the answer, but wanted to make him say it.

"No."

"Why not?"

"Because I love her, and if I want to be in her life, I have to accept her lifestyle."

It hurt to hear him say it. He barely knew her; how could he love her? "Those sound like her words, not yours."

What was this scene to be, Veronika wondered? Maybe Lorelei would claim the whole thing was Veronika's idea? That seemed fairly pedestrian, unworthy of the (Veronika ran a count of the screens congregating outside) thirty-seven thousand six hundred forty-four people taking time away from their own pathetic lives to watch Lorelei live hers. What would Veronika recommend, if she were still on the inside? She'd go with a tearful apology. *Nathan, love, I was so afraid you wouldn't like me for me, so I asked someone who knows you well to help me.*

"Wow, that's a lot of screens," Nathan said.

"Yup. And it's showtime." Veronika opened her door and stepped out. A real, live crowd of people had formed on the sidewalk, drawn by all the screens. They were leaning this way and that, trying to see what was going on.

When Nathan stepped out to meet Lorelei, the look of bright-eyed love on his face devastated Veronika. He and Lorelei embraced on the sidewalk, Lorelei turning her head as she squeezed him tight. With traffic whooshing by, and the live crowd muttering, Veronika couldn't hear Nathan when he spoke. Sighing in frustration, she opened a screen among Lorelei's fans rather than sidle over and appear nosy.

"—had me fooled," Nathan was saying.

"Well, I didn't mean to fool you," Lorelei replied. "I didn't employ her as a coach in the traditional sense. She served as kind of an adjunct—advising and arranging more than guiding."

Oh, what complete bullshit. And, irony on top of irony, they weren't her own words—Parsons was obviously feeding them to her.

"Hey, modern life," Nathan said, shrugging. He looked around. "Do you want to grab a bite? Maybe we could invite Vee."

Lorelei canted her head, smiling sort of wanly. "The thing is, Nathan, I fired Veronika partly because I don't think things are working out between us. I'm just not feeling it, you know?"

A dozen conflicting emotions coursed through Veronika as Nathan reacted, his mouth tightening into an involuntary grimace. Lorelei put a hand on Nathan's shoulder. "I'm sorry."

"No," Nathan said. "That's fine. Sure."

Joy. Anger. Relief. Sympathy. Veronika had never felt so conflicted. Break up with him—Veronika hadn't considered that one, maybe because she couldn't imagine breaking up with Nathan. But, yes, that would ramp up the drama.

Lorelei gave Nathan a big, fat consolation hug, still sporting that sympathetic-yet-smug half smile.

Anger. Veronika decided it was definitely mostly anger she was feeling. Well, shit, if Lorelei wanted drama, Veronika would give her some drama.

"Do you even know what 'adjunct' means?" Veronika asked, sauntering over.

"I'm sorry?" Lorelei said.

"You told Nathan you were employing me as a sort of adjunct, and I'm wondering if you know what it means, or if you simply parrot the exact words Parsons feeds you, with no idea what you're saying."

Lorelei rolled her eyes, just like the mean girls in high school used to. "You think you know me. You think you know why I live a public life. Why I went out with Nathan. Why I'm breaking up with him." Her fingers flew for a few seconds— a graceful, lightning-quick flourish of systemwork Veronika was certain was for her benefit. "I may not be as transparent as you think."

Veronika folded her arms. "I'll tell you what I think. I think Parsons just fed that entire speech to you. I bet he fed you this line as well..." She worked her system, painfully aware of her own lack of grace and style, until she located the recording she wanted—from the argument she'd had with Lorelei the first time they'd met—and enlarged it so everyone could see and hear Lorelei self-righteously proclaim, *"And just for the record, all of my lines are my own material."*

No one reacted. No one seemed to care that Lorelei had lied through her teeth, to all of them.

"Who's Parsons?" Nathan asked.

"Parsons is her other coach. Excuse me—her *director*. He feeds her every syllable that comes out of her smarmy little mouth." Veronika made a show of looking around. "Maybe he's in the crowd right now." She worked her system, enlarged a picture of him in the air. "Here he is. Has anyone seen this man?"

"Well, that's the thing," Lorelei said. "I was going to explain, but you didn't give me a chance."

"Oh, you were going to explain?" Veronika folded her arms. "Why don't you explain?"

She turned to Nathan. "I have been working with an adviser. Again, not a coach in the traditional sense, but someone to help me navigate the complexities of living a public life, and…I've fallen in love with him." She turned toward the crowd. Parsons stepped out, head down, hands in pockets. His grand entrance.

Veronika turned her face to the sky.

51

Veronika

Veronika retrieved a pebble by her feet. She leaned far over the railing so she could see the choppy water far below, centered the pebble just below her face, and let it drop.

It seemed a long, long time before it made a tiny splash.

Turning away from the water, she leaned against the railing, closed her eyes, listened to vehicles whoosh by. She never thought she'd come back to this spot, but since Lycan was alive and well, it still felt like her sanctuary—a place to reflect, more than a place of tragedy.

Veronika had prayed for Lorelei and Nathan to split, but now that they had, she didn't feel the elation she'd anticipated. She felt angry, and sad for Nathan, who was taking it much worse than Veronika would have guessed. Mostly, though, she felt petty and frustrated that she cared so much about all of this, that her life revolved around petty crap.

This was not the life she wanted to lead, but somehow she couldn't pull herself out of it and lead a life of consequence.

A life like Sunali's. Veronika didn't care much for Sunali's abrasiveness, but she admired Sunali's guts. She respected Sunali, who lived for something larger than herself. You could psychoanalyze her motives—she was clearly driven by a profound rage at being abandoned by her son in the bridesicle center—but her actions were pure, and honest, and worthy of respect. And now she had the resources to do even more. No more meetings in her living room. Learning about the contents of Kilo's will was the important event from yesterday, not Lorelei's childish antics.

Ironically, Sunali could now execute Lorelei's idea of unleashing ten thousand bridesicles on the city if she chose to, although Lorelei herself seemed to have lost interest in Bridesicle Watch. Maybe Veronika should continue volunteering, although she doubted Sunali would offer her a seat at the strategy meetings now that the group was well funded enough to attract seasoned professional protesters. Still, there was no shame in serving in the trenches for a cause you believed in. And she most surely believed in this cause. Seeing what Winter had gone through, and continued to go through, talking to Winter at the party about what it had been like to be in that crèche...it had moved Veronika deeply. If only everyone could speak to Winter. If only everyone could feel what Winter had felt.

Veronika's eyes snapped open. She spun back toward the river, clutched the railing, her mind suddenly racing.

If only everyone could feel what Winter had felt.

"Oh," she said aloud. "Oh, that would be incredible."

Was it possible, though?

She pinged Lycan. He popped up in a screen almost instantaneously.

"Your new technology...is it far enough along to be used now, if it's for a good cause?"

52

Mira

Mira was glad when she saw it was Sunali again. Then again, who else would it be? No men were going to visit the oldest woman in the place. She was both twenty-six and one of the oldest people on Earth. It was hard to reconcile.

Maybe Sunali would be willing to wake Jeannette again. She wondered if there was any way Sunali could arrange it so they could speak directly. The possibility filled her with such intense longing she almost blurted it out. Better to wait for the right moment.

"It's good to see you again. I would have fixed the place up if I knew I was going to have a visitor."

Sunali smiled. "It's good to see you, too, Mira. I think about you."

It was comforting, to know there was someone out there who knew she was in here.

Sunali started to say something, then caught herself, rolled her eyes. "I have to keep checking myself, to avoid falling back on phrases that are nonsensical in here. Like, 'I won't take up much of your time.' So let me just tell you why I'm here. I could use your help again."

"I'll do anything I can."

"I was hoping you'd say that." It was hard to believe Sunali had once been like her. She was so fully, vitally alive. "What I need is simple, really. I just want you to imagine you're talking to everyone in this city. Pretend they're all listening to you right now. What do you want to say to them?"

"What do I want to say to them?" Mira repeated, because she couldn't think what else to say.

"That's right. Take all the time you need."

Mira almost asked Sunali if she could take a year. If she did take a year, would she age a year? She doubted it. The dead don't age.

What did she want to say to the people out there? That she missed splitting a Peterman's Double Chocolate Stout with Jeannette at the Green Leaf, and playing keep-away with Gordon, their slate-blue borzoi, in Crotona Park. That she missed bickering with Jeannette about who did more of the housework, missed seeing her wander past in a baseball cap and antique PF Flyer sneakers. She would give anything for five minutes with Jeannette. Just five minutes, and after that they could lock her away in this freezer for eternity. She would take that deal, if someone offered it. But no one was offering deals.

She looked at Sunali and said, "Please help me. Please, I'm afraid. I'm so lonely and afraid. I don't want to be in this box anymore. Can't you please get me out of here?"

Sunali fiddled with something beneath the midnight-blue blazer she was wearing. She was beaming. "That's perfect. Absolutely perfect." She stood. "Mira, I can't thank you enough."

It took Mira a moment to understand. Sunali hadn't realized Mira was talking to her.

Sunali reached toward Mira, closed her hand around the air over the space where Mira's hand must be. "This is going to help us more than you know. I can't say how, but I'll come back and tell you...after." She raised her eyebrows. It reminded Mira of the way that first man who woke her—Alex—had raised his eyebrows. "I'd better go."

She wanted to ask Sunali if she could talk to Jeannette, but was suddenly afraid. Sunali had promised to come back, and she was Mira's only hope of being waked again. If she asked too much, Sunali might not return.

"All right," Mira said. Though it was far from all right.

53

Rob

Walking the streets of Low Town, past the pizza joints and dream parlors, everything reminded him of Winter. It was as if they'd walked these streets together a thousand times, and each corner, each stingy strip of green lined with benches, was stamped with a memory they shared. Maybe it felt that way because Rob found himself having silent conversations with an imaginary Winter as he wandered, his lute case dangling from his left hand. He kept thinking of things he wanted to tell her, funny stories he wanted to share. He wanted to revel in his newfound freedom, wanted to feel happy for Winter, but all he could do was brood.

Crossing the gray steps in front of the Museum of Natural History, he found himself wishing things were back the way they'd been, with Winter in her crèche, the two of them packing so much into five-minute conversations. It was a sick thought. He needed to get out of his head.

Maybe a change of scenery would give him a new mind-set. It was time he moved back to the city. He could probably rent a cube in a marginal neighborhood for two thousand a month. His dad probably preferred he keep living at home (though he'd never say that out loud), but Rob was twenty-seven. He belonged on his own.

Rob crossed into the park, past banks of sunlamps set on enormous T-shaped posts that kept the foliage alive in the shade cast by High Town. He picked a bench set across from a fountain that reminded him of the fountain inside Cryomed, even though they looked nothing alike, took out his lute and began to play.

It was impossible to make the lute play what he felt. It was not a sad instrument; its sound was inherently cheery. Which was probably why Rob had been drawn to it in the first place. He tried playing songs with sad, forlorn lyrics, at least, tried unsuccessfully to pour every drop of his heart and mind into them, so there was nothing left to devote to Winter.

When that didn't work, he decided to compose a song for Winter. He tried to capture her staccato laughter, the way she scrunched her lips to one side when she was thinking, her slightly knock-kneed walk, the flecks of gold in her eyes.

There was a woman across the lawn, heading toward Rob. Rob squinted, trying to make her out. She was bent forward, moving stiffly, clearly in distress.

Rob dropped his lute. "Hang on." He ran to help her.

As he drew closer, it became clear that something was very wrong with her. Her face was bone white, her lips midnight blue. She reminded Rob of Winter, dead and frozen in her crèche.

"Please, help me," the woman said as Rob drew closer. "Please, I'm afraid." There was so much need in her voice, such aching desperation.

Rob reached out to help her, but his hand passed through her arm as if it was so much smoke...

Suddenly he was terrified, and felt utter, bleak despair like he'd never known. She had no hope; she would be dead again in just a few seconds, and she knew it. She was trapped in a coffin, her living face attached to a corpse. Rob sank to his knees, sobbing. It was intolerable.

And then it passed, and Rob was all right.

"I'm so lonely and afraid," the projection said, panting with fear. "I don't want to be in this box anymore."

Rob stepped back, examined the image—a screen without the screen. Someone was going to get a hefty fine.

"Please, help me..."

Rob turned toward the voice—it was the same voice, but coming from behind, and farther away.

Outside the park, on the sidewalk across from the museum, the same projection was telling a woman she was afraid, so lonely and afraid. The woman was covering her face with her hands, muffling a wail of despair. On the steps of the museum, two more projections climbed the stairs toward people coming out. Rob couldn't hear them, but knew they were asking for help because they were lonely and afraid and didn't want to be in a box anymore.

As soon as they were finished begging for help, each of the women moved on, toward another person.

Rob laughed out loud. The explanation was suddenly so obvious. It had to be Sunali. How was she generating those terrible emotions, though? Rob had never felt anything like it; they had felt so utterly, horribly real.

Rob ran back to the bench to retrieve his lute, then hurried toward the streets, wanting to see it unfold.

Movement caught his eye: a body, falling from High Town,

plunging toward the roofs of Low Town, arms spread, loose dress flapping wildly. His breath caught for an instant before he realized it was another projection of the bridesicle.

He spotted another, falling toward the river. Then another.

Out on the street, traffic was at a standstill, drivers standing beside open doors, staring at the falling bodies, at the ghostly white women limping painfully from person to person, begging for help.

"Brilliant," Rob said under his breath.

He probably should see if there was anyone who needed help, but instead he returned to his bench to finish composing the song for Winter—not just about Winter, but for Winter—as the bodies rained down from High Town.

When he finished, he played it through, flawlessly, as if he'd been playing it for years. He sent an audio recording of the performance to Winter, with a simple text message: *I wrote this for you.*

54

Veronika

"I think we're on the cusp of a new age, of awesome changes." There was a drop of foam on the end of Lycan's nose.

Veronika swept at it with a napkin. "Yet you jumped off a bridge. When I hear you talk about your work, so excited...I don't know, there's such a disconnect."

"Work and life are different things. If I could work all the time, I'd be happy all the time."

"Then why don't you?"

Lycan thought about it. "I don't know. It gets lonely."

Veronika barked a laugh. "What you need is a wife. *Then* you could work all the time, comforted by the knowledge that you have a neglected wife at home."

Lycan didn't laugh. "If I had a wife, she would always come first."

He was such an earnest soul. He and Rob were similar in that way—incapable of sarcasm, unable to laugh at others. The complete opposite of Nathan. And her.

Lycan cleared his throat, which he seemed to do almost incessantly when he was nervous. "By the way, assuming everything goes well, do you want to do something to celebrate? Maybe a celebration dinner at my place?"

"Sure, that sounds great." Veronika looked around for Nathan. He'd sent a message nine minutes ago saying he'd be there in five or six.

Lycan checked the time. "It won't be long now." He stuck his hands under his arms and squeezed, leaning forward in his chair. "I'm nervous. If something goes wrong, it could end my career."

It had taken Veronika a while to convince Lycan to help them. When Lycan explained just how enormous a risk he'd be taking if he helped, Veronika had been sure he'd refuse, given that he hadn't even been willing to donate money to help Winter. But in the end he'd surprised her, and once he'd agreed, he worked tirelessly.

Lycan was peering up at the thousand-story buildings that surrounded the massive Liberty Med Courtyard. He looked down at the hole that opened onto an expansive view of Low Town. Their seats were impressively close to the doughnut hole, providing them with the full, dizzying effect. Greenery bloomed among the tables, warmed inside an invisible containment barrier. It made nearby trees, with their naked winter branches, look dead.

"I should come to places like this more often. You get into patterns, going to the same places all the time." He shrugged. "Or to no places at all, besides home and work." He checked the time again, licked his lips.

"Hey, hey." Nathan pulled up the third seat at their table, looked from Veronika to Lycan. "Just call me *rueda de tres*."

He was not snapping back from the breakup with Lorelei

in typical Nathan fashion. There were dark circles under his eyes, and maintaining the roguish smile appeared to be taking a great deal of effort. Referring to himself as the third wheel insinuated that she and Lycan were a couple. Veronika let it go.

There were four or five bumps under Nathan's shirt, at the shoulder. He was doing bugs to ease his pain.

"How are my two geniuses today?" Nathan asked.

"I'm peachy." Veronika checked the time. Any minute. Nathan had no idea what was about to happen; Sunali's people had been deadly serious about leaks, and understanding just how important the element of surprise would be, Veronika had told no one, not Nathan, not Rob, not her sister. It would be fascinating to watch Nathan's reaction. To watch *everyone's* reaction, for that matter.

Lycan gasped, wide-eyed.

Veronika followed his shocked stare and spotted a woman approaching their table. Only it wasn't a woman, it was the projection. The bridesicle was shivering, her skin white with a blue tinge, her hair caked with ice. Nathan lurched to his feet, his chair clattering to the floor as he hurried to help the woman, who looked about to collapse.

"What's the matter with you?" Veronika asked Lycan, who was all but trembling, his face gray.

"I know her," Lycan said.

"Please, help me," the woman said. "Please, I'm afraid."

Nathan reached for her outstretched hand; his own hand passed through it. He sank to one knee, like he'd been punched, his breath rattling.

"I'm so lonely and afraid," the bridesicle pleaded. "I don't want to be in this box anymore."

"Oh, that is magnificent," Veronika said as the bridesicle

limped toward her. She glanced at Lycan, who was shaking more than Nathan. He was making a keening sound in the back of his throat. Veronika went over, shooshed like a mother. "Why are you so upset?"

Lycan's attention was drawn by something a few tables away. Veronika followed his gaze, toward another copy of the same bridesicle, making the same desperate plea to another patron. Lycan seemed mesmerized by the sight of her. "Of all the women to choose from, they chose Mira."

Lycan's answer to her previous question suddenly registered. "Wait, did you just say you *know* her?"

That got Nathan's attention as well.

"You recognize her?" Nathan said.

Lycan nodded, his eyes fixed on the apparition.

"From where?" Veronika asked. She watched, fascinated, as six or seven bridesicles wandered the courtyard. The nearest one turned, headed toward Lycan. Lycan leaped from his seat and hurried toward the arched exit.

"You knew this was going to happen, didn't you?" Nathan asked Veronika.

"Yes. But we were sworn to secrecy." She raised her voice, called, "Lycan, wait," but he kept going. She opened a screen beside him.

A bridesicle wandered around a corner, stepped right into Lycan's path. Lycan skittered around the image, away from her outstretched hands, her bluish fingertips. He was acting like he was seeing a ghost, like she was haunting him alone, rather than the entire city. Yet if the bridesicle had been someone Veronika knew who had died, she might react similarly.

"How did you know her?" Veronika asked Lycan, who was heading for the micro-T station.

"We dated."

Veronika studied one of the wraiths as she stepped around a chair. She was beautiful, her tousled hair midnight black, her eyes almond shaped. "You dated this woman?" She tried not to sound dubious.

"At the bridesicle place. I was curious..."

Now they were getting somewhere. "Lycan, *stop*. Please."

Lycan slowed.

"Okay, you visited her. Why are you so upset?"

This seemed to calm Lycan, but he still looked miserable as he leaned against a wall. "I did an awful thing. I lied to her, got her hopes up, and then I dashed them. It was right after that when I jumped off the bridge."

"Oh, sweetie." Veronika signaled to Nathan that she was leaving, then headed toward the exit. "Stay right there, I'm coming."

Lycan nodded, wiped his nose on his sleeve.

Now it made sense. He dashed a dead woman's hopes of escaping from hell, then the woman shows up at his table, pleading for help. Yeah, that could rattle anyone.

What didn't make sense was why, of all the women at the center, Sunali and Lycan had chosen the same one.

Lycan greeted her with a fierce hug, as if it had been years since they last saw each other, not five minutes.

"Come on, I'll take you home. You need a double shot of Blue Devil."

"I don't like the supercharged stuff." He sniffed.

"You can make an exception this one time," Veronika said. She jolted in surprise as a bridesicle slammed to the ground a dozen feet from them. She landed with a convincing thud, and lay unmoving as blood bloomed around her face. "Shit, that startled me. Imagine if you had no idea what was happening."

Veronika opened a half-dozen screens at random locations around High Town and Low Town. There were bridesicles everywhere. Not ten thousand, as Lorelei had originally suggested, more like a hundred thousand. They were incredible. So haunting, so terrifying and beautiful.

Bridesicles leaped from sky bridges, from rooftops, from micro-T tubes. They rained down on Low Town like pale, lovely snowflakes. Never in the streets, though; they'd taken Lorelei's advice on that front as well.

"Can I ask why you chose this particular woman, out of all of them?"

Lycan shrugged. "Because she'd been there the longest. I thought that would make her different from modern women. Simpler."

"Sunali must have picked her for the same reason—the longest-suffering bridesicle." In fact... Veronika used her system to check the info cloud that had been dispersed to support the event, and tapped into one nearby. One of the first things it mentioned was the bridesicle's status as the "longest-serving detainee."

As they walked in silence, Lycan now relatively calm, something else clicked into place. "That was why you refused to visit Winter. You didn't want to go back."

"I'm never going back to that place," Lycan answered.

55

Rob

Rob leaned his lute against the wall by the door, marked his clothes and shoved them down the storage tube, unpacked a box of toiletries, a couple of photos, and he was finished moving in. The place was beyond tiny; eighty square feet wasn't much, especially when you had no windows to help open things up. Maybe a few floor-to-ceiling mirrors would help.

He put in a reservation for the rotating kitchen he shared with three adjoining rooms, then grabbed his lute and went out for a walk. The apartment was small, but the city was large.

A passing businesswoman carrying a boxed lunch dropped a two-dollar coin into his case. Rob nodded thanks, went on singing "Song for Winter." He played it every third or fourth song, but no one stayed around long enough to notice how repetitive his playlist was.

Off in the distance a juggler was working the granite steps of the Museum of Natural History, but she was too far away to catch more than snippets of his music.

He was beginning to think of this as his bench. It was nice, to have a bench. It wasn't a busy part of the park, so not the most lucrative location for a busker, but that was all right. Rob enjoyed the solitude.

He was hungry, he realized. Rob didn't want to go back to his apartment to eat, so he decided to visit the Biryani cart across from the museum. He reached down to pluck some coins out of his case, then froze, startled by an envelope sitting in the case. He picked it up, turned it over to find his first name written on the front. How had it gotten in there? He thought he would have noticed someone dropping something as old-fashioned as an envelope into his case, unless they dropped it from behind him. He slid his finger along the seal, drew out a folded sheet of light-blue paper.

Rob,

I don't think I've written on paper since the third grade, but this is the only way no one on my end can possibly read it.

It's beautiful. Every time I listen to it, I cry.

The leaves outside my window are rustling like dry paper. The cat, stalking bugs outside my window, is a paper cat. My life is a paper life, the waning sun a light bulb.

As you can see, I'm no poet.

I couldn't ignore your lovely gesture, but, please, no more.

I miss you.

W

Rob read the note over and over, trying to glean every scrap of meaning from the words, wishing there were more of them.

56

Mira

Mira was sitting beside her father in a movie theater. She was four years old, waiting impatiently for the commercials to end and the movie to begin. It was a Disney movie, but she couldn't remember which one. The scene was remarkably vivid, but Mira knew it wasn't real. It was a dream, or a memory, or something in-between.

"Four years old today. What a big girl," Dad said. "Four is when memory begins." He was rubbing her little back as he talked; she loved when he did that. "When you're all grown up, this could be your oldest memory. Us, sitting here right now. This is a good day. Try to remember this one."

"Daddy," Mira croaked. She struggled to open her stiff eyelids.

"Hello again, Mira." It was Sunali.

Mira smiled, her head clearing somewhat. "I was just remembering something my father said to me when I was little."

"Did you have a good father?"

"I did. I miss him."

Mira expected Sunali to say she missed hers, too, but she didn't. Instead she took out a flat screen the size of a pack of gum, held it where Mira could see. "I want to show you what we accomplished with your help."

Mira drew in a breath, startled by how different the city looked in the recording. It was still recognizable as High Town, probably during rush hour, but the pedestrians were *gliding* along the sidewalk with careless ease. Vehicles small and large threaded among each other in a dizzyingly complex dance. Dozens of colorful tubes lined the buildings, crossing high over the streets. Still more vehicles glided along the outsides of the tubes. There were scores of drones hurrying about, resembling big plastic bugs.

Then Mira spotted herself on the sidewalk, her skin ghostly white, her lips as blue as a bruise, her hair and eyelashes frosted with ice. She walked up to a man sitting on a bench sipping coffee from a pouch, and said, "Please help me. Please, I'm afraid. I'm so lonely and afraid. I don't want to be in this box anymore." Then she reached out toward the man. Her hand passed through him, and the man gasped. Gaping at her, he said something that Mira didn't hear, because her attention was on another Mira approaching a small crowd waiting for a micro-T. "Please help me," this Mira said. "Please, I'm afraid. I'm so lonely and afraid."

"My God, What are they?" Mira asked.

"They're just images." Sunali put the screen away. "I'm sorry, I forget how long you've been in here, even though I went through it myself. They're only images, but people are fooled, because it's illegal to display full-body images like these in public. And for added impact, whenever the images came into contact with someone, we made it so the person felt what you were feeling when you made this recording."

Mira wondered if she would even be able to function in a world like that, if ever she did get out. "Did you get into trouble for doing this?"

"Oh, yes," said Sunali, sounding nonchalant. "I've been slammed with huge fines, a few injury lawsuits, although my foundation paid all medical bills resulting from the event. Prison isn't out of the question, but I can probably buy out my sentence instead." She waved it away. "I don't care. No one was badly injured or killed, so I'm happy."

Mira wasn't sure what to say.

"*Everyone* is talking about it, Mira. There's a dialogue going on, from micro to macro channels, about bridesicles." Sunali reached out as if to touch Mira, her fingers brushing close to Mira's shoulder. "Everyone is talking about *you*. The whole world knows who you are."

"You gave them my name?"

Sunali shook her head. "They used your likeness. It matched a photo of you from the US Army archives."

"Does that mean I might get out of here?"

Sunali ran a hand through her hair, which was clumped into big strands that reminded Mira of Medusa. "It's hard to say. But it's possible. It's possible." She sounded like she was trying to convince herself. "Anyway, I wanted to show you what we've accomplished, you and I."

Mira had grown sensitive to summing-up words that meant she was about to be dead again. Words like *anyway*. As far as she could tell, Sunali had no reason to visit again, so it might be years, or decades, before Mira was next revived. The thought of her body lying frozen in this wall, with her not asleep, not unconscious, but simply nonexistent, was intolerable. "Please don't go yet. Can I have just a few more minutes?"

"Sure. Of course." Sunali waited, eyebrows raised.

Mira didn't know what to say. She didn't want these minutes to talk about her plight, she just wanted to *be* for a few more minutes. More than that, she wanted to see Jeannette, missed Jeannette so badly it burned. What it would mean to hear her voice, just once.

"I miss her so much," she said aloud.

"Who?" Sunali asked.

"Jeannette."

Sunali nodded understanding.

"Please, can you wake her again? Can you tell her I'm thinking about her?" Mira searched Sunali's eyes, desperate. "You know what it feels like to be where I am. You know what it must mean to me, don't you?" She still wasn't used to begging people for things, things as basic as being alive, or seeing the woman she loved.

Sunali nodded. "Yes, I do." She thought for a moment, then stood, her screen clutched in both hands. "Hold on. I doubt Cryomed is going to like this, but fuck them." Then she was gone, without ending Mira's session first.

Mira was elated to have time to be awake, time to think. She wondered why Sunali had left her alive this time, and what Cryomed wasn't going to like. Surely they didn't care if she and Jeannette communicated through Sunali. She couldn't wait to hear what message Jeannette would send to her, wished she'd had time to think of a message more profound to send to Jeannette than "I'm thinking of you."

A vivid, three-dimensional image sprang to life above Mira: a gray face, looking down at her from inside a crèche like hers.

351

"Mira?" The voice was a croak, but the face—the face was—

"Jeannette? Oh my God, Jeannette." She was older, but otherwise hadn't changed much. She was still so beautiful. Mira wanted to say a thousand things at once; they piled together and left her mute.

Jeannette's eyes crinkled, her lips forming a stiff smile. "You look *awful*."

They laughed and laughed, because what else could they do? Mira understood that these moments, these few, incredibly precious moments, were an utter fluke, more than she could have dared hope for, and she understood that when they were over, she would never see Jeannette again.

"I missed you, when you died," Jeannette said. "I missed you so much. You were the best part of life."

"Miss Van Kampen," a disembodied voice cut in, "facility regulations prohibit the use of communication devices of any kind. Please disable your screen immediately."

Mira heard Sunali's shouted response loud and clear through the screen. "Go fuck yourself."

"Yeah, go fuck yourself!" Jeannette shouted, as loud as the air tube would allow, her eyes never leaving Mira's.

"Go fuck yourself," Mira chimed in, then giggled like a child who knows she's being naughty, but doesn't care. Male voices, speaking urgently, drifted from below. They were coming to get the screen.

"I love you," Mira said.

"I love you, too, Speedy."

Mira opened her mouth to laugh, surprised and delighted to be reminded of the nickname Jeannette had given her the first time they met. Then everything went black.

57

Rob

There was an assertive thump on the floor—the resident below Rob pounding on his or her ceiling. Rob stopped playing, set his lute aside and drew one knee up to his chest.

All he wanted to do was play. It was strange: after killing Winter he hadn't been able to *look* at his lute. This new flavor of pain left him unable to do anything *but* play. The problem was, he didn't particularly want to play for an audience, although he'd have to get some gigs before too long, or go back to working at the reclamation center. He was burning through what little money was left in his account, after returning that final anonymous donation.

He wondered what Winter was doing at this moment. Was she on the island? Maybe off at some important function with Red? Her note had said, "no more," but the last thing she wrote was, "I miss you." Would she get angry if he tried to contact her, if he sent something to tell her he missed her, too?

There was a knock at his door. For a single, irrational second he thought it might be Winter, but beyond all of the other reasons it couldn't be her, it wasn't a ping through his system, it was an old-fashioned knock. Someone who didn't know him, maybe a neighbor looking to bum a beer. He struggled to one knee, then to his feet, crossed his apartment in three strides, and opened the door manually, just a crack.

It was Winter, in a screen.

He yanked the door open. "*Hi.*" His lungs felt empty; he couldn't seem to get any air into them.

Winter floated in without a word, eyes downcast.

"Are you all right?" Rob asked.

"I don't know. Not really, no."

Rob took a step toward her, then hesitated, irrationally afraid that she'd bolt if he got too close, even though she was nothing but a screen.

Her screen rotated to take in the apartment. "Not much of a place. You must be one of those guys who spends all of his money on irresponsible things."

"Mostly on women. I went out with this woman who bled me dry."

She rotated to face him. "You were going out with her, were you?"

Rob shrugged. "It felt like it. After a while."

"Yes, it did." She bit her bottom lip, a gesture that had become so endearing to him. "The song is beautiful. You're going to be famous one day."

A screen acted much like a crèche, Rob realized. They could speak, but there could be no physical contact. "I wish you were really here."

"That would be a very bad idea. A terrible idea."

"I don't care. I still wish you were here."

"All right." The voice came from behind him. Rob spun around: Winter—the real, flesh-and-blood Winter—was standing in his doorway.

"Hi," she said. She took a step into the room, looked around again, then brushed her hair back behind her ear as Rob stood there, speechless. "This can only end horribly. For me that doesn't matter much; I'm in a pretty unpleasant situation as it is. But for you..." She let the implications hang there in the three feet that separated them.

Rob closed the distance between them. He touched her shoulder, which was bare, and pale from three years hidden from the sun. He slid his palm behind the back of her neck, felt her hair brush softly against the backs of his fingers. Winter melted against him, rested her head on his shoulder, her lips a whisper from his neck.

The world went silent. There was nothing but this embrace, nothing to think or worry about, nothing that possibly needed to be done, nowhere to go. As he inhaled, he felt Winter exhale, tickling the hairs on his neck. He exhaled, felt Winter draw air through parted lips. With this woman in his arms, he could solve any problem.

"Can we stay just like this for about a month?" Rob said.

Winter drew back, out of his arms. "No." She reached up, released the clasp on her shirt, and let it slide off.

When he woke, Winter was sitting on the edge of the bed, sliding on a boot that probably cost a month of Rob's pay. Winter saw he was awake, smiled wanly. "Got any suggestions for a good lie I can tell Red, if he asks where I've been? I don't have much experience with lying. I'm guessing you don't either."

Rob thought of the card from Penny he'd kept hidden from Lorelei. That had been more deception than lie.

"I guess I should feel guilty about this, but I don't," Winter said. She was finished dressing. "Before I died and went to bridesicle hell, maybe I would have."

Rob bunched the sheets across his lap, sat up. "Do you have to go? I could get some coffee delivered."

"That sounds lovely, but I should get back."

"Just don't tell me this was a onetime thing and that I can never see you again. I don't think I can stand to hear that again."

Winter folded her arms and sighed. "That's what I was planning to say, but I would just be fooling myself. Again."

Rob stood, wrapped his arms around Winter. "Can we plan something? This way I can look forward to it."

"I wish we could go out to dinner, but...too risky."

"Dinner here, then. I'll get a delivery from Luigi's."

"*You'll* get it? Rob, I've got money coming out of my ears. Dinner's on me."

58

Veronika

Veronika rode past Lemieux Bridge. It stretched toward the river, the high sweep of its expanse like a harp with golden strings. She smiled.

Just go through the motions until it stops hurting, she subvocalized, then took a sip of the blueberry coffee she was holding. *It's old advice, but it's all I've got.* For an instant Veronika forgot she was addressing Nathan, because she'd said the same thing to Rob just yesterday. She may have used the exact same words.

I know everyone thinks this, Nathan sent, *but I'm not sure I'll ever get over her. This—* He stopped, trying to regain his composure.

It was weird being the whole one, the shoulder to be cried on. It was also weird that suddenly her happiest male friend was *Lycan.* As Rob and Nathan agonized over their respective lost loves, Lycan was finding himself. Veronika thought she deserved at least a smidgen of credit for that particular turnaround.

I wish I knew how to help you, she sent. She took a swig of her coffee.

Rob pinged her. Great, heartbreak in stereo. She invited him to join her.

I appreciate you listening, Nathan sent. *I know I'm saying the same things over and over. I'll let you go.*

Rob's screen popped into the passenger seat as Nathan signed off. Rob looked...surprisingly good. Happy. Beaming, even.

"What happened to you? Ten hours ago you looked ready to ask Lycan for tips on bridge diving."

"This is borderline rude, not waiting to tell you this in person, but I can't wait. Winter came to my apartment last night."

"No *way*." Veronika bounced in her seat, unable to control herself. "She just showed up? In person?"

"Yup."

"What happened?"

Rob smiled. "She loves me."

"God, I hope you guys know what the hell you're doing." If Red caught them, the legal consequences would be devastating. Beyond that, the research indicated that affairs almost always ended badly, leaving nothing but pain and regret in their aftermath.

"Well, under normal circumstances I'd never think of being with a married woman, but these aren't normal circumstances."

"No, they're not. Normally you're not risking the wrath of a billionaire."

"Where are you headed?" Rob asked.

"To Lycan's for dinner."

"Let's talk more, when we can do it IP?" Rob said. "You've

been such a good friend, I wanted to tell you as soon as possible, even if that meant via screen. It's just between us, okay?"

"Sure thing."

They signed off, and Veronika was alone in her silent car. Veronika envied Rob's earnestness, how deeply he trusted his own emotions, even if that trust was probably misguided in the case of Winter. It seemed obvious that Rob's obsession with Winter sprang out of his need to take care of her. He'd sacrificed everything to keep his promise to her, and when you make someone the center of your life like that, she's going to end up on a pedestal.

As Veronika's Scamp swung into the garage under Lycan's apartment complex, it occurred to her that she could get a sense of how compatible Rob and Winter really were, just to satisfy her own curiosity. She'd constructed a profile for Rob months ago, but never used it. She retrieved it now, ran it against the profile she and Nathan had constructed for Winter, minus the parts that were fabrication, and...

Her coffee pouch slipped from her fingers, plopping to the seat. "You're kidding me." Point nine-seven. If Veronika had tried to find a match for Rob, and started from a sample of ten thousand prospects, she would have been lucky to find one match that good.

With a sigh, she climbed out of her Scamp, stepped into the lift. Rob had run over a woman who was all but perfect for him, making it impossible to ever be with her. What a mess.

In the hall, she pinged Lycan to let him know she was there; the door to his apartment swirled open. She stepped inside, yelped, took an involuntary step backward.

Lycan's place had become a sumptuous dining room, complete with chandelier, high-backed brass chairs, antique drone servants. It was instantly familiar to Veronika as a scene from *Wings of Fire*. Lycan was sitting at the table, foot crossed over knee, dressed in the signature twenty-first-century garb of her secret, embarrassing crush—Peytr Sidorov. Blue jeans and a layered white banquet shirt, his shiny white shoes rounded at the tips.

Hand trembling, obviously nervous, Lycan rapped on the dining table. "It's all real. Not an interactive."

And to think just a moment ago Veronika had been thinking about how grounded Lycan was becoming. The door to the kitchen had been replaced by gold curtains; they swished open and a drone entered, carrying a silver tray. It held out the tray to Veronika, offering little crab-shaped appetizers. She took one, held it between two fingers. "What is going on?"

Lycan grinned. "It's a surprise. Remember a few months ago, when you left me in your living room and invited me to play an interactive to pass the time while you worked?"

"Yes," Veronika said uneasily.

"Out of curiosity, I checked which you played the most. Then I bought my own copy."

Veronika took a good look around Lycan's living space. There were vases filled with flowers everywhere, frescoes of maidens in billowing dresses on the walls. "And then you had your home decorated to match it?"

Lycan swallowed, nodded.

This was too bizarre for words. Veronika resisted the urge to back out of the room and run away. They'd been treading that odd ground between friendship and intimacy for some time, and Veronika had been comfortable there. But this...

"Lycan this is...a little over the top, don't you think?"

This was not a dinner planned for a good friend, or even for someone you were treading that odd middle ground with.

Lycan only shrugged, his big hands gripping the ornately

carved arms of his chair, his foot dangling over his big knee, looking ridiculous in that white shoe.

She tried to entertain the possibility that that dopey shoe was on the foot of a man she could love. But she was in love with Nathan, and Nathan was single again, so there was hope.

Trying to set that aside, she imagined sitting in her kitchen drinking tea with Lycan on a Sunday morning. Or the two of them in bed on a Friday evening, Veronika's hair brushing Lycan's face.

No fireworks; pulse slow and steady.

Hey, hey, Nathan sent, interrupting her reverie. *What are you up to? Free for dinner? On me.*

Veronika felt a thrill, then surveyed the sumptuous spread the drones were laying on Lycan's giant banquet table. The candlesticks on it were freaking works of art. Were they authentic eighteenth century? They sure looked it. Of course she had to stay, after Lycan had gone to all this trouble. The prospect of dinner with Lycan didn't fill her with the mad, crazy excitement she felt at the prospect of eating with Nathan. *On him?* They *always* paid for their own meals. Had Nathan finally recognized what had been right in front of him all this time?

Can't, she subvocalized. *Having dinner with Lycan tonight.* She knew what his reply would be: Bring him along. Make it a party. The more the merrier.

Can't you reschedule? She was surprised. Nathan wanted it to be just the two of them. Definitely not like him.

Can't do that.

She took the seat across from Lycan, lifted her spoon.

"Acorn Squash and Raspberry Soup," Lycan offered.

It was terrific, though her attention was primarily on

trying to sort things out rather than on the soup. She'd been the one who pushed Lycan to be bold, to take chances. Well, this was bold. Weird, but bold.

"Have you seen what's going on with Bridesicle Watch?" Lycan asked. His forehead was sweating, his voice a stress-induced octave higher than normal.

"I haven't checked the feeds in the past few hours. Anything new?"

"They've got ten thousand screens parked outside every entrance to the dating center, heckling anyone who goes inside—customers and employees alike. They're ID'ing them, spreading their photos and info all over. Only guys wealthy enough to own copters can visit unmolested."

"Sooner or later they're going to have to agree to Sunali's reforms. Skintight. And you deserve a lot of the credit. It took guts, what you did." Veronika lifted her glass, and, after a moment's hesitation, Lycan scooped up his as well.

He was a strange mix. He'd actually patronized the bridesicle center, yet he was risking everything to reform it. He'd been reluctant to help Rob visit Winter, yet he'd spent a fortune to impress Veronika with this dinner.

Across the table, Lycan ate his soup. Their spoons clinked in the silence. She should say something chatty and pleasant, but now that she was thinking about the Rob-and-Winter thing, it was niggling at her.

"Can I ask you something?" It was rude, but she had to ask. "When the rest of us kept pitching in to help Rob visit Winter, you never did, until I asked you. Was that because of your bad experience at the dating center or something?"

Lycan looked incredibly uncomfortable, as if the soup was caught in his throat. "No. I just, I don't know."

She studied Lycan. His eyes were pleading for something. Forgiveness. Understanding.

She smiled. Decided she should just let it be. "I'm sorry, that was rude. You've done more than anyone could possibly expect, and more."

They ate their soup, talked about Bridesicle Watch, his research, her work. There was no witty repartee, no crackling insights about the relationship between cryogenics and existential terror.

They started on a vegetable soufflé.

Lycan cleared his throat, turned his head from side to side, as if he was trying to loosen it. "I hope I didn't give you the wrong impression with all of this. I just..."—he struggled for words—"wanted to thank you for being such a good friend."

Damage control. He sensed she was uneasy, and was trying to walk it back. How many times had she done that with Nathan, tossed something flirtatious out there and then laughed it off?

"No, no. I get it. It's wonderful, it's an absolutely wonderful gesture."

Lycan smiled uneasily, nodded.

She didn't love him. Not the way she loved Nathan. She kept checking herself for a spark, for that feeling she got on the first warm day after a cold winter, but all she felt with Lycan was...comfortable. Safe.

As the drones cleared away the dessert dishes, she hugged Lycan good-bye, squeezing tighter than normal, trying to convey her appreciation, to signal that everything was okay between them. She couldn't help but see the disappointment in his eyes as the door swirled shut.

Is your invitation still open? she sent to Nathan as she rode the lift down. *I've had dinner, but maybe drinks?*

Absolutely, he replied.

She headed toward her Scamp, the first twist in Rainbow Tower almost directly overhead.

Lycan pinged her. She opened a screen back in his apartment. "What's up?"

"I want to tell you something, but you have to promise you won't ever tell Rob, or Nathan."

"Sure, I promise."

"I did give money to Rob. I'm not cheap, and I'm not selfish, I just have my own way of doing things." There was a hitch in his voice. Her thoughtless question at dinner had wounded him deeply.

"I'm so sorry I asked about that. I know you're not selfish. Not after what you did—" She stopped, considered what he'd just said. "Wait, you *did* give money to Rob?" She stopped walking, glided a few feet on her momentum before sliding to a full stop. "*You* were the anonymous donor?"

"Yes." He sounded almost defensive.

"Holy shit. I thought it was Sunali. Why didn't you say something?" Veronika felt as if she had something caught in her throat. Lycan's stinginess toward Rob had always seemed unlike him. Now everything slid neatly into place.

"Then it wouldn't be anonymous, would it?"

"Why did it have to be anonymous?"

"I don't know. I don't like to draw attention to myself. The old guy with the money. I wanted to fit in with you and your friends."

Only half aware of what she was doing, she turned, headed back toward Lycan's building. "You gave Rob, like, fifty thousand dollars."

"It's just money."

The front door to Lycan's building let her in. In the lobby, she stepped into one of the capsules and headed up.

"You're a good person. Do you know that?"

Maybe she should give him a chance. She didn't love him the way she loved Nathan, but maybe that wasn't the only way to love someone. Maybe what she'd always thought of as "settling" was just a different sort of love. Maybe she under-valued feeling safe and comfortable. Maybe she undervalued kindness, and overvalued wit and poise.

She knocked on Lycan's door, the old-fashioned way.

The door swirled open.

"*Hi.*" Lycan sounded overjoyed to see her.

Veronika collapsed her screen. "Hi. I came back because I wanted to say this IP." Suddenly she felt nervous. She actually had no idea what she'd come back to say.

Lycan waited, his eyebrows raised.

"You're a good guy, and I like you." Veronika cringed inside. What a line. Pathetic. "And—and I'd like to reciprocate. I'd like to invite you to dinner at my place. I can guarantee you it won't be nearly as elaborate as the meal you planned—"

"No," Lycan interrupted, stepping on her last few words, "that doesn't matter. I'd love to come. Thank you." He wrig-gled his nose, one of his other nervous habits.

"Great."

"Great."

Once again, Veronika headed into the street, wonder-ing if she could ever be happy with someone like Lycan. She laughed out loud at the thought. When had she ever been happy, anyway?

Lycan pinged her. Laughing at the absurd circularity of this evening, she opened a screen in Lycan's living room again.

"Do you remember when we met in that pizza place, and I was having a panic attack?" he asked.

"Sure."

"You asked why I was having it, and I said I didn't know." He cleared his throat. "I did know—I was just embarrassed to say. It was because I was going to see you."

A warmth washed over Veronika, like she was standing on a beach, soaking in the sun.

59

Mira

or the first time, Mira found no one looking down at her
hen she woke. There was nothing to see but the ceiling far
ove, and part of the wall. She waited, expecting a face to
pear. Had Sunali waked her, then been called away, or left
use the bathroom? Surely it was Sunali.

"Hello?" Mira called.

Nothing but the faint echo of her own horrible graveyard
ice. Maybe there had been some technical error in her
èche that accidentally woke her? That would be wonderful;
e'd have time to herself until someone noticed.

"Mira Bach," a woman's voice said.

Mira waited for a face to appear, then realized the voice
d come from farther above, where the warning had come
om when Sunali let her speak to Jeannette.

"Yes?"

"Do you recall saying the following during your last meet-
g with Sunali Van Kampen?"

A brief pause, then she recognized her own terrible dea
voice, on the verge of hysteria: "Please help me. Please, I'ı
afraid—"

She was in trouble. Although, she wondered, what els
could they possibly do to her. Put her in prison? Beat her wit
a stick? "Yes, I remember." How could she forget? It wasn
as if she got the opportunity to speak very often.

"What were your intentions in saying it?"

Did they record everything that went on in here? It wa
probably safe to assume they did, that they'd already reviewe
Sunali's visits. "I was speaking to Sunali; I was upset. I didn
know she was going to use my words the way she did." Mi
was trying to recall what she'd said to Sunali leading up
her outburst. Did she come across as complicit?

"Congruent with Cryomed policy," the voice said, "v
have revived you to inform you of a change in your statu
You're to be relocated to the main storage facility, whe
you'll be preserved for the remaining five hundred forty-fo
years stipulated in your insurance policy."

"*Wait.* I didn't do anything wrong." She wouldn't have tl
slightest chance of speaking to Jeannette again, or of beiı
revived.

"The decision is not contestable," the voice said.

"But I didn't—"

She wasn't given a chance to argue.

60

Rob

ırough the window of the train, Rob watched a micro-T
ıscend from High Town, dropping almost vertically, and
ondered if Winter might be on it. It was headed to Grand
ıntral, so it was possible. But it was too far away, and mov-
g too fast, for him to make out individual faces.

Six o'clock, you said? Veronika sent, and Rob replied by
ınding a thumbs-up.

He wiped his palms on his pants. They were slick with
▪eat, not from nervousness, but just because he was flat-out
cited. He had no doubt his dad and Winter would hit it
f. Winter would be able to relax out in the suburbs, where
ere was little chance of a camera catching them together. It
ıuld be nice to be able to hold Winter's hand in public, or
t his arm around her waist. In the city, that was only pos-
▪le in his room.

The train stopped at Grand Central. Rob hopped out,
:ated the wall with the giant clock in it, and found Winter

already waiting, one foot propped against the wall. As they planned, Rob kept walking, knowing Winter would follow. He boarded a train to the suburbs, spotted Winter boarding two cars down.

When the train pulled out, he crossed through the car separating them, took the seat behind her.

"Hey, you," Winter said, turning sideways in her seat.

Rob grinned. "Hi. Hope you like Superfood."

"Veronika's bringing something as well. But even if she didn't, I grew up eating Superfood."

"Your whole childhood?"

"It depended on who Mom was married to. At times we were pretty well off, then she'd get bored with whoever she was married to and leave him, and we'd be in the streets. I got whiplash from all the change. Mom thrived on it."

Rob nodded, thinking how different her upbringing had been from his. He'd been poor, but always just somewhat, and everyone else in the neighborhood was poor too, so it felt normal.

"So, were the times you were homeless the worst part of your life? Besides being dead, of course."

A man a few rows away glanced at them, then looked away.

Winter laughed. "Being dead isn't part of life, so it doesn't count." She thought for a moment. "I'd have to say the low point was Ty."

"Ty?"

"My boyfriend in college. He broke up with me, but neither of us could afford to move out, so we went on living together as roommates. Pretty soon he was going out with someone new, one of those women who dress like clowns. Bright red hair, colored face paint?"

"Oh, I know them." There had been a clique of clowns in is school. Liz Faircloth, who lived down the road from him, ad become one, showing up for the walk to school one day earing bright, primary colors, with blue corkscrew hair.

"Soon she was pretty much living with us, and I was sleep-g in a corner of the living room while they had loud sex the bedroom, with her laughing her crazy fake-clown ugh—" Winter broke into laughter herself. "When did peo-e start doing that, where their whole identity is tied to some ok?"

"No idea."

Two boys, maybe twelve years old, burst into their car, ggling like mad. Rob watched as they ran past, hit the door the far end, and disappeared into the next car.

"Life with my mom wasn't all bad. I don't want to give u that impression," Winter said, when it was quiet again. Once mom opened a day-care business in our apartment. e just kept packing kids into the place."

"Hold on. These were the good times?" Rob laughed.

"It was chaos, but it was like having twenty brothers and ters. Mom was utterly incompetent as a caregiver, so we ere free to do whatever we wanted, as long as we stayed in e house."

"How long did the day-care business last."

Winter shook her head sadly. "Maybe three months. Mom et husband number three, and we moved into his house."

They talked nonstop to the burbs. Rob wished the ride uld go on for hours, but soon they were at the end of the e, on the walk to Dad's house, in the shadow of Percy tate.

"That's where I worked, while you were in the minus hty," Rob said, pointing to the reclamation center.

Winter squinted, trying to make out details of the facility "Looks depressing."

Rob shrugged. "It wasn't that bad." Memories of thos grueling, soul-wrenching days flashed through his min Back then this landscape had looked so different, so muc filthier and smellier, without a system filtering his senses.

Rob disabled his system, surveyed the suburbs in the raw They were passing an old, partially collapsed motel his sys tem had edited out entirely, including the mother bathing h children with water dabbed from a rusty frying pan.

"What are you doing?" Winter asked, watching him.

"I disabled the sensory filters on my system. I spent so lon seeing this place in the raw that I'm kind of used to seeing that way. I think I prefer it."

Winter tapped her own gorgeous, wildly expensive system then looked around, inhaling deeply. "Wow. I see what yo mean. It's a completely different place." She nodded. "I' going to keep mine off too, so we're seeing the same things.

To say nothing of smelling the same things. The air w rife with a pungent industrial odor.

"I can't help thinking of my brother, out there somewher living a Raw Life," Winter said. "I miss him. I didn't alwa agree with him, but I respected his conviction." She looked Rob. "In a lot of ways he reminds me of you."

Rob smiled, basking in the compliment. "Did you ev think you might want to go find him? Were you ever tempt by the Raw Life?" He tried to make the question sound li casual curiosity, but it was more than that, really. If she ev decided to bolt, if *they* ever decided to bolt, a raw communi would be a possible destination.

Winter sighed, a little wistfully. "Not really. I like the pa of the city. I would miss being connected to everyone, to everything."

Rob nodded, though he felt slightly disappointed. He wanted to ask if she thought she could at least tolerate a Raw Life, if it meant the two of them could be together, but it wasn't fair to ask. The risk would be enormous for her, much greater than for him.

"Don't be thrown if Dad introduces you to the image of my mom that he's got wandering the house."

"Do I pretend she's a live person, or how do I treat her?"

"He won't expect you to play along or anything. Maybe just comment that she was pretty, or something. He'd like that."

It was so strange, to think Winter and his dad were about to meet. Rob couldn't help wondering about the significance of it. Did Winter see it as coming home to meet the parents? Again, he reminded himself of Winter's situation. They couldn't ever be a couple in the typical sense. Unless they ran away and disappeared.

"This is it." Rob pointed to his house, second on the right on Appleby Street. Part of him wished Winter hadn't disabled her sensory filter, so the house would appear less dilapidated than it was.

"It has a good feel to it. A warmth."

Dad opened the side door before they had a chance to knock. He grinned at Winter, spread his arms, and when Winter hugged him, he squeezed her tight, rocked her back and forth. When he finally broke away to look at her, there were tears in his eyes, as if he'd been reunited with an old, dear friend. It wasn't until Winter sniffed that Rob realized he was crying too.

Dad put an arm across Rob's shoulder, and led them both into the house. Mom was sitting at the kitchen table, but to Rob's surprise, Dad didn't introduce her to Winter. Instead he went to the cabinet, lifted out a pot.

"Do you want some tea?" he asked.

"I'd love some." Winter approached Rob's mom almost reverently, studied her for a moment. "Your wife was beautiful, Mr. Mashita."

His dad turned, smiling a little sadly. "That's kind of you to say, and I must agree. And call me Lorne. We've known each other for two years, even if you didn't know it."

"Oh, I did." Winter peeked into Lorne's business room. "May I?"

"Sure," Lorne said. "I usually charge six dollars for the tour, but I'll give it to you for free." Lorne flipped on the lights.

Winter walked around, arms folded. She lingered for a long time at the Wall of Fame, studying photos, especially the old ones, chuckling at some of the goofy poses.

Finally, she turned to face Lorne. "This is a good place. You can feel it, just standing here."

There was a tap on the front door. Rob half expected it to be a customer looking to get an after-work haircut, but it was Veronika, Nathan, and Lycan. Each was carrying a stay-fresh food container.

They had dinner, the six of them—seven if you counted Mom—and everyone seemed to have a wonderful time except Nathan, who was polite but distracted, and hollow-eyed.

Veronika had told Rob a few days earlier that her friendship with Lycan had morphed into something more. Not a romance, she insisted, but an NPMC—a "nonplatonic monogamous companionship." Seeing them together, you wouldn't know anything had changed, except that instead of

374

nostly looking at his hands, Lycan mostly looked at Veronka. He also spoke more, seemed more connected to the group, even cracked a couple of jokes. Nathan, on the other hand, spent most of the evening looking off into space. Evidently Lorelei's new romance was popular with her viewers. Rob imagined it was difficult, hearing about everything your ex-girlfriend was doing on the microfeeds.

Lorne was showing everyone the expression Rob had made the day Peter sauntered in and asked if someone was interested in information about a bridesicle, when Rob was pinged.

It was from Peter, a text-only message. Cryomed was going to announce the closing of their facilities in the morning.

Rob leaped from his seat. "*Holy shit.*" He enlarged the message so everyone could see it.

"Holy shit," Winter echoed as they gaped at the message.

Cryomed was closing their bridesicle facilities. All of them. They weren't reforming their practices, they were simply pulling the plug on the entire program.

"Why would they do that?" Veronika asked. "Bridesicle Watch wasn't demanding they close the whole thing down, just make the process more humane."

Why would they do that? Rob sent to Peter.

The reply came promptly. Rob posted it for all to see.

The program was not a huge revenue source for Cryomed. Easier to shut it down than to institute the reforms. Plus, this way they go out on their own terms, appear stronger.

Rob shot back a quick subvocalized reply. *I know that's exactly what you wanted to happen. Your wife is at peace. Thank you.* He'd gotten what he wanted, but sitting beside Winter, Rob couldn't help feeling guilty.

"Good. Good for Sunali," Winter said, fighting back tears.

Rob wondered if it *was* good. Fewer women would now have a chance to be revived. If not for the program, Winter wouldn't be sitting next to him, squeezing his hand.

"That's right," Veronika said. "Good for Sunali. She did it." She patted Lycan on the back. "With some help."

"With a lot of help," Rob said. "From both of you." He raised his glass. "Vee and Lycan, congratulations."

Lycan, who had been staring at the news feed, didn't lift his glass. "What about the women who don't have insurance though? What happens to them?"

"Surely they have to move them to the main facility," Veronika said. "After the black eye they took over the way they were treating them."

"It doesn't matter," Winter said. "Either way, they're better off." She looked around the table. "I know I owe my life to that place, but believe me, they're better off."

Lorne nodded, thoughtful. "No one would know better than you."

Winter rode back to the city with the others while Rob took the train. They met back at Rob's apartment and made love in his pullout bed.

Afterward, they lay clutching each other, as if anticipating a hurricane that would pull them apart.

"I wish I could feel happier, after what happened today," Winter said. "All I keep thinking is, it doesn't affect me at all. I'm still an indentured servant."

"I've been thinking the same thing. I'm glad the dating center is closing, but I was hoping the protests would force the government to outlaw lifetime-marriage agreements."

Winter nodded. "I guess I should work on being grateful. By all rights I should be ashes right now."

Rob turned his head and kissed her temple. "I'm definitely grateful that's not the case."

"Maybe you should send Red a thank-you card."

She clearly meant it to be a joke, but the words stung.

"I want *this* to be my life," Winter said.

Rob kissed her temple again. They stared up at the yellow-ing plastic ceiling.

"So why did you decide to become a teacher?" Rob asked.

Winter rolled on her side, propped her head with her hand. "I'd be lying if I said I went into it because I wanted to make a difference. The truth is, it was one of the few degrees I could afford, one of the few doors I could find out of poverty. I specialized in English because it was the cheapest teaching degree they offered. Once I was in the classroom, all that cold-eyed pragmatism melted away. I got to know the stu-dents, all of their stories, and it stopped being about me."

"I pulled up a recording of you teaching, when we were doctoring your profile. You're pretty awesome. Do you have any plans to go back?"

"I can't. I have to be available when Red needs me, for lun-cheons and stuff."

Rob only nodded. By silent assent, they'd both stopped railing against the unfairness of Winter's situation. It only served to make their time together less pleasant.

"Your father is a wonderful man," Winter said into Rob's neck. "There's so much love in him. It's as if he's ready to burst, he loves so much."

"That's a good description of him." Rob thought of what his father had learned about Mom with the lie-detector appli-cation. "I think the hard part is, he loves so much he never gets as much love back as he gives. As much as I love him, I'm not capable of returning all the love he gives me."

Winter leaped from the bed like she'd been goosed. "Shit. Red just pinged me."

Rob jumped up to help her find her clothes as she frantically pulled on her panties.

"He *never* contacts me when he's out of town."

"We need to come up with a good answer, when he asks why there was a long delay in lifting your block."

Winter pulled her system on, grabbed the sock Rob was holding out to her, pulled it on while hopping on one foot. "Shit. He'll want to know what I'm doing in Low Town, in a residential area."

"Did you know anyone who lives around here, before you died?"

"No," she said. "*Yes*. Keener Piven. He taught history. Assuming he still lives in the same apartment." Her fingers flew across her system; a map with a flashing red dot materialized. "Yes." She pulled her boot on and sprinted for the door; it opened just before she plowed into it. She disappeared down the hall.

Moving more slowly, Rob went into the hallway, took the catwalk to the window at the front of the building so he could watch her leave.

Winter slowed as soon as she hit the sidewalk. A screen opened beside her an instant later. From his angle, Rob couldn't see Red very well, but even so, the sight of him sent a prickling mixture of disgust and dread through Rob. Not for the first time, he wished the old man would die, once and for all. But that was unlikely; with revivification he was almost guaranteed to live another twenty years at least, unless he was run over by a train, or his island collapsed on him.

61

Veronika

Veronika wasn't sure what to do with herself while she ate.

She watched the news for a while. They were still talking about the great bridesicle protest, and Cryomed's announcement. There was an entire documentary about the woman whose likeness had been used in the protest—Mira Bach—although they didn't know much about her beyond where she had lived, that she had been employed by the US Army, that she died in an industrial accident. Veronika wondered why no one had gone to the bridesicle place to interview her. It wouldn't officially close for another three weeks. Maybe Cryomed wouldn't allow anyone to see her.

A rap on the door startled her. She popped a screen outside to see who it was, saw it was Nathan, and opened the door.

"Hey, hey," he said. "Have you eaten yet? I brought Sishwala."

One of Veronika's favorites. "Wow, I was going to eat a sandwich."

Her drone set out dishes, and they talked about the closing of the bridesicle program, and about Rob and Winter. Nathan didn't bring up Lorelei at all. He seemed less morose than he'd been, but rather than being his old upbeat self, he seemed preoccupied, on edge.

"So how are you feeling?" Veronika finally asked.

"I'm feeling stupid," Nathan answered, as if it were a perfectly legitimate response.

"Oh? How so?"

Nathan set his fork down, looked at Veronika, and cleared his throat. "I think I let the perfect woman slip through my fingers."

"Lorelei didn't slip through your fingers, sweetie, she bit them off."

"I'm not talking about Lorelei." He took a sip of water. "I'm talking about you."

"*Me?*" Veronika almost dropped her fork.

Nathan nodded. "I've been thinking about my life, the choices I've made, my trouble with relationships. Through all the ups and downs, all the shit, the one constant good thing has been you."

Veronika wasn't sure what to say. For the past four years she'd been waiting for Nathan to say exactly this. Handsome, charming Nathan. He was talking fast, probably hopped up on bugs and caffeine.

"I didn't realize just how much I enjoyed having you around until you weren't around anymore." Nathan closed his mouth, waited for Veronika to say something.

Veronika studied his face, his firm jaw, his smoky-brown eyes under perfectly manicured eyebrows. She knew every curve, every line, the placement of every whisker on that face.

Nathan set the fork down, evidently finished, although

he'd only eaten half of his lunch. "It's funny. Friendships are Catch twenty-twos when you're single and in your thirties. Friends are your life rafts. You try to help each other meet people, you confide in each other, you spend Thanksgiving, Valentine's Day, all those emotional land-mine holidays together. But sooner or later one of you is going to meet someone and be gone into the world of couples."

This wasn't about her, she realized. Not really. He wanted to hang on to a lifestyle that was disappearing, and she represented that lifestyle. He was terribly lonely. He had lots of friends, but no one he could talk to besides her. His other friendships were wafer-thin.

"I'll always have time for you. I'll always be your friend."

He lifted his fork, studied it for a moment, as if there might be an answer caught between the tines. "I know. And I'm glad you're happy, I really am."

Happy? Probably not the word she would use, but she let it go. Maybe she was selling Nathan, and herself, short. Maybe she didn't represent the lifestyle Nathan was clinging to, maybe she was his Lycan. Safe and kind. Comforting, if not capable of quickening the pulse.

Veronika wished she had a time machine, to send this moment back to herself at a point when it would have put her right over the moon. It was a shame, really. "I really do mean it. I'm not going anywhere."

"I know. But you're not going to want to go out much. It's just the reality of not being single." He leaned back in his chair, folded his arms. "It's funny, I never outgrew the things I loved when I was twenty. I still love crowded bars, prowling the streets on Friday night, looking for the places where things are happening. Stopping in for a slice. But you stop fitting in—"

Suddenly, they had company. Lorelei had popped into the room via screen, unannounced.

"Sorry, I thought you'd be alone," Lorelei said. In a downbeat tone, she added, "Hi, Nathan."

"No, I actually have friends," Veronika said. She had to admire how incredibly adept Lorelei was at the subtle insult. "What can I do for you, Lorelei?"

"Nothing, just popped in to say hello." Without her entourage? Unlikely.

"So how you doing, Nathan?" Lorelei said. "Good to see you again."

"You, too."

Veronika guessed Nathan's heart was hammering. He was holding a big grin in place, overdoing it a little.

"I wanted to apologize for springing everything on you so suddenly. I didn't give you much warning."

"No, I appreciate you being direct. It's one of the things I admire about you."

Lorelei smiled brightly. "Thank you. Not everyone appreciates that quality."

Somehow Veronika got the sense that comment was a swipe at her, but she didn't see how it applied. Maybe it was her innate paranoia—a trait almost no one appreciated.

"I wanted to congratulate you," Nathan said. "Your idea brought the mighty Cryomed to its knees. Very impressive. Creativity—there's another of your admirable traits."

You're laying it on a little thick, Veronika sent to Nathan.

I'm not laying it on at all, he shot back.

Poor Nathan. It was hard to believe that a few minutes earlier he'd been professing his love for Veronika.

Then *Lorelei* pinged her privately. *This is all very awkward. Can you get rid of him? We need to talk.*

382

What about? Veronika sent, as Lorelei and Nathan continued to chat.

Parsons and I broke up. We had a dazzling view of the city as a backdrop. Close to a quarter of a million viewers.

That surprised Veronika, although it probably shouldn't have. *Congratulations,* she sent.

The thing is, I'm not sure if the argument was real or not. If it's just for drama, and we're going to get back together, that's skintight, because it played well. If it's real-real, then, I liked him, you know? Plus, I lost my director.

Another surprise. Lorelei could be hurt by someone. *I'm sorry. What do you need from me?* It was also hard to believe Parsons would bail at this point. Lorelei's star was rising; she was doing interviews on the macros, taking all the credit she could for bringing down the bridesicle program. Not that she didn't deserve some of the credit.

I want to talk about employing you, full-time.

Veronika stifled a laugh. Nathan glanced her way, puzzled, before refocusing his attention on Lorelei.

Full-time? Veronika could be the new puppet master, steering Lorelei to even greater heights. She could build on Lorelei's notoriety as one of the architects of Bridesicle Watch's victory, create a new, more socially conscious persona, use Lorelei's fame to do good things in the world.

Sorry, not interested, Veronika sent. *Can't drop my clients like that, plus, it's outside my area of expertise.*

Across the table Nathan was laughing, his eyes bright, probably thinking he had most of Lorelei's attention, hoping he was winning her back, unaware that his rival wasn't Parsons, it was Lorelei's lifestyle. Nathan had no chance with Lorelei because getting back together with him would be a rerun. Lorelei had to keep her material fresh.

62

Rob

A black corrugated-steel grate rattled as he stepped on it and passed back onto the gum-stained sidewalk. Old-fashioned storefronts lined the streets, with doors and windows instead of the wide-open look of the modern stores in High Town, where invisible containment barriers kept the heat and cold out.

Moving kept the anguish at bay. Moving among old, solid things was especially therapeutic. Seeing Winter occasionally was better than the hopelessness of thinking he'd never see her again, but it was more painful than he'd thought. He'd never been the affair type, had never even gone out with a woman who was supposed to be exclusive with someone else.

He lived for any word from Winter, though they were few, because Redmond might get suspicious if he checked her communications and found a bunch of text messages or screen visits to Rob. They'd risked going to a virtual movie together the night before, in an old 1920s-art-deco setup to see a flat black-and-white film from that time, but it wasn't the same. Moving those silly avatars around, pretending the squeeze he felt inside his glove was Winter's fingers on his.

God, he hated Redmond, hated his entire family for how they treated Winter. He recalled the story Winter had told him last night, how Red's son Lloyd made her sit down and finish a berry wrap she'd left half-eaten, because she had no right to waste their food.

Rob cut down a cobbled side street. He needed to get out of his head. All day, he thought the same pointless, repetitive thoughts. He couldn't banish them even for ten minutes, couldn't drive them out with music or conversation or drugs—

He jolted to a stop as Winter popped up in a screen directly in front of him. She was crying.

"Red found out about us. He's going to have me interred in a debt camp."

Of course he found out. At some level Rob knew he would. He suspected Winter had as well. "Run. I'll meet you—"

Winter shook her head. "I'm trapped. There's no way off this *fucking* island-on-stilts. I'm a hundred feet above the water."

Rob headed toward the Christopher Street Pier a block away, with Winter's screen gliding beside him. He could steal a boat.

"How did he find out?"

"He got suspicious, so he had a winged camera the size of a fly following me. It was in your apartment with us." Winter looked behind her, as if she was afraid someone might be eavesdropping. "I begged Red to release me from my contract. I told him I loved you, that I could never love him. He recorded it all as evidence."

385

Heart pounding, Rob slowed to a jog as he reached the wharf. He leaned over the railing separating the walk from black water. There were dozens of old wooden boats creaking in the shallow waves, moored with rotting ropes or plastic cord. He trotted down corroded concrete steps, unmoored one of the boats that had oars.

"What are you doing?" Winter asked.

"Tell me how to get to you." He climbed into the boat, grasped the oars, then paused. The boat was probably some poor guy's livelihood. He pulled off his High Town shoes and tied them to the mooring rope, as compensation.

"Rob, stop. There's no way down to the water. I just wanted to say good-bye, to tell you I love you."

"There must be a maintenance ladder. Something."

"There's no ladder."

Rob was swinging the boat around, aiming the nose toward open water.

"Rob, listen to me, there's no way down. I'd have to jump—"

She went silent. Rob stopped rowing. He worked his system.

"How high up are you?"

"Rob, even if it's possible, we can't do this. You'd never be able to live in the city again. *Any* city. You'd never see your father again, or Veronika, or any of your friends."

His face would be in the criminal database. Any time his likeness was caught by a public camera, the authorities would be alerted automatically.

"I knew what I was getting myself into when I came to your apartment that night," Winter said. "Don't worry about me. I'll be okay. Debt camp will probably be an improvement."

"Just tell me how high up the estate is."

Pause. "It's a hundred eighteen feet."

A quick query told Rob it was possible to drop up to one hundred fifty-eight feet without sustaining serious injury, *if* you landed just right—feetfirst, with your head tilted back to minimize the likelihood of your neck breaking on impact. Then again, a drop of forty feet could kill you if you hit the water wrong. If you drifted too far forward, your ribs would puncture your aorta on impact; too far back and your spine was snapped.

"Tell me how to find you."

"No. I can't do that."

Rob huffed, frustrated. They were wasting time. "Winter, I'm glad Red caught us. I don't want to have a few hours with you once or twice a week, hiding in my apartment. I want to be with you all the time. The only reason I didn't ask you to run away with me before this was because it wasn't fair. You'd be taking most of the risk. Now that's not an issue. So let's go, let's run away while we still can."

After a long pause, a red light appeared on the horizon, to the left of the Statue of Liberty. "I'm two point six miles from you, in the upper bay." Another pause. "It should take an amateur rower an hour and forty-four minutes."

"I'm guessing that estimate is for people not rowing for their lives," Rob said. The nose of the little skiff lifted out of the water on each pull. If he still had the soft hands of a musician, he probably would be looking at savage blisters after this trip. Hopefully the long hours at the reclamation center would pay off, not only in calluses but in endurance.

"Where are you now?" he asked.

"In my room. I'm not locked in." She shrugged. "Where would I run?"

Rob was terrified, but also excited. His belly felt like he was in an elevator, falling swiftly. They had no choice now—they were going to be together, unless they were caught. It would be hard, but they'd be together. That was all he wanted.

"Do me a favor?" Rob said. "Connect me with my dad." He didn't want to take his hands off the oars even for an instant.

As he rowed past the Statue of Liberty and Ellis Island, Rob said good-bye to his father. Lorne told him he was doing the right thing. Rob promised to get word to him when they were safe, somehow. He didn't even know where they were going. It would be safest to get out of the country, but they had no way to pay for transport. Their accounts would be frozen as soon as Winter was discovered missing.

Rob also said good-bye to Veronika, and left it at that. The rest of his friends would have to hear it from Lorne or Veronika.

After an hour of rowing, the nose of the boat was no longer lifting out of the water. His fingers were raw. The oars rubbed in places that lifting and moving and plucking things did not. Rob had no idea how long they had before the authorities came for Winter. He couldn't help imagining there was a copter in the air at this very moment, on its way to get her. He glanced over his shoulder. The estate island was glowing red, maybe half a mile away. Rob clung to the oars and tried to push with his legs to make up for the stiff, exhausted state of his arms.

Tiny waves lapped the sides of the boat, tilting it this way and that as Rob stared up at Redmond's estate. Now that he saw how high a hundred and eighteen feet was, it seemed far, far too high.

Winter's screen, which had accompanied him during the entire trip, was tilted up to take in the height as well.

"I don't know about this," Rob said.

"No, me neither."

They stared up in silence. Rob looked each of the pillars up and down carefully, hoping Winter had missed some important detail. There were no details to miss; they were nothing but slick gray-carbon fiber. Likely Winter had opened a screen and examined each one up close.

"I'm coming," Winter said.

"Are you sure?"

"Yes. I'm out of my room."

Rob's heart began to pump faster. She was really going to do it. When she got to the edge, would she change her mind? Possibly. He couldn't imagine climbing over the low fence that surrounded the estate and jumping from that height.

"I'm in the elevator. Oh, crap." Her screen disappeared.

"What is it? Winter?" No reply. Rob was tempted to open a screen up there to find out what had happened, but that could only make things worse. So he waited, his mouth dry, his heart hammering, wondering what he would do if he didn't hear from her again. What could he do? Row back to shore.

Winter's screen reappeared. "I'm here. I bumped into Lloyd's wife, Kidra. I told her I was going to see Red, to beg him to reconsider. I'm outside. There's no one in sight."

Rob thought he caught a glimpse of movement above.

"I can see you," Winter said. "Okay. I can do this." Feeling like his heart was going to explode, Rob watched her climb over the fence, then turn and face the water. "Oh, God, I don't know."

"Keep your head back, hands at your sides."

"I'm so scared. I don't know if I can do this."

Maybe it would be best to convince her to go back inside and wait for the authorities. Better she live in a debt camp than drown. She was right there, though. So close. In a few seconds she could be in the boat.

"I'm going to count to three," he said. "On three, you jump. Don't think, just jump. On three. One. Two—"

"I don't know. I don't know."

"Three."

She jumped.

Suddenly she was falling, her clothes billowing, her red hair like the tail of a comet. Her hands were pinned to her sides, her feet together, head back. Rob had a flash of that other bride-sicle, falling in ten thousand places at once. But she hadn't been real—no bones that could break, no aorta to puncture.

Winter hit the water. Without waiting for her to surface, Rob rowed frantically toward the spot where she'd hit, leaving her still-open screen behind after catching one quick glimpse of her—her face barely visible in the dark water, obscured by bubbles, eyes wide.

When he reached the spot, she wasn't there. He stood up in the boat, looked all around.

She wasn't there.

"*Winter? Winter?*" The boat rocked dangerously as he bent over and peered into the dark water, trying to catch a glimpse of her, wondering if he should dive in, swim down, and try to feel around for her.

Desperate, he looked at her screen, still hovering a hundred feet away, hoping to get some clue as to where she was. Instead he caught a glimpse of movement in the water, fifty feet beyond the screen, almost in the shadow of the estate. It was Winter, thrashing in slow motion, her face disappearing as each swell passed over her.

"Winter," he shouted. He dove in, the cold water a shock that left him spluttering as he swam, calling her name, urging her to hang on.

She was under water when he reached her, her face a blur receding into darkness. Rob dove, grasped her by the shoulder, and drew her up until they broke the surface together.

Her eyes were open; Rob didn't think she was breathing, but he wasn't sure. Treading water, he pulled her face to his, held her nose and blew into her mouth.

Nothing. He tried again. It didn't feel like the air was going in. He had to get her into the boat.

He swam on his side, doing his best to hold Winter's head above water. The boat was drifting away from them. It had been a hundred feet away when he left it, now it was three times that. He redoubled his effort, tried to flatten out so he could kick on the surface of the water, but he couldn't manage it while holding Winter.

Winter vomited water into his face.

"That's it, love. That's it," Rob said. He turned her so she was facedown, tried to thump her back. She vomited again. "That's right. Get it all out."

Winter fell into a coughing fit, her chest and stomach spasming. She took a long, squealing breath and coughed more.

"We have to get to the boat," Rob said, nearly shouting. "Can you hang on around my neck?" He spun around, wrapped Winter's hands around his neck, squeezed them together. "Hold on tight, as tight as you can." Winter dug her fingers into his collarbone. "That's right."

Rob swam a breaststroke. It was easier now, but the boat

seemed impossibly far away, drifting toward the Verrazano Narrows Bridge, which separated the bay from the ocean.

"What happened to the boat?" Winter asked, so soft Rob could barely hear.

"It's drifting away on the current."

Winter's legs started thrashing. It took Rob a moment to realize she was trying to kick, to help. They were feeble kicks, but it was nice to see she could move her legs.

"Are you all right?" he asked. "You're not hurt?"

"Don't talk. Swim."

So Rob swam, struggling to keep his face above water while bearing Winter's weight on his shoulders.

Soon the boat was noticeably closer.

And closer still. As they closed in, the boat seemed to be flying across the water, intent on staying out of Rob's grasp.

Rob kept swimming.

63

Veronika

Veronika wiped her eyes, but the tears kept coming.

She wanted to open a screen over the bay to see how Rob and Winter were doing, but it was too risky. If she watched, there was a risk of inadvertently giving away their location to the authorities. The moment Rob tossed their systems into the bay, Veronika closed the screen she'd been watching from, high above the bay, knowing she'd never set eyes on either of them again.

Across the big banquet table, she caught Nathan's eye. He smiled.

It's sad, but still a happy ending, no? he sent.

I'm happy for them, terribly sad for me, she sent.

Nathan nodded. He stood, gestured for everyone's attention. It was a large gathering, mostly Bridesicle Watch people, but also some of Winter and Rob's friends, whom Veronika had invited after the news of their disappearance became public. The room quieted.

"Before the formal festivities begin, I'd like to propose a toast to my two friends." Nathan raised his glass of champagne, originally intended to toast the demise of the bridesicle program. That could wait. "To Rob and Winter. Wherever you are, wherever you end up, you're where you belong. Together at last."

Veronika stifled a sob as she drank. Lycan reached out, patted her back. "I'm sure they'll be all right."

Sunali got everyone's attention and gave a little speech. She lavished praise on Veronika, and Lycan, and even on Lorelei, although the latter was clearly an effort. They toasted the fall of the dating center.

"Now I want to tell all of you something firsthand, before it leaks," Sunali said, after the toast. Veronika was struck by the woman's presence, the sense of power and purpose she exuded. "Cryomed is going to announce that it is returning all of the 'salvage' bridesicles to their families for burial."

Sounds of surprise and outrage rose; Sunali raised her hands for quiet. "They want to make Bridesicle Watch seem responsible for these deaths, that we forced the closing of the dating program, now look at the terrible price these poor women and their families must pay."

Veronika couldn't help thinking that if the closing had occurred a few weeks earlier, Winter would have been one of those women.

"Right after their announcement, we will announce that Bridesicle Watch will revive all of these women."

"*All* the bridesicles?" Lycan asked. Veronika was startled by his voice; it wasn't like him to speak in front of so many people. His graduate student was handling all of the interviews surrounding the rollout of his emotion system app, because he was too nervous to speak in front of the camera.

"No, Lycan, unfortunately we don't have the funds to revive everyone in the program, only those who'd otherwise be buried. It will drain most of our remaining funds, but with the dating program closed, Bridesicle Watch doesn't have much reason to exist anyway. So, we're going out with a bang."

"What about Mira?" Lycan asked.

Sunali nodded. "Mira will be first. My plan is for her to be at my side at the press conference, if she's willing. And we'll revive a few other women who'd otherwise go back to the main facility, to repay favors owed."

Lycan nodded, went back to looking down at his hands.

"I want to talk to Sunali for a minute," Lycan said as people were filing out of the banquet.

"About what?" Veronika asked, but Lycan was already halfway across the room. Nathan motioned to her; Veronika held up a finger and hurried after Lycan, who strode up to Sunali like someone mustering his courage for a confrontation.

"I want to be the one to tell Mira she's being revived," Lycan said.

"*Wait a minute*," Veronika said, before she could stop herself.

Sunali ignored Veronika, canted her head at Lycan. "I don't understand. Why would you want to be the one to tell her?"

Lycan was looking at Veronika, surprised by her outburst.

"Can't you let Sunali do it?" Veronika asked. "You can speak to Mira once she's out."

Lycan shook his head. "It wouldn't be the same. This is important to me, that I do this."

"You *know* her?" Sunali asked.

Lycan explained, haltingly, clearly uncomfortable to be confessing his bridesicle sin to the founder of Bridesicle Watch.

When he finished, Sunali looked at Veronika. "And you're uneasy about this because of their past?"

Veronika nodded.

"You don't have anything to worry about," Sunali said.

It was a remarkably patronizing thing to say, as far as Veronika was concerned. Of course Veronika was being foolish. Of course a woman as stunning as Mira wouldn't be interested in Lycan, unless she was dead and trapped in that unholy hell. But to come right out and say that? Her hackles up, Veronika asked, "And why is that, Sunali?"

"Because Mira is gay."

Already prepared with a comeback for what she'd expected Sunali to say, Veronika swallowed it, let out a stunned peep in its place.

"How do you know?" Lycan asked, looking beyond surprised.

Sunali explained. Mira had asked her to pass a message to a woman in the main facility, whose name was Jeannette. Jeannette told Sunali that she and Mira had been partners. Mira never mentioned that to Sunali, evidently afraid of being pulled from the bridesicle program if anyone found out she wasn't hetero. After doing some digging, Sunali had discovered that in the early days of the dating program, Cryomed had simply plucked longtime residents of the minus eighty without much effort at screening the women, orienting them, or getting their consent.

"I really want to be the one to tell her," Lycan said. "Please."

64

Rob

The night air was chilly, but rowing kept him warm, even though he was shirtless after tossing his system overboard. He'd been happy to discover Winter was wearing a shirt underneath hers. Smart girl.

She was still sleeping, curled in the bottom of the boat.

The boat rose on a particularly high wave, plunged down the far side. He was getting used to it somewhat, no longer convinced the boat was going to capsize each time they went over a big wave.

Without his system, he had no idea how long he'd been rowing; all he knew was he needed to get about thirty miles up the coast to ensure they weren't caught by any surveillance cameras. It was going to be hard, adjusting to having no access to information like that, now that he was systemless.

"You know, it's still not too late." Winter was awake, looking up at him. "Take me up the coast, drop me ashore, row back. There's no evidence you were the one who helped me."

Rob almost laughed. "Like I told you, I'm glad we got caught. It's you and me now."

Moving gently, cautiously, Winter worked her way into the seat across from him. "Head nod. You and me."

The lights along the coast were growing sparser. A good sign. "That was quite a jump you made."

"Relax, then follow the bubbles."

"Come again?"

"I paid a cliff diver for a consult before the jump. He said the key was to relax as much as possible right before impact, and then to remember to follow the bubbles back to the surface, because I'd end up deep underwater."

"I wish he'd mentioned that you weren't going to surface anywhere near where you went under."

"That would have been useful information."

Rob looked up. The dark sky was beautiful.

"So, where are we heading?" Winter asked.

"Up the coast, then inland. I was thinking we could try to find a raw community that will take us in."

Winter took a deep breath, exhaled slowly. "Sounds good."

"Do you have any idea where your brother might be?" It would be nice to have someone they knew, out in the raw lands.

"The last time I heard from him, he was heading toward Montana."

"That would be a long walk." Rob rowed just with the left oar for a moment, trying to bring the boat back parallel with the shoreline. "I'm worried about how we're going to buy food." He looked at his bare chest. "And a shirt."

Winter grasped a chain around her neck, drew out a small pouch dangling from it. "Jewelry. Not much, but it's quality stuff."

"You are incredible."

"Hopefully it will keep us fed for a while, but eventually we're going to have to figure out something else. Have you thought about what it will be like, to live like this?"

Of course he had. It was going to be hard. No friends, no family, no access to Superfood as a last resort. On top of that, the thought of having no remote communication, ever, was almost inconceivable to him. Not even an outdated hand-held? It would be like having one of his senses amputated. But it was a tradeoff. He'd be with Winter.

"I'll be with you," he finally said. "If that means not getting to watch my favorite shows..." He shrugged. "I can live with that."

Winter grinned. "I'm going to miss *Purple Daydreams* and *Tempest*. Those are my favorite shows, by the way—if you hate them we might have a problem."

The swells were getting higher. Rob looked over his shoulder; in the distance white crests topped many of the waves.

"You know why I'm sure we'll be okay?" Rob asked.

"Why?"

"Because we're used to hard times."

65

Mira

"Mira? Can you hear me?" The voice came from a billion miles away, from another galaxy.

Where was she? She waited for the disorientation to clear; she could barely string thoughts together.

"It's me. Lycan," the voice said.

Lycan. She could picture him. He'd been...someone important to her.

Then it came back to her, in layers, beginning with Sunali, her removal from the program, then speaking to Jeannette, then Lycan. She opened her eyes.

Lycan was leaning over her, smiling. "I've got awfully good news."

"Good news," she said. The words felt strange on her lips, as if she was speaking in a foreign language.

"Yes. You're getting out of here. Sunali is paying for it, but my research helped make it possible. You remember Sunali?"

"I do," Mira heard herself say. She thought she must be imagining this conversation. Maybe this was her true death. Maybe her time in the minus eighty had ended, and they were pulling her from the crèche, and this was some final spark of light that came before true death.

But how would a soul know the difference between true death and the death of the crèche? Surely it couldn't.

"I wanted to be the one to tell you. After what I did to you, I wanted to tell you the good news."

Her mind had cleared enough to be certain she wasn't imagining this, or dreaming it. Lycan was here. And she was in a different place—the walls and ceiling were less ornate, more hospital than palace. This must be the main facility, where Jeannette was.

"Sunali can really do that? She can afford to get me out of here?"

Lycan grinned. "She really can. She inherited a fortune. Her organization did, anyway."

"Can you give Sunali a message for me? Tell her I want her to revive Jeannette instead of me. She'll know who I mean. Can you do that?"

Lycan was grinning. "It's all taken care of. *I'm* going to revive Jeannette for you."

This wasn't making sense. Mira wondered if Lycan was delusional. This was real, but they were only words, spoken by a man she didn't know. "Are you sure?"

Lycan tapped in the air for a moment, and words appeared above her face, partially blocking Lycan. "That's a legal document." He pointed out a line near the bottom. "My DNA-coded signature. I borrowed most of the money against my future earnings."

For the first time, Mira dared allow a sliver of hope to break through. Lycan reached to remove the document, and Mira said, "*Wait*. Please. Let me read what it says."

It said Jeannette was going to live, to breathe, to speak in her own beautiful voice again.

"Satisfied?" Lycan asked when she'd finished.

"Yes. Thank you. So much."

"You can thank me the next time I see you. We want to have you and Jeannette over for dinner as soon as you're both able. 'We' is me and my girlfriend. Her name is Veronika."

It was inconceivable to Mira, she and Jeannette walking into a room together, sitting down, eating.

All Mira could think to say was, "I'd like that."

"Good. I'm glad. I'm glad you're not angry at me. I'll see you soon, then."

"Yes. Soon." Although still, she couldn't quite believe it.

Lycan reached up.

Mira   jolted   awake before she hit the Mira.

Acknowledgments

I'm deeply grateful to my editor Tom Bouman, and to my friends and fellow writers Ian Creasey, Rachel Swirsky, and Laura Valeri, who provided incredibly insightful feedback on the first draft of this novel.

Warm thanks to my friend psychologist Jim Pugh, who provided indispensable input as we mapped out this novel on a napkin at Moe's. I miss our lunches.

As always, thanks to Codex, my online writing community, and to Clarion East and Taos Toolbox, for their roles in my development as a writer.

Thank you, Sheila Williams, editor of *Asimov's*, for publishing "Bridesicle," the short story on which this novel is based.

Thanks to my wonderful wife, Alison, for her support and love, and to my parents, who are always there for me.

Finally, this novel wouldn't exist if not for the people at Orbit, and my agent, Seth Fishman. I mean that quite literally: they suggested I turn my short story "Bridesicle" into a novel. Thanks to Orbit for believing in this novel before I'd even written it, and to Seth, for his masterful guidance and wisdom.

extras

www.orbitbooks.net

about the author

Will McIntosh is a Hugo Award winner and Nebula finalist whose short stories have appeared in *Asimov's* (where he won the 2010 Reader's Award for Short Story), *Strange Horizons*, *Interzone*, and *Science Fiction and Fantasy: Best of the Year*, among others. His first novel, *Soft Apocalypse*, was released in 2011 and his second novel, *Hitchers*, was published in February 2012. In 2008 he became the father of twins.

Find out more about Will McIntosh and other Orbit authors by registering for the free monthly newsletter at www.orbitbooks.net

Prologue

Game Face

This is not the end of the world, Ross told himself.

He closed his eyes as a low hum began to sound around him, heralding the commencement of the scan. The effect was more white-out than black-out, the reflective tiles filling the room with greater light than the fine membranes of his eyelids could possibly block.

He should look upon all of it as a new start; several new

starts, in fact. Yes: multiple, simultaneous, unforeseen, unwanted and utterly unappealing new beginnings. Welcome to your future.

As he lay on the slab he conducted a quick audit of all the things that had gone wrong in the couple of hours since he'd stepped off his morning bus into a squall of Scottish rain and a lungful of diesel fumes on his way to work. He concluded that it wasn't a brain scan he needed: it was a brain transplant. Nonetheless, as the scan-heads zipped and buzzed above him, for the briefest moment he enjoyed a sense of his mind being completely empty, an awareness of a fleeting disconnection from his thoughts, as though they were a vinyl record from which the needle had been temporarily raised.

'Hey Solderburn, are we clear?' he asked, keeping his eyes closed just in case.

There was no reply. Then he recalled the capricious ruler of the Research and Development Lab telling him to bang on the door if there was a problem, so he deduced there was no internal monitoring.

He opened his eyes and sat up. It was only a moment after he had done so that he realised the tracks and scan-heads were no longer there. He did a double-take, wondering if the whole framework had been automatically withdrawn into some hidden wall-recess: it was the kind of pointless feature Solderburn was known to spend weeks implementing, even though it was of no intrinsic value.

There was still no word from outside. Solderburn probably had a lot of switches to flip, so Ross was patient, and as he didn't have a watch on, he only had a rough idea how long he'd been sitting there. However, by the time the big hand on his mental clock had ticked from 'reasonable delay' through 'mild discourtesy' into 'utterly taking the piss', he'd decided it was time to remind the chief engineer that his latest configuration included a human component.

The bastard had better not have sloped off outdoors to have a fag. Seriously, was there any greater incentive to stop smoking than having to do it in the doorway to this dump, looking out at the rest of the shitty Seventies industrial estate surrounding it?

Ross got to his feet and extended a fist, but before he could deliver the first of his intended thumps, the door opened, though not the way he was expecting. Instead of swinging on its hinge, the entire thing withdrew outwards by a couple of inches, then slid laterally out of sight with the softest hiss of servos.

WTF?

Beyond it lay not the familiar chaos of the R&D lab, but merely a grey wall and the grungy dimness of a damp-smelling corridor.

So Solderburn *was* taking the piss, but not in the way Ross had previously believed. This was the kind of prank that explained why the guy had ended up working here in Stirling, rather than winning a Nobel Prize. He must have slid some kind of false wall into place outside the scanning room. Ross walked forward, stepping lightly because he suspected Solderburn's practical joke had some way to go before it reached the pay-off stage.

He looked left and right along the passageway.

All right, so maybe it was time to revise the practical joke hypothesis.

There was a dead end to the left, where the way was blocked by three huge pipes that emerged from the ceiling and descended through a floor constructed of metal grilles on top of concrete, into which sluice channels were etched in parallel. There was a regulator dial on the right-most tube, sitting above a wheel for controlling the flow. A sign next to it warned: 'DO NOT MESS WITH VALVE'.

It was a redundant warning in Ross's case: he wasn't going near it. Even from a few yards away, he could feel the vibration of flow in the pipes, indicating that enormous volumes of fluid must be passing through the vessels. It sounded like enough to power a small hydroelectric station. Even Solderburn couldn't fake up something like that.

In the other direction, the corridor went on at least twice the length of the lab, condensation beading its walls. He could hear non-syncopated pounding, its low echo suggesting something powerful and resonant that was being dampened by thick walls. This thought prompted him to glance at the ceiling, which mostly comprised live rock, occasionally masked off by black panels insulating lines of thick cable.

He began to make his way along the corridor. Light was provided by strips running horizontally along the walls, roughly two feet above head height. Ross assumed them to be inset, but if so it was a hell of a neat job. They looked like they could be peeled right off and stuck wherever they were required.

There was another light source further ahead, a dim blue-green glow coming from behind a glass panel set high in the wall on the left.

The corridor trembled following a particularly resonant boom from somewhere above. Ross could feel the metal grates rattle from it, the air disturbed by a pulse of movement. It felt warm, like the sudden gust of heat when somebody has just opened an oven door. There was still no rhythm, no pattern to the sounds, and yet Ross found something about them familiar.

As he approached the panel, he could see a play of coloured light behind the glass, constant but fluid, as though there might be a team of welders on the other side of it. Please, he thought, *let* there be a team of welders on the other side: hairy-arsed welders with bottles of Irn-Bru and Monday-morning hangovers, toting oxyacetylene torches and forehead-slappingly obvious explanations for what was going on. Perhaps he had ended up at one of the factories on the estate, somehow?

The panel was high, so Ross had to stand close and stretch to get a look through the glass. As soon as he did, he caught a glimpse of someone on the other side and promptly threw himself back down low, out of sight.

It wasn't a welder; or if it was, it was one who had utterly lost it at some point and started grafting stuff to his own face.

In his startlement and panicked attempt to hide, Ross tumbled backwards to the deck, a collapse that felt less painful but sounded altogether more clangingly metallic than he was expecting. If the hideous creature behind the wall hadn't seen him as he peered through the glass a moment ago, then he had surely heard him now.

He had to get moving, and hope there was more than one way out of this corridor. It might be prejudiced to assume that the man he had seen meant him any harm purely on the basis of his unfortunate appearance, but it was difficult to imagine anybody with a penchant for soldering things to his coupon being an entirely calm and balanced individual. Besides, Ross's alarm hadn't been inspired purely by the fact that the guy would have a bastard of a time getting his face through airport security; it was the look Ross had briefly glimpsed in that nightmarish visage's eyes: wild, frantic, unhinged and, most crucially, searching.

It was as he uncrumpled himself from a heap on the floor that he discovered any attempt at flight was futile, and for a reason far worse than that this mutilated horror might already have cut off his escape. His eye was drawn, for the first time since emerging from his cell, to his own person rather than his surroundings, and a glance at his limbs showed them no longer to be clad in what he remembered pulling on that morning. Gone were the soft-leather shoes, moleskin jeans and charcoal shirt, replaced by a one-piece ensemble of metal, glass and bare skin, all three surfaces scarred by scorch-marks and gouges.

He looked in terrified disgust at his forearm, where two light-pulsing cables were visible on the surface, feeding into his wrist at one end and plunging beneath an alloy sheath at the other. His legs were similarly metal-clad, apart from glass panels beneath which further fibre-optic wiring could be seen intermittently breaking the surface of skin that was a distressingly unhealthy pallor even for someone who had grown up in the west of Scotland.

His chest and stomach had armour plates grafted strategically to cover certain areas whilst retaining flexibility of movement by leaving other expanses of skin untouched, and there were further transparent sections revealing enough of his interior to suggest he wouldn't be needing a bag of chips and a can of cream soda any time soon.

Trembling with shock and incredulity, he hauled himself upright, finding his new wardrobe to be impossibly light. His movement was free and fluid too, feeling as natural as had he still been wearing what he'd turned up to work in.

Was it some kind of illusion, then?

No. Of course. He had fallen asleep during the scan. It was a dream.

Except that normally the awareness of dreaming was enough to dispel it and bring him to.

Ross looked himself up and down again. There was no swirling transition of thoughts and images bringing him to the surface, no dream-logic progress linking one bizarre moment to the next.

He approached the glass again. He could see two vertical shafts of energy, one blue and one green, seemingly unchannelled through any vessel, but perfectly linear, independent and self-contained nonetheless. Reluctantly, he pulled his focus back from what was behind the glass to the reflecting surface itself.

Arse cakes.

He looked like he had faceplanted the clearance sale at Radio Shack. It was still recognisably his own features underneath there somewhere: even that little scar on his cheek from when he'd fallen off a spider-web roundabout when he was nine. He recalled what a fuss his mum had made when he needed stitches. Everything's relative, eh Mammy?

Another muffled boom sounded, moments before another shudder rippled the air. He could hear lesser percussions too, like it was bonfire night and he was indoors, half a mile from the display. It was hardly an enticement to proceed down the corridor, but what choice did he have?

He strode forward on his augmented legs, surprised to discover his gait felt no different, his tread lighter than the accompanying metal-on-metal thumps suggested. There was absolutely nothing about this that wasn't absolutely perplexing, not least the aspects that felt normal. For instance, as he followed the passageway around a bend to a T-junction leading off either side of an elevator, he was disturbed to find that he seemed instinctively to know where he was going. Was there something in all this circuitry that was doing part of his thinking for him? He wasn't aware of it if so; though the fact that he probably wouldn't be aware of such a process was not reassuring.

He stepped on to the open platform of the elevator and

pressed his palm to the activation panel. A light traced around his atrophied fingers at the speed of an EKG and the platform began to rise.

He looked again at the leathery grey of his hand. It gave a new meaning to the term dead skin. He thought of all the times Carol had ticked him off for biting his nails, of her rubbing moisturiser on his cracks and chaps in wintertime.

Carol. No. Not yet.

He put her from his mind as the elevator reached the top of the shaft, where his faith in instinctively knowing where he was going was put to the test by his arriving somewhere he was dangerously conspicuous. No narrow passageway this time: he had reached some kind of muster point or staging area, and was rising up into the centre of it like it was his turn on *Camberwick Green*.

He got there just in time to see a group of figures – each of them similarly dressed by the Motorola menswear department – march out through a wide doorway. They moved briskly and with purpose, two halves of the automatic door closing diagonally behind them as the elevator platform came to a stop, flush with the floor.

The booms were louder here. The smaller ones sounded like muffled explosions somewhere beyond the walls, but the big ones seemed to pulse through the very fabric of whatever this place was. He could tell when one was coming, as though the entire structure was breathing in just before it; could sense something surge through all those pipes lining the walls. It was like being inside a nose that was about to sneeze.

He was absolutely sure of which way to head next, but it wasn't to do with any weird instinct or control by some exterior force. It was simply a matter of having observed in which direction the platoon of zombie-troopers had shipped out and of proceeding in precisely the opposite.

They'd had their backs to him so he couldn't get a clear view of what they were all carrying, but the objects had been metal and cylindrical, and he considered it unlikely they were some kind of cyborg brass section that had just been given its cue to hit the stage. Given how little sense everything else was making right then, it was always possible that the latter was the case and they were about to strike up 'In the Mood', but Ross strongly suspected that the only thing they were in the mood for was shooting anybody who got in their way.

He proceeded towards his intended exit at what he realised was an incongruously girly trot: hastened by his eagerness to get away but slowed short of a run in case it should be conspicuous that he was making a break for it. His head spun with awful possibilities, trying to piece together what could have happened. It had to have been the scan, he deduced. Whether intentionally or not, it had left him in a state of suspended animation and his body had been stored until the advent of the technology that currently adorned and possibly controlled him.

Neurosphere. Those amoral corporate sociopaths. This was their doing. There was probably a clause in his employment contract that covered this shit, and as he'd never bothered to read the pages and pages of legalese, he'd had no real idea what he was signing. Now he could be working for them forever, part of a manufactured army. But in that case, why hadn't they erased or at least restrained his memory? Why was he not a compliant drone like the others he'd seen? Perhaps something had gone wrong with the process and he was the lucky one – retaining his memory and his sense of self and thus able to testify to Neurosphere's monstrous crime. Or perhaps he was the really *un*lucky one, trapped in this condition but not anaesthetised by merciful oblivion, and unlike the others he'd be conscious of every horror he was about to witness, or even effect.

He had no idea what year it was, or even what century. Chances were everyone he ever knew was gone. There might be nothing in the world he would recognise.

The big doorway opened obligingly as he approached, its two halves sliding diagonally apart to reveal another corridor, brighter than he'd seen before. Light appeared to be flashing and shimmering beyond a curve up ahead, and with nobody to observe him, he ran towards it.

'Oh,' he said.

The source of the flashing and shimmering on the far side of the passageway turned out to be a huge window opposite, easily twelve feet high by twenty feet wide, through which Ross could see what was outside this building. He hadn't thought he could ever look into another pane of glass and see a more unsettling sight than the one that had met him only a few minutes ago when he glimpsed his own reflection. Clearly it was not a day to be making assumptions.

The first thing he noticed was the sky, which was a shade of purple that he found disturbing. It wasn't so much that there was anything aesthetically displeasing about the colour itself; it was, to be fair, a quite regally luxuriant purple: deep, textured and vibrant. It was more to do with his knowledge of astronomy and subsequent awareness that, normally, the sky he looked up at owed its colour to the shorter wavelengths and greater proportion of blue photons in the type of light emitted by the planet's primary energy source. What was disturbing about this particular hue was not merely that it could not be any sky on Earth, but that it could not be any sky beneath its sun.

Worse, its predominantly purple colouration wasn't even the most distressing thing about the view through the window: that distinction went to the fact that it was full of burning aircraft. There were dozens of them up there, possibly hundreds, stretching out all the way to the horizon. It looked to be some kind of massive extraterrestrial expeditionary landing force, and its efforts were proving successful in so far as landing was defined as reaching terra firma: all of the craft were certainly managing that much. However, controlled descents executed without conflagration and completed by vessels comprising fewer than a thousand flaming pieces were, quite literally, a lot thinner on the ground.

Ross felt that inrush again, that sense of energy being channelled very specifically to one source, then heard the great boom once more, and this time he could see its source. It was a colossal artillery weapon, sited at least a mile away, but evidently powered by the facility in which he was standing. Its twin muzzles were each the size of an oil tanker, jutting from a dome bigger than St Paul's Cathedral, and its effect on the invasion force was comparable to a howitzer trained on a flock of geese. Each mighty blast devastated another host of unfortunate landing craft, sending debris spinning and hurtling towards the surface.

He had no sense of how long he had been standing there: it could have been thirty seconds and it could have been ten times that. The spectacle was horrifyingly mesmeric, but the car-crash fascination was not purely vicarious. Everything Ross saw had unthinkable consequences for himself. Instead of being merely lost in time, he now had no idea which planet he was even on.

He could see buildings in the distance, only visible because they were so large. The architecture was unquestionably alien, as was the very idea of building vast, isolated towers in an otherwise empty desert landscape. And still something inside him felt like he belonged here, or at least that his environment was not as alien as it should have been.

'It's an awe-inspiring sight, isn't it?'

When Ross heard the voice speak softly from only a few feet behind him, he deduced rather depressingly that he must no longer have a digestive system, as this could be the only explanation for why he didn't shit himself.

He turned around and found himself staring at another brutally haphazard melange of flesh and metal, one he decided was definitely the estate model. The newcomer was a foot taller at least, and more heavily armoured, particularly around the head, leaving his face looking like a lost little afterthought. He looked so imposingly heavy, Ross could imagine him simply crashing through anything less than a reinforced floor, and couldn't picture walls proving much of an impediment either. Wherever he wanted to be, he was getting there, and whatever he wanted, Ross was giving him it.

'Yes,' Ross agreed meekly, amazed to hear his own voice still issuing from whatever he had become.

'You could lose yourself in it,' the big guy went on. His tone was surprisingly soft, perhaps one used to being listened to without the need to raise it, but not as surprising as his accent, which was a precise if rather theatrical received pronunciation. Clearly, as well as advanced technology, this planet also had some very posh schools.

'Perhaps even forget what you were supposed to be doing. Such as joining up with your unit and getting on with fighting off the invasion, what with there being a war on and all.'

His voice remained quiet but Ross could hear the sternest of warnings in his register. There was control there too, no expectation of needing to ask twice. Very bizarrely, Ross was warming to him. Maybe it was the programming, same as whatever was making him feel this place was familiar.

'Yes, sorry, absolutely … er … sir,' he remembered to add. 'My unit, that's right. Have to join up. On my way now, sir.'

'That's "Lieutenant Kamnor, sir",' he instructed.

'Yes, sir, Lieutenant Kamnor, sir,' Ross barked, eyes scanning either way along the corridor as he weighed his options regarding which direction Kamnor expected him to walk in.

He turned and made to return to the staging area. Kamnor stopped him by placing a frighteningly heavy hand on his shoulder.

'Are you all right, soldier?' he asked, sounding genuinely concerned. 'You seem a little disoriented. Do you know where your unit even is?'

Ross decided he had nothing to lose.

'I have no idea where *I* even am, sir. I don't know how I got here. I have no memory of it. I'm not a soldier. I'm a scientific researcher in Stirling. That's Scotland, er, planet Earth, and this morning, that being an early twenty-first-century morning, I had a neuroscan as part of my work. I was still totally biodegradable; I mean, an entirely organic being. When I stepped out of the scanning cell, I found myself here, looking like this.'

Kamnor's face altered, concern changing to something between alarm and awe, and everything that it conveyed seemed amplified by being the only recognisable piece of humanity amidst so much machine.

'Blood of the fathers,' he said, his voice falling to a gasp. 'You're telling me you were a different form, in another world?'

'Yes sir, lieutenant, sir.'

'Blood of the fathers. Then it truly is the prophecy.'

Kamnor beheld him with an entirely new regard, readable even in his alloy-armoured body language.

'The prophecy?' Ross enquired.

'That one would come from a different world: a being who once took another form, but who would be reborn here as one of us, to become the leader who rose in our time of need. That time is at hand,' he added, gesturing to the astonishing scene through the huge window, 'for our world is under attack, and lo, you have been delivered to us this day.'

Ross half turned to once again take in the sky-shattering conflict in which he had just been told he was destined to play a legendary role. A host of confused emotions vied for primacy in dictating how he should feel. Sick proved the winner. He recalled hearing the line: 'Some men are born great, others have greatness thrust upon them.' He wondered if that also applied to heroism. He had no combat training, no military strategy and tended to fold badly in even just verbal confrontations.

He was about to ask 'Are you sure?' but swallowed it back on the grounds that it wasn't the most leaderly way to greet the hand of destiny when it was extended to him. He settled for staring blankly like a tit, something he was getting pretty adept at.

Then Kamnor's face broke from solemnity into barking, aggressive laughter.

'Just messing with you. Of course there's no bloody prophecy. You've been hit by the virus, that's all. Been finding chaps in your condition for days.'

'Virus?' Ross asked, his relief at no longer having a planet's fate thrust into his hands quickly diminished as he belatedly appreciated how preferable it was to the role of cannon fodder.

'Yes, sneaky buggers these Gaians. They hit us with a very nasty piece of malware in advance of their invasion force: part binary code and part psychological warfare. Devilishly clever. It gives the infected hosts all kinds of memories that aren't really theirs. Makes you think you're actually one of them: a human, from Gaia, or as they call it, Earth. It uploads all kinds of vivid memories covering right up until what seems like last night or even this morning. Like, for instance, that you're a scientist from, where was it?'

'Stirling,' Ross said, his voice all but failing him.

'See? It's really detailed. Convinces you that you just arrived here, plucked from another life on *their* planet. But don't worry, it wears off. It's full of holes, so it breaks down: I mean, hell of a coincidence they all speak the same language as us and even sound like us, eh? The virus auto-translates what they're saying. Don't worry, you'll be right as rain soon enough. We find that shooting a few of the bastards helps blow away the mist. So how about you catch up to your unit and help them spread the spank?'

Ross ... was his name even Ross? He now knew officially nothing for sure.

This couldn't be true. These memories were his. They weren't just vivid and detailed, they were the only ones he had. Surely there would be some conflict going on in there if what Kamnor was saying was right. Yet as he stood before this terrifyingly powerful mechanised warrior, it occurred to him to wonder why the lieutenant would be so patient and understanding even as war raged on the other side of the hyper-reinforced window. Furthermore, there was that disarming sense of the familiar, even of positive associations, ever-present since he'd arrived here. For the moment, he'd just have to run with it, see if the mists really did blow away.

'I don't know what unit I'm with, lieutenant sir,' he admitted.

Kamnor reached out a huge, steel-fingered hand and tapped the metal cladding that Ross used to think of as his upper arm. There was a symbol etched there, a long thin sword.

'You're with Rapier squad. Mopping-up detail, under Sergeant Gortoss.' He gestured along the corridor in the opposite direction from where Ross had just come.

'Turn left at the first pile of flaming debris and look for the most homicidally deranged bastard you can find. Ordinarily he'd be in a maximum-security prison, but when there's a war on, he's just the kind of chap you want inside the tent pissing out.'

'Yes sir,' said Ross, by which he meant: 'Holy mother of fuck.'

'You remember how to fire a weapon, don't you?'

'I'm sure it'll come back,' he replied, making to leave.

Kamnor stopped him again.

'Well, before you go I would suggest you take a quick refresher on how to salute a superior officer.'

Kamnor saluted by way of example, sending his arm out straight, angled up thirty degrees from the horizontal, his metal fist clenched tight.

Ross was inundated with unaccustomed feelings of gratitude, loyalty and pride, driving a determination to serve and please this man. He had read about leaders whom soldiers would follow into battle, kill for, even die for, but never understood such emotions until now.

He sent out his right arm as shown, his shoulder barely level with Kamnor's breastplate, clenching his fist once it was fully extended. As he brought his fingers tightly together, a long metal spike emerged at high speed from somewhere above his wrist, shooting up into Kamnor's mouth, through his palate and into his brain.

It was a tight call as to who was the more shocked, but Kamnor probably edged it, aided by the visual impact of blood and an unidentified yellow-green fluid spurting in pulsatile gushes from his mouth. He bucked and squirmed but was too paralysed to do anything else in response.

'Oh Christ, I'm so sorry,' Ross spluttered, trying to work out how to withdraw the spike back into his wrist. 'I didn't mean it, I just …'

But Kamnor was way past listening. He fell to the floor, pulling Ross over with him, his arm still linked to Kamnor's head by the rogue shaft of steel. The blood subsided but the yellow-green fluid continued to hose, while one of Kamnor's great feet twitched spastically, clanking and scraping on the metal grate lining the floor.

Ross heard a hiss of pistons and saw the double door at the end of the corridor begin to separate.

'Oh buggering arse flakes.'

Through the widening gap he could see six pairs of metal-clad legs making their way towards the passage. In about one second they were going to spot this, and it wasn't going to look good.

How did you get this bloody thing out?

A clench of his fist had extended it, he reasoned, but so far merely unclenching wasn't having the corresponding effect.

He opened his hand instead, stretching out his fingers. This prompted an instant response. He felt something twang at the end of the spike, like the spokes of an umbrella, then felt a sense of rotation and heard a soft, muffled whir.

The incoming troop made it through the doorway as the spike withdrew, liquidising Kamnor's face and spraying Ross with the resulting soup as though he had lobbed the poor guy's head through a turbo propeller.

He turned to face them, the end-piece of the spike still spinning and sending blood, flesh and other matter arcing about the corridor.

'It's not what it looks like,' he offered.